The Tides of March

The author grew up in the Welsh towns of Port Talbot and Pontypool, where many of his family worked in the coal and steel industries. He moved to the Southwest in his twenties and has spent many years exploring the rich lands and seascapes of Devon and Cornwall. From a very early age he has held a deep fascination with Japan and the East, a beguilement that continued to feed his imagination into adult life.

After receiving a nasty head injury from an accident whilst riding his motorcycle, on recovery, he has been strangely left with a strong desire to write and create stories. Currently residing in Berkshire with his wife and their faithful German Shepherds, he enjoys mountaineering, skiing, rugby and despite everything – still likes motorcycles…

Also available in both ebook and audiobook formats.

THE TIDES OF MARCH

S D Price

潮の世
Tides World

POD 7 PUBLISHING

CONTENTS

To Dad, who provided the youngster with all those hand-me-down books; he showed me so many windows into other worlds and their infinite possibilities.

PART ONE

Prologue

The Japanese, having transitioned from centuries of isolationism, now exhibit a remarkable capacity for assimilation, at least on the surface, as they present themselves as a modern, Western-oriented society. This transformation is most evident in their dominance across various manufacturing and technological sectors, a testament to the substantial investments and unwavering work ethic of the Japanese people. Japan's rich tapestry of culture and tradition, honed over centuries, remains a fundamental underpinning of its society.

This aspect of the country has often been misinterpreted by Western cultures, initially through ignorance and later through arrogance, throughout Japan's history. To this day, many people continue to misread Japanese actions as mere appeasement or acceptance, failing to grasp the nuances of their complex society. A misinterpretation that overlooks the astute strategic thinking inherent in Japanese culture and the subtle sleight of hand that is always taking place. While everyone smiled at the fluffy rabbit on display, the bowler hat that it sprang from was being measured, quantified and analysed, before being copied, improved and marketed. The Japanese have always firmly understood that true power can manifest itself in many forms.

At the end of the Second World War, one of Japan's fundamental challenges that had contributed to its entry into the conflict – the scarcity of natural resources – remained as pressing as ever, if not more so.

From the 1930s onwards, Japan's deficiencies in natural resources created a critical need that was skilfully exploited by both its political and military leaders. They adeptly linked the country's demand for essential materials, vital for a modern, expanding nation, with Japan's martial heritage. This strategy led to catastrophic consequences for those nations that possessed the resources Japan sought.

This self-perpetuating cycle of insatiable expansion, which began in Korea, extended to China, and then spread across Asia and into the Pacific, created an escalating spiral of need. This expansion formed a fragile bubble that grew increasingly tenuous as it encroached upon territories controlled by more powerful adversaries. Ultimately, this led to its inevitable and catastrophic collapse.

Post-1945, following the disintegration of its hegemonic ambitions, Japan embarked on a quest for a new approach to satisfy its energy needs. Intriguingly, the answer lay in the very element that had precipitated its ultimate capitulation.

For the Land of the Rising Sun, its aggressive wartime actions inadvertently set the perfect stage for the very force that led to its swift surrender: the advent of the atomic age. This new era, marked by the devastating impact of nuclear power, further compounded the suffering of its people, already deeply scarred by the brutalities of war, etching a new, formidable chapter into their daily lives.

The devastating introduction of this new, unparalleled power into the human realm brought the Japanese people not only profound sorrow but also critical lessons. One key lesson was their ability to transcend the immeasurable suffering they had endured and envision a future for their nation and its people, beyond the shadows of their traumatic past.

Japan's destiny would not be marked by disintegration or isolation, responses that might have been expected under such circumstances. Instead, by enduring the seemingly unendurable and shouldering an even greater burden of hardship, Japan discovered a path of resilience. This path revealed the potential advantages of the very power that had once caused their downfall.

The birth of the nuclear age would not only drive Japan to develop a globally dominant economy but also to become one of the leading users of nuclear energy in the world. It would remain one until March 2011...

The sea beguiles one like no other, it is like the passion of a volatile lover. Violent storms once rode out can always be abated by the gentle balms, that bring consoling forgetfulness. A light breeze over a soothing swell, anaesthetises, re-charming the passion-raged soul, along with its powerful amnesia, creating a mollifying oblivion.

It is the ultimate selfish desire, which only heals the distress within those who are coveted, just enough for them to endure the next frenzied emotional typhoon, thus allowing the cravings of their wanting attraction to return again and again.

Always will it be so, that the potent sea and the passionate lover be confident in the eternal consumption of their addiction. Forever drawing each to the fate, that is perpetually written for them.

The Ogress Adachigahara

4

CHAPTER ONE

11 March 2011, 13.35 Coast of Fukushima

The fishing boat's hull gently slapped against the light swell of the Pacific waters. Stood, brace-legged on the very point of the boat's prow, Kurosawa Hikaru gently swayed in harmony with the short lapping movements of the small vessel. His breathing naturally cycling within him, his knees gently flexed to absorb the water's soothing rhythms, harmonising with the movements as he allowed his spirit to attune to the powerful age-old forces of the deep ocean currents, held in abeyance beneath him.

He turned his face to the rays of the sun filtering through the midday light haze, controlling his breath, seeking inner calm amidst the clamour of the bustling fishermen behind him. By focusing on his breathing, he gained a few more moments of tranquillity. He brought his mind back to the immediate task of ladling the last of the bait fish over the guardrail of the craft's bow. The oily, puce patterns of the small, bloodied fish hitting the water evoked a childhood memory of the autumn cherry blossoms of Fukushima Prefecture.

As the final bait vanished into the Pacific, its fish blood mingling with the vast ocean, his fleeting memory of the blossom faded, yielding to the relentless uproar of activity that surged behind him. Ending his brief meditation, he turned to look along the full length of the open deck. The *Michi Maru* was a tuna fishing boat, long and narrow, constructed in the traditional Japanese style; a craft built to cut through the sea at speed when called upon. The sleek bow gave it the ability to chase the fast and agile tuna shoals once they were located by the boat's powerful 'Fish Finder' sonar. Moreover, and most importantly, this feature enabled the *Michi Maru* to swiftly head for shore upon the emergence of unyielding, turbulent weather on the horizon. However, this requirement for swiftness was a trade-off. For, in lumpy waters, at slow speeds or worse, at rest, when the tidal swells were strong, its slender draft made it wallow like an overweight sow drunk on fermented chestnuts. This movement of the craft could induce seasickness, even in some of the most seasoned of sailors, but it was a price worth paying for the promise of a quick catch and a safe return to shore.

The *Michi Maru* could hold about twenty-three crew but had only eighteen souls on board that day. The ones topside now split either side of Kurosawa, were running from the bow backwards to almost the stern. Fifteen men in all, each with a fishing pole, skilfully whipping Blue Fin Tuna out of the bloody waters over their heads and onto the decks behind them.

The fishing poles bore a resemblance to the Tenkara variety used in river fishing, but these demanded individual skills for hooking and efficiently despatching the fish, embodying an industrial essence in their design and use.

An array of jets which ran around the hull of the vessel just below the deck, sprayed outwards with constant streams of water agitating the sea around the craft, masking its outline to the fish below.

In conjunction with the water spray was the live bait Kurosawa had been scooping over the side, these two elements acting as a dynamic lure continually drawing the fish in. Behind him fish were being repetitively arced out of the frothing sea by the fishermen. Skill and ingenuity combined became a deadly attraction for the remarkable creatures that did not have the capacity to resist. Fish after fish were being efficiently whipped out of the water, each one ending up on the sloping deck behind them, landing with a violent slap as their solid, muscular bodies hit the steel catchment chute. The surface of the deck was drenched with a mixture of sea water and fish blood, from where the barbless hooks of high-tempered, carbon-rich steel, had been ripped out of their mouths by the recoiling power of their carbon fibre poles. It created a slimy mess that contributed to the slippery fate awaiting the hapless victims, as they were funnelled along chutes across the sloping decks into the hold below.

The fisherman remained focused on recasting their lures, economic in the rhythmic consistency of their motion, creating a kind of perpetual kinetic energy that they continually imparted into the pendulum action of the Tenkara rods. The Pole Men steadily took one fish after another, in a deadly dance of strike, whip and rip. The tuna, unable to resist the ship's allure, would only end when the shoal had ceased to exist, or the hold was full.

Kurosawa had used the day's labour to lose himself in the repetition of his mechanical task, employing it as a temporary balm for his ever-troubled thoughts. To him these trips were a kind of aquatic basket weaving, a type of occupational therapy of the sea. But now the bait had long gone, along with the hours of his waking meditation. He got up from his seat next to the tank that had held the little fish and started to cross from his station to the bridge to tell the captain that the bait had been consumed. He was about to open the door to the wheelhouse, when it flew open, almost hitting him. The captain suddenly stuck his head out of the doorway, directly into Kurosawa's face. He began frantically shouting and wildly waving his arms in the air, as he pushed past Kurosawa and came out onto the deck.

'Stop! Stop, the hold is full, stow the poles and start cleaning up top-side – and make sure the catch is well iced when you have stowed it all below.'

He had said little to the captain during the trip out into the

Pacific, other than during the initial brief introduction. An exchange facilitated for him by Kengo, an acquaintance who was one of the regular crew members and that had been a minimum of the social perfunctory requirements to secure him the job on board. The captain had not offered his name to Kurosawa, he had been preoccupied with getting the boat ready to disembark, so it had been a brusque, cursory meeting. To the captain he was just another dayworker, which suited Kurosawa fine.

The nameless Captain, known for his minimalist communication, treated Kurosawa with the same concise orders he gave to the rest of the crew, a dynamic Kurosawa preferred. Yet, in a fleeting moment of unexpected face-to-face encounter, the captain glimpsed a peculiar expression on Kurosawa's face before he quickly diverted his eyes to the deck. That brief, unsettling expression left the captain feeling uneasy, a rare occurrence in their otherwise straightforward transactions.

Some of the crew were still hooking in a few more fish before they were told to withdraw their poles. With no further room in the hold, these tuna were ripped off the flashing lures with a flick of the wrist, the pole and line snapping like bullwhips as they struck the fish off their hooks and back into the sea. With mouths torn and gashed by the hooks, the tuna made bloody trails through the water as they frantically swam away from the boat to freedom.

Kurosawa waited until all the poles were out of the water before removing his safety hat and visor and moving aft. He had been hit by a rogue tuna before, some of which could weigh as much as thirty kilograms; even the lighter ones could pack a significant punch after being launched off the line. Also, being caught on one of the vicious looking fishing hooks was not a pleasant experience. Several of the crew sported scars from the pitiless barbs. He soon realised that many of the crew were keen to show off their battle scars from this particular occupational hazard. Several of the scars Kurosawa had been reluctantly exposed to on the journey were located in rather unconventional places, making him grateful that the trip out had been a brief one.

The crew started to clean up as the captain pulled the boat about. They were about fifty kilometres off their home Port of Namie as the *Michi Maru* headed in. Its bow rose out of the waters as the captain applied more power and its sleek hull started to pick up momentum. It quickly reached its cruising speed of fifteen knots on the flat, calm sea. This was the optimum speed for good stability to allow the crew to stow the gear, sort the fish and still get to Namie by early afternoon.

Kurosawa busied himself helping the crew, he definitely was not a fisherman by trade, but liked to go out with one of the boats four or five times a year. He was no stranger to graft – indeed as with most Japanese, he found honourable labours carried out diligently brought with it spiritual solace. Namie was a small town, and he knew many of the fisherman there; fishing boat skippers were ever willing to take on unpaid deck crew or *Kōhanshu*. They were often short on crew, so an extra pair of hands, particularly one they didn't have to share the haul profit with, was always welcome. As most fishing villages around the shores of Japan, Namie struggled to compete with other industries in the area, possibly because they did not involve being out in all weathers for low pay, being smacked by a fish, caught on a hook or possibly falling overboard and drowning. Consequently, getting a place on board was usually not an issue.

The problem was he had already made the decision to go on board that particular day…

★ ★ ★

At around 14.00 the port started to materialise on the horizon; a misty haze of pastel colours as if someone had painted a vivid watercolour where the grey sea met the duskier land. Though it had been overcast for most of their trip into the Pacific, the weather had held for the main part, the waters calm.

Until they reached the harbour and had to start unloading their lucrative catch, the work for the time being was done. The crew sat around the deck in small groups of contentment,

9

smoking and chatting amongst themselves, some were passing a flask around, each accepting a sip of sake before passing on to the next man, taking satisfaction from an honest day's labour.

Kurosawa was leaning against the bridge, feeling the tendrils of a light breeze on his face and tasting the sea salt in the air. They were about half an hour out, this was the moment in the trip that he usually felt calm, cleansed and energised, and was the reason he took these little voyages in the first place; today though, something was amiss. He started to experience a deep sense of anxious foreboding, a sensation he was well-acquainted with, though typically perceiving it in others rather than himself. This feeling, unfamiliar in its internal origin, intensified his unease. As he let his mind start to internally examine the emotion, he was interrupted by the wheelhouse door swinging open again. The captain had locked the helm in place and stepped out of the bridge to stand next to him. He arched his neck and surveyed the sky and then the horizon.

'No shite Hawks,' he said simply.

Kurosawa followed his gaze. The captain was right, the fishing boats were normally mobbed by gulls on the return journey, looking for scraps from the boats. But today he could not see a single bird in the sky. He looked at the captain.

'That is very odd,' said the captain, pulling on tendrils of his wispy beard. 'Very, very strange.'

Kurosawa saw a look of perplexing apprehension on the man's face. Seeing such a look on such an experienced sailor was troubling and he was about to ask what he thought was going on when they both felt it.

The boat suddenly seemed to momentarily slow and pull backwards. A low moan of alarm went around the crew in the stern of the *Michi Maru* as they also felt the sea beneath them create the contrary swell. It was not just the boat that had slowed, the surrounding sea did so as well. Although the vessel continued to motor forwards, the very sea it was moving on was regressing, turning their small piece of the ocean into a kind of alarming watery treadmill for a few seconds. The uniquely odd sensation not only unbalanced everyone, it also caused a strange sickening feeling in the pit of their stomachs. The hull gave a little shudder, slowed slightly for a moment and then chugged on.

'What the fuck was that!' shouted one of the now totally spooked crew.

The captain began to bark orders at his crew to put on lifejackets and secure everything that had not been stored below. The underlying fear that he was struggling to control portrayed by the tremor resonating in his voice.

Although the situation was disconcerting even to him, Kurosawa stood on the deck calmly observing the panic starting to erupt all around him, for the moment untouched by its effect. It was not that he had the great emotional control the Japanese where famous for, it was that any danger perceived or real he came into contact with did not elicit the response from him that generally affected other humans. He had come into this world a rare freak of nature and those lacking an emotional attachment to dangerous events tended to have a short life span. His reactions were always clinically dispassionate, accompanied by reflexes that were swift and often deadly. Although Kurosawa harboured a distinct personal response to fear, he was adept at detecting it in others. This skill was not only due to the palpable veil of fear currently enveloping those around him, but also stemmed from his innate, profound ability to assess and understand others.

The captain stared at Kurosawa, who, he suddenly became aware, had not reacted to his commands.

'You too,' he barked, trying to camouflage his fear with anger at Kurosawa's perceived disobedience.

'What?' Kurosawa said.

'Put on your lifejacket, you fucking idiot,' shouted the captain into Kurosawa's face, pushing a life vest against his chest.

Kurosawa looked at his leathery, weather-beaten, whiskered face with eyes like hard, black stones. Thirty years at sea, spending endless hours enduring ravaging storms and scouring sunlight, had carved features constructed of deep lines and pock-marked crags upon his face. His skin looked as thick and as tough as overcooked pork rind. The man was using anger to create a mask for his own growing anxiety. This façade was effective for most people, it projected the desired qualities of leadership and control needed to take command in difficult situations and seemed to be working on the crew.

However, Kurosawa's perception went beyond surface appearances; he saw the inner truths people radiated, the core of their being that no external disguise could conceal. When close to others, he perceived these truths as distinct auras. It was a talent he had held since a child, only in later years did he realise that this was a rare gift. He had honed this ability into a practical tool, enabling him to interpret individual auras against a spectrum of emotional states. This skill allowed him to decipher an array of unconscious feelings emanating from those around him. Presently, the aura of the captain was emitting waves of extreme terror.

Kurosawa found this disconcerting; his capacity for self-preservation now tuned to maximum. Still ignoring the captain's command to put on a lifejacket, Kurosawa regarded the man before picking the right tone to ask,

'What is it captain? What is wrong here?'

The manner in which the question was posed prompted the captain to view the unassuming man, who had spent the day quietly on his ship, in a completely new light. The person he had originally been introduced to earlier that morning before they left the harbour had seemed very different to the one in front of him now. That man had been slightly stooped, with rounded shoulders and an almost constantly bowed head. He had spoken in a most effeminate of voices, not very manly at all. He had pigeonholed him straight away as a 'city guy,' possibly even gay. Not that he cared about that, he could put his dick wherever he liked, as long as he didn't bother him personally and it did not become an issue with the crew. The captain saw himself as modern and inclusive in that way. In his many years' experience of being at sea, he found 'mariners' to be much less intolerant of a man's sexuality than one would have thought possible in the perceived macho world of seafarers. There was a saying he heard often during his time as Petty Officer in Japan's Maritime Self-Defence Force – *This years 'givers' were next years 'takers'* – it could be a lonely life being at sea after all…

However, that person had seemingly vanished into thin air and the person in front of him now was not the same weedy, shy, little runt, who had come on board that morning. Stood before him was a tall, perfectly proportioned individual with one of those wiry, muscular frames, in the same way a dancer's physique was set out, powerful, yet balanced. His voice had also changed, very different to the weak, reedy tone he had heard throughout the day, he now projected such an air of menace, that for a moment it unnerved him almost to the point where it superseded his original terror. This was no mean feat considering the captain's current disposition – he had just been wondering if he had any spare underwear on board.

'I'm not sure,' he said, feeling compelled to respond to the stranger's question.

'And what exactly is it you are not sure about, captain?' There was that compelling voice again, well spoken with perfect modulation like a judge or a general giving one no option but to comply or respond.

'I think we are about to get into some serious trouble.'

Kurosawa held his gaze firmly and said, 'We are only twenty minutes from port, why not dump the fish and put the engine to full speed and head in?'

The captain looked out of the cabin window at their home Port of Namie, now only a few kilometres away.

'Dump the catch, yes, but if we were to head into the port, I think it will get us killed. We must turn about and head back out to sea… if it is not too late.'

Kurosawa, although not quite certain what was going on,

realised he must depend on the captain's experience and accept his concerning intuition.

He nodded in agreement saying, 'Yes, I agree this is what we must do, captain.'

'What! Dump the tuna after eight hours of backbreaking fishing. Are you out of your fucking mind, skipper?' said one of the crew who had appeared unnoticed behind them. 'And you, Kawaii boy! What the fuck has this got to do with you, keep your trap shut or I will put you in that stinking bait box you have been sitting on all day!'

The captain now understood there was nothing cute or feminine about Kurosawa, as the crewman had implied by calling him a Kawaii boy. He stared at the sinewy limbed man who now stood behind Kurosawa, along with the rest of the crew who had now gathered around the outside of the bridge. The man was known as Jōji and was one of the permanent members of the crew. A hard-working hand, but prone to being a loudmouth and who also had an excessive taste for sake, a straw-covered flask of which he now pushed in the direction of a crew mate to his left. As he did so his undone life yellow life vest opened up and he heaved out his rib cage to throw some extra emphasis to his point, it made him look like a puffed-up Yellow Bunting.

Murmured grunts of approval for bird brain's sentiments echoed around the rest of the crew in his support but they were presumptuously short lived. Kurosawa turned around to face Jōji and then instantly hit him squarely in the ribs with the flat of his right hand. The deck hand's scrawny frame folded like a rice paper kite that had been struck with a baseball bat. He ricocheted backwards into the crew members standing behind him, taking them all into the gunwale, with several of them almost accompanying each other over the starboard side.

Mmmm…not a dancer then, thought the captain, looking at the crew members scrambling to stop themselves going overboard. The surrounding fishermen, taken aback by the sudden transformation, quickly engaged reverse and scrambled away from Kurosawa, releasing a short chorus of surprised cries as they did so. The figure now standing before them bore little resemblance to the unassuming Hikaru they had encountered earlier in the day. This man exuded an intense, almost intimidating aura that left them feeling uncomfortable.

The sudden display of violence disturbed the crew, not because he had struck one of their shipmates, because this was common enough for rough fisherman, it was more the way he had moved to deliver the blow. Most spent their time at sea doing hard physical work in harsh conditions or, if not at sea, in many of the bars around Namie waiting to go to sea, with neither element suffering fools gladly; sudden altercations were common to both domains.

Slowly turning to face them, the twist of his pivoting body was like a spring being wound into compression or a bow being drawn ready to fire. His feet, hips and upper body moving efficiently, totally balanced, coiling up to release an economic strike of fluidity and force that was perfectly weighted for the desired effect – to stun but not permanently damage its victim. They were also troubled by his face; they simply didn't recognise it. To be fair most had not made eye contact with Kurosawa since he stepped on board. His hair, a rich black, was styled with a floppy fringe that cascaded over his face, often concealing his features. Kurosawa habitually walked with a bowed head and a stooped gait with his shoulders curved inwards. This posture, combined with the veil of his hair, made it challenging for anyone to catch more than a fleeting glimpse of his countenance.

At the time they had not noticed or even cared about this behaviour, lots of young men were a little eccentric in their ways. He had given no offence, politely responding to anyone who had talked to him. He just got on with his tasks and kept to himself, giving the impression of a shy introvert, so they had left him to it.

Because of this most of the crew had not really gained a reasonable look at his face. Now though, they had an extremely good view of his features and they did not like what they saw. Kurosawa's head was now erect, his stance unnervingly held in a challenging manner, the once loose and untidy shirt which was now buttoned up around his inner T-shirt, extenuating the 'V'-like ratio between his hips and his shoulders. Both garments were now tucked into slacks that no longer hung baggily under his crotch, but neatly pulled up and belted around his waist. His long fringe was still there but pushing through the jet black hair there appeared to be the snarling face of a demon. 'Oni,' cried Kengo with a whispered hiss of astonishment, citing the demon from Japanese mythology and synonymous with a popular video game.

The apparition, which had more in common with an exquisite carving than a human being of flesh and bone, gave them a look that pinned them like a butterfly, sticking them straight through the thorax to the spot with a sharpened look of deep, dark, malicious contempt, radiating from a face of razor-angled symmetry.

If the face had been a sculpture, then it would have been one that would have made even Leonardo proud to have created both DaVinci and DiCaprio, though it had to be said the mouth was a little strange. His upper lip was drawn tightly over a row of white incisor-looking teeth, with a canine breaking past his lower lip on either side of the jaw. There also seemed to be far too many teeth in there for a normal person.

The captain now realised what he had seen in Kurosawa's face earlier; he had seen that look before but it was not on any human, it was the look of an absolute lack of compassion and empathy to be found in the expression of a Great White Shark. He was aware he needed to take back control, events were unfolding around them faster than an Origami Master could unravel a poor student's work. And to say that the crew were now more than a little disconcerted would be more of an understatement than a Tomioka Tessai painting. Kurosawa stared down the crew; for some reason they all felt as if his dead-eyed gaze was on each of them alone. It was not a good feeling. Before the captain could say anything, Kurosawa began to speak. The pitch of his voice had changed again, now a deep tone resonating intimidation in every syllable as he said in a low measured drawl, 'Either you arseholes go over the side or your fish can, what's it to be?'

The crew quickly shot glances at each other and then looked towards the captain for some support against this demon.

'Look lads,' he said, his voice steady yet tinged with resignation, 'It's clear that something's amiss, and if my hunch is right, we're on the brink of a monumental challenge. Whatever it is, it's imminent and it's going to hit us hard. We must prepare ourselves.'

They lowered their heads in compliance and subserviently shuffled off to start bringing the tuna up, first picking up their colleague who had been winded by Kurosawa. They quietly grumbled to each other as they went.

The captain watched them go thinking, *it really does take a lot to stop a sailor from bitching.* He pushed past Kurosawa and, sticking his head out the bridge doorway shouted, 'And be quick about it, you bunch of sake sodden layabouts,' adding some further chastisement to try and reassert his dwindling authority as the boat's skipper. He turned to Kurosawa. 'And unless you're fucking a sea devil, I would put this on,' he said slapping a life vest onto Kurosawa's chest. 'Believe me, if I'm right you are going to fucking well need it!'

He took hold of the helm and turned the boat about, setting a course heading back out to sea. Kurosawa put on the lifejacket as he watched the men reluctantly dispose of the catch over the side. They got about half of the catch out before they heard a sound coming over the horizon like several jet turbines powering up in chorus. They all stopped what they were doing to listen to the strange foreboding resonance.

'Stop gawking like a bunch of *Shojo* virgins on your wedding night, you dozy cunts. Get yourselves below,' shouted the captain, his voice now quivering with fear.

The men who were unloading fish off the boat's aft quickly got themselves into the lower quarters. Five of the crew who were working forward squeezed into the bridge, standing behind Kurosawa and the captain they all focused through the cabin windows over the bow to the horizon beyond.

Strangely, the horizon appeared to be approaching at an alarming rate, far quicker than the boat's current speed could account for. Moreover, it was rising rapidly in height, creating an increasingly imposing and surreal spectacle.

They all now realised they had been too late in coming about, their dash for the safety of the deep ocean had failed. The wave that ran across the horizon in front of them, imbued an overpowering feeling of menace as it began to soar above them, progressively building ever upwards into a wall of primeval disturbance.

They were witnessing one of nature's great terra-forming forces in action; part of its armoury of creation that had shaped the planet for eons. Kurosawa could not help but appreciate the beauty of its naturally evolving form. The daylight darkened above them as the very sky itself withdrew from the hellish scene, seemingly giving way to the deep grey mountain of water that continued to ascend, creating a massive watery arch high above them.

To the men on the boat the huge wave seemed to pinch in on itself and momentarily take the shape of a striking cobra as it bore down upon them, the crest breaking into a ridge of iridescent tendrils. The sight froze Kurosawa, again not in fear but in an instant of grudging appreciation for this nemesis of mother nature. He realised from the abrupt anguished screams around him and the strong smell of excrement that was suddenly filling his nose, that many of the crew did not share his immediate feelings of admiration for their mutual circumstances.

The captain spun the wheel and brought the boat fully about, steering directly at the approaching wall of water. He rammed the throttle lever forwards, putting down as much power as he could; the diesel engine roared into life, the craft's single propeller surging the craft onwards.

As the vessel started to climb up the face of the mountain of water the captain struggled with the helm, trying to keep the small craft square to the oncoming wave. Up they rose, their momentum still pushing them along the surface, with the huge mass of the wave itself continuing to propel them inland. They were making no headway back out to sea; the craft was quite literarily like an insect on flypaper stuck to the front of the monstrous wave.

They continued to climb the wave until the *Michi Maru* was almost vertical, its rapier-shaped hull cutting through the water on either side. The captain held firmly onto the ship's wheel, bracing his feet against the bridge's console to steady himself.

Kurosawa found himself thrown back into one of the rear corners of the wheelhouse, crashing into several crew members. He locked his body into place there, finding purchase on the bulkhead and deck by spreading his hands and feet wide from his body, pressing his spine almost flat against the corner. A dreadful howl seemed to accompany them as the wave closed around the vessel as they attempted to ascend the face of the great swell of water. He could not tell whether the eerie sound came from the men on board or the wave itself.

The kinetic energy of the valiant fishing boat now began to dwindle, coming to almost a dead stop just as they reached the frothy pinnacle of the wave. For a brief moment the *Michi Maru* began to fall rearward, dropping backwards, slipping down the moving waterfall. Then, with a great lurch forward, the vessel crashed down the far side of the monstrous swell. The engine let out a piercing wail, its propeller briefly slicing through the air as the ship crested the wave. The vessel's slender stem arched dramatically towards the sky, pivoting like a dancer caught in a fluid, graceful leap. The captain frantically pulled back on the T-shaped throttle, before the prop, now finding itself free of any water resistance, smashed it and the motor to pieces. The engine, suddenly released of any load, now found itself free to roar into the red zone, with a hammering self-destructive rattle of steel on steel, as the internal mechanical revolutions of its crankshaft and pistons smashed together.

The fleeting relief the men felt from surviving the initial onslaught, was quickly eclipsed by a gripping sense of dread. A second, menacing whitecap loomed ahead. Although this roller was marginally smaller than the first, the *Michi Maru* had not landed squarely, having slewed to her aft side as it reground its hull into the waters. Her engine was also still recovering from its violent oscillations causing the craft to lose most of its speed and all of its control.

The collective relief of the surviving crew was instantly abashed by this new and immediate precariousness. To the crew it had become personal, there was no doubt now in their minds that the sea was trying to kill them and would show no mercy in its endeavour to do so.

CHAPTER TWO

11 March 1945, Nanjing China

The woman was chained to one corner of the bare cell. Once beautiful, she was now in a pitiful state. Her hitherto sleek, long, black hair was bedraggled and matted, torn out at the roots in places, revealing several raw and festering patches on her scalp. Her face bore the harsh evidence of brutality, with both eye sockets bruised and swollen into prominent, disfiguring lumps, nearly sealing them shut. Her lips were split and weeping and most of the teeth on the left-hand side of her mouth missing or shattered. Her body, frail and emaciated, bore silent testimony to the unspeakable horrors she had endured. She had faced repeated violations that left deep, irreparable scars, both physical and emotional in a way that defied recovery. What was left of her clothing hung in soiled rags from her emaciated body, the remaining pieces of cloth barely covering what was left of her breasts; the once fine, full, pertness of which she had been so proud, now devoured by her body's need for nourishment. Not much was left of the spirited young daughter of an influential Manchurian Mandarin, her very existence, like the beauty she had once been, now lost for ever.

Despite the repulsive incredulity of the thought, she found herself measuring her situation against the ghastly yardstick of torment endured by others in that place of unspeakable evil.

By this grim standard, a disturbing realisation dawned upon her: amidst the sea of suffering that engulfed all its captives, her own condition, as harrowing as it was, had to be seen as comparatively fortunate.

Her name was Ying Yuewu, a name that had weathered storms of unimaginable adversity. Initially taken as a political hostage during the Japanese invasion of Xinjing, the capital of Manchuria, she had witnessed first-hand the shift from a contentious occupation to an outright massacre of her people. Those years under Japanese captivity were marked by unspeakable brutality, a barbaric testament to human cruelty. Yet, it was her subsequent confinement in this house of torment that cast a chilling light on her past sufferings. Here, in these suffocating walls, the depths of her ordeal took on an even more harrowing dimension, redefining her understanding of despair.

Ying stared across the gloomy, stinking cell to where three men were being confined in a set of wooden stocks on the other side of the chamber. The men sat with their backs to the wall, on a near freezing stone floor, strewn with a worthless layer of straw and sawdust. Their feet were held firm in the timber device, locked around each ankle, testament to the enduring efficacy of its ancient design. Each man's foot showed signs of varying degrees of putrefying frostbite; from the initial stages of painful, blackened swelling to the grotesque finale where rotting, gangrenous flesh clung desperately to the darkened, skeletal remains of their feet.

The men had been taken beyond the normal thresholds of suffering a human could endure, and now lay in a state of twitching semiconsciousness, praying for that blessed relief that could only be accommodated by death.

Ying turned away from the men's suffering, pulling on the chain that was attached to a steel collar around her neck. The chain itself passed up through a metal ring anchored to a corner of wall half a metre off the floor. From this point it snaked along the rough blockwork towards the doorway where it was securely fastened. When the guards came to rape her, they would first pull the chain through the ring, dragging her down onto the floor, securing it to pin her down before abusing her.

This treatment had continued for several months and during this period the men in the stocks had been replaced many times. Now even the foulest of the guards had stopped visiting her since the disease had broken out within her. Even the most desperate of her captors finding little attraction in what was left of her body. It mattered not now, what else could happen to her? She had made a deal that would allow her to escape, of sorts. Though she had not gone into this pact lightly, she had been left with one last small thing that she could use to bargain with – perhaps it was not that small really, maybe she had just underestimated its value; but it was too late now for the deal had been struck and it was one that could not be broken.

The door to the cell abruptly crashed open and in marched three uniformed men, two of them were Korean guards she knew only too well, the third man was tall and thin and, although he wore the uniform of a major in His Majesty's Japanese Imperial Army, he was in no way a military man. Major Kurosawa Shinji despised the military as much as he despised himself for being part of it. He briefly glanced at her, his gaze emotionless as he passed by, but beneath that mask an acknowledgement of her terrible condition. He turned towards the guards, eyeing them with a disdainful air of disgust. They avoided his gaze, wondering what he expected them to do for entertainment in this shit hole they had been assigned to.

He had a small, black leather medical bag with him, which he placed on the floor, opening it next to the feet of the men in the stocks. The two guards stayed back, more to remove themselves from the foul gangrenous stink the men's feet generated but also to give the young scientist room to work. He took out a metal probe and tweezers and carefully inspected each man's feet in turn. Not one made a sound during the morbid inspection; one was comatose and the other two just looked at him blankly as he picked at their flesh. He was aware they had reached the far side of despair, their horrific injuries and morbid neglect having crushed them, forcing the destruction of mind, spirit, and soul. Even the specimen with the initial stages of frostbite was losing the will to survive, crushed by the terrible futility of his situation. As Shinji observed the three men, he believed himself devoid of empathy, long eroded by his time in the unit. Yet, confronting the gravely afflicted figures before him, a flicker of pity – reminiscent of his early days in the facility – unexpectedly stirred. This fleeting sentiment scratched at the emotional shield he had meticulously built, a defence meant to preserve his sanity amidst the facility's horrors.

Back then he had been a young graduate just starting his studies for his PhD in Biological Science. At that time Tokyo had still felt like a city trying to modernise itself. Western culture and dress permeated all areas of society, even Christianity had been more widely accepted than it had in the past. He had even toyed with Catholicism in his freshman years at university. However, he had found it too morally constrictive, returning to his native Shintoism, missing the closeness to the wonders of nature that his family's historic religious beliefs brought.

Shintoism embraces the duality of life, acknowledging the necessity of both darkness and light for true balance. Turning the other cheek was problematical to the Japanese, although they understood the importance of duty and obligation regardless of any pain that may bring. They may not react philosophically to a slap to the face, but it was within their nature to endure life's challenges. Shinji had not realised the significance of endurance back then, along with most Japanese the concept of endurance was more a personal experience rather than the collective one it would become. It was a surreal period in Japan's history. The country he could see now had been on the cusp of two totally opposite destinies, unfortunately for him he could only see the one that he wanted to be part of. Tokyo had been full of hope and excitement as Japan reached the zenith of its drive to modernisation. It was 1937, and to him the 'Moga girls', who were still parading through the streets in Western men's clothing, seemed to be more of a reality to Japan's collective state of mind than the reports of its modernised army fighting Chinese bandits in Manchuria. All that changed when he had received a visit from his supervising professor. Shinji was informed that he had been given a great honour, he had been chosen by the army to work with the medical services. Because of his work on tissue regeneration, it had been decided that his research and experience in this field could be of great military benefit. He had been selected to join the growing ranks of academia, summoned to dedicate their expertise in service of the Emperor.

He would be required to undertake a short period of basic military training, after which he would be given the rank of 'Major' in his Majesty's Imperial Army. He had of course vigorously protested at first, he was a scientist not a soldier; his father before him a banker, and although he was proud of the family's Samurai heritage within his ancestry, he knew the military life was not where he saw his future heading.

Fortunately for him, the professor was far more politically astute and worldly wise than the immature researcher he was at that time. He calmly explained to him that although he was being asked to volunteer for this role, in essence it was a command. To refuse it would not only be seen as a great dishonour to himself, but also to his family. He tried to make him realise the possible dire consequences of snubbing his country's powerful martial establishment. At the very least he would be forced into an existence far removed from the privileged middle-class life he now enjoyed. The professor would have no choice but to terminate his studies at the university and cast him out into an academic wilderness. This would be the minimum he could expect. If he foolishly rejected the 'opportunity' he was being offered, far worse could befall the young man and his family... Did the professor not understand where Japan was heading? What it had become, insidiously under all their noses these last twenty years. Kurosawa Shinji could not believe what he was hearing, let alone grasp the situation at that time, but now, now he understood it all too well. Fate had raised its irresistible banner of martialism and, if he wanted to survive, he had no choice but to follow it.

Within the next three months he was posted to Mainland China, eventually finding himself standing alone outside the main gates of the inner cordon of a huge concrete complex. It was euphemistically called 'Epidemic Prevention and Water Purification Department'. In reality it was the epicentre of the notorious Unit 731, the human experimentation centre for biological and chemical warfare. During his time there he would witness the cruel demise of thousands of innocent people in an unfathomable scope and scale of hideous atrocities. However, in an attempt to emotionally compensate the perpetrators of such horrors, the captives were never regarded as people, or even as human beings, they were colloquially referred to simply as 'Logs'. The dehumanising term used was to create acceptance of the degrading barbarity that they daily inflicted on the stream of helpless souls that passed through the macabre process of systematic scientific live human experimentation. It had been a long war in China, he had spent many years at the facility and, as some people can, he began to normalise the abhorrent repugnance, slowly allowing himself to be conditioned by the system to the barbarity of what they did.

Then, at the beginning of 1945, unexpectedly he had been granted a short furlough to the mainland of Japan. The trip jolted him out of the cowardly malaise he had allowed himself to succumb to in China. From the moment he stepped off the plane the devastating evidence of the homeland was immediately dreadfully apparent. First in the physical destruction that wreathed every path he took, and then materialising in subtle ways from his interactions with the populous. They now realised they were utterly beaten, even if they could not or would not admit that openly. Within them he could see the meaning of what it truly meant to endure. It was obvious to anyone who had the courage to look, that the impact of the war had altered the nature of every man, woman and child who had survived this far. A longing for the end of this war, with the underlying desire for a new beginning, was profoundly palpable. But what that new paradigm would look like no one could conceive, only that there must be a 'something'; 'somehow, somewhere', in a time yet to be understood, for those who had the will to survive for their country's future.

He closed his bag and drew himself away from the 'Logs'. Yes, that had always been the answer to his conscience, to never allow himself to consider them as members of the human race or even human specimens. His strategy was to keep thinking of them as devoid of any humanity, just spongy, leaky, stinking lumps of rotten wood, there for him to exhaust their limited utility and then to be disposed of once their gruesome purpose had been served.

He turned away from the men, striving to reclaim the comforting reassurance of his former self; the one that enabled him to cope, especially in the presence of the guards and his colleagues. Aware of the importance of projecting the right persona in front of his superiors, he was meticulously cautious, ensuring that his outward demeanour remained unflappable and composed.

Shinji glanced at the woman chained to the corner and found her staring back at him, deep within the swollen, puffy folds of her battered face, he could see slithers of bright green within her pupils that seemed to suddenly start glimmering like polished jade. Her lips started to move as she tried to speak in a strained whisper, it was all her battered body could manage, he thought he heard a few words that sounded Japanese. One of the guards grabbed the chain where it ran next to him and pulled violently through the retaining ring, slamming her head into the wall behind as it yanked on her steel collar.

'Shut it, bitch,' he screamed, angry that a prisoner would dare embarrass him in front of an officer. He moved in to kick her in the face, but Shinji intervened and commanded, 'Stop! Step away from her.'

Respectfully the two guards did as they were told, allowing him to come forward and bend down level with her head.

One of them whispered to the other, 'He must like them … well broken in.' The other gave a restricted snort in response.

Shinji, registering their irreverence, turned towards the guards. All the Korean guards were common, base, uneducated men; Korean conscripts such as these had been on the lowest rungs of Japanese society before the war. They now enjoyed a level of power over people that they would once never have dreamed was possible, revelling in the horrific behaviour they could now indulge themselves in. A whiff of insubordination hung in the toxic air and began to feed the contempt he had always held for them.

'Do you realise that there is a blast experiment to be carried out in the Outer Field Area Five tomorrow?' Shinji said.

The Major's tone unnerved them, they knew he was not one of the more sadistic scientists that worked there, the ones who really enjoyed their work, but he was an officer and officers were always trouble.

'Yes, sir, it is written on the weekly schedule for 09.00,' replied both men together, coming to stiff attention.

'And how many Logs are to be used?'

'Eight, sir,' they both answered smartly, as a creeping air of apprehension began to form around them.

'Yes, eight, eight perfectly fresh specimens, for a particular experiment involving a new pathogen. However, the two children from the selected group were strangled by the remaining six adults – to save them I suppose,' his voice trailed off for a moment, the sickening comprehension of his statement catching him off guard. Quickly recovering himself he said, 'In any event we are now two Logs short for meeting the experimental criteria. Perfect specimens such as yourselves are challenging to come by now, as you know. Word has irrevocably got out on what we do here it seems. So, I would like you both to volunteer, to make up the numbers.'

The two guards visibly paled. 'Us, sir?' stammered one.

'Volunteer, sir?' whispered the other.

'Yes, you two…' he intoned slowly, with a light smirk. 'Is it not your duty to die for the glory of the Emperor?' He looked directly into their terrified faces, contemptuously saying, 'Are you refusing to lay down your miserable lives for his Majesty?'

The two guards said nothing, one started to tremble slightly. 'Good,' said Shinji. 'I'm glad that is settled. Once I have finished here, we will go together to tell Colonel Arai that his experiment will now be saved by the fortunate windfall of your unselfish sacrifice. He will be delighted to utilise the superior Korean stock for an essential comparison. This will demonstrate how the wounds he inflicts on you will accelerate the spread of the disease, intensifying the contrast between your group and the Logs. I'm sure you will both receive a medal for this – posthumously, of course – once you eventually succumb to your wounds. But your family, no doubt, will be greatly honoured by your selflessness.' Shinji broadly grinned at the men, saying, 'Now, wait outside for me.'

'Yes, sir,' mechanically replied both men before shuffling out of the cell.

He knew that he would never be allowed to use the guards in experimentation, but they, alas, did not. All the same, he would play them along as far as he could, it would teach them a lesson for their insolent behaviour towards him.

Shinji returned his attention to the tortured woman before him. She was still looking at him with the same strange effervescent, emerald glint in her eyes. It seemed like there was someone else, some other being, deep inside her, using her eyes as peepholes to look out of the battered and broken body. She began to whisper again, her voice was hoarse and rasping, indistinct, but he still believed it to be Japanese. Odd, he thought as he leaned in closer to hear what she was saying, 'What was that?' he asked, in a quiet enquiring tone. He was taken aback when she replied in a strong powerful voice, in a Japanese dialect he did not recognise, a voice that was definitely not hers.

'I can offer redemption only for every other male heir of each generation, but I will give you the choice when the redemption starts.'

He was about to react angrily to this latest bout of insolence, coming from a half dead Log, but something in the unnerving tone of her voice and the hypnotic glower of her gaze, stayed him. 'I don't think you're really in a position to bargain,' he tentatively replied.

'No, it is you, Kurosawa Shinji who holds the weaker position, you just don't realise it. Give me what I need, and I will give you a valuable gift in return, which is more than you deserve, as you well know "BoyBoy". If you refuse, I will strip you of everything, and this curse shall extend to every subsequent generation bearing your name.'

He was stunned that she knew his full name and used the childish nickname his mother would call him by as an infant. How could she possibly know that? 'Who are you devil, what is it you want?' he weakly said, his reply sticking in his throat.

'Don't play me for a fool, Major,' she hoarsely spat at him. 'There is only one thing I could want, as do they.' She pointed a bruised, bony, finger in the direction of the three frostbitten men. 'Release us from these now worthless vessels, that is your only gift to give. But understand, this offer of redemption is only for the first male born to every other generation. He will experience harmony as long as he shall live, for the next, there will ever be angst.'

Standing away from her, Shinji was visibly shaken. After a few moments he released the catch to the flap of his leather holster with his right-hand and then drew his Nambu 8mm pistol. He looked at the weapon; it was customary for officers to purchase their own side arms, which at the time he had thought outrageously strange. In all his years of military service, although he had been involved with the murder of thousands of people, he had never discharged a weapon against anyone. In training they had been forced to kill live pigs that had been tied up to make it easy for them. He had dispatched the animal with a single shot, much to the annoyance of the instructor who had wanted them to hear it scream in pain to add to the shock of killing something for the first time.

He raised the weapon, aiming it at the woman, and cocked it, ready to fire. Then, in a sudden change of heart, he let it drop, allowing it to dangle loosely from his extended right arm.

'Think of the child, Major, Ichirō's future is in your hands now, as are the fates and prospects of your line from this moment onwards.'

His body went visibly weak on hearing this and believed he was about to pass out. Regaining his composure, he asked, 'How do you know about my son?' he demanded. 'You could not possibly know that!'

'What I know is that you have two paths before you and unfortunately both will be hard roads to walk for you, whichever you choose. Only the future of your son or his issue can be secured with the right choice – if you have the fortitude to take it that is, for you have shown nothing but weakness thus far in your life. One would be wise to remember how the gods despise such feebleness, Major.'

He struggled to regain his self-control. Had he finally succumbed to madness? It was not possible for the woman to know so much about him – no one did. With difficulty he brought himself back under control.

'Who are you?' he hissed at her.

'That is the wrong question, Major. *What* am I, is what should now be concerning you.'

'What then? A Witch?'

'Yes, there is here now in this cell, a witch of sorts. It is not this shattered wretch before you now, for she is all but broken. I am making this generous offer on her behalf.'

It was true, as far as he knew the woman did not speak Japanese and her voice now held an unnerving depth. It was still hers but had claimed such a disturbing resonance that he seemed to be hearing as much inside his head as from her voice. He was failing to resist its reasoning and slowly that persuasive force overwhelmed him.

She looked at him realising that he was about to agree to the bargain. There was just one final piece to conclude the pact.

'You are given until the next new moon to decide the cycle of which generation will experience lifelong contentment and which perpetual discord,' she added.

This time it was the woman who let out a relieving sigh, as he raised his pistol to her forehead. He did not understand what had happened or why he believed her, but he did.

Anyway, he reasoned to himself, what did he have to lose by killing another few Logs now. He had recently seen the orders that had come in to start shutting the unit down, all its inmates would die soon enough.

He pulled the trigger twice in quick succession, putting the rounds into the socket of her right eye. The back of her head erupted against the stone wall behind her and she slumped forwards, her shackles stopping her from falling totally to the floor. He turned and fired in quick succession at the heads of each of the semiconscious shackled men until the pistol's chamber action locked open.

He mechanically started to remove the now empty clip; its six cartridges spent. As he reached into his leather magazine pouch attached to his belt to replace the clip he had expended, the two guards crashed back into the cell, both in a state of panic at hearing the sound of gunfire.

Just as he turned to face them, he caught sight of an ethereal movement by the woman's body. He quickly turned back to her but there was nothing to see. He was certain he glimpsed presence in his peripheral vision – a ghostly, wraithlike presence. It was a blur of shifting colours, from white to greyish black, wrapping momentarily around her before disappearing. For reasons beyond his understanding, a peculiar serenity began to permeate his being, soothing the fear and anxiety that clung to him just moments before. For the first time in years, he experienced an empowering sense of control over his destiny. It wasn't a surge of euphoria, but rather the emergence of a comforting contentment, signalling a pivotal turn in his journey. He sensed he had reached a crucial juncture, with the path ahead gradually revealing itself, inviting him towards a future he was now ready to embrace.

Coming back to the present, he became aware of the puzzled scrutiny of the guards observing him.

'Clear this mess up,' he snapped at them before they could question him as to what had happened. 'And when you've done, come and see me in my office. I will ask Colonel Arai to meet us there,' he added sadistically.

CHAPTER THREE

1 March 2011

The diminutive Suzuki noodle van had served Takada Satoshi well over the time he had spent living in Fukushima. To him it may have been dwarfed in size, but in stature and utility, it was a giant, something he felt they both had in common.

There was a sign that covered each side of the all-white vehicle that said, 'FRESH NOODLES COOKED WHILE YOU WAIT OR BROUGHT TO YOUR DOOR – DAILY.' He had not delivered any noodles fresh or otherwise from his little van for many years. Though, to anyone peering inside, they would see every piece of equipment clean and sterile, all tidied away. It was always 'noodle ready,' just in case; all that was required was a modest selection of fresh ingredients.

Though in truth, it would be fair to say, there was not much space left for foodstuffs in the chilled stainless-steel larders that lined the floor along the back of the van at the present time.

He turned the ignition key and the van's little engine faithfully jumped to attention, like an eager pooch, making the vehicle quiver in enthusiastic anticipation, excited at the prospect of doing its master's bidding. He pressed the little red up arrow on a plastic remote-control fob activating the drive motor to the roller shutter door on his extremely compact garage. Once fully open he accelerated out onto the quiet suburban street where he lived, into the fresh, crisp evening air, as the door quietly closed behind him like a shroud covering a lair. The winter had been reasonably mild, but now – the beginning of Spring – it felt like an unseasonal frost was on the way. He was not that concerned; his little van had four-wheel drive and did well in poor conditions. When he had operated his noodle run, he had never missed a day. After all, reliability and duty to one's customers was an unquestionable expectation of Japanese culture regardless of one's occupation.

It was quite dark when he reached the secluded area of countryside two hours later. He had meticulously scouted out the area several weeks earlier and knew exactly the position he needed to stop on the highway. Halting at the side of the road, he deftly engaged reverse gear on the column change lever situated beneath the steering wheel. With a satisfying clunk, followed by a small jolt from the gearbox, he began reversing the little Suzuki up a disused and rather overgrown track that meandered off from the main road up into the shallow hills beyond. The track he knew led to some fallow fields, up along a gently sloping bank that fell away to a star-lit horizon. He knew the owner of the pastures had retired, and with no one in the family willing to carry on the farming business, he had shut up shop long ago. The land had not been farmed for many years and would probably remain so for some time. Ideal for his purposes that night and into the future. He turned his baseball hat around, so the peak lay over the back of his neck and pulled an LED headtorch over his forehead. He switched on the light, got out and retrieved a spade, mattock pick, a lightweight groundsheet and a plastic twenty-five litre can of petrol from the back of the van. He pressed the car's locking fob and secured all its doors and headed up the track into the folds of the hills.

Following the bright sphere illuminating the ground before him, he briskly made his way up the track. Within twenty minutes of walking, he found the spot he was looking for – a dip in the ground that couldn't be seen from the road.

He marked out approximately one metre square in the turf by cutting its edge with his spade, stamping the tool below the root line on each penetration. He then dissected from the cut perimeter neat lines, crisscrossing from one side to the other, creating small oblongs, each precisely matching the spade's blade in both width and length.

He pushed under the first clod of grass, neatly lifting the turf intact with its life-giving roots undamaged by the spade. He laid the pieces gently to one side, placing them in a perfect mirror image of the darkened earth square he had cut them from. With the square complete, he rolled out the groundsheet to one side of the bare earthen patch and began to dig, using the spade where he could and the mattock pick to break up the compacted soil as he got deeper. He worked diligently ensuring that not a crumb of dirt from each shovelful fell anywhere but onto the groundsheet.

Within half an hour he was over a metre down, with a sizeable mound of soil on the sheet. He stepped out of the hole and surveyed the labours of his excavation. Deciding that this would be deep enough for his needs, he placed the tools carefully onto the small mound of earth and, with measured haste, returned to the van. *After all it was very bad manners to keep dignitaries waiting*, he thought, chuckling to himself as he carefully scurried on his way to retrieve the body of the once Governor of Fukushima Prefecture.

Unlocking the Suzuki, he began to hoist the woman through the rear doors of his compact van. Her body felt quite rigid after her time being stuffed in the small larder area under the counter. He reached in with his overly muscular arms to encircle the plastic sheet which held her petite body and, very carefully so as not to tear the translucent plastic, he drew her cold, foetal-shaped torso, out.

He held her against his chest with one hand while he closed the doors and locked them with the other. Then, cradling her across the front of his body in both arms, in an almost tender embrace as one might carry a sleeping child, he made steady progress back to the grave he had just dug. He was now committing to what was the most vulnerable phase of the foray. Being caught out in the open in the possession of a dead body at any time, would not be an ideal position for any self-respecting professional killer to find one's self in. The discovery of the deceased, who had been a high-profile politician and had already been overtly missing for several days, would lead to a somewhat all together more challenging situation no doubt. He effortlessly lifted the Governor again, carefully placing her into the pit. He manoeuvred her body into a more compact, foetal position to ensure a proper fit. With meticulous attention, he made sure every part of her, along with the plastic covering, was well below the surface. Taking a small penknife out of his pocket he made an incision in the plastic sheet, slitting it open along most its full length. He poured the remainder of the petrol into the grave, moving the nozzle up and down to ensure that every part of her body was saturated with the fuel.

He peered down at the broken and battered body of the Governor, watching as her clothes soaked up the flammable liquid. She had not died well, but he had not expected her to. The woman had no honour – that fact had been already made apparent to him long before he had decided to kidnap her.

He had eventually received all the information he required. It had taken a few days of rigorous interrogation, but nothing too exotic. Using the usual practices of psychological and physical torture had given him all the information he wanted.

Although she had been a professional politician of strong will and undoubted fortitude, for a female in their late forties, of fragile disposition, she was never going to put up much resistance to the insidiously destructive techniques he had applied to both her body and soul. Towards the conclusion of her torture, he felt a surge of satisfaction upon obtaining not only the essential information he sought, but also a collection of captivating, unexpected bonus insights. Watching, waiting for the petrol to soak into the corpse and saturate the soil beneath it, he pondered on what she had revealed to him. It always fascinated him with many of his victims, that even as they saw the end growing near, with all hope lost, adrift in a miserable sea of agony and desolation, something held them back from releasing that final grasp on the fading threads of existence. At that critical moment, a mere hint of redemption often proved to be enough to persuade them to relinquish their deepest secrets, despite their blatant disregard for the permanent consequences of their degradation.

So many people truly do not appreciate life until it is all far too late, he thought, as he set fire to a box of matches and threw it onto the body. He retreated rapidly from the inevitable fireball that would follow.

Even from where he was standing, he could feel the heat of the cleansing flames, their scorching scourge removing any trace of himself from the body. The heat was good, it was the light that came with it that concerned him.

While the furnace crackled and rendered the body to ash, he walked the short distance to the top of the hill that overlooked the main road and kept watch as the flames did their work, until they steadily died out about ten minutes later.

He returned to the pyre, the smell of burnt flesh and plastic catching in his nose and throat. He looked down at what was left of the body, which was very little. Globs of blackened, melted plastic were stuck at numerous points around the woman's remains. If her body were ever found, he was confident that only the teeth and DNA could potentially reveal her identity. However, he was assured that nothing about her would trace back to him, leaving no forensic evidence to connect him to the discovery. He had been careful not to break any bones, and all of her soft tissue had been consumed by the flames, with most of her skeleton no more than a powdery shadow.

Reviewing his handiwork, he meticulously cut away some singed edges of grass and then began to back-fill the grave, being careful not to spill any dirt onto the grass surrounding the hole. He methodically compressed the soil over the corpse using the flat side of his spade. To ensure an even surface, he also jumped on it, leaving a gap of approximately one hundred centimetres from the surrounding ground level. This gap was necessary to accommodate the turf, allowing it to be laid flat and seamlessly blend back into its original environment. He quickly reassembled the grassy jigsaw, returning it to the same orientation as it was taken. He then pulled up the corners of the sheet, retaining the remaining unused dirt within it. Securing the bunched ends of the plastic within the grip of one hand, he retrieved the rest of his gear with his other and set off back to the noodle van.

The track leading to where the vehicle was parked had a drainage ditch running along one side. As he walked alongside the ditch, he released one corner of the plastic sheet allowing the soil to trickle in as he went, leaving the first rain shower to melt it back into the ground and obscure its origin.

With a final check of the area, he got in, started the vehicle, and quickly drove off. He had arrived from an easterly direction, he now turned north onto the main road in the opposite direction to the way he had come.

The journey back was longer, which would mean less sleep before his early shift in the morning, but he never took unnecessary risks having learnt the lessons of his craft well.

He was confident her body would never be found. Spring would be here soon enough and the grass would grow strong and succulent around the grave. In the unlikely event that she was discovered, there was nothing to trace the body back to him, the only secret she could give up now was her identity.

It was the identity of others that concerned him now because the Governor's information had radically shuffled his list of suspects. Several had now been elevated across his deadly threshold of complicity into that zone where she had once taken the prime position. He was surprised that he had overestimated her importance, which concerned him as he was not a man who liked surprises at all. When one is surprised by an event, it indicates a lack of control, a true marker of sloppiness, which in his experience could lead to fatal mistakes. He had no reservations regarding his own ability to protect himself whatever circumstances evolved before him. However, the killing of innocents had never sat well, even on his stunted conscience. Undoubtedly, the Governor had committed several misdemeanours that, in his view, amounted to capital offences. Therefore, by the esteemed principles of Takada's law, she was justifiably deserving of her dreadful fate, based solely on those.

He drove on into the creeping dawn, back to Fukushima City to begin his shift at the restaurant that serviced the hotel where he was employed as a chef. It was 04.30 when he arrived to start the day's work. He parked his van in the car park beneath the hotel and made his way up to the top floor to start preparing the kitchen for the morning's breakfast rush.

He collected a fresh apron and chef's hat from the linen store and put them on. Adjacent to the kitchen island, he crouched down to unlock the cupboard beneath, where he stored the implements of his secondary, expertly honed craft. He carefully extracted a robust brown canvas knife wallet, secured by two brass buckles at each end. Adorning the space between the buckles was a leather patch, elegantly embossed with the words 'Ritz Paris', signifying its distinguished origin. He unbuckled the wallet and rolled out an exquisite set of extremely high-quality knives, mainly of Japanese origin, but also some of European design. He lovingly ran his hands over them, these were the tools of his trade, but also much, much more. A set of good knives is all a chef requires to get work, but it is also a passport to go anywhere in the world.

This set of blades, combined with his masterful skill, had made him welcome at some of the very best restaurants in many countries during his career. He withdrew one of the knives from its protective sheath within the wallet, holding its blade close to his face for inspection. He could tell just by looking at the edge alone that it was a Japanese blade. The profile of the cutting edge being the epitome of what made Japanese knives stand out against all others. The edges of European knives, and their swords for that matter, were sharpened from both sides, into a 'V'-shaped cutting edge. This was fine for heavy work, such as chopping through thick bones and joints when one was in a hurry, but to a Japanese chef, useless for the correct preparation of any type of food.

The cut of the food was regarded as divine to this culinary art. All types of food, whether they were meat or fish, fruit or vegetables, could be enhanced in appearance and taste by the slice of a blade that would leave a molecularly smooth surface in its wake. To achieve this required the chiselled edge of the traditional Japanese design. These blades were continuously flat on one side with only the opposite edge honed to extreme sharpness. This allowed for the most delicate and exquisite of cuts to be made and used expertly, could turn a mere chef into a culinary maestro.

Some of the dishes he had created in his career had been masterpieces, and through these fleeting works of art he had built a reputation for excellence with restaurateurs in kitchens located in the East and the West. They were always eager to procure the services of the Japanese chef, even if he never seemed to stay very long at any one establishment. That chapter of his life, marked by a deep love for gastronomy, now felt like a distant memory, overshadowed by other, more extreme passions. Yet, as he reflected on the unpredictable and often surprising nature of life's journey, he entertained the thought that perhaps, one day, he might reclaim his position among the world's culinary elite.

CHAPTER FOUR

3 March 2011

Matachi, their driver, had to swiftly, and abruptly veer the car to the roadside with a sense of urgency. This manoeuvre sent a shower of stones flying and tyres screeching during the unexpected halt. This drastic action was compelled by his partner's silent but overpowering emission of gas – a by-product of the digestive turmoil akin to a giant fermentation engine. Once the car stopped, Matachi hurriedly bolted out, seeking refuge at the roadside, safely away from the expanding noxious zone that had begun to envelop the vehicle.

'I feel sorry for your proctologist,' called Matachi from a radius of four metres away from the open side of the vehicle.

'Don't have one,' replied Tekiō, who had also now thrown open the passenger-side door. Initially he had felt very pleased with his creation, but even he now felt the need for fresh air. He pressed the rear trunk release button to get a better flow of air though the car.

'Not anymore anyway, because he probably fell in during your last colonoscopy and is still being digested inside you somewhere, decaying with the rest of the biomass in there,' called back Matachi. He changed position to take advantage of the direction of the wind, the force of which was just strong enough to keep Tekiō's foul aroma at bay.

Tekiō continued to savour the final lingering's of his masterpiece in olfaction. Then called the 'all clear' to his partner who was still standing in the field next to their car.

'It's gone now, it's safe to come back in – I promise,' he added.

Matachi carefully began to make his return to the large Toyota as if he were approaching a suspected IED.

'I thought we agreed before we started out that you would remain in full control of your disgusting bowels! And actually, if I remember correctly, it was one of the conditions that I put in place before I agreed to take this case with you. Fukushima is a large place and there is going to be a lot of "car time" involved in this job.'

'Yes, yes, apologies boss,' said Tekiō, 'I just forgot myself for a moment, it sort of slipped out.'

'Really! Well don't get dementia, or we will both be screwed,' retorted Matachi.

'It's all your fault actually.'

'Really, how did you work that one out?'

'Well, if you had not been driving like the usual pussy you are, we would be there by now and not have at least another hour to go.'

'I was obeying the speed limit, nothing wrong with that, you should try it. That is if we ever find a car large enough to allow your fat carcass to fit behind the steering wheel!'

'That's mean, boss, very low. Listen, let's fire up the blueys so we can get a wiggle on.'

'Eh… okay, but just this once, we would not wish to give the local boys a bad impression of us.'

'You mean other than the fact that between the two of us we have managed to "put down" more criminals than most departments have in their entire history.'

'They were all justified and appropriate responses, carried out during the legitimate performance of our duties as police officers.' He looked at Tekiō challengingly. 'They were unfortunate outcomes that evolved from difficult situations, nothing more wouldn't you say.' He responded as a statement rather than a question.

Tekiō stared back silently, the expression on his large oval face a picture of noncommittal inscrutability.

That line was there again, the invisible thread of morality that weaved through the centre of their profession, one that each of them ran close to at times, but approached from opposite sides. Matachi always aligning to the legitimate position, trying to keep them honest, within the law. Tekiō held more of a predisposition to principles of fairness. To him the law was but an abstract framework that he loosely operated within. In his perspective, what seemed right could be mistaken, and what was wrong could, at times, be considered the most appropriate course of action.

His stoic expression finally gave way to a lively display of animated creases as he let his unspoken thoughts be overtaken by an easy, familiar grin. He remarked, 'No doubt, if their superiors weren't aware of us before, they would have certainly looked us up by now.'

That smile Matachi knew could be replaced in an instant by emotions that were far more unnerving, but he let it be, best not to pick at old wounds.

'I am just pointing out, that it would be helpful to try and keep our Fukushima colleagues on side, at least for a while,' he responded.

'Well, that will be a waste of time for a start. Would you cut someone any slack if they turned up on your patch and took a case out of your hands? Because that is exactly what we are about to do; march into their HQ and demand every single piece of information they have on everything and anything to do with this governor's disappearance. Then we are going to push them all away to the side lines, keeping them there in a holding pattern, until we need gofers to run errands for us. Of course, they will be all smiles and bows on the outside, but that will only be because the Chief would have that ornate swagger stick of his up their boss's arse and then swivel him around a bit.'

'That may be so, but at least try not to choke anyone out in the toilets again… please…' said Matachi, recalling Tekiō's latest physical transgression.

'Sure boss, no problem, I told you that was just a little misunderstanding. So, let's get a move on shall we.'

Matachi, flicked the switch for the in-built blue lights hidden beneath the bodywork. The back and front of the vehicle began strobing with a bright effervescence. Gunning the Toyota into life, he accelerated out onto the highway.

The two men who sat in front of the large Toyota Land Cruiser, were both detectives, one held the rank of Inspector, the other a Sergeant, however, these were not ordinary detectives – if ever there were such a thing as an 'ordinary detective'. If there indeed was, then this odd pairing must be regarded as extraordinary.

They officially worked for Tokyo's Criminal Affairs Bureau, within the Organised Crime Investigation Division. However, you would not find them on any roster or police roll call, for they worked in the shadows as a uniquely qualified team who reported directly to a Senior Commissioner in the Tokyo police force.

In the eyes of the public, the two detectives appeared as contrasting as night and day. Physically, they differed considerably – Matachi, was average height for a Japanese, slight of build, with a dapper dress sense that was poles apart from his associate. Tekiō was huge by any human standard at two metres tall; a badly dressed ball of extremely intimidating fat and muscle would be an apt description. Both men supported distinct regional accents, that stuck out and even grated sometimes on others.

They had both arrived at this station in life from two unique and completely diverse perspectives. One, had once been a reasonably successful Sumo wrestler, the other forging an extremely lucrative livelihood as a very capable stock-market trader. Each from Japan's privileged élites, one had their roots in an ancient caste, the other born of the country's relentless drive for the future. Despite their cultural divergence, there was an unbreakable synergy of brotherhood between them that had been forged in the searing fires of shared adversities, a bond that each knew only death could destroy.

Their contrasting physical appearances often gave rise to a clichéd image, which they were not averse to exploiting for effect. They would sometimes play the roles of the bumbling duo, the archetypal ‹little and large› team of simple-minded cops, seemingly sharing a single brain cell between them. This act, however, was nothing more than a strategic pretence, designed to lower the guards of those they encountered. The moment they engaged with someone of interest, the veneer quickly dissipated. Both detectives were, in fact, exceptionally sharp and intuitive, with a subtle yet unmistakable air of menace lurking beneath their disarming exteriors. Their combined intelligence and cunning often caught their targets off guard, transforming any initial sense of ease into a profound discomfort, whenever they chose to reveal their true capabilities.

The pair's method of work was unusual, specialising in the unorthodox, with associated idiosyncrasies that their high-ranking superiors had been forced to reluctantly accept because of their astounding results. For, although it was not openly known, the two of them were the most successful detectives in the history of the Tokyo police department, which basically meant they were the best in Japan. Their unparalleled track record spoke volumes: the number of cases solved, criminals brought to justice, vast sums of money recovered, notorious crime syndicates dismantled and a significant body count. Their approach to law enforcement was uncompromising; they had zero tolerance for foolishness, particularly when it manifested as aggression or the ill-advised brandishing of weapons in their vicinity. They never took risks – a principle etched into their very being through years of navigating the perilous and unforgiving landscape of crime-fighting. Their methods, while unorthodox, were borne out of necessity and honed by experience, making them an unstoppable force in the realm of criminal investigation. They were a highly trained and motivated, professional unit, dedicated to eradicating serious crime. There's a saying that fortune favours the brave, and indeed, their impressive collection of commendations stood as a resolute testament to their courage. However, their remarkable success wasn't solely attributable to their readiness to deploy uncompromising violence when necessary. Their effectiveness stemmed from a blend of keen intelligence, strategic acumen and an innate understanding of the criminal mind, complementing their physical prowess. This multi-faceted approach allowed them to outmanoeuvre and dismantle criminal operations in a manner that brute force alone could never achieve.

Their fundamental method of work was a game changer in the world of Japanese policing. They were an epitome of what was modern Japan, a combination of the traditional, seamlessly bonded with cutting edge technology.

For one modest department within the Tokyo police service, Inspector Matachi Tadataka had changed the ineffective way the authorities had been dealing with fiscal corruption. He had brought into the police force the science-based technologies that ran through the world of finance, then used them to follow the revenue streams of substantial organised crime operations working within business and politics.

The initial façade of Matachi's operation, which once appeared distant and detached from the brutal realities of organised crime, was abruptly shattered as the impact of his early interventions became evident. What had begun as a seemingly remote and uninvolved endeavour, quickly transformed into a direct confrontation with the harsh underbelly of criminality. The effectiveness of his initial actions peeled away any illusion of detachment, thrusting him into the very heart of the conflict and exposing him to the raw barbarity that defines the world of organised crime.

The response of those of the criminal fraternity he was

affecting had been brutal, and at that time he had been forced to make a choice – return to his old, comfortable, privileged life or take serious issue with those who had hurt him and continue with the programme he had initiated.

Back then he had never been an aggressive or violent man and certainly never became involved in any physical confrontations, but despite his disposition, he would not consider himself a coward. He informed his superiors of the conditions acceptable to him, if he were to continue with his critical work for the police service. They reluctantly agreed with one very important stipulation of their own. It turned out that the 'condition' was a far bigger one than he had expected. Kondō Takehiko, better known by his Sumo nickname, Tekiō, had reported to him for duty a few days later. They had been an inseparable partnership ever since that day, ten long years ago.

The men were now travelling from Tokyo to Fukushima Prefecture. They had been tasked, to take over a highly politically-sensitive case – the mysterious disappearance of the Governor of Fukushima. This incident was now being connected with the disappearances of several other people and, in addition, to a number of what at the time had been considered as 'accidental deaths'. The individuals in question were either all local politicians or industrialists and, with the exception of the governor, to date, had indeed all been male.

Apart from the normal levels of cooperation one would expect of regional police forces, it was highly unusual for police units from other prefectures to directly intervene in the issues of another force in a different area.

Although only the two of them would be actively working the case in the field, they had been assured of receiving significant support. Their superiors had promised to give strong consideration to any additional resources or assistance they might need during the course of their investigation. This promise of backup, though not immediate, provided a safety net, ensuring they would have access to the necessary tools and reinforcements to effectively navigate and resolve the complexities of the case.

A great deal of political pressure was being applied to their superiors to find answers as to what was happening in the area — and quickly. They had been left in no doubt that something very serious was going on in Fukushima Prefecture and their presence on the ground was immediately required.

CHAPTER FIVE

3 March 2011

Making himself comfortable on the rocky edge running along the clifftop ridge, Kurosawa took in the rugged view of the bay as it bowed around to his left-hand side. He had driven through the night so as to arrive at the waters around the Shima Peninsula before sunrise. Below him on the shoreline were a group of about ten women, busying themselves in their final preparations before they started work.

Four or five of them were gathered around a Kamado stove they had set up on the beach earlier. There was a flurry of fiery sparks from its cast-iron doorway as one of the group opened it to re-stoke the fire consisting of the charcoal and small logs that they had brought with them. Others were stacking wicker baskets and folding woven fabric sacks into piles. To stop their trappings from being blown away by the fresh inland breeze, they used one of the many rocks that lay around the rugged shore to weight them down.

Each of the women was wearing some type of wetsuit. Several were of the more modern neoprene type, but most were the old-fashioned rubber variety. Each had a tight-fitting hood attached, which created a circle around their faces, running from just under the lower lip then curving upwards, cutting across the eyebrows, creating a moon-like face in all of them. The divers equipped themselves with large, circular diving masks that were meticulously designed to fit the contours of their faces. These masks enveloped every inch of their exposed skin and features, with the exception of the area around the mouth.

The ladies paired up to examine one another, checking the fitting of the masks to the diving suits, ensuring the seal of the mask fitted perfectly to the edge of their hoods. Once content with their safety checks they retrieved the rest of their equipment, consisting of flippers, nets, buoys and, most importantly, the main tool of their profession – the 'Awabi-Okoshi' hooks.

For these womenfolk were the 'Ama', a band of free divers, who trace their origins back five thousand years, existing then as today by plying their trade around the shores of Japan. Each of them was capable of diving to around twenty metres on one breath, staying down for nearly a minute, while they dug around the sea bottom using their hooks to prise out sea cucumbers, octopuses, lobsters and the prized Abalone crustaceans.

He now watched as the small group of divers waded out into the surf and then started swimming to the fixed orange buoys that bobbed up and down in the swell, about one hundred metres out.

It was March and the sea temperature was around sixteen degrees centigrade. They would stay out in the water for one and a half to two hours, continuously diving for the whole period. Even with the protection of the wetsuits it took a particularly hardy type of person to brave those waters. For these ladies, this was no recreational pursuit, for most of them it was their main livelihood. Their harvest, drawn from the abundant riches of the sea, was highly prized as culinary delicacies. Their primary clientele consisted of gourmet restaurants renowned for their exquisite menus. Consequently, most of their days spent diving proved to be highly profitable.

On reaching the floating buoys that had been tethered to the seabed, the divers began to take a few sharp, quick breaths, followed by one long, full one, held it and then immediately dived below the surface. Their flipper-swathed feet briefly breaking the surface as they majestically swooped down, harnessing the propulsion generated by their powerful legs through the movement of their flippers, driven purposely to the seabed below.

Attached to the securing ropes of the buoys were open-topped nets. As the divers returned briefly to the surface, they would deposit the fruits of their forays into these from their own smaller mesh sacks tied to their waists, before snatching another breath and returning to the rocky sea floor to continue winkling out the tasty creatures that were secreted away there.

By some Japanese they were regarded as one of the country's 'living treasures'. Kurosawa watched them in amazement working to harvest the ocean's bounty, their fortitude and skill combining to entertain him with their aquatic ballet.

Remarkably, the small group, had an average age of around sixty years. This number was somewhat deceptive, as it was skewed lower by the presence of several younger members, whose lithe and graceful movements resembled those of mermaid-like ballerinas. Despite the varying ages, the group's collective experience blended the wisdom of the elders with the vigour of youth. It was one of those women in particular that had compelled Kurosawa to drive through the night, to take on the gruelling journey from his home in Fukushima.

He had tried to single her out during the dive, but bobbing up and down in the swell, one rubber-clad head with a glass bowl stuck across the face, looked much like another.

The sea now started to become choppier. The snorkellers had been in there for well over an hour and he could see they were starting to struggle to catch their breath on returning to the surface, as the waves began to rush in on them from every angle.

Several of the crew had lost friends and relatives to the sea and its vagaries in their time, and consequently understood that no one's life was worth a bag of shellfish. So, seemingly without any orders being given, the group began to complete their final dives and then started to untie the net bags and swim back to the shoreline.

As the buoyancy of their haul within the lattice sacks was lost as they reached the shallows, they struggled to drag them up onto the gravelly beach. He thought about going down to give them a hand, but then other women emerged from sheltering on the other side of the cove, pulling small carts behind them. The trolleys looked as though they had been cobbled together from bits of scrap metal as they rolled down on sets of old car wheels to the water's edge. They threw the bulging bags of seafood onto each cart in turn, helping one another to lift the heavy sacks, before pulling the day's catch up onto the beach.

All the fisherwomen were now ashore. Some began to warm themselves around a roaring open-air stove that sat outside of their wooden hut, while others commenced the process of sorting and weighing the catch. This group worked as a team and shared the bounty equally. From what he could see; he knew who would be buying dinner tonight he thought.

Some of them started to help each other out of their wetsuits, after first carefully putting their face masks away in padded bags to protect them from becoming scratched. One of them pulled back her rubber hood to reveal a shock of short cut, bright blue hair, still relatively dry from being sealed tightly in place and which stuck upwards in a series of crazily angled spikes. She was laughing at a comment one of the others had said to her; to Kurosawa the women seemed to radiate life and vitality. He watched the woman with the bright blue hair, her full figure athletically filling her suit as she stood there at the centre of the gathering. That's my girl, he thought.

Coming down from his vantage point, Kurosawa trekked back across the ridge towards a small line of shacks and beach-houses that sat alongside the municipal carpark. The Ama were already starting to congregate around one of the larger, but more ramshackle huts, as he arrived. He kept a respectful distance from the group as the final stragglers arrived to join the exuberant gathering. The ladies seemed to create a festive atmosphere, freely laughing, and hugging each other, invigorated by the intoxication of their successful foray.

As he looked on, some of them, a few still in wetsuits moved inside the building to remove and store their precious attire, returning in casual clothing to assist with the loading of several small vans that had turned up to take away their fare.

He finally glimpsed the unmistakable blue hair of his Ikuko; she was at the rear of one of the vehicles helping to load the last of the sacks inside. Upon noticing him lingering near his Prius, she quickly slipped on a denim jacket over her T-shirt and baggy sweatpants. After calling out farewells to her close-knit group of friends, she exchanged a few final waves and warm hugs. As she departed, a handful of her friends made teasing remarks that, although inaudible to him, prompted a playful blush to colour her cheeks. With a mixture of amusement and anticipation, she gracefully made her way towards him.

'You made it then?' she said coming right up to him, close enough for him to smell the scent of the ocean on her body; mixed with the natural release of her pheromones, it was a heady mix. Yet, it was the sudden emergence of her aura that truly captivated him. It appeared as though she had stepped through an intensely vibrant, arch-shaped portal, materialising from another realm. This ethereal vision unfolded as she closed the final few metres separating them, entering the range of his heightened perception. Her approach seemed to bring the very air around her to life, with her aura intensifying in luminosity and colour, casting an otherworldly glow that left him deeply affected.

'Of course, I told you I would be here early,' he replied, as he struggled to control the intensity of feelings her sudden proximity generated within him.

'And Hikaru always does what he says he will, don't you my love,' she said, flicking away the strands of his long dark fringe away from his eyes. She brushed the edge of his angular cheekbone, as she moved in to kiss him on the lips. 'So where

54

are you taking me for lunch today, somewhere nice, I hope? Breakfast was a long time ago and I have built up quite an appetite for some reason.'

'Well, as you're the one buying, somewhere expensive I was thinking!' he said holding her close to him with his hands around her waist.

'You know for a rich boy you are tighter than some of those clams I dredge up!'

'What makes you think I'm rich?'

'I have seen your house, you know, and as far as I can make out, you do not actually have any kind of job. Unless you regard running a rake around that sandpit of yours as an occupation?'

'I told you the house is not mine, as such. It is held in perpetuity to the Kurosawa name, it cannot be sold if someone legitimately linked to our family line is still alive. As it has been for over three hundred and fifty years. Anyway, if I was rich would I be driving around in one of these?' He released her and tapped the roof of the Toyota.

'You're not fooling anyone, you know. You drive this because you're one of those well-off "Green" types, a wanna-be Eco Warrior, wanting to keep a low profile. Just the upkeep of your place would be hard enough to maintain, even if you did work full time. On my granny's grave, I am sure I have no idea what it is you spend your free time on.'

Kurosawa pointed to one of the older ladies standing in the group behind her.

'Isn't that your grandma over there?' he asked.

'Not that one, I meant the crazy one on my mother's side.'

'What's crazier than a woman who has spent her life free diving on a daily basis, to depths that would shred the lungs of a normal human?' he said, trying to distract her away from one of her frequent exploratory excavations into his life.

'Yeah, I will have to tell you about her someday. Her motto was, "It is nobler to burn within the furnace of one's heart than

55

flicker in the shadows of regret"… and she lived by that saying… and then died by it.'

'Mmmm, interesting,' he said, opening the car door and inviting her into the passenger seat.

'So why the sudden need to see me, other than the obvious fact that I am quite irresistible of course?' she asked as he got into the car.

'I have to go away for a week or so, my sister has asked me to accompany her on a business trip to Okinawa. She is trying to offload some leftover stock and is taking lots of samples with her. Some of the textiles are quite bulky and she has not been well lately, so she is worried she may struggle carting them around, not being the robust type like you,' he nonchalantly lied.

'Hey, so you are going to do some actual work for once!'

'Well, I would not go that far,' he said smiling at her, still feeling the strength of her presence physically and ethereally.

'Do you think that your sister will ever return from living in Tokyo? It would be nice to finally meet her.'

'I'm sure you will one day soon, she is just so busy with her business problems, it's been quite a hard time for her lately.'

'Yeah, I'm not trying to be pushy, it's just she does seem to be a little illusive. We have been an item for over six months now and the most I have seen of her is that picture you have in your room of you both as children.'

'She is a very private person; I can assure you she means no offence by not visiting for a while. She can see that I am happy, so she is very glad about that. Listen,' he said, trying once again to change the subject. 'I'm not that hungry right now, for food anyway! Why don't we go back to the hotel and order some room service?'

She smiled at him, 'Sounds like a plan. How fast can this green machine go?!'

CHAPTER SIX

3 March 2011

Outside the Municipal Police Headquarters in Fukushima City, Matachi was carefully peeling off a parking penalty sealed in a very sticky plastic bag from their illegally parked Toyota's windshield, failing in his attempt to not leave any gluey residue on the windscreen. The ticket, a consequence of their late arrival at the police station and then being confronted with a full car park. A civic meeting being hosted at the station with local dignitaries from around the prefecture, the cause of their parking dilemma, forcing them to find an alternative parking solution. Unfortunately, as it turned out, one that had been in violation of the local parking restrictions.

'That went better than I expected on the whole, don't you think?' said Matachi.

Tekiō extended one of his giant arms almost fully across the hood of the car and plucked the ticket out of Matachi's hand, his sausage-like finger and thumb performing a weirdly delicate action for such chunky digits. Lightly pinching one of the less sticky corners, he stared down at the offending notice.

'Yes, it did, but don't you think that was a bit surprising, odd even?' said Tekiō over his shoulder, as he began to walk down the street to where he had spotted a parking warden furtively peeking at them from behind some legally parked cars that were sitting a short distance in front of theirs.

'I did get the impression that they seemed almost genuinely glad to be offloading the case onto us I must admit,' said Matachi, continuing the conversation with Tekiō as he walked away from him down the line of cars towards the warden.

The man, on seeing he had been spotted, turned around, pretending to find something interesting in the storage tail box of his tricycle as Tekiō approached.

'Hey, Meter Maid,' growled Tekiō.

The man turned around. He was very short even for a Japanese and wore a smart, deep blue, cotton uniform and peaked cap with 'traffic attendant' written across it. He had to arch his head back to look Tekiō in the face. His eyes appeared far too large for his face when seen through the extremely thick lenses of his spectacles.

'How dare you address me in that fashion!' the man said, outraged by a demonstration of such bad manners.

Typically, the traffic warden encountered little resistance from those he issued tickets to. Most individuals readily acknowledged their mistake, often accompanying their admission with a customary, grovelling apology. They expressed regret not only for their parking violation but also for the inconvenience caused to him by having to issue a ticket.

The warden readily lapped up the endorphin fix this self-righteous satisfaction provided, and though the pleasure still consummately fed his ego, its potency had waned somewhat over the years. This had caused him to rely on these now rare encounters to give him a more potent hit. There were not many of these in general, it being culturally unacceptable to create a shameful disturbance in public. Though times were changing in Japan and with the accompanying lowering of standards, there were always a few that tried to argue their way out of being ticketed and these were his favourite offenders. Putting such individuals in their place was by far the most rewarding part of his job.

He had been secretly watching the two men approach their car, the reactions of motorists finding a ticket on their windscreen still a gratifying part of his job. So, when one of them started walking towards him, he could not believe his luck. He had slowly released the safety catch on his arsenal of lofty sarcasm as he pretended not to see one of the men approaching. His view had been partially obstructed, so he had not been viewing the two men directly, keeping his gaze down as the first man approached. When he had finally turned to face his rude assailant, he was surprised to find such an extremely large man who now stood uncomfortably close to him. Tekiō's sizeable frame now seemed to obscure everything as it filled his view. His demeanour of insulted self-righteousness, fading beneath the intimidating shadow of Tekiō.

'Don't you see who I am?' he countered, noticing Tekiō's enormous hands.

'Oh... oh... I'm sorry,' replied Tekiō mockingly.

That's better, thought the parking attendant, readying his arsenal of belittling banter, unfortunately for him totally missing Tekiō's contemptuous tone before he could start his tirade. Tekiō carried on talking over him.

'But you see, I could not give a flying fuck who you are!'

His officious tone breaking slightly, the man said, 'You cannot address me in that manner, do you not understand that you are dealing with a city official?'

'Really! Well, you can – city official this – out of my fucking sight,' he said, holding up the ticket in front of the man's face. The attendant was astonished at the rude and brazenly aggressive behaviour he was being subjected to.

'Once the penalty notice has been issued it cannot be unissued, you will have to go through the appeals process,' adding helpfully that, 'the details are on the back of the notice.' With a trembling hand, the warden attempted to show Tekiō where the information was on the ticket.

Tekiō swatted his hand out of the way with an audible smack, then reached down and stuck the sticky packet onto the man's chest, pinning it there with a heavy prod of one of his oversized fingers. The attendant took an involuntary step backwards from the force of the interaction. Before the man could protest, Tekiō pulled out his badge and held it down in front of his face.

'If we get any comeback on this fucking parking penalty, I will come and find you, scrunch you into a ball, then stuff you in that fucking box, you gobby little shitbag,' he informed the man, pointing at the small storage pannier attached to the rear of his trike.

Not waiting for a reply, he turned and 'swagger-barrelled' his way back to where Matachi stood. It was the same intimidating saunter he had used during a match in his competition days, after he had defeated a fellow wrestler.

'Making friends with the locals I see, excellent, dear boy. Now if you have quite finished terrorising the populace, we have some work to do.'

'It's past lunchtime, you know I can get rather tetchy if my blood sugar levels start to get low.'

The two men climbed into their SUV, Matachi taking his usual position in the driver's seat. 'Ah, that explains it then, feeling a bit hypoglycaemic, are we? We will get a snack later, right now make yourself useful and put this address into the car's GPS system,' said Matachi, handing Tekiō a pink sticky note as he pulled the car out into the traffic.

Tekiō began punching in the address he had been given onto the touch screen of the car's internal navigation system. Matachi was always amazed that he could do this so adeptly with such large fingers.

'Where are we going and who are we going to see?' enquired Tekiō.

'City Hall, let's see who is keeping the governor's old seat warm,' replied Matachi, pleased that Tekiō's fascination with the parking attendant had abated. The man had such a low tolerance for anything he perceived as bullshit. It seemed such a base emotion for a detective to hold as a starting point to any interaction. To Tekiō everyone was a potential arsehole until proven otherwise.

Over the course of their decade-long partnership, Matachi had grown to realise that Tekiō's depths extended far beyond what was immediately apparent – and what was apparent was already quite remarkable. This insight began to dawn on him shortly after they were paired as partners, a partnership that had initially been formed under reluctant circumstances. Ironically, it was a shared experience of profound tragedy that had ultimately brought them together, marking an inauspicious yet pivotal beginning to their relationship.

Back then Matachi was the whizz kid rookie, the geeky mathematician brought in by the Tokyo police under a new initiative to exploit skills and expertise not normally found in the ranks of policemen. His job was to bring disorganisation to the realms of organised crime. Though not by the usual tactics of raids, arrests and interrogation. They were the old ways and using the same old methods produced the same old results.

A new strategy was required and Matachi had been chosen to deliver it by building algorithmic programs that could discover, track and analyse where and how they were making their money. What mathematicians called 'Big Data' was the key; the more information that could be collected, the more powerful the magic of the application of statistical bias became. Once he had activated his programs, there would be no hiding from the insidious nature of the data gathering mechanisms. If you were an entity in the universe, of any description, you generated data. It just required the appropriate tools to collect and analyse it. With the data in your possession, one could build an intricate picture of what essentially was the business model, illuminating in stark relief the operational protocols and philosophies of the crime syndicate.

The moments and whereabouts of key elements such as money, commodities and people would become visible. And with that visibility would come the ability to manipulate and interdict those flows. To have the power not only to generate evidence to arrest and successfully prosecute, but also the ability to create chaos and sow confusion and internal suspicion by maliciously manipulating those processes.

Within the world of organised crime, it was almost too easy for Matachi to infiltrate their enterprises and discover their design and operation strategies. Whatever they did and whatever they had done – it was recorded. Wherever and whenever they did it – it was recorded. Even doing nothing was no defence against his digitised data collection and cyberised probing; it did not make you invisible, on the contrary, banality was its own marker. If one did everything or did nothing, one was always doing something. There is no such thing as a neutral act, a lack of action as important as any enterprise.

A tutor of mathematics at Tokyo University had told him once that: *If an element exists then by the very nature of its existence it can be detected by its effect on space and time as a pattern. Scale is irrelevant here, each event is registered, regardless of size or configuration as a disturbance. All one is required to do is take a measurement of it to reveal the ghost in the machine. The esoteric mathematical patterns are always therein their mystical simplicity.*

What this meant for the crime gangs was, no matter how banal their action or inaction, however obscure its occurrence was or innocuous the activity initiated, each could be measured as a data point. With everything being recorded and fed into his substantial number-crunching array of servers, the Tokyo police department had built it into the basement of their HQ Building. He understood the precept that data knows no right or wrong, it bears no grudges, makes no preconceptions, it has no agenda of its own, it just exists, awaiting analysis to transform it into information. And this is what he achieved, exponentially building on each event, until he had constructed a rich seam of raw data. The efficient armoury of the statistician was then put to work, using his toolbox of methodologies to mine on occasion the colossal amounts of data collected, but also to gather valuable insights from quite modest input.

The final step of this process is the contextual interpretation of its relevance. The data is manipulated with the selection of statistical techniques, where it is made to give up its secrets and tell its story, through being regressed, codified and trended, presenting opportunities to be acted upon. This manipulation of data is used by every major corporation in the world to second guess the needs of its customers and the aims of its competitors, delivering spectacular results.

That had been Matachi's domain for many years. He was a master of the intellectual skills required to build the programs and apply the principles required to glean extremely useful information. He was now using those skills for the benefit of the police department.

He had turned his unique abilities initially to the underworld of organised crime. With results in the form of arrests quickly following, as he uncovered how the network of gangs moved and laundered its ill-gotten capital. In all honesty, it had not been problematic to locate the Yakuza's pot of gold. To him it may as well have had a big fuck-off rainbow emanating out of it, with a flashing neon sign saying, 'Here I am.'

He had created for the police a detailed masterpiece of the workings of organised crime in Japan. A depiction that showed the detailed positions of people and finances, how they got there and where they would go next. He detailed the relationships of the criminals and their legitimate business associates. His programs had exposed the many different factors and environments the crime syndicates operated within, providing a range of venerable targets. Once the police departments began to act on that information, the impact on the organised crime regimes was immediate and devastating. Several high-profile arrests followed within the ranks of the Yakuza gangs and their legitimate confederates.

Unfortunately, to Matachi, his work held no real relevance to

63

his then daily reality, he was too much the fledgling in his career to understand the implications of the stratagems he had set in motion. Actions that would impact on the lives and livelihoods, not to mention, 'honour' of some very dangerous people. He was oblivious to the fact that the pot of gold he was trying to tip over would release some very nasty Leprechauns.

He had been the first, and remained the only, Doctor of Mathematics to become a full-time policeman, not only in Japan but as far as he knew within any country's police force. Back then his egotism had run alongside his naivety in its lack of limits. At that time, the battle to break up the Yakuza gangs was at its height, and it was a war his intelligence-driven strategy was winning. He was striking at the vitals of the organised crime syndicates and causing them great pain. Accolades from his superiors were bestowed on him as his successes grew. Regrettably it grew alongside the apathy of his growing conceit, which was deluding him of the reality of the situation he had manufactured.

Matachi deceived himself that he was fighting these gangs in a kind of virtual ecosphere, insulated from the reality he was creating. He rarely got involved in the real consequences of acting on the information he provided. He paid scant attention to the actual taking down of targets he highlighted, or the raiding of establishments that were fronts for the spectrum of illegitimacies he uncovered. These matters, soiled with the tragically affected lives of real individuals, were not his concern.

Detectives seldom work alone and because of his inexperience in more general police work, he had been given an experienced partner as a guide and mentor, though he was still technically her superior, because his fast-track route into the police force came with the rank of Inspector. On the rare occasions when he would have accompanied her in the interrogation room, she had done all the talking, leading the situation totally.

Izuko was a skilled detective, he understood now that her understanding of the nuances of her craft were far beyond his at that time. She just needed to understand the line of questioning he wanted her to pursue and she did the rest. Her manipulation of suspects was masterful; if there was any information of value to be uncovered, she would draw it out.

After his brief excursions into the realm of real-world policing, he would retreat into his subterranean lair, a domain ruled by advanced supercomputers. Here, in this digital sanctum, he callously processed the information harvested from his ventures. Each piece of data was meticulously analysed, used solely to refine his self-serving methodologies, further detaching him from the nuances and realities of any existence beyond police work.

He was happy to be lost in the surreal domain of mathematical economics, where he linked the tangible to the abstract, creating discoveries and hypotheses that amazed his superiors. He had thought then that he had found his true vocation in life, enjoying using his skills for the good of humanity, bringing societal riches rather than commercial ones.

Then the sudden violent death of Izuko had changed all of that. He could still see her broken and bloodied body lying beside her car in that fucking, shitty underground carpark.

Death had not come quick to her; she had fought back and paid the price. And it had been his stupidity and inexperience that had caused her death. The disgusting reality of the life he had ignorantly been working in, had unveiled itself to him in the most horrific of manners. Ignorance is not bliss, it is just ignorance, a dangerous unawareness that can become a pitfall for fools.

He knew the gods had punished him for becoming so arrogant, for allowing hubris to consume his soul. His isolation from reality was bringing a destabilising imbalance into his life. When you only lengthen but a few spokes on your wheel of life, the universe has no choice other than to deliver you a bumpy ride. There had been no time to grieve then as they were at a critical juncture in the operation. His superiors had offered him compassionate leave, a standard requirement in these events and one that was normally rigidly enforced for the wellbeing of the bereaved partner and their colleagues. But it was not a normal time, they were at a critical point in their operation, success here would put Tokyo's organised crime network on the back foot for years to come. They needed him to carry on, to put his anger and grief on hold, while they completed the final stages of the operation.

In murdering Izuko, the gangs had found a way to hit back at the police. It was evident that he could be next, so they had assigned a new partner to him – a specialist in close protection. Just a temporary precaution they said, his security was paramount he was told.

It was important to Matachi to keep working, it was not a hard decision really, he wanted revenge for his partner's death and the best way to get back at them was to complete his work – for now anyway.

So, he had been introduced to Tekiō and from that point on the guy had not really left his side. Though at first, even after the horrific shock of losing Izuko, Matachi could not see the worth of his new partner. Izuko was no mathematician, but she was very intelligent, he found working with her insightful, often giving logical challenges to his work. She was also a first-class detective who could be tough at times, definitely not a fragile flower. She had been known as the 'Steel Pearl' in the department and with good reason. In addition to this she had been a lot easier on the eye than Tekiō. For a while he had felt that he had swapped a goddess for a lumbering hippo and he was resentful. Feeling confused, he believed they had given him some dispensable meathead minder for his protection. A bullet blocker, who he was to drag around with him everywhere he went.

He was ashamed now for feeling so resentful of Tekiō back in the early days of the partnership. He put it down to his grief over Izuko and had not looked beyond the appearance of a scowling fat man. He mistakenly believed that the man's only talent was his large size, useful as a shield in case of gunfire. As it turned out Tekiō had a deeper soul than he had first realised and, being Tekiō, not only refused to take shit from anyone but also understood human nature extremely well. His Sumo training had paradoxically enhanced the natural empathy that was at his very core, although to be frank that core was quite a way down and not accessible to everybody. Tekiō understood what Matachi was going through, and for a large guy managed to give him space when he needed it; he seemed to appreciate when he needed to be left to himself.

His work involved long hours staring at computer screens in their modest high-tech dungeon and sometimes he would forget that Tekiō was even there. He seemed to blend into the surroundings, no mean feat for a man of two hundred kilos and two metres in height. Tekiō's insightfulness ran deeper than knowing when to keep his mouth shut. Many times, when Matachi's mind would once again begin to wander to the weakness of melancholy and he would stare at the screens but not see them, lost in a sea of despairing self-loathing, Tekiō would make him start with his deep powerful voice, shocking him out of his apathetic disdain with abashing irreverence, shouting something along the lines of… 'Hey Geek, I need to take a shit, and would like to get some fresh air. I have been trapped in this dump with you for fucking hours. While I'm gone use one of those boring algorithms to find us a nice place to eat. Make sure you book one with a booth with a bench, my arse has a dislike for those fancy fucking chairs.'

Then suddenly his despondency would be replaced by annoyance for his direct manner. He would irritate him with the perceived familiarity of his profanity, after all just who was the superior rank here! Then he would be absorbed with the task of booking a restaurant – with seats that Tekiō's fat arse could fit into.

Tekiō would return, from invariably blocking up their only lavatory in the basement with one of his giant-sized evacuations, and off they would go.

At the restaurant, Tekiō would then proceed to get him

inebriated whilst listening to his drunken sorrows, saying little, except to offer to pour another glass of sake, never taking 'no' as an answer, until he had become semi-conscious. Later he would half carry, half drag him out of the restaurant, with one hand holding the scruff of his jacket, like a normal-sized person would hold a scrunched-up plastic bag and put him in a taxi and take him home. Matachi owed much to the giant for his kindness during those dark days, and it was a debt that he happily accepted.

On their arrival at the Municipal Civic Building they found themselves identifying who they were to a wide-eyed attendant at the reception desk.

'We are here to see Matsumoto Hirofumi,' Matachi informed the obviously nervous young man sat behind the long desk with several similar receptionists.

'Matsumoto san,' repeated the man mechanically back to them.

'Yes, that is what I said, Matsumoto Hirofumi. We would like to talk to him – right now,' Matachi said slowly and deliberately. He was standing in front of Tekiō, who loomed behind him projecting his usual air of menace, both holding their detective badges up to the face of the young man.

The receptionist, now feeling rather intimated by their imposing presence and brusque manner, foolishly repeated, 'Matsumoto-san?'

A deep, exasperated breath behind Matachi informed him that Tekiō's arsehole threshold was being dangerously tickled by the man's repetitive answers.

Realising that he was not doing himself any favours here, he quickly answered, 'He is not at work today; he has taken some annual leave of absence.'

'How long has he been off work?'

'I am not sure I am allowed to share with you that personal information.' The young receptionist faltered in his answer.

Just as Matachi felt Tekiō's gut pushing him in the back as he moved forward to probably start throttling the man, a female receptionist intervened.

'It's OK, Saigō-san, I will deal with this matter,' she said to the much-relieved man. She looked at Matachi and introduced herself as the office manager.

The detectives again revealed their IDs and immediately Matachi felt that something was not quite right, so he got straight to the point. 'This is official police business. We are looking for Matsumoto Hirofumi; we need to know when he was last in work and his address.'

'And we won't be asking again,' emphasised Tekiō over Matachi's shoulder for good measure.

'Of course, sir. Saigō-san, open the vacation schedule.' The receptionist leaned over his keyboard and tapped on several keys with one hand, operating a mouse with the other. The manager looked at the screen hidden out of sight below the top of the long desk. 'He called in this morning to say he needed to take some leave, no explanation logged,' she informed the detectives.

'Address?' demanded Matachi.

The woman pushed past the receptionist and logged in with the higher clearance required for this level of personal information. She wrote down the address on a notepad, tore off the sheet and handed it to them.

'Thank you, Office Manager-san,' said Matachi accepting the piece of paper. With a parting scowl from Tekiō at the hapless receptionist, they headed back out of the building, both realising that it was highly unusual for any worker, let alone a high ranking official, to take a sudden leave of absence.

They retrieved their car from the adjacent multi-storey car park opposite the building and made their way to the address they had been given for Matsumoto. Within twenty minutes they found themselves on the outskirts of Fukushima City outside a row of traditional looking houses, along a street in the residential suburb of Iizaka-onsen. They parked their car outside a small Shinto shrine at the end of the road and made their way on foot to the house.

Tekiō rang the bell, waited a few moments but as no one came to the door, rang it again.

'You stay here and keep trying the buzzer and I will go around the back,' ordered Matachi, making his way down the street to find a route to the rear of the building.

Having no luck with the bell, Tekiō tried banging the door with his hand. Usually, the noise of a fist hammering at one's door seemed to instil more of an immediate response in his experience. He was about to deliver another series of solid hits when the door opened to reveal Matachi standing there with his pistol drawn.

'Oh, do please come in,' he cordially said.

Tekiō purposefully drew his own personal weapon and followed him in.

'I do not think there is anyone else in here – alive that is – but we better check all the rooms. Downstairs is clear-ish, let's try upstairs.'

The two men, carefully covering each other, professionally searched all the upstairs' areas in the methodical manner in which they had been trained. They made sure each room was empty of occupants with the minimum of disturbance as it was a potential crime scene.

'All clear,' called Tekiō, backing out of the toilet, the final room on their search pattern.

'You had better put these on,' said Matachi, pulling out a set of plastic overshoes from his inside jacket pocket, handing a pair over before he started putting them over his own shoes. Tekiō looked questioningly at his boss as he did the same. 'Now follow me, you are not going to believe this old chap.'

Matachi led Tekiō back downstairs and into the main living area of the house.

'By the way, I think you are about to thank me for not stopping for lunch!'

CHAPTER SEVEN

5 March 2011

The road to hell was indeed paved with good intentions, thought Uchida Zenjirō. As head of one the largest civil engineering consortia in Japan's atomic energy sector, he was regarded as the pinnacle of leadership in this field. He was venerated by the great and the good of Japanese captains of industry and politicians alike and regarded as a living bastion of the codes underpinning corporate business in Japan – or at least for the time being.

He now realised that years of accolades had blinded him, leading to a string of questionable decisions. It had taken a lifetime, but he had finally reached an inflection point. The once shadowy inevitability was now starkly clear: a reckoning for his dubious past actions loomed, threatening disaster due to his unquenchable thirst for power.

Even in his seventy-seventh year, his voracious craving for control was as intense as ever. With age came a deeper understanding: the more one ages, the more desperately one clutches at life's reins. Establishing the Fukushima Nuclear Power Plant was the crowning achievement of his extensive career. He had schemed to ensure its secrets would remain long after he transitioned into an ancestral Kami, entering the underworld of Yomi-no-kuni, the dark after life realm of the dead.

If it were not for him the plant would have never been built in the first place. Of course, he fully understood that at the time he was putting into place measures that could be considered at best, questionable and unethical, and in most cases unscrupulously corrupt. The position of the conglomerate's backers was that failure was not an option, and results would be demanded of him at any cost. However, it was clear to see now that mistakes had been made.

What other choice did he have? The sheer scale of the project's challenges turned what would normally be insurmountable difficulties into everyday realities. The expenditure required in dealing with these issues had been enormous, billions of Yen in fees, on a budget spiralling out of control; costs that had to be recovered from somewhere to avert the collapse of the venture. He had been under enormous pressure to deliver this project on time, and in full. That meant meeting the financial commitments had become critical to its success. The project had struggled technically from the outset, which quickly developed into financial stresses.

Compelled to make it work, he staked everything on the project, fully aware of the dire consequences of failure. This stark reality was underscored from its conception and frequently reiterated by his influential overseers.

The decommissioning bond alone would eventually reach hundreds of billions of Yen, which was more than the entire cost of the combined project construction price.

Each construction contract included an automatic ten per cent markup, a significant amount but dwarfed by the Japanese government's ninety per cent subsidy. This substantial government funding was committed not only during construction but also for ongoing contributions long after the plant's completion. The costs escalated on a sliding scale, increasing as more of the six reactors became operational and the massive turbines started generating electricity. Despite this substantial support, managing the cash flow to keep the project on track was a high-stress endeavour, stretching resources to their limits. Initially, he had assigned low priority to the issue of the bond, considering its cost irrelevant unless the plant achieved success. Yet, as his efforts began to bear fruit and the plant unexpectedly sparked into life, those additional costs morphed into a relentless, self-amplifying burden. At the time, he hadn't grasped the potential profitability of the seemingly unattainable bond. That realisation became apparent later. Back then, the bond was just one of several significant challenges that needed to be addressed efficiently to prevent them from bankrupting the construction budget.

Undoubtedly slowing down the construction timetable was not a viable option. The plant's output could not be reduced or the revenue curve they had predicted from selling the power to the consumers, would not be met. In addition, the grants and loans they had secured from local and national government, were performance related. They would only receive the agreed subsidies in relation to the facility's construction schedule. Once the site finally became operational, the remuneration model shifted to be based on the plant's output, as it began to channel millions of watts of power daily into the national grid.

Uchida's unscrupulous instincts were always to follow the money, so this is where he began to focus his attention. The two most lucrative revenue streams were always the decommissioning bond and the construction costs. He employed two strategies, each part as audacious as the other. For the latter, eye-watering sums were required to pay a range of contractors who were involved in every aspect of the design build and construction activities for the Fukushima Plant. This was indeed a rich vein, but it would need to be carefully quarried so as not to bring the roof down on himself. The bond was managed by a 'reputable' banking organisation, yet it was entangled in a dubious scheme. Operating through an independent entity, he had been orchestrating a sort of 'shorting' operation with these bankers. They had arranged for large sums to be siphoned off as 'loans'

– a blatantly illegal manoeuvre. However, legal boundaries had never deterred the banking sector from exploiting other people's equity for profit. The interest accrued from loaning out billions of Yen was substantial and it was a scheme he felt compelled to perpetuate.

Uchida's troubles began when he started devising the dubious strategies needed to feed the project's insatiable avarice.

The second of his strategies was as audacious as the first and had involved making a deal with his lawyers overseeing the contractual obligations held by the main companies engaged in the massive project. He had arranged a meeting with the Notary Partners, a band of jackals he knew to be as disreputable as himself – well almost. For years, he had been a client of theirs, and their scant scruples mirrored his own – a fact he always kept in mind with cautious awareness during their interactions. The three elderly men who managed the firm, always present at every meeting, appeared so withered by life's trials that they seemed more than merely aged. The corpse-like dryness cried out for moisture, almost as if they would suck the very life out of you if you came into close proximity. But it was more the predator-like demeanour of the three, parchment skinned, sharp skulled creatures, rather than their appearance, that unnerved Uchida the most.

With a meeting arranged he had made the journey by bullet train to a plush steel and glass tower block in the business area of Tokyo City. He had arranged to meet the cadaverous trio at the headquarters of a highly respected law firm under their control. He had been shown into a beautiful oak panelled room, that was at odds with the modern building it nestled within. After completing the meticulous formal introductions, a ceremony that even their persistent solemnity couldn't overlook, they had all taken their seats around one end of a huge, highly polished, red oak table. Uchida started by illustrating an interesting offer he would like to propose to them. His primary strategy was to siphon money from the main contractors through a form of legalised extortion. In exchange for their aggressive tactics, he offered them a twenty per cent kickback on any costs recuperated from the subcontractors involved in the build, over and above their standard fees. His sole condition was that the project remained on schedule and did not violate any of the stringent safety standards required for constructing and operating a Nuclear Power Plant. As long as those red lines were not crossed, then they were free to use any means at their disposal to coerce the construction companies reimbursing the syndicate.

At the meeting's conclusion, the three members stood and bowed, a gesture that sufficed to seal their agreement. The deal was set. The law firm would then unleash its most aggressive lawyers, licenced to exploit any contractual breaches. They would target the profit margins built into the business' agreements, using obscure penalties and ambiguous clauses in the contracts to siphon revenue from the principal contractors. This relentless legal assault threatened to decimate their profits, pushing many to the edge of bankruptcy, with a few possibly going under from the voracity of the legalised onslaught to come.

This was the point where his oversight allowed the law of unintended consequences to seep into his plans. Putting such a fiscal squeeze on had left the construction companies in a difficult position, the only way they could break even was to start cutting corners. Because of the very high level of regulatory compliance the government's administration of the nuclear industry demanded, the corners cut, were trimmed extremely covertly. The quality of the building materials was reduced to the bare minimum as were the quantities. Elements such as concrete, cabling, electronic components and steelwork; wherever a lower standard could be sidled past the regulators, it was done.

These actions did take a considerable amount of pressure off the amount of cash being burned. However, due to his greed, Uchida could not resist just one final squeeze that was available to him. So, it was to the very design that he now turned his attention. The core of the plant's fabrication could not be touched, enshrined as it was in the gold standard of specifications the nuclear industry unequivocally stipulated. Consequently, he turned his attention to the peripheral safety requirements. Within the confines of the emergency planning scenarios for potential events of a catastrophic disaster, he discovered a lucrative loophole that could be made unwittingly far leaner with a little careful paring.

His initial action was to suppress a critical report detailing the potential effects of an earthquake, which could significantly disrupt the seabed of the Pacific, potentially triggering severe seismic consequences. It had sounded like far-fetched nonsense to him at the time. The report stated that if an earthquake struck with a magnitude that exceeded 8.0 anywhere along the Fukushima coast, it would have the potential to develop a wave that could exceed fifteen metres at the point of landfall.

The document had concluded that: *even a relatively low-level seismic disturbance could, if the localised geological conditions were compromised, cause catastrophic tectonic disruption to the planet's crust, enabling an explosively kinetic energy to be unleashed into the plates of the coastal seabed, that could move them both linearly and vertically.*

What a pile of 'Gomi' he had thought back then. These people seemed to have combined the most destructive possible aspects of every seismic event in the history of Japan and rolled them all into a single worse-case scenario. It was obvious that they gave no consideration to the geographic location of these earthquakes in relation to the location of the plant, in addition to which none of which had ever occurred around Fukushima. And who uses emotive phrase like 'unleash a catastrophic series of events' in a technical report? Sensationalists playing to the crowd, he was having none of it.

He proactively addressed the baseless claims by commissioning several reports to assess the probability of the event in question. His goal was to determine the likelihood of its occurrence. He felt a sense of relief when one of these new analyses presented a more optimistic risk assessment. However, all the reports unanimously highlighted the high potential hazards of such an earthquake and its aftermath, vividly depicting the catastrophic consequences should such an event occur. He gravitated towards the more favourable report, which concluded that the plant was more likely to be compromised by the immense upheaval from a direct seismic impact of an earthquake, as opposed to being overwhelmed by a wave, even if it were exceptionally large. This evaluation was based on a detailed analysis of the potential risks posed by tectonic forces.

Uchida, equipped with a hypothesis that suited his needs – one that aligned with his strengths – was now engaged in managing risks. However, these were risks he deemed acceptable, focusing on optimising the plant's main construction elements in a way that maintained safety.

There was one area of design and build that could not be touched and that criteria had been rigidly adhered to it. The actions he had taken were of one level, but he was not foolish enough to mess with the reactors and their immediate protective surroundings. Indeed, it was possible, in theory at least, that this construction was so robust that it could be lifted up out of the ground and resituated somewhere else and still maintain the required level of atomic safety. Its structural integrity would be uncompromised, still able to maintain control of the reactors via a complete spectrum of extensive technical redundancy for all critical operations.

So, now encouraged by this information, he pushed through several redesigns. Some of these involved building a less substantial breakwater along the plant's docks and lower flood protection walls on the seaward flank of the site. He also ensured that the less expensive option was taken, that of siting the emergency backup diesel generator units below ground, with reduced protection from flooding, rather than embarking on the far more expensive route of constructing 'tanked' casements for the units or locating them at an elevated position within the plant. He had truly believed that these were acceptable risks he had taken when one considered the bigger picture. And indeed, for the next forty-five years he had been proved correct. Too late he had remembered the adage that a 'reliable probability will always better a speculative prediction.'

Finally constructed in 1971, the plant had gone from strength to strength. With its six reactors operating, it had the potential to produce an enormous 4.7 GW of power.

But the course he had fixed for the project would not be a fair one, for by then the road to disaster had been well and truly laid, set to arrive at its final disastrous destination. For forty years all would be fine. In tandem with the plant's success as a major contributor to the national power grid, he became richer and more powerful. It was then that the Universe began to conspire to punish his avarice.

His initial challenges arose abruptly and inexplicably, defying any logical explanation he could grasp. At the time, these incidents were sufficiently concerning, yet his understanding of potential catastrophes was naively limited to human-related scenarios. He failed to recognise that beneath Heaven and Earth everything is interconnected.

Those tribulations began with an insignificant civil servant's innocuous quest for power that had been enlightened by a sudden and late-in-life aspiration for political ambitions. Driven, almost entirely it seemed, by principles of altruistic egalitarianism – in Uchida's opinion the very worst type of politician. The man had been a useful idiot to his greater cause for many years, his self-righteous socialism, easily hijacked to manoeuvre in support of his own agenda. The fool's main objectives were manipulated, like a child turning a balloon with an ant crawling on its surface, thinking it was getting somewhere but actually going nowhere.

But then, after a stupid oversight by his contact in the Financial Services Agency (FSA), the governmental financial overseer, the man had stumbled upon something he should not have seen.

The official had been one of those dependable, incorruptible types that Uchida particularly despised. There was only one way of dealing with that type and that was to burst his illusory balloon emphatically. There would be some fallout from his untimely passing but that could be handled.

What was most concerning to him was the sudden disappearance of one of his key conspirators, Iwasaki Shizuko the Governor of Fukushima. A most well connected and helpful woman, who imbued some of the important fundamentals required within politicians – naturally corrupt, with extremely low levels of integrity, and an insatiable lust for power.

She had first come to his attention in the late nineties, demonstrating her skill as a masterful political manipulator of human emotions. She had helped tie the growing anti-nuclear lobbyists in more knots than a Kinbaku bondage master – and he ought to know. Iwasaki had infiltrated the ranks of unions, community groups and small business sectors, working her insincere magic on them all, with promises of support, development, and funding, little of which of course continued to materialise after the plant was completed.

She had been instrumental in his plans then and now, for such an ally to vanish overnight was deeply disconcerting. The larger issue was that this sort of event draws unwarranted attention. It was not long before he heard disquieting whispers of questions being raised in government circles. Even more worrying, was the talk of a move to assign a task force to investigate the matter.

Having unknown quantities poking around in his affairs, which were of a highly delicate nature, would not be conducive to a good night's sleep for him or his confederates. He had been required to call in several markers from his network of dubious political contacts, to introduce some interference to the proposal. In addition, offering a few incentives to like-minded associates, some of whom were also feeling overly exposed by this latest development and who were in a position to influence the unwanted appointment.

Thankfully his efforts had succeeded with less effort than he had anticipated, and he had managed to appropriate a reduction in the task force to just two policemen. The Commissioner having been persuaded to handle the case as a standard missing person's incident. Uchida had not been able to find any more details about the two officers, other than one was an academic type and the other a bully. It sounded like they were already out of their depth before they even arrived. Even though the detectives had been dispatched, and were already on their way to Fukushima City, he felt confident that they would be bumbling around for years before they found anything of any significance. His hope was that they would quickly abandon the case altogether.

There was just a small concern scratching in the recesses of his mind, the Commissioner was known as a straight draw. Because of his uncompromising position on the sanctity of the law, he had been content to make enemies during his rise to the top, as long as his credibility remained intact. So, it was out of character for him to unreservedly downgrade his force to such a weaker element. Was it that he was forced to succumb to the greater political pressure that had been brought to bear? Or could it be that the man had misjudged the situation? Whichever it was, it really didn't matter if he couldn't understand why or how the Commissioner had been outmanoeuvred, the important thing was that he had been...

CHAPTER EIGHT

5 March 2011

The head wobbled across the cedar wood floor, spinning congealed blood from its neatly sliced through neck. This caused a line of the sticky, gelatinous liquid to splash across the left side of Matachi, leaving dark red strokes across the front of his immaculately tailored, contemporary cut, pale blue suit, along with a single congealing spot on his left cheek. The head then came to rest about half a metre in front of his feet.

'Hope you've had your Hep shots, boss?' affably proclaimed Tekiō. He was dressed in a much less fashionable suit. Even with his excessively large body, the garment for the most part appeared too big for him, the jacket hung from his back like a sack draped over a barrel. The bottoms of the slacks bunched up into a mess of creases and folds, like stamped on paper lanterns, hung over his worn and scuffed leather shoes, touching the floor at the heels. This was at odds with the sleeves of the suit, here they seemed far too small, as the suit struggled to contain the appendages within, the seams running along them looked stressed and solid, as if someone had packed them to bursting with sand.

'Yes, I have,' snapped back the blood-spattered Matachi angrily, as he took out a handkerchief and thoroughly wiped the globule of blood off his face. 'I told you to be careful when you picked it up – did I not?'

'He bit me!' exclaimed the big man. 'So I had to let him go, boss. Why did you have me move it anyway, isn't that interfering with the crime scene somewhat?'

Ignoring the question, Matachi carefully squatted down to examine the head which had come to rest laying on the left side of its face, after slipping out of Tekiō's hands and bobbling across the floor.

He observed the bloodless, pale features of what looked to be a Japanese male, undoubtedly the recently deceased Matsumoto Hirofumi. The lips were drawn back over his teeth that were quite close together and did actually look like they were biting down, the eyes were naturally open on a face that was a frozen picture of utter serenity. The man had a full, silvery head of hair, and he guessed his age at late forties to early fifties. The manner of his decapitation was most intriguing – apart from the fact he had been decapitated in the first place that is – as the line of the cut through the neck must have entered level with and under the chin and been drawn down through the throat to exit under the back of the skull. He deduced this from the direction of the tendrils of cartilage from the throat, and the small bits of shattered vertebra that had combined to create a pattern in the flesh of the neck, that followed from the path of the blade as it had cut across, neatly dissecting the man's neck.

The line of the cut had not been straight across, but had been drawn down to create a wedge shape across the incision line from the front to the back of the head. It was that gristly wedge that had supported the skull so precisely upright on the cabinet, almost like a trophy. The murder weapon had undoubtedly been a sword and, if the cut had been produced on purpose, the one who wielded it was without doubt a master of his craft.

'Dead men don't generally bite, Tekiō. And yes, in answer to your question, my shots are fully up to date,' said Matachi, the man in the once nice blue suit trying to head off his partner's next question.

'I'm telling you, boss, return of the fucking walking dead here bit me, right there on my little pinkie.' Tekiō held up the small finger on his right hand to emphasise his point.

He looked at Tekiō's 'little' rubber-gloved finger, which was as big as three of his own fingers combined. Their protective gloves were coloured black and made his hands look like a piece of child's balloon art.

'Unlikely,' he said.

'What about HIV?' persisted Tekiō, ever the germaphobe.

'You can only get HIV through sexual contact or some sort of transfusion,' he replied. 'And there is no real inoculation for it anyway. Was there anything under his head after you threw it on the floor?' he asked, gesturing at the inlaid mahogany cabinet the head had once been mounted on.

'You sure about that, boss? I saw on the internet a video of some guy saying you could catch Aids from breathing the same air as someone who had it, if you were close enough!' asserted Tekiō as he approached the cabinet.

His protective overshoes made tinfoil rustling sounds as he carefully selected blood-free areas of the floor to place his rather large feet. He turned to look back at Matachi. 'And you would have thrown the fucking thing too, if it had bitten you!' he added. 'That's utter BS, and Aids is the disease, HIV the virus, they are two different things. You should stick to downloading porn instead of trying to watch that educational stuff, Tekiō. That reminds me by the way, been meaning to ask, can you still reach your dick these days?'

'That's nasty, boss, why have you got to say offensive stuff like that, I have feelings you know, I can be hurt,' said Tekiō as he slowly peeled off from the top of the cabinet an object wrapped in tin foil, sticky with congealed blood, that had been hidden under the head. He held it up for his superior to see.

'Again, unlikely,' retorted Matachi. He looked at the scarlet, goo-covered, foil packet, it was the reason why he had asked Tekiō to break crime scene protocol and move the head for him. Neatly folded around its edges, it was about forty millimetres in length and about ten millimetres wide, tapering slightly at one end.

'Tekiō?'

'Yes, boss.'

'Carefully bag up that piece of evidence please before that bites you as well,' he said as he handed Tekiō a sealable plastic evidence bag.

Tekiō did as he was told, firmly sealing the bag before handing it back to Matachi. He looked at the rest of Matsumoto-san lying stretched out on the hardwood floor of the living area. 'You're so funny, boss, do you want me to pick up the head and put it back?'

'No, Tekiō, thanks ever so much for offering, but I feel that I have gotten enough blood on me for one day. Anyway, you know what they say, "once bitten, twice…"' He let the sentence trail off before adding sarcastically, 'If you would just retrace your steps back to me without causing any more contamination of the crime scene that would be just so amazing, thank you.'

Tekiō did as directed, carefully stepping around the stretched-out torso of Matsumoto, which lay prostrate on its front, the torso's arms neatly pressed to attention along either side. Having successfully circumnavigated the pool of blood that had formed in front of the body without further incident, he handed the foil packet to Matachi at the doorway.

Matachi held the bagged sachet up for them both to look at, with Tekiō stooping so he could get a closer look. 'What do you think it is, drugs?' he asked.

'Not sure,' answered Matachi. 'Let us leave this place to forensics and we will examine it back at the office. And by the way, I am leaving it to you to explain to them why the head is on the floor.'

Matachi turned and made his way into the hallway, Tekiō

followed behind him, with a belligerent smirk on his face, saying, 'What about tetanus, boss?'

Matachi did not respond, other than to shake his head and retrace his steps to the front door. Tekiō followed grinning like a Kaomoji's emoticon. 'Hey, boss.'

'Yes, Sergeant.'

'Can we get that bite to eat now?' said Tekiō. 'My arse is snapping at the grass I'm so hungry!'

CHAPTER NINE

5 March 2011

How's business?' asked Kurosawa of the petite female as he sat down opposite her. She was seated at a corner table, located at the back of a reasonably busy restaurant in downtown Fukushima City.

'Glad to see you have not lost your sense of humour, brother,' responded the woman.

He beamed warmly at his sister in return. She wore a masculine styled, navy-blue pinstripe trouser suit, perfectly tailored for her female form. Her black, shoulder-length hair, was cut in an exquisite style, feathered around the neck and fringe into locks of individual wisps that fell around her perfect Oriental features. Her style a seamless combining of the spheres of business and fashion. Kurosawa Azumi was the epitome of a successful Japanese businesswoman.

'I see that you are still somewhat upset about the "incident". It was over a year ago now; I would have thought that it would have been all water under the bridge for you by now,' he said, his smile now turning into a mischievous broad grin.

'Cute, brother, you know the litigation from this could ruin the both of us. It would be terrible if you had to give up the family home – *our* family home – which now seems to be your personal bachelor pad, to pay for some of the damages.'

Kurosawa's smile did not drop a fraction at his sister's barb.

'What I know is that you are very good at business, the kind of entrepreneur that skilfully diversifies her risks. The only ones who will be paying any damages are the banks, which have been entangled in your strategically advantageous deals, leaving them extremely vulnerable. Also, the insurance companies are implicated, especially considering the meticulously crafted policies you secured with them. And even if you had not protected our investment, all our eggs are not exactly in one basket are they, sister…?'

'Mmmm… tea?' she said, now smiling back at him and taking up the side handle of the Kyūsu earthenware teapot and pouring him a cup without waiting for his reply.

'Thank you, sister.' He checked the mirror tiled wall behind her before asking, 'So what's the job?'

'Our friends at the "Firm" have declared some unease. They have a concern that our cousins across the sea may be connected to several, what had originally been regarded as seemingly unconnected events. They need clarification that the recent death of a number of key individuals is nothing more than just the standard Japanese undercurrent of our institutionalised corruption. I have been giving my press badge quite an airing lately and there are a few indicators that concur with their thoughts.'

Kurosawa stared at the zone of energy that flickered around his sister, the darkening of the edges emphasising her concerns.

'Their propensity for worry, appears to have significantly increased as of late,' he said.

'Yes,' she replied, 'the latest display of the extension of our cousins' reach has refocused their minds somewhat.'

A waitress appeared at their side asking if they would like more tea. They both smiled and Azumi thanked her for her attentiveness but said they were fine for the moment. Kurosawa waited until she had gone before resuming the conversation with his sister.

'But I cannot see where our particular talents would be required here. This sounds more like a case that law enforcement should be handling.'

'They also see that as a possibility, so they have mobilised a specialist team on it. Don't know that much about them, other than they are regarded as some sort of super sleuth outfit, trained to utilise high-end analysis tools. We already have full oversight of all their reports and lines of inquiry. It seems they have really hit the ground running and are working through a series of leads. It looks like they are a couple of geek analysts who spend their time crunching data to extract information. They were probably selected for the non-intrusive, low-key approach, so they did not muddy the waters unduly. We will just feed off them as necessary.'

Kurosawa reached for the teapot and refilled their cups. 'And our next move?'

'In a preliminary report they have flagged a Professor Takeuchi who used to work at the Fukushima Nuclear Plant. It appears that she took an "enforced" disability retirement package, after a curious accident at the plant a few years ago. The police unit do not regard her as a priority, their leads are focusing them on financial and political corruption aspects, not espionage. This is as expected, they are not looking at this case through the same lens as us. Our friends, however, see her as a higher priority. The view of the police is that she has possible incriminating knowledge concerning elements that could be politically damning, which, needless to say, the Firm pretty much couldn't give a flying fuck about. The main issue is that she may have inadvertently discovered information that is of far more interest to us.' Azumi took a sip of her tea. 'They see her accident as "no accident" shall we say.'

'Botched elimination?'

'Quite likely, so tread carefully. We would not want your pretty face blemished would we, brother?' she said, her grin briefly revealing the similar fanged canine arrangement as his own.

He lowered his voice as some customers exited the tea house passing their table. 'Okay, what is the play?' he said once they were out of earshot.

'Firstly, we need to assess the area where she lives. We may have to pick her up at very short notice at some point, so you had better get down there and make an evaluation.'

'And what are your plans, sister?'

'I am staying locally for a few days; I have another meeting with our friends. I will continue to track the progress of the police unit and keep you updated of anything they uncover, then I may return to the mill.'

'Ah, still working closely with your manager, ensuring that everything is being correctly looked after,' said Kurosawa, the teasing smirk returning to his face. 'After all we would not want any of that delicate equipment to seize up from lack of use, would we!'

'Ah, and you should be careful my wise brother, that your own equipment does not get rusty, you do realise the corrosive effect that sea water can have?' she replied, tilting her head at him, with just a slight curl of her upper lip, a single incisor giving the merest hint of a mocking sneer.

Kurosawa looked back at her, the same deathly blank expression reflecting deep within her dark eyes as he held within his own.

Holding his gaze, she teased, 'So, tell me how is your mermaid?'

'She is very well, full of life. She sends her best regards and wishes me to tell you that she can't wait to finally meet you one day.'

'One day, yes, one day perhaps. But we both know that our futures are locked into our past. We must stick to our plan, think how far we have come since childhood, the sacrifices we have made to survive.'

'I know, sister, I understand that if we are to have any chance of a real future for our Clan, we need to maintain control of ourselves and it. We feed the beast and the beast feeds us.'

'We feed the beast and the beast feeds us,' his sister repeated.

CHAPTER TEN

5 March 2011

In retrospect, that really had been quite stupid, thought Takada. He had decided to grant the man an honourable death and he had nearly paid the ultimate price for it, when the two policemen had arrived unexpectedly.

Before then it had been relatively easy to enter Matsumoto's home through the back courtyard entrance during the early hours of the morning. There was a simple deadlock on the rear door of the house and no security system, as was common for many Japanese households. General crime rates in Japan were some of the lowest on the planet, so installing a home security system might seem unnecessary. For most people it would be regarded as a waste of time and an insult to one's neighbours.

As expected, he found the man in bed... but alas not asleep. He was sitting cross-legged on his futon, in perfect stillness, his back resting against the wall, his aged features exaggerated by shadows from the small lamp beside him. It was almost as if he had been waiting for someone to arrive. He watched Takada enter in profound stillness; his hands folded across one another on top of the covers. The official merely nodded, his gaze fixed on Takada's sheathed short sword, the gloves covering his hands and his unmasked face. In this silent acknowledgment, he resigned himself to the inevitable fate these details foretold. Seeing that Matsumoto was calm and sensing no immediate threat from the official or indeed a desire to escape, Takada knelt down near the man, sitting on his feet and placing his sword to his left side. An unspoken understanding of the circumstances enveloped them, creating a shared, silent acknowledgment of the situation at hand. For a few moments they settled in silence before beginning a negotiation of the damned. Takada offering honourable, painless repentance, in exchange for a full disclosure of Matsumoto's downward slide into corruption.

This was not how he usually conducted such interrogations. He generally followed a process whose fundamentals had been laid down by masters of their trade for generations. It was one designed around instilling feelings of ever-increasing trepidation that progressively moved the victim along the periphery of fear, until reaching a state of absolute terror.

The first of the psychological levers applied started with his instilling hope within the victims, allowing them to grasp at the possibility they may survive the ordeal. The infliction of physical discomfort kept to a minimum, the victim, coerced by their anxieties alone into freeing their exhortations. This first stage was usually the most productive, if the stresses were applied appropriately, a wide range of intelligence could be provided by the correct application of this principle. The relevance of this information then being cross-referenced with the interrogator's existing knowledge.

Once this method had been exhausted, the application of various elements of physical torture were applied in relation to more targeted questioning. The intensity of the suffering applied steadily increasing, until the impact of its physical debilitation on the individual had reached a point of irretrievable retraction. If the brutality was professionally applied, then its effect was to hold the victim against a threshold of excruciating torment, while allowing them to comprehend that the devastation applied to their bodies was not a condition they would want to live with, even if the option of surviving were available to them.

At this point, choice was simplified into two realms, continue in agony or accept the offer of a quick end. If the interrogator was a true artisan of his trade, then the victim would realise that the final outcome was the same; the interrogator would have received all the testimony he required, and the victim would be dead. The route to that final destination was the only thing that differed.

Of course, this was not always the case, humans were a bizarre and diverse entity, with some not strong enough to endure such a journey and, a few extraordinary individuals, able to even withstand it.

Matsumoto-san, however, fell into the category of the 'Confessor' – willing to reveal everything he knew to Takada. The official not only freely answered every question he asked of him, but he also provided him with a story, that even with his experience of corruption, was one of such degradation he had found it incredible. The information he gleaned went far beyond confirming what he already believed to be the state of degeneracy that had permeated the integrity of Japanese politicians and business élites.

The civil servant had painted a picture that had gone far beyond his suspicions of the conspiracies which he already knew existed in principle. The ones that were woven deep into the interlaced fabric of Fukushima's influential and privileged networks of power.

Matsumoto-san had offered a great deal more than to confirm his level of understanding of the degree of corruption involved, his revelations surprising even Takada's hardened consciousness. In his experience there were some lines that even the most committed criminals or deplorable reprobates would not cross. That marker was treason. For Takada it was a special kind of degenerate that would sell out one's own country.

This had also been the final element that had convinced

Matsumoto that he had strayed beyond the confines of moral decency, and his code of honour could only be fulfilled by one's ultimate sacrifice.

Takada realised that the man was basically an honest and honourable individual, who had been drawn in by the insidious translucent nature of a corrupt world, that teased him with subtle innocuous attractions over the years. He had only wanted to be a decent politician, a virtuous force for good. But slowly, piece by piece, he had stretched his political morality by granting requests of favour for counter-favour, in effect trading his scruples to move his own agenda forward for what he thought was the greater good. It was a sacrifice that finally locked him within a fraudulent inescapable dominion.

Matsumoto had seen no way to free himself from the situation he had become entangled in. Then, one by one, his co-conspirators began to vanish or meet with mysterious ends. Some of those individuals had been instrumental in maintaining the web of corruption surrounding the Atomic Plant's construction. He was uncertain as to whether someone had decided to clean house internally or whether there was some power struggle taking place amongst the corrupt cabal. Whatever it was, he concluded they were now being hunted down. Though the thought terrified him, he realised this could be his way out of the dishonourable mess that he had become embroiled in.

His pacifist nature and Catholic faith had prevented him from taking this own life, so he decided that given the opportunity, he would make a pact to divulge everything he knew in return for an honourable exit. Also, he was aware it would give him the chance to make a statement to the nest of vermin he had lain with for far too long. Then, when he heard someone entering his house that evening, he set his mind to accepting his fate and put his plan into effect.

It took several hours to fully hear the man's story and it was early morning before he had finished. After listening to what Matsumoto had to say, Takada had agreed to his request for an honourable death and to forego indulging in his own perverse recreations. As he escorted the man downstairs, he tried to put aside the concern that perhaps he was mellowing as he steadily moved beyond middle-age.

There was no doubt he took great pleasure in killing a particular type of person. But on numerous occasions lately, he had found himself showing a disproportionate amount of empathy with many of those he came into contact within his daily life. Though to be fair, most of his colleagues and associates would not generally regard him as the friendly and approachable type.

Before taking Matsumoto downstairs, he instructed the man to call his office to say he had been struck by an extreme bout of food poisoning and would not be in for a few days. He held the phone while Matsumoto repeated exactly what he had been told to say.

Once in the living area, he directed Matsumoto to kneel down, with this head leaning slightly forward, chin up, hands clasped together behind his back. Before he knelt, he asked Takada to open the centre drawer of a wooden bureau at the side of the room. Inside he found a memory stick. Matsumoto told him that the data stick contained highly treasonable evidence backing up what he had just divulged to him, fully implicating many of the highest-ranking conspirators' involvement. Matsumoto had received this information a little over a week ago, anonymously, from someone who had foolishly thought he was not involved in the corruption. The stick had been accompanied by a note that said the files on it were strongly encrypted and a key to unlock the files would follow directly, though he had received nothing as yet. Takada pocketed the stick, although he was not sure of what use it would be to him. He had limited access these days to the kinds of personnel who could decipher such information. Matsumoto then knelt on the floor as directed and, just before he was about to strike, Takada had an idea. He then removed the man's head in one perfect sweep of his sword. After first wiping the blade clean of any blood on Matsumoto's cotton pyjamas, he replaced the sword in its sheath. He then went into the kitchen and began looking for some tinfoil to wrap the memory stick in. Knowing there may well be a tracking device inside, he knew the foil would act as a faraday cage, preventing any possible electronic emittance from the memory stick while he worked out what he would do with it.

While he was searching for some foil, Takada heard the sound of machinery outside. He went back upstairs to peer out of the window overlooking the main street. A work crew had appeared and were busy deploying a 'Mobile Elevating Work Platform', adjacent to one of the streetlights. The men seemed in no hurry in their siting of the MUWP, being very precise and safety conscious, ensuring that the machine was fully stable before sending a work crew aloft.

Takada berated himself for taking far too long on his assignment. He couldn't risk leaving the building as the workmen would have a very good view of the surrounding area from their vantage point. It was imperative he was not seen leaving Matsumoto's house. He was left with no alternative other than to settle himself down and wait until the workmen had completed their task.

Three anxious hours later, the workmen had left, and he was completing his final checks in readiness to leave. He was put off balance when he suddenly heard the doorbell ring, followed by some aggressive hammering on the door and the loud call from a policeman to 'Open Up'.

From the muted conversation on the doorstep, he gathered there were only two officers. When the conversation stopped, he suspected that one of them was making his way around to the rear of the building. Takada was now left with the choice of fighting his way out, fully aware of the consequences that would follow, even if he were to be successful, or to hide.

He looked at the large, antique, oak dining table at the far end of the living area which was a sister piece to the cabinet he had taken the memory stick from. He made his decision.

The detective had entered the premises very noisily calling out to the owner to make him aware of his presence. Takada listened as the detective made his way through the house until he entered through the open door of the living room. He heard the shocked expletive as he witnessed the scene that Takada had laid out in the room for him.

As expected, the guy had drawn his weapon and started to search the room, being careful not to upset the crime scene. Finding no one else present, he moved to the front door to admit his partner, informing him that he had cleared the downstairs area, and they should work their way upstairs.

Once Takada heard footsteps on the stairway as the men began to search the upper rooms, he carefully lowered himself from his braced position under the table. He had been there for only ten minutes, pushing his hands and feet into the broad depths of its wooden apron. His concern had been more for the structure of the table flying apart from the force he had been applying, than for the physical strength required to maintain his position there. He quietly extracted himself from under the table, concentrating on the sound of the policemen's footsteps above. Rising to his feet he admired his handiwork; his idea of placing the head on the bureau had given him the added benefit of drawing their attention away from the table.

Takada was about to complete his escape while he still had the advantage of the men searching upstairs, when he made an impulsive decision.

He fully understood that the motive that drove his next action was, in the main, of a personal nature and emotionally complex. His psychosis was heterogeneous in form, function and execution, however, ultimately it had to feed the twin hungers of benevolence and brutality. The rules that guided these needs were interchangeable, violence could be deemed compassionate and kindness seemingly sadistic, which was to him psychologically helpful, as both entities had vivacious appetites.

The dilemma he found himself in was that he functioned

within a set of boundaries that were as comforting as they were controlling. Regardless of his motivations, good, bad or indifferent, he operated within a code, and all of those he came into contact with became, by default, unwittingly part of that covenant.

During his time spent with Matsumoto some very disturbing details had come to light. These being far beyond the qualifying motivations that had first attracted his attention to the group of unworthy individuals he was hunting. Those reasons now paled in light of the recent revelations bestowed on him by his victim. He would never admit to being out of his depth. However, the support network he once could rely on was no longer available to him, perhaps it was time to enlist some new allies – so he placed the foil-covered stick under the head and, by doing so, covertly enrolled his new subjects to the cause.

Having made his way back to his noodle van parked a few blocks away, he decided to observe who his new, unwitting associates were. He pulled his van to the end of the street, pointing away from the house and waited.

Within twenty minutes he was rewarded with the appearance of a very odd couple in his wing mirror. A slim, dapper individual wearing an expensive suit led the way, followed by a mountain, in the shape of a human being, dressed in a very poorly fitting outfit.

They may have looked like poor caricatures of Laurel and Hardy, but there was something else about the pair that he found quite perturbing. The big man was unmistakably a kindred spirit – one always recognised one's own – and most definitely someone who was no stranger to killing.

He had seen enough for now; he bestowed a parting leer to his new partners in crime and drove away before the local plods arrived. As a final courtesy to Matsumoto, he had agreed one other final indulgence for the man. Perplexingly, he was uncertain as to why he had acceded to his request. Murdering people for free, on the whims of others, was not a deed he generally did – he really must be getting soft. But as today was his day off, he felt lifted by the promise of some extra curriculum activity. It would also be an interesting footnote for his new unwitting partners.

CHAPTER ELEVEN

6 March 2011

'Are you going to eat that?' said Matachi, looking at the uneaten pieces of tempura on Tekiō's plate.

Tekiō pushed back from the table, in the manner of 'Hara Hachi Bu' – the Japanese custom of calorie restriction by physically moving oneself from the dining table, leaving a portion of food remaining on the plate.

'No, help yourself, I'm full,' he said, trying to hide his resentment as he watched his boss lean over and start removing the last pieces of tasty tempura off his plate, then consuming them with an exaggerated zeal.

'Really? I think it would take a bit more than a single plate of tempura and a bowl of noodles to fill you up,' said Matachi, reaching over the table with his chopsticks to pick the last few tasty morsels off Tekiō's plate.

'You know I have a glandular problem,' said Tekiō.

Matachi loudly scoffed at this comment. 'Bullshit,' he said, 'more like a secret Mr Motto Sweet Dumpling problem. You do realise that consuming food in secret is a sign of an eating disorder, don't you, Tekiō?'

'Who says I eat in secret? No one knows what I do in private… no one, okay.'

'Tekiō, dear boy, it has come to my attention over the years, that you have a very complicated relationship with food. I think it could be bordering on the bipolar end of the spectrum. On occasion, I have witnessed you eat like a starving bear. Then, and I think this is driven by feelings of gluttonous guilt, you pretend to eat like a sparrow with his beak wired up around me. And yet you weigh what, two hundred kilos? Unless you are able to break both the laws of biological science in addition to those of physics, you are in denial of your problem. Lying, not only to me, by the way, but more importantly to yourself. But that is the way of it for those people unfortunate enough to suffer from eating disorders.'

Tekiō put two enormous fists on the table either side of him; he looked like he was about to chuck some salt in the air and go into 'Tachi-ai', the intimidating pose a Sumo wrestler takes just before he attacks his opponent.

Matachi kept up his playful teasing. 'Let's look at the facts, shall we? Firstly, the sheer energy your body expends to simply keep you alive and mobile, especially considering your stature. And yes, while there's a significant amount of, let's say, non-muscle mass, I must admit there's also a fair share of muscle hidden in there somewhere,' he said with a wry smile. Tekiō, reacting to the mock criticism about his muscularity, responded with a mix of a frown and a pout. He flexed his arm, causing a massive bicep to swell impressively, straining against the fabric of his jacket as if it might rip through at any moment.

Not intimidated in the slightest, Matachi continued with his cutting appraisal. 'I would estimate that it would require you to burn around two thousand calories a day minimum, just idling. I know you train quite hard at the Dojo with your old Sumo cronies at least twice a week when you can, so the effort of throwing your great lump of a carcass around, that's got to be another one thousand calories burned per session. But sometimes I estimate I do not ever see you consume more than five hundred calories a day. Unless you are the most efficient lard arse that ever walked the earth or can absorb energy from the ether, you are secretly binge eating like a ravenous Korean at a dog meat soup festival.'

'You don't know that,' said Tekiō.

'Tekiō as you well know, and I do say this from a position of humble acceptance, of my superb record of solving intricate and complicated cases. I am, without the merest hint of a breath of doubt, a great detective. However, that being an undeniable truth, it takes very little deduction on my part to work out your fundamental problem. You're a fat bastard – pure and simple,' said Matachi, happily ramping up the rhetoric.

'Ah, you! You're hardly the great detective you think you are, merely average at best,' Tekiō shot back sharply. 'Any successes you've had, stumbling blindly through cases, you owe entirely to the formidable shadow I cast. My presence alone intimidates and loosens tongues more effectively than an uptown Geisha shedding her kimono after a corporate tea ceremony.' His words were laced with a blend of jest and truth, highlighting the dynamic of their partnership.

'You can loom and intimidate as much as you like, dear friend, but it was not a great deal of use to us earlier was it. I feel that poor Matsumoto-san was beyond responding to your particular talent of terrorisation old chum,' Matachi sarcastically replied. 'It's just as well you have my good self and the unlimited resources of a fine police department behind us for just such an occasion, when your skill set meets its limitations.'

Tekiō pulled a face that resembled someone who had just chewed on a wasp. He wondered to himself if he were to place one foot on Matachi's trunk, taking hold of a single arm, how long it would take to pull it out of its socket.

'About two seconds,' he unconsciously muttered. 'Sorry, Tekiō, I didn't quite catch that?'

'Nothing, what's the background on Matsumoto then?' he asked, quickly changing the subject, somewhat cheered by the imagined vision of his mutilated superior.

Matachi opened his tablet and started scrolling through his analysis to date.

'Well, it seems Matsumoto-san has held a long and distinguished career in local politics. He first became politicised as a student whilst at Okinawa International University, leaving there with a First in Social Policy & Public Administration Studies in 1983. He became politically active within the first year of his studies, taking part in a sustained campaign and general support for the removal of American Forces from the Island. Afterwards this picture was taken with him holding a placard displaying the words: *Murder and Rape of our People is not Protection of our People.*' 'Catchy,' said Tekiō as he took the device from Matachi.

On it was displayed a photograph of a very young Matsumoto standing with a group of demonstrators, all holding similar banners. It was taken outside the gate of an American Air Force base. 'He was consequently arrested and charged with civil disobedience,' continued Matachi. 'At that time, Young Matsumoto-san here was found not guilty of the charge at the subsequent magistrate's trial. But that did not stop him from being arrested numerous other occasions for civil unrest over the years, as he continued to support the cause to remove the US Military from Okinawa. Surprising he was acquitted on every occasion on all cases brought against him. That is until six months after he graduated. When, seemingly frustrated with the lack of progress of his cause, he decided to take more direct action. Breaking into an American base and painting the slogan, "Go Home Yankee Killers who are Bad Flyers" on the side of an aircraft hangar.'

'I like it, that's much better,' interrupted Tekiō.

'He escaped without being caught but was recognised by one of the responding Japanese police officers and later arrested once more. This time though it didn't go so well for him. His then girlfriend refused to corroborate his story about him being at her apartment that night. He picked up a six-month suspended sentence and a fine and was banned from being within a kilometre of any American base.'

Tekiō chuckled, 'I bet they're not still an item after that.'

'Have you finished?' said Matachi.

'I'm just saying, you know women, they are a breed apart. Never try and understand them and don't try to get them to understand you, my grandfather used to say.'

'Really, and there's me thinking you were single because you're fat. Have you finished sharing your relationship theories? Can I go on now?'

Tekiō's face reverted to wasp mode.

'Thank you, detective,' said a smirking Matachi. 'Still holding a taste for politics, but now very curtailed from his activities in Okinawa, Matsumoto decided to join the anti-nuclear campaign and moved to Fukushima to start being a political pain in the arse here. Though now with a strategy of subversion, rather than direct action.'

'Always better to be in the boat pissing out, than outside the boat getting pissed on,' interjected Tekiō.

'Correct, well mostly,' added Matachi. 'He then secured a position within local government and started his infiltration of local politics. Then it seems the hormones stopped fuelling his radical zeal, the hairs on his balls grew greyer, and he became assimilated into the realities of life.'

'You mean he grew up?'

'Yes, though he still retained his fundamental values of righteous morality. He had steadily worked his way up the political pole, taking on the role of Commissioner of "Fixed Assets" at the last local election. Until fairly recently he had remained a loyal civil servant, ensuring the good people of Fukushima Prefecture received value for money in lieu of their local tax payments. He was a supporter of maintaining civil rights and liberties and seen as an irritant to bullish lobbying by powerful business interests, trying to push through what was seen as some civically unfavourable legislation in the local council chambers. It also looks like he was an ardent advocate of decentralised reform of regional governmental institutions, supporting the devolution of power from national government bodies to local ones.'

'More power to the people crap,' said Tekiō, holding up his right hand clenched into a massive fist.

'Precisely, but he was not an elected official, he held a powerful position but was appointed to it by the governor. He made no secret that he held aspirations to become an elected official though. It appears he was positioning himself to run for Governor as an independent candidate, levering his support within the communities whose interests he had served so faithfully over the years. His base was particularly strong with groups opposed to the building of the Fukushima Nuclear Plant; he has caused a lot of grief for the stakeholders advocating its construction. Luckily for them he was ten years too late in seriously interfering with the project starting, but it looks like he really put them through the grinder on several occasions. Then, I presume, trying to add some weight to his campaign, he started to press for an inquiry into historic funding irregularities that he had uncovered.'

'I see,' said Tekiō. 'He did realise who he was actually upsetting and what they were willing to do to put an end to his interfering in their affairs?'

Matachi nodded in agreement as he adjusted the pearl studs on his shirt cuffs, adjusting the sleeves until they were both symmetrically aligned with his suit. 'Yes, and he began to feel the consequences of their interventions. Just as it was all looking reasonably positive for his bid for governor to get underway, they started unravelling his life. He had been confronted by long buried skeletons from his past. They dug up his record for the charge of criminal damage, the one he was convicted of way back in the eighties. In addition, details of several of the cases that he had quashed were brought out for a public airing. Though legally, it could not stop him from running, politically it did not look good. He was by then, well and truly smeared by rumours. Then to further cast doubt on his character, a series of unsubstantiated accusations were leaked out by parties unknown. Though none were proven, speculation along the lines that he had managed to cover up many other unsavoury facts about his life, started to become the overriding narrative. It all combined to irretrievably damage his reputation. With confidence in his integrity as an honest broker evaporating faster than the credibility of prime ministers visiting the Yasukuni Shrine, his power base soon began to erode. He quickly realised that his quest for a career as a politician had been well and truly thwarted. He was then left with really no choice other than to go back to working for a living.'

'But then his ego kicked in,' deduced Tekiō. 'He couldn't just leave it there, could he? Not for a man who wears his honour like a suit of armour. With that amount of "lost face" he had to take action. So that was when he started poisoning the political Miso soup bowl they were all chugging from.'

'Correct,' said Matachi, 'he started looking around for those accountable for his problems. However, I do not think he knew who was ultimately responsible for attacking him. Just a list of potential suspects, who he then proceeded to do everything he could to try and upset. I think he was trying to flush out some answers as to who was behind the slandering, but it would appear that all he managed to achieve was to lose friends and make even more enemies and at an alarming rate.'

'And some of those enemies turned out to be the extremely serious types,' said Tekiō. 'By the way you are doing it again.'

'Doing what?'

'Repeating the word "correct" over and over, in that condescending tone you use. You know exactly what I mean, the headmaster voice talking down to his pupils. You know full well it annoys the living shit out of me.'

'No, I'm not,' said an affronted Matachi before continuing. 'His medical records show that he was currently taking antidepressants, prescribed to alleviate some mild anxiety he had been experiencing. We can be fairly certain that these mood changes were brought on by the shame and embarrassment he felt for these alleged, and visibly perceived, failures on his part.'

'Ah, possible suicide brought on by psychological issues then!' said Tekiō, grinning at his own joke.

'Well, although there is actually no sign of any struggle or forced entry into the apartment, the scenario of cutting one's own head off and then setting it on the furniture, I feel we can legitimately rule suicide out.'

'And managing to hide the foil package under there as well was probably a bit of a big ask of the recently decapitated Matsumoto-san,' helpfully added Tekiō.

'That said, there is still more than a little intrigue regarding his demise. After all it is not every day that someone literally loses their head in the living room of their own home!'

'Correct! Someone is definitely trying to send a message here...'

'Fuck you!' interjected Tekiō.

Matachi ignored him and carried on speaking.

'What that message might be and to whom it is intended is what we need to explore. Our equipment should now have arrived at the Fukushima Precinct HQ so we need to get back there so I can start adding the latest data we have into our system. We also need to find out what is in this interesting packet,' he said, patting the top pocket of his jacket. 'Anyway,' said Matachi, changing the subject as he spotted the waiter bringing over the card machine so they could pay, 'that's enough about the case. Where was I earlier? Ah I remember. You do realise that eating disorders are a sign of mental frailty?' not able to resist one last dig as he paid the check. The waiter kept his head down and lowered his eyes.

'And do you realise I am quite capable of lifting you up and snapping your scrawny back like it was a rotten chopstick, boss?' said Tekiō, moving the conversation to where he was most comfortable, making violent threats.

The waiter's head was now horizontal to the floor, as he tried to make himself as obscure as his position would allow. 'Gangsters,' he thought. He kept the tableside etiquette to a minimum. Quickly ripping off the paper receipt from the card machine, he thanked them, gave a couple of bows in quick succession, and swiftly scurried away to the safety of the kitchen.

'Of course, Tekiō, my dear boy, it's one of the reasons I keep you around,' said Matachi, with a genuine smile on his face as they both got up to leave.

The niceties of their luncheon behind them, they got into their large, unmarked police Toyota and began to drive back into the city centre to return to the police station. Matachi drove, as usual, whilst Tekiō, putting the seat back into recline, took out a cotton handkerchief and placed it over his eyes, soon drifting off into an afternoon siesta.

Evidently sleeping off his huge lunch, thought Matachi, looking over at the enormous torso gently rising and falling as Tekiō had quickly placed himself into a state of sleep. For all his bulk, and that bulk was considerable, Tekiō was also a master practitioner of several martial arts, not just the incredible skills of a Sumo wrestler. The ability to switch off and recharge at will, Tekiō had informed him, was one of those talents he had gained during his extensive training.

Matachi thought that this was total and utter bullshit unless they taught the ancient art of 'fat lazy bastard' at his Sumo stable.

CHAPTER TWELVE

8 March 2011

Professor Takeuchi Hiroe lowered herself down onto her heels with some difficulty, by the side of her modest herb garden. She moved her right arm painfully, as the withered muscles stretched the tightened skin that had been scarred by scalding burns. Out of necessity she wore a tight-fitting surgical sleeve that ran from her wrist right up to her armpit. A similar sleeve covered her right leg. She was told it would help with the healing of the scar tissue, but it was a constant irritant, particularly come bedtime.

There had been a slight storm last night which had also disrupted her sleep, then in the morning she saw the wind had caught one of her potted bay leaf trees. It had blown over on to its side and rolled onto the stone garden path that meandered through her vegetable patch. She looked at the pot forlornly; now a delicately built lady with only a fraction of her energy left to devote to her beloved garden.

She had been full of vitality once, even in her late fifties she had been strong and healthy. Back then cultivating the garden had been a great joy to her, spending long hours tending to her modest crops in those happier moments during her time away from her precious work at the Facility. She would spend many hours on the physical joys she found in weeding and nurturing her beautiful flowerbeds and vegetable plots. Happily labouring, her back bent double with the effort of planting next year's bounty, digging over the ground with spade and fork. Now though she struggled even to do the lightest task and relied on a gardener a few days a week to attend to her allotment's needs. Unfortunately, he had already been once that week and was not due to return until the next.

That being the case she could not allow the large terracotta pot, that still held the miniature bay leaf tree, to be blown around the garden by the wind. It had already done enough damage, crushing a line of parsley and coriander. She resolved to at least attempt to upright the toppled pot, planning to leave it in place for the gardener to relocate later. Observing the pot, she estimated its weight to be around thirty kilograms, a hefty load for her to manage in her frail state.

She righted herself from a squatting position with some effort and shuffled over to where the tree lay in a horizontal position. The pot's exterior was coated with a mixture of soil and remnants of the crushed herbs. It swayed slightly in the gentle breeze. She anchored it with her stronger left foot, and, despite the discomfort, bent down to grip the slender trunk of the sapling firmly with both hands. She endeavoured to hoist the tree back on to its base, using her body as a counterweight. This effort involved extending her frail right leg behind her, trying to balance the considerable weight of the pot.

It started to lift slowly, but just as she got it almost vertical, a sudden gust of wind blew from the opposite direction, pushing her off balance. The tree dropped back onto the stony pathway, pulling her with it. She lay there for a moment, exhausted from the exertion, prostrate along the obstinate pot, limbs spread either side of the vessel, her head resting on the tree's thin trunk. A great swell of frustrating anger rose up inside her and she gave a cry that was half sob and half yell, infuriated with the pathetic being she had become. It was then that she became aware she was not alone in the garden.

She painfully turned her head to look down the garden path towards the main gate.

Coming up the path, approaching her quite quickly, was a short, stocky man dressed in plain, loose-fitting, beige clothing, wearing a surgical mask with the hood of his lightweight jacket pulled up over his head. As he advanced towards her down the path, he seemed to hold his right arm rigidly down his side. At first, she felt embarrassment, thinking that it was a bystander who had seen her fall and was coming to assist her.

She started to try and push herself off the terracotta receptacle, but her feet started slipping on the damp soil the pot had earlier trailed onto the path. She held her left hand up with an embarrassed wave to the man.

'So sorry,' she started to say, 'I am fine, thank you, thank you, for coming to help me, but there is now no need.'

She managed to push herself onto her knees and turned to look at the man. It was then she noticed he was wearing tight-fitting, cream-coloured rubber gloves on his hands, not of the domestic lightweight variety, but similar to the ones they wore in a lab for heavy duty work where there was a risk of possible contamination.

Up until then she had not been concerned by the surgical-type mask he wore covering his lower face. Wearing such masks was common in Japan, a cultural requirement even, in some circumstances it would be regarded as very poor etiquette for someone to go outside their homes if they had a cold without covering their face. But she suddenly felt very uneasy as the man quickly approached her.

Her worst fears were realised as he reached down and grabbed her violently by the hair with his left hand, roughly angling her head to one side. She tried to scream, but he had placed his right foot into the back of her left calf, pinning her there as he screwed her head around, twisting her spine into an excruciatingly painful spiral, until she was unable to move. She desperately tried again to scream but because of the torsion being applied to her body she could barely breathe.

She stared at him pathetically, then watched in horror as a long-bladed knife, half a metre in length, dropped smoothly out of his right-hand sleeve, its ornate handle falling neatly into his gloved hand. He held it there a moment, perfectly in line with his outstretched arm, pointing at a slight angle towards the rear of his body. He had now extended and twisted her head so that she was almost looking back over her shoulder directly at him. The burns on the right side of her face looked vivid and angry from the tension applied to the skin round her head by his grip on her scalp, and distorted her appearance even more. The blade flashed in the faint morning sunlight as he whipped it above his head in a hypnotically fluid action.

She knew she was about to die, but even though the life she lived now had become a miserable shadow of what it had been in day's past, particularly during these last few bitter and painful years, she realised her desire to live, to live any life, was as strong as it had ever been. His left hand released her hair and she managed a small whimper as her assailant drove the blade into a sweeping downward arc.

When she was younger, she used to have a disturbing recurring dream. In the dream she was among several captives tied and bound in a kneeling position, while a man went along the line with a pistol and shot each captive in turn in the back of the head. As each one was shot, she became more and more terrified, but accepting of the fact that there was nothing she could do. She just kept telling herself over and over again, 'It will be over in a minute, it will be over in a minute.' One brutal jolt and she would no longer experience the fear, she would feel nothing, just a release from the growing terror. By the time it came to her turn to be killed, she thought her heart would burst within her through the mounting anxiety before the shot was finally fired. The man finally pulled the trigger, but there had been no violent smack into her skull, just a dull click; he re-cocked the pistol and pulled the trigger once more, again, just an empty click. All the while her terror grew and grew, she screamed inside for them to get it over with and then just as she could take no more, she would wake up and realise it was just a nightmare. The same terrifying debilitating feeling returned to her now as the short sword fell onto her neck – awaiting her death to take away her terror, just as in the dream.

She was suddenly shaken out of her mesmerised state by a great ringing clash of steel on steel and then promptly received a momentous kick up her backside, which launched her back over the large pot. As she slipped off and fell back onto her right side, she saw a second man who seemed to have appeared from nowhere. He was holding a much larger sword and had blocked the downward swing of the assailant's blade.

The second man was tall and looked more athletic than her muscular nemesis. She glanced at his face and saw a look that was as both terrifying as it was strikingly handsome. The young man's hair, a cascade of jet-black strands, hung over his sharply defined granite cheekbones, draping across eyes that bore a lifeless, stone-like quality. In the midst of her harrowing ordeal, she unexpectedly felt ancient emotions resurface, emotions she believed were long extinguished. These newfound stirrings for her unlikely saviour were complex, stemming from more than just gratitude for saving her life.

Kurosawa, though somewhat preoccupied, felt an inward smile as he detected the faint change in her aura. Where there is life there is lust, he thought…

The two combatants squared off against each other, blade against blade as each pushed back against the other, testing for advantage. Metal clashed against metal, as neither gave backward quarter. Then just as her saviour's sword was almost touching the face of the assassin, he feinted backwards. Then, just as suddenly, he surged forward again, using his stocky build to push hilt against hilt, thrusting Kurosawa's blade away and towards the floor. The move momentarily allowed him the fraction of time and space he required to disengage.

They faced off at each other, outwardly emotionally blank,

senses assessing every nuance of their opponent. Both held their swords angled towards each other's torso, the tips almost touching. Their legs were bent, and both were set in a wide low stance, feet feeling for the uneven surface of the path beneath them. With the ground muddy and uneven ground on either side of the pathway, there was no other space to manoeuvre in, confining them to moving forwards or backwards on the cobbled track.

Kurosawa observed the spectrum the man had generated around him, it portrayed a fearless acceptance of his fate. Declaring that he was here now and the reality of the now was all that mattered. Kurosawa recognised the man would accede to die in these next moments, if that was what the consequences of upholding his honour decreed.

Each now had made his deadly evaluation of the other, with the mutual realisation they were both skilled with the sword mortally evident. The assassin started to edge rearwards slightly; for a moment his opponent did not follow, then with a slight feint to his opponent's front foot he attacked, Kurosawa's long sword clashing against the shorter weapon as his strike was immediately blocked.

Their duel quickly developed into one of strike and counterstrike. A ringing blur of steel filled the small garden with a shattering crescendo of metallic sound, while sparks flinted off their weapons' case-hardened edges as they were continually smashed into each other. The shorter sword held its own against the more powerful, longer blade, but its wielder knew it was but a matter of time before the katana would gain the upper hand against his lesser weapon.

As with any martial art, if you remove the violence, it is like a game of chess. The assassin realised he was being manoeuvred into a trap, for the man he fought was recognisably no less a master than himself.

Kurosawa pressed home the advantage of the longer weapon, in doing so putting the pieces into place for the final deadly move of checkmate. The assassin thought if he were to die today, he would make sure he did not die alone. He readied himself to accept the final fatal blow and used his last reserves of energy to lock the blade within him, determined to hold its place just long enough to drive his own weapon into his opponent's throat. Suddenly there was an ear-shattering scream as the woman found her voice. Both men froze for an instant and then a steel trowel hit Kurosawa in the back of the head. It was not a significant blow, but it was just enough to stop him from driving home his advantage against his adversary. With a final sweeping parry to the longer Katana, the assassin twisted away and darted for the garden gate. Kurosawa followed, but the brief distraction of the blow to his skull distracted his reactions, giving the man just enough time to safely disengage. He reached the gate in time to see him running into the street beyond, hiding his sword under his jacket as he ran. He watched as he slipped into a small printing shop, disappearing inside.

Kurosawa returned to the professor and found her collapsed on the floor. He knelt beside her to check her condition and he could see that she was still breathing. He left her side and retraced his footsteps to the point along the wooden-panelled fence where he had climbed over to enter the garden. Reaching the other side, he retrieved the scabbard for his sword from where he had left it leaning against the outside of the wooden screen. He swiftly returned to the professor's side; she seemed to have fainted and was lying on the floor beside her precious overturned pot. He gently lifted her up in his arms, as light as a feather, feeling the emaciated frame of her skeleton through his calf-skin gloves. He carried her back into the small cottage and laid her onto a thickly padded armchair.

Checking her condition, he could find nothing outwardly wrong with her other than a few scrapes and scratches. That is if you accepted in the first place her emaciated and burnt condition. He poured a tumbler of water, placing it on the table beside her chair. He put his head next to her and whispered, 'Professor-sama, you really do need to work on your aim.'

Picking up her telephone, he dialled the emergency services number carefully with a gloved hand and laid the handset next to the water. He left the unconscious woman and exited the cottage the way he had come in. Back out on the garden path he looked at the rusty garden trowel lying on the cobbles. He removed one of his gloves and rubbed at the back of his head where the trowel had made a slight cut in his scalp. He thought of the lethal clash of fine killing steel that had taken place there, with not a scratch taken from either opponent's blade, but he had been wounded by a badly thrown rusty trowel. He licked the small droplet of blood off his finger, ninety per cent of accidents really do happen at home he thought as he retraced his steps, deftly hopping from the stones and rocks scattered through the scientist's garden towards the boundary. Athletically flicking his legs into a scissor kick, he jumped back over the fence, landing lightly on the balls of his feet on the tarmac road on the other side.

Kurosawa quickly made his way across the small access route that ran alongside the professor's cottage, at the same time pushing his sword under the left side of his jacket, pulling the hilt tight up into his armpit, then dropping his left hand down the side of the blade, holding it in line with his leg. He would not have raised any suspicion to anyone watching, unless they were directly looking at his left side and noticed the slightly rigid movement of his arm and leg, the end of a dark Katana scabbard protruding along his thigh. To a casual observer there was nothing unusual about the plainly dressed man that could have attracted attention, other than the fact he was a little taller than most Japanese.

He turned right and strolled down a line of quiet residential houses, keeping his left side close to the walls and fences that bordered their gardens. Turning left into a small side street with a line of parked cars against one side, he halted at the rear of a pale blue Toyota Prius. He flicked open the trunk and quickly placed his sword inside. He took out a disposable plastic refuge bag and a second pair of shoes, these were comfortable leather

116

slip-ons, not like the trainers he was currently wearing. He placed the muddy trainers into the bag and, removing his lightweight jacket and leather gloves, he deposited them in the bag along with the trainers. Tying the handles into a knot, he placed them into the trunk alongside his sword and climbed into the driver's seat.

The assassin had been good, an excellent swordsman. If his opponent had also held a Katana, it may have been a very different tale to tell. It had only been the woman's good fortune that he had been there and mere chance that he had spotted her assailant as he conducted his reconnoitre of the area prior to making his entry. Even so the man's presence there had been a shock for a number of reasons, not least that he intended to dispatch the woman with a sword. They had known that the professor was a person of interest, but not interesting enough to have killed. They needed to find out why. Talking to her would now be out of the question because she would undoubtedly be put under police protection.

The swordsman though was a potential lead, one that he needed to understand. The killer would wonder how he had been detected, but he knew the assassin would not panic. He was certain the man was a professional of some sort. In which case he would realise that if he had been fully discovered, he would have been attacked at a more discreet time with a greater force than just one adversary, so would deduce it was an unfortunate coincidence. The murderer would return to whatever type of socially camouflaged life he created for himself. He would be more guarded, without a doubt, but would not want to break the protection of the established protective routines he had fashioned, practising the daily habits and customs he had contracted within his social interactions with others. He would continue to hide in plain sight, applying the skills of his tradecraft to those who existed around him, as proficiently as Kurosawa applied his.

He needed to find out who he was and why he had targeted this nuclear scientist. He would send a description of the man within the flash report he intended to send to their handlers at

117

the Firm. There could not be that many short, stocky, skilled swordsmen, at this point in history at least, operating as assassins, even in Japan. Kurosawa was contemplating the day's events as he entered his family home; an old traditional Japanese villa set in the foothills of Fukushima. He let himself in through the kitchen and laid his sword on the modest table in the centre of the room. He opened the door to the wood-burning stove that lay at the heart of his comfortably functional, rustic kitchen. He placed the plastic bag that contained his shoes, coat and gloves inside on top of the neatly stacked logs. Striking a match, he lit the kindling beneath them, closing the iron door as they caught alight, widening the draught and flue mechanism to draw more air into the burner. On the mantle above the old fireplace was an old sepia photograph of a young aristocratic-looking Japanese man, dressed in a dark formal suit, finished with a top hat. He was standing on top of a row of steps in front of an imposing building. The photographer must have been situated at the bottom of the steps, for there was an upward focused angle to the shot. Framed behind the man was the entrance to the grand building, over the doorway, a hardwood sign spanned across the pillars either side bearing the name 'Kyoto Imperial University' with the date scrawled in pen at the bottom of the picture – 7 March 1938. His grandfather looked so young, fresh faced and innocent in the picture. The few that there were taken of the man after the war, were of a very different looking man. They portrayed a haunted and hunted specimen, exhausted by a lifetime of horror and self-repulsion.

Three years after this photograph was taken, his country had set in motion events that would change its fate forever. In 1945, his grandfather had engaged in an act that had a similar effect on the Kurosawa lineage. The repercussions of his actions, resonating through generations until this very moment. The price of embracing evil and making pacts with demons.

The smoke from the burning textiles in the iron stove began to turn acrid and caught in his throat. He slid the panels facing his inner courtyard fully back to allow the stench to exhaust itself into the cool evening air. He stepped outside onto the raised deck that ran around the edge of his inner courtyard; he looked down upon his Zen stone garden that lay almost a metre beneath him. He gently focused on the contours of the raked, grey sand that he had created that morning. He followed its lines around the five small boulders of granite that lay within the garden, where they protruded at odd angles into the sky, or lay lengthways on their sides. The spiritual space of the garden never looking the same, always presenting a different viewpoint for one to explore. A true quality of any masterpiece of art is its ability to portray an unending range of emotions and feelings, dependent on the observer.

Next to the garden was his featureless, hardwood training area, with boards darkened to almost black from centuries of exposure to the elements. Its exterior was polished into a lacquered sheen by traditional natural treatments of beeswax and regular usage. Although the surface held a burnished gloss, when it was dry it gave a good firm footing. This side of the enclosure, however, never changed from a comforting constant where he knew every knot or crack in its solid wooden veneer. He looked forward to clearing his mind with his daily practice in the morning, but for now he needed to talk to his sister, for whom he had a number of questions that he hoped she would have answers to.

CHAPTER THIRTEEN

8 March 2011

The room they were given at Fukushima's police headquarters was by no means palatial, but it was, as they had requested, secluded, which suited the two Tokyo detectives perfectly. They were used to working in dungeons through necessity due to the level of secrecy required by their work. The basement room they occupied back in Tokyo, which had been their base for nearly ten years, was not that much larger than the one they were allocated here.

In one corner of the room, neatly stacked side by side were three robust, locked containers, each one meticulously crafted from moulded toughened plastic, reinforced with sturdy metal edging. The steel bands were riveted at regular intervals, encircling the crates, enhancing their durability. The containers, in a rich brown hue, were secured by silvery metallic straps, giving them the appearance of ancient treasure chests reminiscent of those found on a pirate ship.

Tekiō began checking the caskets, satisfying himself first that they had not been tampered with, before breaking the seals on two of them and unlocking them with keys he alone held.

Within was a selection of specialised equipment from their base in Tokyo. It had been delivered to them via a second police team from their headquarters in the capital. It held the more portable elements of what Matachi described as his 'Engine Room'. There were several laptops, all dedicated to individual functions, each operated in isolation from each other. There was a selection of printers and scanners that were 'slaved' to only one of the laptops and then only via a hard-line link. All WiFi connections had been permanently disabled or removed from the units entirely. The heaviest item was an uninterruptible power supply unit, known as a 'UPS', basically a very powerful battery. It, once connected to the mains, would be left in a state of continuous charging, storing electricity as it did so until it topped out at around two thousand volt-amperes. It would instantaneously maintain the supply of electricity to their systems in the event of a general power outage, coming online within thirty milliseconds. Also, there were three auxiliary monitors and, most importantly of all, two server 'Blades' which, although modest in size, were similar in dimension to a large laptop. These were the most powerful instruments they had brought with them and able to store, calculate and compute vast amounts of data.

Both detectives started to connect the various devices using the bundles of cabling and power units that had also been couriered to them within the crates. With very little discussion the men arranged the equipment into two workstations; Matachi's layout configured with two of the monitors and all but one of the laptops. This was the business end of their digital operation; Tekiō's desk was laid out with the support equipment. They had placed the Blades and UPS next to each other on the floor, adjacent to one of the power supplies for the room.

Within a few hours they had managed to bring all their tech online. With one final test of their cyber security systems, using the highest degree of protection, Matachi began sending his first situation report to his boss via their encrypted protocols, using a bespoke WiFi over a Peer 2 Peer secure system. He had designed the system himself and knew it to be extremely secure.

Tekiō had begun to examine the object they had recovered

earlier from beneath Matsumoto-san's head. Donning some sterile gloves, surgical face mask and safety specs, he started to carefully unwrap the bloodstained foil from around the article.

Matachi having completed sending his update, moved behind Tekiō to observe what he was doing. For a big man Tekiō's dexterity was similar to that of a surgeon when it came to close-up work. His large fingers delicately manipulated two sets of tweezers with unwavering precision, as he neatly unfolded the foil back across its original crease lines. It was the same skill set that had seen him graduate as top of his class at the Military Ordnance School at Okinawa, his American instructors amazed at his ability to successfully disarm a variety of explosive ordnance. Fold by fold, the wafer-thin aluminium was peeled back onto the plastic sheet Tekiō had laid on the desk.

They were soon looking at a larger than normal USB data stick, it was blue in colour with a pale white strip of paper adhered to one side. Matachi put on a rubber glove and reached in to pick it up, whilst Tekiō retrieved their forensic kit from one of the briefcases that he had brought with them. He took and marked a series of swabs from different sides of the stick as Matachi held it for him, then carefully dusted it for prints, gently blowing the powder onto the device with a small puffball before lightly brushing it with a fine-haired, bulbous brush. The stick was clean of any prints, so Matachi took it over to one of his laptops and plugged it into a port in its side.

'Anything on it?' enquired Tekiō.

'There is a single file written to it but looks like it has been encrypted.'

'A job for the Spaniard?' asked Tekiō.

'Yes, just bringing him online now.' Matachi searched his laptop hard drive for a document entitled the 'Spanish Inquisition' and opened it. Inside was a single file called the 'Inquisitor'. He placed his curser on it and dragged the file over to where the encrypted document lay on the auxiliary drive section of his computer. He dropped it onto the file. The document folder then changed colour from blue to grey, followed by a steadily increasing noise from the hard drives within the server's blades as they whirred into action.

The 'Inquisitor' was a fully automatous, multi-faceted hacking tool, combining a range of code and security breaking protocols that worked in conjunction with a master-controller system. It used the various weapons in its armoury as a supercomputer played a game of chess. Moving its pieces in a coordinated manner, altering its strategy and tactics as required, to break down the defences to reach its ultimate goal.

A small digital clock appeared in a pop-up menu in a corner of the laptop's screen, displaying a window announcing '24H:47M To Breach'; as they watched it jumped to '25H:16M To Breach.' 'Looks like this will take some time,' said Matachi. 'Let's find out where forensics are in this place and hand them the swabs from the stick, it will also give us an opportunity to see if they have discovered anything interesting at Matsumoto's house.'

'What, more interesting than the fact he got his head sliced off?' said Tekiō. 'I bet that shook the fuckers up; you can be sure these yokels have never seen anything like that before!'

'Yeah, I do get the feeling that nothing very exciting ever happens in Fukushima. These latest events must have come as quite a shock to them.'

The detectives left their newly acquired base of operations, Tekiō hanging back to lock the door behind them. The two men were, as individuals, highly trained and competent detectives, however, as in any high-performing team, the partners had a demarcation of responsibilities between them. An order that had self-evolved from their particular skill sets and experience, into an inventory of appropriate functionalities. It was like two pyramids of accountability that broaden out as it cascaded downwards, merging and overlapping as it did so. At the top of one was 'Security' above the other 'Cyber' – Matachi was the specialist in the latter, Tekiō took care of the former. They both understood each other's strengths and weaknesses totally, allowing them to compensate and complement one another, as if in a self-perpetuating, performance-enhancing ballet, that as it played out amplified their abilities, turning them into a formidable entity.

They made their way through to the main floor of the headquarters where they were met by the Station Chief who they had introduced themselves to earlier that day. Commander-san purposefully strode at them in full uniform, complete with an ornate swagger stick. His name was Nomura and as he approached them, they could see from his expression and demeanour that he was not the same jovial, chipper character they had met that morning.

'I see that you have both made quite a start with your inquiries,' he said not hiding his sarcastic tone.

'Good afternoon, sir, it would appear so,' replied Matachi, maintaining cordiality, trying to defuse any confrontation before it arose. He wondered what had caused such a change in the officer's manner from the initial meeting that day.

'I can see now why you were sent to assist us; it appears that you are able to create cases as well as solve them,' continued the Commander. He was a tall man, and he was trying to use his height to intimidate Matachi, ignoring the considerably taller Tekiō standing by his side.

Matachi was not sure what was going on with the guy but his patience with the man was wearing thinner than a Geisha's conscience and they really did not have the time for this. They both knew what the situation was here; the man had been informed by his superiors that his team would not be involved in the case unless requested by the two Tokyo detectives.

'That is very kind of you to say so, sir,' replied Matachi, also dropping any pretence of camouflaging his own sarcasm.

Taken aback at Matachi's unhesitant and disrespectful reply, he dropped the barbs, reverting to pulling rank instead. He bore his gaze down at Matachi and started issuing commands.

'I would like to see your full report concerning everything you have discovered in your initial inquiries and also the particulars of the Matsumoto incident on my desk by this evening.'

'I see, sir, unfortunately I have already made my report to Commander Ōno,' said Matachi very matter-of-factly.

'Good, then you can give me a copy right now.'

'I'm afraid that will not be possible, sir. Any and *all* information we will gather on this case will only be presented by us to Commander Ōno. Apologies, sir, I was under the belief that you had been informed of this aspect?' said Matachi innocently.

'You do understand failing to respond to a direct order from a superior officer is a serious offence?' said the Commander, trying a different approach.

'Yes, indeed, sir, that is exactly the case. Which is why you will not be receiving any updates directly from us – at all – at any time – during the full period of our secondment to this prefecture. If that will be all, sir, we really need to get on.'

The Commander looked like someone who had forced a ball of Wasabi paste into his mouth, his face burned with the fire of indignation, the thread-like veins in his cheeks looked like there was molten lava running through them. The man took his swagger stick from where he had been holding it beneath his arm and touched Matachi on the chest.

'There is an insubordinate piece of shit on the end of my cane,' he slowly and deliberately said, almost spitting each word out in turn.

Matachi sensed Tekiō was getting twitchy, he could demonstrate diverse levels of twitchiness, and all of them were a very dangerous portent of bad things about to occur. He needed to defuse the situation quickly.

'Well, it's not on my end, sir,' he retorted, pushing the baton to one side with a wave of his arm and striding past the now quite shocked man. He hoped that Tekiō was following him, and was relieved to only hear the sound of the big man's footsteps following behind him; luckily not the screams of anyone in pain or a body hitting the floor.

When they were out of earshot from the Commander, Tekiō announced, 'I hate fucking officers.'

'But Tekiō, I'm an officer!' 'Exactly, case in point.'

'We really have to work on your anger management issues, Sergeant.'

'Really! Do I have to highlight to you that my lack of anger management has saved our lives on numerous occasions?'

Matachi ran a quick reflection on an assortment of unsavoury incidents in their past, that on the whole were probably best left there – in the past. 'Good point, I duly retract my earlier statement. Ah, here's the Forensics Lab,' said Matachi, silently welcoming the diversion of their arrival at the department.

They went inside and introduced themselves to the laboratory staff and were directed to one of the female technicians working there. Her name was Kondō-san and she had been assigned exclusively to support them with any forensic issues they had. Matachi thought she seemed a little mature to be working as a technician, putting her age around the mid-forties. The woman seemed perfectly pleasant and helpful, quite a contrast to the interaction they had been involved in a few minutes before. Tekiō handed her the swabs he had taken off the memory stick. She looked at the labelling on the sides of the protective plastic tubes covering the swabs. There was scant detail written there, just Matsumoto One, Two and Three respectively on each receptacle.

'From what did you take these exactly?' she asked.

Tekiō, kept quiet, waiting for Matachi to decide what to tell the technician.

'They are just some areas of significance that we are especially interested in from the Matsumoto murder crime scene,' he responded, being liberal with the truth.

'I see, and may I enquire where exactly are these significant areas that interest you?'

Tenacious, thought Matachi. He needed to be careful with this one. It was totally against procedures to remove items from a crime scene, and although they did not generally constitute much attention to regulations – unless it suited them to do so of course – it never paid to advertise such transgressions.

'His spectacles,' he said, picking an obscure item that they may not have covered in their search. 'We have a suspicion someone else may have held them prior to his death. They were folded and neatly placed on the other side of the room, seemed odd to us, we being detectives 'n all.' He smiled at her after making his joke.

She did not smile back.

'I am sure we would have run similar tests on the item. If we haven't already, then we would certainly have done it in due course. You could have simply made a request for us to test them; we have been told to fully accommodate any request you make, after all.'

He realised that she was not really buying his story, but that didn't matter, just that there was one is all that mattered.

'Apologies, very sorry indeed,' said Matachi. 'I did not mean to infer that you didn't know how to run a crime scene. I am sure we will quickly get used to each other's idiosyncrasies.'

She looked at them disdainfully. 'Like dropping the victim's head onto the floor, you mean?' she replied.

'Yes, that was an unfortunate lapse in professionalism on our part there,' said Matachi, glancing at his colleague.

'Bit me,' whispered Tekiō.

'I'm sorry, did you just say – "Bite me!"'

'No, no, the head bit me when I picked it up. Or it seemed to at the time. Gave me a bit of a start, so I dropped it.'

'But why were you picking it up in the first place? It was a crime scene!'

Matachi could see this conversation was going south fast, so he decided to interject before Tekiō dropped them right in it.

'That would be my fault,' he said. 'I'm afraid the head looked like it was about to topple off onto the floor, so I instructed the Sergeant to gently place it back onto its original position on the cabinet. Clearly in hindsight not a great move, but I can assure you, it was undertaken with the best of motives.'

Tekiō's relief at his colleague's interjection on his behalf was palpable, she was a great deal scarier than the commander 'I am sure it was,' she said.

She gave them a look that was both disapproving as it was disbelieving and took possession of the swabs that Tekiō had been holding outstretched to her, like a chastised schoolboy offering an apple to a teacher. An awkward moment of silence passed between them, which Matachi was about to put an end to when his cell phone rang.

'Detective Matachi,' he announced to the caller.

As he listened, he turned and started heading out of the building. He made a goodbye bow in the direction of the forensic scientist, at the same time gesturing to Tekiō to follow him. His obvious sudden sense of urgency portraying the need to override the normal requirements of courtesy.

'We are on our way. Make sure you have enough personnel to fully secure the house and the surrounding area,' he said as he hung up.

'What's the gig?' asked Tekiō.

'We have got another one, this time it's two guys, seen chopping away at each other with swords in someone's cabbage patch!'

'You are fucking joking. Has someone pissed off Mifune Toshiro? I heard he lived around here.'

The two men arrived at their Toyota, this time legally parked within the station grounds.

'Unlikely,' said Matachi, unlocking the car. 'Firstly, he lived in Tokyo and more importantly he has been dead for over twenty years.'

'Precisely, that's enough to piss anyone off.'

'Stop dicking about and do something you're good at, programming the GPS,' said Matachi, handing Tekiō his phone.

'Open the first text on the list, it is the address of some Professor of Physics house.'

Tekiō began to feed the address into the device. Then said, 'Boss, do you think it's us?'

'What is?' Matachi replied a little perplexed.

'The weird shit that always seems to go down when we start a case. We start off and everything is fine and normal. We are on the bad guy's trail – then wham, it all starts going sideways quicker than a Tokyo Drift Jockey taking a cindered corner.'

'That thought has crossed my mind from time to time, that perhaps we have become some sort of crime-orientated, self-fulfilling prophecy machine. We are assigned complex and unusual cases, so our cases become complex and unusual.'

'Still,' said Tekiō, 'look on the bright side, it's great to see swords making a renaissance in the world of serious crime again don't you think?'

CHAPTER FOURTEEN

8 March 2011

The universe was conspiring against him, Uchida was sure of this, it appeared he had upset the Gods again somehow. In addition to his recent woes, now his associates from across the sea had made an unannounced visit – to his home! The audacity of foreigners was beyond bad manners. It had been a mistake to allow them into his scheme, an obvious error on his part, he could see that now. But one cannot move forwards by thinking backwards. There is no such thing as a perfect plan, every strategy drags out mistakes in its wake, like a trawler rakes ups rocks into its net along with the fish it pursues.

As a young student his teachers had taught him that the 'imperfection of a plan, was its perfection', a stratagem that unfolds seamlessly, not encountering issue, was a weak one of narrow formula and, by default, free of any ambition. It was hammered into him by his tutors that – 'The plan is not the goal', it is the route you have decided to take. Over focus on perfection here and it is here that you will remain, stuck on the path. Provision the journey well, as you must, but execute to the objective. Arrival is the time for consolidation, throw out the rocks then… but remember even a rock can have value.

He had followed this doctrine his entire career and its returns had been bountiful. Striking out for his goals without inhibition – only turning to cleanse the path in retrospection. As the greats had done – Alexander, Toyota, Caesar, Samsung, Genghis, Apple – not worrying about what carnage was created in the pursuit of their goals. The 'ends' always focus on the ends, never the means. Now though he seemed to have dredged up some stones that were too large to jettison.

The man had accused him of being complicit in the disappearance of the governor and the one who had initiated the 'accidents' that had befallen several other minor officials. His indignation at such an accusation was only matched by the preposterousness of it. Why would he do such a thing, that was so obviously not in his self-interest? The loss of key individuals had undermined the whole operation, causing him grave issues that he was actively trying to correct. It was evidently nonsense to suggest otherwise.

They also had some concerns about a freelance reporter from Tokyo, known as Kurosawa, who had been asking a number of questions of key people involved in their network. They wanted to know what he had said to her. The last thing they needed was the Press undertaking some investigative journalism.

Yes, of course he knew of her, however he could assure them that he had not talked to her directly. She had become a bit of an annoyance it was true. Mainly because she did not work directly for a company, so it was difficult to apply the pressure he would normally put any inquisitive journalist under. The problem being she was not only a bit of a free speech evangelist she was also a woman of means and had not taken up their offer of a number of generous bribes to stop asking questions and harassing his associates.

He was told that their assessment of the situation was different and that their appraisal led them to believe he was readying himself for a clean extraction from the venture. He was clearing up loose ends and covering his arse before making his final move to retirement. Which, of course, they saw as understandable; he had after all been the project's principal architect and master puppeteer from the beginning. Now in his seventies and still in good health, it would be an ideal time to start enjoying more of the fruits of his labours. This could be tolerated, but only within the framework of managed transition. They were not looking to take a greater cut from him, if that was his concern, he should be assured by now that they were not in it for the money. That was just a lucrative side line as far as they were concerned, a welcome addition to the Great Leader's coffers, no doubt, but it would always be the technology that would be of real value to them. The details of how a modern nuclear power-plant operates being far more important than mere money to the regime. If he wished to leave, he could do so and with their blessings, as long as he did not compromise the operation. He detested working with Koreans, they all had a chip on their collective shoulders from the past, whichever side of the 49th Parallel they came from.

Struggling to contain his seething fury, he adamantly refused to abandon the remarkable enterprise he had single-handedly built. The very idea of relinquishing control of his incredible creation to anyone, especially barbarians, was unthinkable and intolerable.

Secretly he wished he had not become so involved with them, but although this was a view that he had never openly advertised, it did not take a genius to work out he may have some regrets over the decision to bring them on board in the first place. He really did have to give them credit for how they had achieved such a deep infiltration into his organisation. They had been more sophisticated in their approach than he had thought possible for such a backward people.

A lesson there, he thought, not to allow one to be swayed by one's personal prejudices. Admittedly, overriding millennia of cultural indoctrination proved challenging. His thinking processes, undoubtedly influenced by subconscious conditioning, were unmistakably affected in this incident.

He had resigned himself to be shackled to those Gok iburi

132

bastards, for the time being anyway. He had definitely not put anything into play at the moment, to the contrary, so they had no evidence to back their bullshit hypothesis.

He had soon realised that the aggressive response had been a test, to see how he reacted to such forceful and direct accusations put directly to his face. It soon transpired that he had passed that test.

The ill-mannered fellow seemed to become quite conciliatory after he had been totally honest with him regarding his position. He had quickly realised that being open and transparent was the way forward and out of this potentially hazardous situation.

This was an easy and obvious position to take, given the fact that he did not have anything to hide – well in regard to this little episode at least – and he did not fully know what it was that they actually knew. He let the truth as such do the talking for him, his responses unquestionably corroborating what information they did have.

However, at the end of the discussion, although they had established that it was not either of them that were carrying out these actions, the only other thing they managed to do was highlight the unknowns, of which there were many, and all very concerning.

Someone was coming after them that was evident, but it did not look like it was any type of anti-crime unit, intelligence service or rival organisation. With the exception of the governor, those who had gone missing or met their ends, were connected, but not directly, none of them knew of the involvement of each other by name, scope or detail. The governor did know most of this, but she disappeared after the events that had befallen the others.

The only event that had occurred after her disappearance was the recent decapitation of Matsumoto. A fitting end for the slimy, difficult bastard no doubt, but he was not in their pocket at all, quite the contrary, he had been about to cause some major problems for them and he had needed to act quickly to curtail his machinations. He had plotted his downfall personally, expertly cutting his political legs off metaphorically, rather than his head literally. That aspect of his death had made no sense at all.

The two bumbling detectives, though, had shown considerable foresight in singling the man out for a visit, an action which he put down to beginner's luck for the moment. When he finally did receive access directly to their systems, he would be a lot more comfortable. The fact that this simple matter had not been implemented yet, was becoming annoying, what was he paying these policemen for after all!

The shocking discovery they had then made was a rather disconcerting. It pointed to an unknown actor or actors, whose motives were unclear. A message was being sent with this ritualistic killing. What it was and to what end he had a suspicion they were about to find out, for he was certain the gruesome message was for them.

CHAPTER FIFTEEN

8 March 2011

Squatting down on the stony garden path, Matachi pulled on a pair of latex gloves and shook open another one of the ubiquitous evidence bags. He had just been told a story that would not have gone amiss in the tales of the *Seven Samurai*, but without a doubt he believed the old lady's story. He reached down and picked up a rusty old trowel by its wooden handle, he turned it over in his hand, inspecting it perceptively, then he gently placed it into the bag and sealed it.

'Everything okay, boss?' asked Tekiō, coming out of the cottage doorway.

'It's all good, big boy, all good.' Matachi looked at the trowel through the bag. 'I think we just got our first real break.'

'Really, boss, you sure about that. You believe the old lady's Ninja showdown story?'

'I do and once I get the lab results back on this thing, it will confirm it.'

'OK, boss, whatever you say, boss, after all you're the boss, boss.'

'Tekiō, dear boy, stop breaking my balls and try and make

yourself useful please. You can start by picking up that plant pot that's rolling around, before someone else gets hurt by it.'

Tekiō walked over to the plant and reached down with one hand, grabbing the tree by its small trunk. He lifted it up as if it were a radish, holding it out towards Matachi.

'Where do you want it?' he asked, followed by a loud crash, as the large flowerpot slipped away from its incumbent shrubbery. Matachi looked at Tekiō, who was holding the bay tree out towards him with one hand, its root ball now exposed at its base, and then down to the smashed terracotta pot strewn across the pathway.'

'Are you some new kind of fucking idiot?' he said, staring up at Tekiō. 'Are you intentionally trying to contaminate every crime scene you attend from now on?'

'Sorry, boss,' he replied, projecting his best apologetic face, which Matachi felt definitely lacked a proper level of sincerity.

'Don't tell me – the flowerpot bit you?'

Tekiō said nothing, just placing the compacted root ball of the small tree onto a soft piece of earth on the edge of the herb garden. He then began to gather up the larger pieces of the broken terracotta pot and put them to one side of the pathway, before walking back inside the cottage to apologise to the old lady.

Matachi looked across the rows of planted herbs to the area of the fence where the old lady had said her saviour must have appeared from. He could just make out some footprints in the softened soil that looked like they ran to and from the fence. From the ones closest to the path, he could see the feet were large for a Japanese. There also appeared to be the pattern of a sports shoe imprinted there. The imprints seemed deeper and more pronounced leading towards the path from the fence; plainly the man had been in a hurry to cover the ground, rushing to make his intervention in the professor's defence.

Leading away from the scene, the imprints were far lighter, barely perceptible as they trailed back to the fence. This must have been the route he had taken to make his exit. He did not want to disturb the area, so left it for the forensic team to look at in greater detail.

He followed Tekiō into the cottage. The sergeant had not yet been able to tell the woman of his accident as the paramedics were still trying to persuade the old lady to go with them. But she was having none of it, thankful for their initial assistance, she was now politely, but firmly, telling them to leave her alone. As Matachi walked into the cottage, one of the paramedics had hold of her arm trying to lead her to the ambulance outside. He saw her glance at the plastic-coated trowel in his hand, noticed the expression on her face and thought he had better tell them to let her go before someone else got a smack around the head with a garden implement.

'Are you sure you are okay, Takeuchi-san,' he said. 'I would say you have been through quite an ordeal today, both physical and emotional, perhaps it would be wise to go with them?'

The woman forcibly prised the fingers of the paramedic from around her left wrist with her right hand, then turning back to Matachi said, 'It is Professor-sama actually, Detective-san, and I am fine thank you, and will be even better when these kind gentleman leave me in peace.'

The paramedic began to wince as she continued to apply pressure to his fingers that he now found were being locked back painfully against their joints. Tekiō was impressed, recognising that she was using a derivative of a standard Aikido wrist lock. Not bad for an old bird he thought.

Matachi gave a dismissing nod to the medics saying, 'I'm sure if you would be so kind as to release the dear fellow, he and his comrade would be glad to be on their way, Professor-sama."

Takeuchi released the man and the two of them quickly gathered up their medical paraphernalia, muttering in inaudible irritation to each other as they did so.

Tekiō grinned broadly at the two men as they left, his admiration for the professor growing.

'We just have a few more questions we would like to ask you before we also leave, if that is okay with you?'

'I'm sure I do not know any more than I have already told you,' she said, retaking her seat near the fire. 'I have absolutely no idea who the two men were.'

'Yes, but that being said, I would've thought it is not every day that two men fight a duel over you. As flattering as that may seem, there has to be a reason for it.'

'I am afraid, Detective-san, I do not have an answer for you to that question either.'

'You once worked for the Fukushima Nuclear Power Company, did you not?'

'Yes, for over thirty years. I was one of the original design specialists for the reactors. Once they were functioning, I was employed directly by the company to oversee ongoing operational radiological safety for the plant. That was until last year of course.'

'That was when you had your accident, yes?'

'Yes… my accident,' she repeated quietly.

Matachi could see he was starting to distress the woman, but continued to press her. 'Would you mind telling us how the incident occurred please?'

'I was undertaking some routine safety maintenance procedures with a team of colleagues, around the primary heat transfer system surrounding the core. The seven reactor units at Fukushima plant are of the BWR variety.'

'BWR?' asked a puzzled Matachi.

'Boiling Water Reactor, basically the intense heat generated by a nuclear pile is used to boil water. Similar to how an electric kettle operates. The difference being that the steam produced from the boiling water is not for making a pot of tea it is used to do "work", in this case to drive a steam turbine connected to an electrical generator. Apart from the fact that is that the water in the kettle is heated by the resistance caused within its element to the passage of electrical photons, whilst within a nuclear reactor, it is through an atomic chain reaction taking place.'

'I see,' said Matachi, appreciating her attempt to simplify an analogy, but confusing him even more. 'Apologies for interrupting, please do continue.'

'The team was about to start its inspection of one of the condensing units, which are an integral part of the steam generation system. This device is used to return the steam vapour to a liquid, where it is pumped back into the reactor to be converted into steam once again, thereby creating more energy to drive the turbines. It is basically an eternal cycle, totally enclosed, that would continue for infinity, all things of course remaining equal.

'Before any inspection of such a system, we would have undergone a rigorous process of isolation, with many levels of checks and counter checks, each one signed off by the requisite key personnel before any work commenced on the system in question. You need to understand that safety is paramount in the nuclear industry; it underpins every aspect of every single thing we do. So, it was with a very high degree of confidence we entered the condenser area to start our inspection. The sudden release of scalding hot, high-pressure boiling water was a totally shocking incident.'

'I bet it fucking was,' blurted out Tekiō.

Matachi, gave him an admonished look. 'Please go on, Professor.'

'Two of the maintenance workers were killed by the initial blast of steam, three of us were badly injured, two of those survivors died very soon afterwards from the extent of their horrific injuries. I was lucky, four of my colleagues were in front of me and they bore the main force of the release.'

'Not that lucky, I would imagine,' said Matachi, looking at the visible scars on her arms and around her neck.

'Everything in life is relative, Detective. In comparison to my friends who were killed, I was very fortunate to survive with just these injuries. If uncovering the truth about the events of that day is the last achievement within my grasp in the time I have left, then it would bring me some measure of solace. Exposing who was really responsible for that avoidable tragedy is extremely important to me now.'

'You did not see it as an accident then?' responded Matachi to the revelation she had disclosed.

'Unfortunately, Detective Matachi, we see other respective worlds very differently to one another. Yours, I have no doubt is filled with coincidences, random occurrences and unexpected misfortunes. In my world, by that I mean the arena of creating power from harnessing atomic energy, we do not have "accidents". They are designed out of the systems that operate the nuclear process from the first blueprints through to becoming fully operational. We work with procedures and methodologies that are error-proofed to a rate of near zero percentages of opportunities to fail. Layer upon layer of interconnected prevention and protection. We just do not take any chances whatsoever with any of the many, many functions that must be undertaken to produce electricity from nuclear energy. Does it create a time-consuming complexity out of what would be simple operations, yes of course, but that is the price we pay for total safety. There are only two elements that could ever affect this condition, human belligerence, and catastrophic acts of God.'

'And which was the cause of your fateful – er – event?'

She shifted uncomfortably in her chair, moving a cushion beneath her injured arm. 'Well, I can assure you, it was no act of God, that I am certain of.'

'You have a theory then – one that you would like to share with us perhaps?'

'Let's say I have a working hypothesis that I am currently testing. Once I have a high degree of proof in support of it, only then will I share it.'

'I see,' said Matachi. 'Professor, have you ever heard of a man called Matsumoto Hirofumi?'

'The name does sound familiar,' she responded, her slight pause before answering being noted by Matachi. 'Why do you ask?'

Both men prepared themselves to assess her reaction to the answer as Matachi said,

'His body was found earlier today at his home, it looks like he, too, was attacked by someone wielding a sword… though I'm afraid he was not as fortunate as you.'

Upon hearing the news, both men observed a subtle quiver of her lower lip, a fleeting sign of emotional turmoil. However, she swiftly regained her composure. Her features shifted into an expression of empathetic concern as she spoke, 'How dreadful, truly horrific – but, detective, how does this relate to me?' Detective Matachi, undeterred by her feigned ignorance, a tactic to divert attention from her involvement, chose to play along with her act. 'Because I believe at least one of the men duelling here today was also the murderer in that case. I am not one to put much faith in coincidences, but I am quite keen on the relevance of correlation. I am sure someone as academically astute as yourself, would agree on this point?'

'Yes, detective, I do see what you mean there of course. I am sorry, it has been a trying day, to put it mildly, I was not thinking logically.'

'Ah, quite understandable under the circumstances, Professor-sama. I think it's time to leave you to get some rest now. We will be on our way, Professor Takeuchi.'

Matachi made a final note, then putting away his stylus and closing the cover on his tablet, he bowed politely to the woman; Tekiō automatically mimicking the action of his superior.

'It has been truly enlightening talking to you,' said Matachi. 'I just wished it had been under more pleasant circumstances. You can be assured that we will be maintaining a twenty-four-hour watch on you and your home for some time to come, at least until we catch the perpetrators of this attack. There's just one last thing before we leave you in peace.'

Matachi could see that his questions were causing the woman some anxiety, but there was one last thing to say before they left. He looked towards Tekiō who was still in mid bow. 'Unfortunately, my colleague here has a small confession to make,' he said as he bowed and began to make his own exit from the cottage. 'I am sorry to say it is more bad news. Sergeant, I will wait for you in the car.' Tekiō gave his Boss one of his – *I'm going to pull your arsehole up over your ears later* – looks. And then, maintaining a respectful distance from her, remembering what she had done to the medic earlier, he started to make his grovelling apology concerning the smashed flowerpot.

Tekiō caught up with Matachi outside on the street where his boss was talking to two uniformed officers who had parked their car opposite Takeuchi's home.

'Thanks for that,' said Tekiō, giving an acknowledging nod to the two men in the squad car.

Matachi finished discussing the security arrangements for the scientist with the two officers and began to walk towards their vehicle, which they had pulled up behind the marked police car.

'No problem, anytime, it was my pleasure, think absolutely nothing of it,' said Matachi, chuckling to himself. 'Did you offer to pay for the damages?'

'Of course, but the old girl would not hear of it. What do you think she is hiding then?'

'That I don't know, but I am sure she does not have a corrupt bone in her body, so it is intriguing that she is hiding something from us.'

'Well, if we can keep her alive long enough for another chat in the future, I suppose we may find out.'

CHAPTER SIXTEEN

9 March 2011

'Service,' shouted Takada to no one in particular. He waited until one of the waitresses came up to his breakfast station, 'Table seven, for the two Gaijin.'

'So sorry, Chef-san, but this is not what they ordered. They wanted a traditional Japanese breakfast,' said the diminutive young waitress bowing her head, not wishing to give any offence.

'What are you called, girl?'

'Maeda Sumire, Chef-san,' she said bowing as she did so.

'Well, Sumire, what nationality are the two men on table seven?' the chef growled at her.

'One is American and the other one I think is English, Chef-san,' she haltingly answered, bowing several times, and worrying where this conversation was going.

The chef moved his face uncomfortably close to that of the waitress.

'Yes, as I said, savages, savages who would not know a traditional Japanese breakfast if I held their faces in a bowl of Miso soup and rubbed salted herring in their heads. And do you know why, girl?'

'No, Chef-san.' She trembled as she lowered her gaze to what the chef had served on the plate. Although she was an experienced waitress, she had only been working at the hotel for a few months. She had already got on the wrong side of this particular chef a few times. Of course, she understood that all chefs were a bit crazy. As anybody would be, who laboured in a hot stainless-steel box, working long hours, busting a gut to lovingly prepare dishes that were rarely appreciated, so it wasn't surprising they were just a little fucked in the head. Sumire realised this and made allowances accordingly. But this guy was a bizarre one. For one thing, he did not like foreigners or academics at all. If he found out one of the guests was a scholar or lecturer, he would become very difficult, as only a chef can.

Sometimes the dishes they would order would suddenly no longer be available, or a really good chef could prepare a meal that was just not quite right, not so much in the taste, but more in the presentation. They say that people first eat with their eyes, well this was particularly true for the Japanese, the look was equally as important as the taste. This chef could deliver a cutting insult with his arrangement of sushi.

Once though she witnessed an occasion when he had gone too far. Inexplicably, an amount of some extra strong wasabi had mysteriously found its way into a visiting Professor of Nuclear Sciences' pudding. She had never seen a man's face get so red, so fast! She thought his head was going to explode. The poor man had never expected his mint green ice cream to turn to molten lava on his tongue. The manager had pulled the chef out of the kitchen to the academic's table to apologise in person over that incident, which he did, very profusely. Bowing so low his head nearly touched his knees, his back bent double. She had thought he was overdoing it a bit bowing like that, but then she realised he was almost wetting himself laughing and needed to keep his head down or the manager or guest would notice.

He also hated politicians. When Iwasaki, the governor, had stayed at the hotel once for a conference, he had called her all the profanities under heaven's vale when she had come down to dinner. This tirade was from the sanctuary of the kitchen, of course, but his voice was blatantly audible in the dining room. Though it had to be acknowledged that the food he produced for her was first class. All courses were on time and a work of art without exception. The waitress had been impressed by his skill, but very embarrassed whilst serving the governor at the table in case she had overheard the amazing litany of expletives that had emanated from the kitchen. She for one, had learnt some enlightening new curse words that day. But nothing had been said and she had left a good tip as well, which the chef refused to have any share in. Stubborn fool, well he won't get a second chance for another tip like that from her, that was certain. Poor lady, it was terrible what had happened to her a few months later, the papers were full of her puzzling disappearance.

The management though, except for the odd chastisement, seemed happy to put up with this particular chef's attitude. A good chef was a valuable asset, the more skilled they were, the crazier the fuckers seemed to be. The management appeared to understand this, and short of him killing someone, seemed fine with his temperament, content to let misbegotten cooks lie.

She had realised that trying to complain about his behaviour, would get her in far more trouble than him. But here we go again, foreigners now were his new flavour of the moment, it seemed. 'Well, I'll tell you why, girl, they are all backward idiots, especially the western ones. They come over here, giggling and smiling at what they see as our quaint little customs and quaint cultural practices. Their stinking, dairy-sodden bodies forever invading your space so close you want to vomit. Trying to be all high and mighty, pretending to fully understand our traditions just from reading a few books and watching some dubbed films. Then they start acting like some fucking pseudo-Samurai. So, give them what they know.' He pushed the plates at her.

He was right about the smell, all that cream, milk and cheese they consumed made them smell disgusting. It had taken her some time to get used to it when she had first become a waitress and had started to regularly encounter foreigners on a daily basis. She had once had an English guy come to stay at her small apartment block. All started quite well; he was very polite and quite handsome for a barbarian. But eventually the residents could not stand it anymore and made the janitor knock on his door and show him where the bathhouse was.

Thank the gods that the school had taught them coping mechanisms to deal with this tricky issue in the first year of catering college. It was all in the breathing she had learned; and never, at any point, no matter what, stop smiling.

She picked up the plates with the few rashers of crispy turkey bacon and anaemic omelette, accompanied by fava beans on the side. She laid the breakfasts in front of the two men.

'Christ,' said one of them. 'Not the Eggo Baco again,' he exclaimed.

'Told you,' said the other. 'That's a 1,000 yen you owe me by the way. It was the same last year when I came here. No matter what you order for breakfast, they just nod and smile politely in agreement and you get Eggo Baco for breakfast.'

The first man turned to the waitress. 'You speaky English?' he said to her, in his best condescending foreigner manner.

She looked at him and glued on her best 'customer not happy smile' as taught in the second year of catering college.

'I will get you some ketchup,' she said, bowing and reversing away from the men's breakfast table, retreating to the kitchen. One of the other female waitresses, slowly rushed (as only a Japanese waitress can do) from her section of the dining floor and intercepted her at the kitchen entrance.

'You got the hell out of there fast, what's up?' she asked of Sumire.

'It's that fucking Takada again, he is such a bastard when it comes to Gaijin. He revels in winding them up. They then get pissed off and I have to deal with the fall-out.'

'Complain to the floor manager about him.'

'Tried that, they don't want to know. I think they are scared of him for some reason.'

146

'Really! Can't think why... maybe it's because he looks like one of those creepy Chikan gropers on the subway and has unlimited access to some very sharp knifes! Anyway, it looks like you will not have to complain to the soggy dumpling that is our floor manager, as *they* are going to do it for you.' She pointed at the table where the two foreigners had called over the manager and were giving him some feedback on the standard of the breakfast service.

'Look, all I am after is some traditional Japanese cuisine. I do not think it is too much to ask – we are in Japan after all, are we not?' said the English guest to the nervous and continually bowing floor manager.

'Yes, sir. Very sorry, sir. Allow me to put this right for you, sir. I will ensure that you receive the breakfast of your choice for the reminder of your stay. If could just bear with me for today?' said the manager in his heavily accented English.

'So tomorrow when we arrive for breakfast, we will receive what we ordered, without question?'

'I guarantee it, sir. Yes, absolutely, without question, sir. I believe you are meeting some colleagues at the hotel today, so I would also like to compensate you for the inconvenience you have suffered. We would like to offer a complimentary lunch for you and all of your party.'

'That is very good of you. There are five of us, but we will not be finished with our meeting until two o'clock. I believe that lunch is served between twelve until two inclusive. Would it be possible to eat around two-thirty?'

The manager realised that this was going to cause some problems with the staff, particularly their chef, but he felt obliged to meet the customer's request. 'Yes, that will not be a problem, sir. Thank you for your patience and indulgence on this matter, so kind,' he said in his best grovelling voice.

With that he turned towards the kitchen, knowing he was about to have a considerably more difficult conversation.

CHAPTER SEVENTEEN

8 March 2011

Matachi opened the car, and they got in. 'Back to the Bat Cave then,' he said.

'Sounds good, let's pick up a snack to eat on the way.'

'There you go again, being led by your ravenous appetite. A diligent officer would be more interested in what was on that memory stick than what was in his stomach.'

Tekiō ignored the remark, asking instead, 'Do you think it will have been breached by now?'

'It's possible, but likelier we will have to wait until the morning. Let's get back and see how it's doing, then check into the hotel we've been allocated.'

'Sounds like a plan, it has been a long and eventful first day. By the way, we passed several roadside noodle houses on the way here, don't forget to pull into one.'

The sun had already set on the gloomy, overcast day when they arrived back at the Police HQ a few hours later. The two men entered the now virtually deserted office area. Most of the day workers had gone home leaving a few stalwarts still working here and there in the facility.

As they approached their office deep in the recesses of the building many of the corridors and rooms were in darkness, but flickered into light in turn as the PIR sensors detected their presence. As they reached their own office, Tekiō came to a halt and held up his hand, stopping Matachi at his side. They had not yet come into range of the PIR operated lights of their room and there was a delay to the area of the corridor they were in, which left their office in darkness.

'What the fuck is causing that!' said Tekiō, pointing through the window.

There was a now a distinct yellowy glow coming from the USB Stick. The two men edged closer to the half-glazed wall that ran around their room. The stick was definitely glowing in the darkness. As they peered forward slightly more, their presence was detected by the sensors and the lights came on in the office and the glow disappeared.

'What are you waiting for?' asked Matachi. 'Go and have a look.'

'You first.'

'I thought you took care of security?' said Matachi, giving Tekiō a look of disgust.

'Looks like an IT issue to me, I will open the door for you,' said Tekiō.

Tekiō unlocked the door and then pushed it open, standing aside to allow Matachi to enter first. They both stood in front of the laptop with its now, quite benignly appearing, data stick protruding from its side.

'Looks fine now,' said Tekiō.

'Yes, but we both know how deceiving "looks" can be – who after all would ever mistake you for being a detective…'

'You are really pushing your luck with me today. I'm telling you, I have limits, I could snap and then I mi…'

'Ah, Tekiō, please do control yourself dear fellow, I was about to say… of such great renown. But you interrupted me, again.'

A grinning Matachi opened the laptop and began accessing it, using a combination of biometric and password authentication. To gain entry to the device required fingerprint, face recognition and a high strength password constructed from a permutation of alpha numeric and symbolic characters. He knew that any security could be breached, given enough time and skill, but that was no reason to make it easy for anyone trying to do so.

The machine's screen came to life with its countdown displayed '04H:23M To Breach'.

'Still seems to be functioning okay. It's picked up quite a bit since we left it to do its thing,' said Matachi, scrutinising the data stick. 'Find the isolation switch for the lights and turn them off.'

Tekiō found the switch, shutting off the room's lighting. They both warily peered at the USB stick, which continued to look perfectly normal.

'Shut all the blinds on the windows,' instructed Matachi. With the room now in near total darkness the two men returned to the suspect stick, which was now clearly glowing along its entire length.

'Don't like the look of that,' said Tekiō. 'Do you think it is contaminated?'

'With what exactly?'

'Radiation, of course, idiot. Making it glow like that.'

'I know you watch a lot of shit on TV and the Internet, but you do realise Godzilla is not a real entity, don't you? And if it were real, its blood would not radiate light even if it was exposed to radiation.'

'How do you know?'

'Because, dear boy, when you were spending your time with your head stuffed up another man's sweaty nether regions whilst grunting like wild boars, pushing each other around a muddy ring, I was busy getting an education. It's a fallacy, radioactive materials cannot glow of their own volition, to achieve radio-luminescence they would need to be boosted, stimulated by another medium to allow us to see the wavelength of any particular radioactive element.'

'So, what is making the fucking thing light up like that then?'

'It appears there is a strip stuck along each side, I would say that it is made of a phosphorescent substance. The stuff that kids' toys and emergency signs are made of. It is a type of material that absorbs light and then emits it when it is placed in darkness, totally harmless.'

'That's a relief but why put that stuff on it in the first place?'

'A good question. The first thing I would say is that it looks like someone obviously wanted it to be noticed, and to be noticed literally in a certain light. The second thing that concerns me is that we now have a number of connections to the Fukushima Nuclear Plant. The Professor worked there, Matsumoto had connections to it through the civic administrative departments and the governor was a long-time supporter of the site.'

'And?'

'My dear friend, regardless of whether it glows or not, it is still possible that it may be radiologically contaminated.'

'What! After all that bullshit you just gave me, you are now telling me that it could be buzzing with radioactivity!'

'All I am saying is, that there are a lot of indicators pointing towards the Plant and the fact that it has been covered with fluorescent material may be a sign; a signal that is trying to point us in a certain direction.'

'Classic, I keep telling you, wherever we go, crazy shit just follows us around.'

'Correct! Would you have it any other way? Let's leave it be for the evening and come back in the morning. We should have hacked into it by then and once we have drawn the information off the stick, we are free to remove the device and get it examined by an expert.'

'By the way, where are we staying tonight? asked Matachi.

'They have put us in the Ryokan Koito hotel, it's not far from here, looks quite nice.'

'Sounds good, let's get this laptop out of sight, just in case it scares the janitor. We had better set the 'Baby Monitors' up before we leave so that we can keep an eye on the place remotely.'

Tekiō began placing the 'Baby Monitors', as Matachi called

them, around the room, covering overlapping angles of view across the door and out of the windows. The devices were sophisticated miniature CCTV cameras that were movement activated. Once initiated they would start recording and send an alerting text to both men's cell phones. They could also be remotely controlled and viewed at any time.

'All set, boss,' said Tekiō. 'Okay, let's go and check in.'

'And get something to eat.'

'And get something to eat…'

CHAPTER EIGHTEEN

9 March 2011 05.00

The makings of a new day drew Kurosawa from his bed; he quickly dressed into his traditional practice attire. As he drew back the shutters that led onto the secluded courtyard, the first tendrils of the dawn had yet to creep through the black night and the haze of a moon could be seen just behind the diluted clouds. Within the rectangular enclosure remained the tranquil Zen garden, with its raked sand and five grey granite standing stones that held hardened memories within that would always bare dumb witness to recollections both modern and ancient. It would be this half of the garden, covered by layered hardwood, that would be his focus this morning.

The whole courtyard was illuminated by lanterns and lamps containing beeswax and oil, flickering in the light breeze, animating the shadows around the five stones. Their silhouettes creating spectres that craned their contours from side to side in watchful station of the deathly still Kurosawa.

It had been several days since he had visited his beautiful Ikuko at the coast. His work caused necessary lulls in their relationship that were unavoidable. She seemed to understand, though her questions were becoming more and more probing as their relationship developed. This was an element he would have to carefully manage, whatever happened between them he could not envisage a time when he could tell her everything, even though he realised how fortunate he was to have found someone like her. She seemed to complement the irregular edges of his personality as perfectly as his character interacted with her temperament. They were both eccentric creatures that would never completely fit into a typical life. Of their true spirits, one was introverted, the other gregarious and expressive, personas that on occasion chafed against the other people whenever fully displayed. She unnerved others with her impolite unreservedness and a willing desire to openly express her liberally extreme views, which often resulted in uncomfortable situations with those who did not know her.

For Kurosawa, it was far less complicated. Apart from a very few people in his life, Ikuko included, revealing to them his true nature openly just scared the shit out of people. He learned from an early age that to get by in this life he was required to pretend he was something else.

The sky above was cloudy but with no threat of rain. Kurosawa only trained with the razor-sharp sword when the weather was good. He stepped lightly onto the deck, breathing in the fresh sea air being drawn inland by the rising thermals on the hills behind him.

Kurosawa was dressed in a dark grey, traditional Japanese training kimono; the overlapping collar concealing the brilliant white inner band. His family's 'Kamon' (crest) was a black disc outlined in white with two downward-angled palm leaves converging towards a symbol of a Shinto shrine. These emblems were thoughtfully positioned – one on each sleeve at the elbow, another on each side of his chest, and a single, prominent one fixed in the centre of his upper back, symbolising his heritage and discipline. The Kamon appeared as gentle clouds drifting above a Shinto temple or a death's head skull, depending on one's disposition. The kimono was secured into a pair of light grey, wide-legged Hakama pants; his feet covered by a pair of black two-toed Tabi socks. A long-bladed Katana sword was pushed through his waistband, the cutting edge curved upwards. He moved to the centre of the arena, feet shoulder width apart, hands hanging loosely at his side. As he inhaled deeply, he visualised his breath's journey with intense focus. The air entered through his nose, creating an imagined path that arched gracefully over the inner dome of his skull. It then descended smoothly down the back of his neck, slipping effortlessly into his windpipe. The breath continued its voyage, filling his lungs expansively, accompanied by the gentle rise of his diaphragm. This process harnessed his inner energy, swirling and gathering strength within him. He directed the air deep into the core of his lower abdomen, centring it at his groin. Here, he held it for a few contemplative seconds, fostering a connection with his inner self. Finally, he allowed the breath to ascend, coursing up through his lungs and trachea, before being released deliberately through his mouth, completing its cyclical journey, and leaving a sense of tranquil energy in its wake.

Kurosawa settled his mind for a few moments using the practice of controlling the cycle of one's breathing, focusing on the mechanical process of air entering and leaving his body, gently moving his perception to a state of wakeful meditation. The technique had been first taught to him by his father when he was a child. It was an exercise that allowed him to forget all other anxieties and flow into the moment. He began to create a stillness in his mind, calming the consciousness within, awareness without thinking, knowing without understanding, being without questioning. He purified himself with the power generated by the cleansing contemplation, repeating the transcendental ritual that allowed him to forget everything and flow into the realm of stillness he was creating within his mind.

An existential doorway opened before him and he drifted through it into a state where he felt nothing, yet sensed everything. He stayed within this phenomenon for a while, playing and experimenting with the primal vibrations that were the essence of the universe.

Slowly he restored his senses back into his body, still basking in the magic that he had returned with. He radiated a pureness that was the essence of life, feeling simultaneously everything and nothing. He had lifted his spirit carefully from its mortal coil and gently balanced it there, somewhere between this realm and the next, by his will alone. He felt its energy drip off and around him, leaving a powerful residue of strength in its wake.

Cultures elsewhere had a name for this feeling – Indians 'Pran', Chinese 'Chi', Polynesians as 'Mana' and the Japanese knew it as 'Ki'. Each culture had their own methods of achieving the cognitive state of mind required to bring one to this level, and how to utilise the force once acquired for both good and evil.

He began to bring his focus back to his mortal body, accepting the pressure of his feet on the wooden floor, the breeze moving across his face and between his fingers, the comforting weight of the sword at his left hip. Gradually re-entering his soul back into the physicality of bone, sinew and flesh, he returned to being 'Kurosawa'… the master swordsman.

Suddenly, without any outward warning, he exploded into movement, stepping back with his left foot, while simultaneously drawing the long blade from its scabbard with both hands, he sliced the air around him with a series of bewilderingly fast strikes. His feet moved across the floor as quickly as the flashing steel cut the deadly arcs that dissected the space around him, moving with speed and precision. He came to a halt as suddenly as he had exploded into movement, the sword held in front of him, body relaxed, right foot forward, perfectly balanced and on the balls of his feet, unmoving. In his imagination three men lay about him in various states of evisceration.

As a finale, his left hand came up and hit the back of the sword, cleaning the blade of any blood that would have settled there had it passed through actual flesh and bone. He clasped the scabbard with his left hand and drew the back of the sword across his thumb and forefinger until the point cleared the scabbard. With clinical elegance he replaced the sword in its sheath and brought his feet back together, returning to his original position, motionless, on exactly the same spot he had started from, in preparation for the next cycle of meditation and movement.

He did this for an hour and felt the cleansing exhaustion of its oscillations. It was nearly dawn, and he needed to get into character for his walk into town to meet the fishing boat on the quayside. He looked forward to his infrequent trips out to sea. The lifestyle he had chosen had become by necessity a very solitary one. He found solace in the interaction with ordinary people, involved in the everyday activities of normal life, even operating incognito as a simpleton.

CHAPTER NINETEEN

11 March 2011 06.30

The two detectives rose early for breakfast the next morning, arriving together to be seated in the dining area at six-thirty. They were given the choice to sit wherever they wished, the room being empty but for a few solitary businessmen fortifying themselves for the undoubtable struggle of the long day that lay ahead.

Matachi kept it light with some tea, grilled fish with pickles, a little rice and a bowl of Miso soup. Tekiō had the same, but he added a four-egg omelette and a bowl of Natto, a popular dish of fermented soy beans. Matachi eyed the pungent beans suspiciously.

'Go easy on that crap or call yourself a taxi, your choice,' he said quietly to Tekiō.

'Left your *ikigai* on the *tatami,* did we?' replied Tekiō, referring to the Japanese philosophy of waking with a positive motivation for life each day. 'And a good morning to you to, boss.'

'I am just saying, I do not want to be asphyxiated again today, thank you very much.'

'Ah, I had forgotten these pleasures, we have not been on a trip away together for a while.'

'Forgot what pleasures?' said Matachi as he slurped his soup.

'That you are not really a morning person are you – more the wake up as a grumpy miserable bastard type.'

'Just hurry up and finish that pig's swill so we can get on our way, we have a very busy day ahead of us. Once we have looked at what was on that data stick, I have arranged to take it to a Professor of Nuclear Physics at Fukushima University so that he can make an assessment. I have no doubt that it is fine, but always best to check these things.'

Tekiō made a final wipe around the inside of his bowl with his chopsticks, sweeping up any missed soya beans. He licked the last few sticky glutinous morsels off them, gave a tight-lipped muted belch, accompanied by a small bounce that shook his whole body.

'Ready,' he said broadly grinning.

Matachi gave him a look of deep disgust. 'Unbelievable,' he said. 'Okay let's go.'

As they left the hotel's breakfast room, they were met by two European men coming into the restaurant engaged in conversation. In unison they both stepped slightly to one side, allowing the foreigners to pass, giving them a polite short bow as they did so. The two detectives smiled back and thanked them. Once they were out of earshot, Tekiō said, 'Don't see many Englishmen in Fukushima.'

'Only one of them is English the other is American.'

'They sounded the same to me.'

'They would.'

'Oh, I can see it is going to be fucking idyllic waking up to you every morning.'

★ ★ ★

Tekiō watched over Matachi's shoulder as he opened the laptop to assess the night's hacking activity by the 'Spaniard.'

'This is going to be a bigger task than first thought,' said Matachi. 'It has broken into the file, but that looks like it was just a protective shell. There are numerous further documents inside, all of them also encrypted.'

159

'Very crafty,' said Tekiō.

'It is not all bad news, at least I can copy the documents off the stick. I will transfer them to a secure area on my hard drive and start the hacking process again on each one independently. At least then we can remove the stick.'

He quickly set about moving the files from the memory stick and applying the Spaniard hacking tool to all of them.

'All done, bag up the stick and let's go.' Tekiō gave him a wary look.

'Stop being such a baby, it's fine, it does not bite. Hurry up, we need to go. We have an appointment in an hour with a Professor Yamaguchi at Fukushima University. I will see you in the car, just need to make a quick call.'

Matachi pulled the large SUV onto the Tōhoku expressway heading for the university. They were making good time since leaving Fukushima City and would be there in an hour or so. Tekiō was as ever gently snoozing beside him, no doubt digesting the fermenting garbage he had eaten for breakfast. He looked so peaceful reclining there, like a giant toddler, sleeping the tranquillity of the pure of heart.

The man was a real contradiction. For someone who could, without a hint of warning, deal out such brutal violence if required, he also held a great deal of empathy for others, even sometimes for those he hurt. Matachi would tease him sometimes saying that he was just a 'big softy' at heart, which Matachi liked to believe he was, the alternative being harder to accept.

His youth had been a painful one, this Matachi knew as a fact. Being his superior officer, he had access to his records where much of what he had done in his life was there. It had made interesting reading. He had been bullied for his size at school, being twice that of his fellow students. He had shown restraint for most of his life accepting the jibes and pranks. Then as he entered his teenage years, there were a few incidents at his school where some of the other kids had got hurt, nothing bad, but a few parents had complained. It was decided to move him to a different school, one that taught sports professionally as well as academics as part of the curriculum.

It was there that he had first been introduced to Sumo wrestling. He had found it a massive challenge at first, struggling with the thought of intentionally hurting someone. For most of his fellow students, raw aggression, and the willingness to inflict violence were not sentiments they generally lacked. However, Tekiō had come to this art from a different perspective and his instructors saw this as a great strength, so worked with him diligently and were rewarded with exceptional progress by the young boy.

After leaving school at eighteen he transferred to a *Heya* or Sumo training stables, to become a professional wrestler. As the years went by and his training progressed, he gradually changed into a 'contender'. To get there the coaches had needed to infuse a great deal of the dynamic 'Yang' force into his natural 'Ying' centred empathetic personality. A great deal of his training was extremely unpleasant, emotionally, and physically, a requirement of the breaking down and the rebuilding of a true warrior nature. Though his career as a Sumo wrestler had been a short one, they had succeeded in creating a formidable force of nature. He had witnessed first-hand the devastating carnage he could inflict when necessity demanded. When Tekiō went to war, he neither asked nor gave any quarter, there was no better man to have on one's side in a bad situation, of that Matachi was sure. He leaned over and slapped the slumbering giant across his chest with the back of his hand.

'Hi, salad dodger, time to wake up, we are here. All you do is eat, sleep and fart. It is that time again when you need to start doing some work for a living. I do hope you are nice and refreshed.'

Tekiō raised his seat up slightly, he could not move to the fully upright position, as even in the rather large Land Cruiser his head would have touched the roof.

'Well, boss, I am surprised that I could get any sleep. The

161

shock of finding a radioactive USB stick in a tinfoil parcel under a severed head, still strangely weighs on my inner calm somewhat.'

'Don't be a pussy and stop acting as if this is your first severed head experience.'

'Ah,' said Tekiō. 'I see that you have shaken off your morning blues and are back to your old self. I think I preferred the grouchy version better.'

'My dear boy, I have no idea what on earth you are going on about. Let's start focusing, shall we. Where is the data stick?'

'I put it in the trunk; I thought the further away from us it was the better.'

Matachi pulled the car into the university campus and slowly drove through the grounds, winding his way on the access road through the neatly cut lawns on either side. He followed the signs for the Physics Department until they arrived at an arrangement of what looked like a group of space-age prefab buildings with a car park set in front of them.

'That must be our man over there,' said Matachi, pointing towards a tall, thin man wearing a classic check waistcoat and a stripy bow tie. 'Credit to him, he did say that he would meet us outside and that he was easily recognisable.'

'No shit. What is it with academic types and eccentricity?'

'That's a bit prejudiced of you, as you know I have a PhD and I am not a bit eccentric.'

'Really! Fuck me!' said Tekiō staring at his boss in feigned astonishment – 'I rest my case your honour.'

They parked up their car and went over and introduced themselves to Professor Yamaguchi. Matachi had explained what they required on making his initial contact with the man. After the standard formal exchange of pleasantries, he led them to a small vacant laboratory inside one of the prefabs.

'Right,' said the professor, 'let's see what you have to show me.'

Tekiō held out the evidence bag that contained the USB stick in. The professor did not move to take it straight away, he first turned around to the bench behind him and put on a pair of thick rubber gloves. He then picked up a pair of plastic tongs before using them to take the bag from a now palpably terrified Tekiō. Matachi, began to feel a little consternation himself at this, but tried not to show it and had no intention whatsoever of catching Tekiō's furious gaze.

He placed the packet onto a fire-retardant sheet that lay on one of the benches. He then retrieved what looked like a portable karaoke machine from a cupboard under the bench. He turned it on by flicking a switch on its side and unhooked a microphone-like attachment from where it was clipped on the machine's side. Adjusting some dials on the top of the device, the professor proceeded to hold it over the USB stick. The Geiger counter made an immediate high-pitched noise like someone playing around with a Fender Stratocaster guitar with a slider tube. Both men gave started at this, surprised after what the professor had said to them on the negligible levels of radioactivity that could possibly be found in phosphorescent paint.

'Hey, Tekiō, will you look at that,' said Matachi. 'Maybe you were right all along, old friend?'

He looked around, but Tekiō was nowhere to be seen, just the fading rumblings of what sounded like a stampeding rhino echoed from out in the hallway. Matachi and the professor stuck their heads out of the doorway into the corridor, 'Your man is quick for a big feller,' said the professor.

'Yeah, he has always been fast over short distances,' replied Matachi. 'You should see him catch the lunch time mobile noodle van if it tries to leave before serving him.'

They returned their attention to the USB stick.

'I don't think it is the stickers attached to it. They are phosphorescent, but only of the type you can purchase in any craft shop,' said the professor. 'But that is not what is giving even this low reading.'

'What is causing it then?' asked Matachi. 'Your machine nearly leapt out of your hands when you scanned it?'

'I had the machine turned up to a high range of sensitivity. I was trying to prove my point that the phosphorescent strip would have very low levels of radioactivity if any at all.'

'Well, you proved something to my colleague that's for sure, he's probably halfway back to the department by now. If it's not the day glow stuff, what's the actual source of it then?'

The professor turned the Geiger counter down and ran the sensor over it again. It still made a noise, but now it was more of a light intermittent crackle.

'It is giving a reading of 0.01 millisieverts, that means it has been contaminated by some sort of radiation. I could tell you the actual source of the contamination by its radioactive signature if you would let me have it for a few days?'

'You can take a sample, but I need the USB stick as evidence. How dangerous is it by the way?' said a smiling Matachi, trying not to show the nervousness that had been growing in him since the Geiger counter had burst into life. He pointed with his head at the USB stick, his arms held circumspectly out the way, hands clasped together behind his back.

'Not a lot really, that reading is quite a low level, you would be exposed to far more if you had been given an x-ray or taken a long-haul flight.'

'Ah yes, yes, I see, Professor-san, but just for my partner's sake, you would not happen to have a suitable lead-lined box perhaps would you, or possibly something similar that we could transport it in?' said Matachi, giving the professor an engaging grin to humour him. 'It's a psychological thing you see, he has become quite unduly concerned over possible contamination from the device. Nonsense of course, but just as a gesture, merely for his peace of mind, my inner karma, and to save unnecessary wear on his shoe leather and underwear.'

The professor looked at the dapper-looking detective in the very fine tailored grey suit. Crime obviously pays for some, he thought.

'I'll see what I can do,' he said. 'It will not be lead lined, but we have some secure anti-contamination sample transportation boxes that may help you.'

'Ah, so very kind of you, sir.'

'May I enquire where you acquired this from?'

'Afraid I can't tell you that. All I can say is that it is part of an ongoing case we are investigating.'

'I see, I did not mean to pry of course, it is just that I have seen this particular type of data storage device before.'

'Really!' said an intrigued Matachi. 'May I ask where exactly?'

'They are of a special shielded type used in atomic research environments. Once they have been brought into those sorts of restricted areas, they are not normally taken out again.'

'That is interesting, thank you, Professor, you have been very helpful indeed.' It was clear the man knew very well where this device originated.

'It is a pleasure to help, detective, and of course my duty,' said the professor, bowing to Matachi. 'Please do tell your partner that there is absolutely nothing to be concerned about with regard to the radiation levels on the stick, it is perfectly safe.'

'I thank you,' he replied returning the bow. 'Oh, and Professor, we are also going to need to borrow one of those please,' said Matachi pointing at the Geiger counter.

Matachi left the Institute carrying a cardboard box in both arms and walked back to the car park, where he found Tekiō lurking at the rear of their Toyota.

The trunk was up and he had broken into the standard police emergency kit, there for use when attending road accidents or similar incidents. He had been wiping his hands on the sterile wipes stored there; in fact, he had used all the sterile wipes he had found in there. He turned to Matachi struggling to pull on the rubber gloves from the kit.

'I told you,' he said. 'I fucking told you it was not right, but no, no, young Einstein here says there is nothing to worry about. What bullshit, that machine nearly jumped out of his fucking hands when he ran it over that poxy USB stick!'

'Listen my little Pikachu, there's nothing to be worried about, honestly,' said a grinning Matachi, staring at the pile of used sterile wipes on the car park floor. Then, not being able to resist, he added,

'You never wanted a family, anyway, did you?'

'That is not funny, this no time to be ridiculing me,' said Tekiō, pulling a rubber glove on so hard that it burst and split across one of his huge palms.

Matachi just managed to stifle a laugh into a short snort.

'Do we need to be fully decontaminated? Will we need to be confined, put into isolation?' said Tekiō as he started picking up the used wipes, carefully using just his fingers where the remnants of the torn undersized glove remained. He placed them into a hazardous materials disposal bag also taken out of the kit. With the tips of his other hand, he pulled off the remains of the rubber prophylactic and cautiously added that to the bag's contents and sealed it.

'Look,' said Matachi, realising that Tekiō was genuinely worried, 'you are overreacting, it's all good. If it wasn't do you think they would have let me out, do you see any guys running towards us with chem suits on to take us away? Mmm... do you? No, so put this in the back and let's get going. We need to make a house call.' He pushed the box into Tekiō's arms.

'What's in the box?' he asked.

'The data stick,' replied Matachi. Tekiō shoved the box back at him, hitting him in the chest so hard it forced him to take a step backwards.

'It is fine, the radiation is very low, way below safe levels of exposure and anyway it's now in a lead box, something I did just for you.' He gave the box back to Tekiō.

Tekiō looked at the box with the demeanour of someone who had been handed a dog turd on a rice cake, but he reluctantly took back possession of the box.

'Where are we going?' he asked.

'The Nuclear Power Station in Fukushima,' replied Matachi.

The box hit him in the chest again, this time with so much force he had to take several steps backwards. Tekiō walked around to the passenger's side and got in.

'Don't be like that, old friend,' said Matachi chuckling. 'I have borrowed one of those machines from the boffin, so you can carry it around with you if you want and do some continuous monitoring. You may look like a bit of a twat, but hey, again, just thinking of you, old boy.'

He put the box in the trunk and joined Tekiō in the car. Tekiō sat, lips pulled into a thin line, with his arms folded over the bulge of his belly.

'It is not going to be another one of those journeys, is it?' he said looking at Tekiō. Getting no response, he sighed and started the car, it was going to be a long ride to the coast of Fukushima in more ways than one he thought.

CHAPTER TWENTY

11 March 1947

Walking briskly down the long corridor, Kurosawa Shinji kept pace with the jovial moustached man at his side. The suit he had been provided with was far too baggy for his reduced frame, the excess material in the trousers flapped around his shins, irritatingly whipping away at his legs as he marched along. He was being taken to meet some Americans by Ishii Shō, an ex-general in his Imperial Majesty's Army. The man had once been his commanding officer and the former commandant of the notorious 'Unit 731'. They had followed their own paths since Japan's unconditional surrender to the Allies, but the general had tracked him down. The two had met many times over the last few months, as Ishii tried to persuade him to come out of hiding. He had been living like a wild beast around the blasted remains of Kyoto since the war ended, foraging where he could, even stealing when given the opportunity.

He had been repatriated back to the mainland, along with all the other academics from the Manchurian facility, towards the end of 1945. After an absence of more than three years, he returned to Japan only to find it ravaged, a stark testament to the country's undeniable defeat in the war. A few months later, the dawn of the atomic age, had been terrifyingly heralded by a series of colossal blasts above Japanese cities, he realised the war was now irrevocably lost.

His wife, a woman he had been virtually forced to marry in haste by his family during a short furlough back in 1942, was now dead. She had drowned in a municipal swimming pool trying to escape yet another destructive furnace created by the barbarously combustible incendiary bombs, dropped from the omnipresent B-29s that daily filled the nation's skies.

The war and his life as he knew it was now over; the honourable thing to do would have been to end his own existence. A path many of his brethren resigned themselves to and it would have been such an easy solution for him also. The problem was honour and duty could make irreconcilable bedfellows. Reputation decreed he should end his life, duty, on the other hand, demanded that he endure.

The woman who he had been obligated to marry, had borne a child from the briefest of unions, following a drink-fuelled four-day pass to Kyoto. Their relationship had been a mistake and should have been nothing more than a transient liaison, born of the sexual liberalism imbued on a people who find themselves at war. If he had learnt anything from the horrors of war, it was that life is never lived fuller than when it is in terminal peril.

It had been a shock when his mother had written to him to tell him that he now had a son. The parents of the boy's mother had contacted his own. She came from a proud Samurai House as did his own family, and once contact had been made by the two clans, there could be no other honourable path to be taken. The two households had looked after them both as best they could as the war relentlessly continued, taking almost everything from them, including their lives, as it progressed to its inevitable appalling end.

Only the boy had somehow managed to survive through it all. He was now nearly six years old and they had been virtually inseparable since he had recovered him from the orphanage on his return to Kyoto.

The boy had been the centre of every decision he had been free to make, since hearing of his birth. He wanted nothing for himself now, his only objective was to ensure that his son would have a full and rewarding life. He needed to show that a measure of good would emerge from the inconceivable evils that he had been involved in. So it was, that he found himself listening to Ishii's bullshit, as the man tried to justify the terrible deeds that they had all committed, by shamefully appropriating them to the name of science and humanity.

The fool had talked to him about the 'rights' and 'wrongs' they had undertaken in the name of the Emperor. Had they not after all just been trying to honourably aid the war effort. Their research had been vital to saving thousands of Japanese lives. It was knowledge gained that could not be now unlearnt, let alone forgotten. It existed and would go on to become the basis of even greater lifesaving research. It was important that he saw the long view, a view that undoubtedly history would eventually take. What he did would be fully understood then; the scale of their great contribution to the spheres of science and mankind recognised for the immense achievement it was.

He was correct in saying that what had been achieved by their insidious work was incredibly valuable to science, no one could deny that, why would the Allied powers go to such accommodating lengths to get hold of the data, if it were not so? However, Shinji knew the real reason why it was so invaluable. It was that it could never be repeated, not by any civilised society, one that valued the true sanctity of humanity.

Ishii became angry at him when he voiced this opinion. Where was the sanctity of humanity when the skies were filled with planes raining down incendiaries on defenceless cities. Had not the Americans alone built atomic furnaces on their land and then stoked them with hundreds of thousands of Japanese innocents!

Why should survivors of such catastrophic events and misfortune bear any guilt, whether collective or personal? Consider historical parallels: do the British harbour guilt over the imperial expansion that led to the enslavement of millions? Or do the Belgians feel remorse for the atrocities committed by Leopold in Africa, purportedly in their name? Of course, not; such notions were preposterous. Similarly, why should we bear such an unreasonable burden of guilt? We were under strict orders to work towards the greater good of our people by any means necessary, and for that, we cannot justifiably be sanctioned. I can assure you the Americans and Russians do not feel even a droplet of guilt about using our research. They have their own burden of guilt to bear and when it was measured alongside the deeds of the Japanese, our misdemeanours paled into insignificance. Even the methods we had taken to gain the information meant nothing in the context of all those millions that have died.

Shinji struggled to believe that any good could come from the despicable deeds they had been willing to undertake in the name of science and the Emperor. The man was right, he needed to see this as an opportunity. The selfish fact was Shinji had scant choice now, not if he wished a better future for his son. He realised that the knowledge he could give the Yankees would only make their military stronger and would aid humanity very little, if at all. But he had done far worse than this in his life, so collaborating with the Allies was nothing by comparison. All that concerned him was whether working with the Americans would give a better life to his boy, if that were the case then that is what he must do.

They entered Ishii's plush, ornately decorated office. Three uniformed Americans raised themselves from the comfortable leather seats where they had been patiently waiting and received them warmly. Ishii gave them a toothy grin, greeting them like old friends as they engaged into a mixture of Western and Oriental greetings.

The meeting turned out exactly as the general predicted. There would be no trial for war crimes, no public admittance of guilt, or damning accusations to bear from survivors and accusers. All he had to do was guarantee his full cooperation and share with them totally and openly, any and every aspect of the work he undertook during his tenure at Unit 731. In return, he would be given a senior place in his old university at Kyoto along with a generous salary funded by the Americans, and many other perks besides. He knew in reality, as Ishii did, they both had no choice. To refuse would have meant arrest and prosecution, closely followed by execution, after joining the conveyor belt of war crimes' trials that were taking place across Japan.

It had seemed like an impossible dream had come true at the time. He walked out of that office with a new life and a potential future for his son. It would be later that he would realise there would be a painful personal cost to him on taking up their offer. He would have to continuously relive in detail every horror that he had inflicted during those horrendous eight years. It seemed that the prophecy he had bargained himself into was now coming true.

In the last few months, on returning to Japan, he had managed to almost forget the nightmare of the domain he had once existed in. The struggle for daily survival in the twisted ruins of Kyoto consumed nearly all of his attention. Now, he was compelled to confront the haunting realities of his past life: the actions he had committed and the solemn pact he had forged.

★ ★ ★

Kurosawa Shinji's son sat contentedly beside him as they drove the newly acquired car up into the rural Fukushima hillside. It was clear how drastically their lives had changed since accepting the American offer. They were now comfortably settled in a sizeable, rent-free house on the outskirts of Tokyo, a generous advance granted to them without even asking. With this newfound wealth, Shinji had swiftly put their affairs in order. They moved into their new home, where a maid and a cook were hired to manage the household and assist in caring for his son. They replaced their worn clothes with fitting, new garments, a small yet significant luxury after the rags they had been forced to wear. With money in hand, even healthy food, scarce as it was, could be procured from the black market. And now, with a car at their disposal, they navigated their transformed landscape with ease.

After six months of working for them, he had answered every question the Yankee scientists had asked of him. Many of the topics they required information on, he had felt embarrassed to give answers to. Describing the experiments, he had carried out on human beings in the genteel offices of academics, seemed grotesque, believing they would be repulsed by his detailed revelations, at the very least to be challenged on the abhorrence of it. However, even when he discussed his experience of witnessing live vivisections, some of which were carried out on American prisoners of war, they remained emotionally detached and matter-of-factly professional.

He found their reaction more unsettling than if they had unleashed their fury on him for the horrific deeds he had participated in. Over the months of probing inquiries, this process evolved into an additional burden he had to bear. He realised that in seeking this path, he had unwittingly made a pact with another devil, and this one, too, exacted its price.

After they had explored all aspects of his experiences, finally exhausting him of every detail of his work, he had been told that his cooperation would no longer be required on such a continuous basis. He unexpectedly found himself free to take up the position he had been offered at Fukushima University to lecture on Biology.

His parents now dead, his family's ancestral home was now his and it was not just out of duty that he would return there. The ruins of Tokyo were no place to bring up a child, he needed a fresh start for his son. The family's large house sat in the beautiful countryside of Fukushima and there was no better place to raise a boy and instil in him a zest for life, not destruction.

He looked down at his Ichirō as they pulled up outside the closed gates to his parents' villa. The boy was always so happy, no matter what their circumstances, he seemed as carefree and unworried as the wind.

Even at first glance it was evident that the house would require more work than he had anticipated, if he were to make it into a comfortable home for them both. His parents had been killed just after he was married, blown to hell by an American bombing raid that hit Fukushima's port. They had been trying to buy some fish at the market there. He tried to put that memory to the back of his mind as he surveyed the property. It had been left to decay ever since that fateful day and had degenerated into a frightful mess. Luckily, he now had some money, his salary from the Americans being not insignificant. He would be able to return the ancestral home to its original grandeur. His mission was to make it into a nurturing home, a place where his son could grow up, protected from the brutal realities of the world outside. They got out of the car and approached the imposing ornate cedar wood double gates. They were not locked but looked like they had not been opened for years, which was probably the case. He placed a hand on each gate and gave them an exploratory push, they both parted from each other slightly. Leaning forward, he exerted more force on one of the wooden gates. It creaked open, laboriously clearing a path through the accumulated garden debris that had gathered over the years of neglect and absence of human presence.

As it parted, Ichirō ran under his arms towards the still majestic villa beyond, keen to explore this new playground. Shinji followed him to the front door, removing a large deadlock key from his pocket – the same one given to him as a child by his parents. He unlocked the front door letting them into the dusty realm beyond. Within he found its décor was now tired, dirty and rundown from the neglect of the last few years since his parents had been killed. However, it still felt more of a home than anything he had experienced in the last ten years.

Ichirō disappeared into the labyrinth of rooms that ran as two wings from either side of the entrance hallway. Shinji turned back out the door to start unloading their belongings, when he heard his son call excitedly from deep within the house. He walked down the hall to the farthest room located at the end of the left-wing. Inside he saw Ichirō staring at a small shrine holding an ancient Samurai helmet, with two swords lain across wooden pegs one above the other. The boy seemed entranced by the objects. 'What are they, Father?' he asked.

'They are relics, son, relics from the past, that your grandfather once cherished.'

'Does that mean they now belong to us, Father?'

'Yes, everything here now belongs to us, Ichirō.'

'But those long knives, Father, what could you do with those?'

'Your grandfather and all the fathers that came before him, could do a great deal with them, my son,' he said remembering the disappointment felt by both his father and himself, when as a boy he had failed to acquire the skills of swordsmanship his father had so desperately wanted him to master.

'What could they do with them, Father?'

'They could use them to write the most beautiful of poetry, my son. Would you like to learn how?' he quietly replied, looking down at his son.

The boy cocked his head to one side and looked up at him with a puzzled expression, the only poetry he knew was written with a brush and black ink. The youngster did not realise then, but all that would change in time. The young boy sagely nodded his head in acceptance of the offer.

'Then I promise you as soon as we get this place returned to being a home again, I will arrange for someone to start giving you lessons. However,' he added sternly, 'in the meantime you are never to touch these swords, is that understood, Ichirō?'

At the stern tone of his father, Ichirō placed his hands behind his back, as if trying to keep them away from the swords. 'Yes, Father,' he meekly replied, not daring to look up.

'Good boy,' said Shinji in a much softer tone. 'Now go and explore the rest of the house while I unload the car.'

As he finished unloading their belongings, he thought how his own father would have been heartened to hear the boy's willingness to take up the offer of being trained in the use of the sword. He himself had been a great disappointment when he showed no interest or aptitude for the fine art of the Japanese sword. On occasion, hard-looking men, who seemed to have menace etched into their faces, would come to the house to train with his father. He had often overheard some of them asking how the young Shinji's instruction was progressing. His father would quickly change the subject, failing to mask his obvious embarrassment at his son's inadequacies.

Ichirō had shown more interest in the swords on first seeing them than he had done in his entire life. His father would never know, but perhaps here was an opportunity to make amends, if only with his father's spirit. He would allow his son to train, perhaps he would respond to the demanding tutelage. Though it would have to be undertaken in secret, the Allies having imposed draconian measures restricting any martial activities. He would ask the general if he knew of anyone he could recommend. He was now dedicated to giving his son every advantage he possibly could. His task was to now prepare Ichirō to take on an even greater burden, for if he was ever to have a child of his own, he must come to understand what would be required of himself and any future offspring. How exactly he was going to accomplish this Kurosawa Shinji was not entirely sure.

CHAPTER TWENTY-ONE

11 March 2011 13.35

It took them just under two hours to reach the power plant, with Tekiō still sulking, first pretending to be asleep, then falling into a deeply vocal sleep, staying in that condition for most of the journey. This had suited Matachi nicely, as it gave him some time to process some of the main events of the case so far and make a few pertinent calls.

He had realised from the beginning the reason they had been assigned the case by his superiors – the disappearance of the governor was without doubt, high profile in its nature. He also fully understood that this event alone would not have been enough of a reason to trigger his and Tekiō's intervention by their superiors. There was more than enough crime being actively committed in Tokyo to keep them busy until retirement as it was... if they managed to make it that far.

He had been informed that, in addition to the governor's disappearance, there had been a series of other unexplained vanishings and suspicious deaths involving local politicians and some notable industrialists. These events, he observed, had occurred over the past six months. Until now, the local police had treated each incident as isolated, failing to connect them due to a lack of apparent logical patterns and their limited scope of thinking, which gave them little reason to delve deeper into potential connections. That had changed, however, with the sudden evaporation of the governor. She had been connected to immeasurably more senior politicians in national government. She herself was destined to join that ruling elite; a fact clearly outlined by the steep trajectory that her career had taken so far.

The woman had gained, then wielded power and influence in high ranking political and business circles. A logical explanation was required to what had exactly happened to her, and it needed to be found quickly.

He had been discretely informed by his boss in Tokyo, that pressure was being applied from the top, from very senior politicians, who now feared a scandal was emerging. Many of them had been, for various reasons, connected to the governor. So, in addition to her network of business contacts, apprehensions were now growing amongst the country's political elite.

Matachi believed there were behaviours going on within the political and business communities of the Fukushima Prefecture, above the normal levels of corruption that one would normally expect in modern Japan.

He had to admit that the assignment intrigued him. He also thought that he and Tekiō could do with a break from the city. A short getaway to the countryside would do them both some good. When he suggested to Tekiō that they take the case, he had said it sounded like a bit of a busman's holiday, but if it gave him a chance to visit the seaside again, a trip he had not done since a child, he was all for it.

If he had realised then that it would be the ocean that would be coming to visit him, he may have reconsidered…

★ ★ ★

The security guard at the gate checked their IDs and asked them to park their vehicle in a small holding car park adjacent to the gatehouse, while he rang their contact at the plant.

A short while later another security guard arrived at their

vehicle and then handed them two passes attached to neck lanyards. He told them to leave their car there, directing them to walk to a small complex that was still outside the boundaries of the main facility. Access to the site designed that a second guardhouse and a set of gates had to be crossed before anyone could gain entry to the main facility.

This aspect came as a great relief to Tekiō, who had been observing the looming line of reactor buildings on the horizon with more than a little trepidation.

The small block of buildings had been designed specifically for essential contact with those visitors who did not require entry into the site proper. They housed several meeting and interview rooms specifically for this purpose.

They were met outside by the Head of the Human Resource Department for the site, along with one of the senior laboratory supervisors, who looked like he was carrying a metal lunchbox with him.

The perfunctory formal introductions were completed, synonymous with Japanese cultural etiquette, including the exchange of business cards by the two senior men from each party. The two detectives then showed them their police credentials, after which they were invited inside. The HR Manager was called Andō Senkichi and his colleague Murakami Osamu.

They found themselves ushered into a small conference room with a series of tables pushed together along its centre to form one large unit. There were a number of chairs scattered around the periphery of the room, with a video conferencing unit sitting at the table's centre and a ceiling-mounted projector hanging over it, pointing towards a screen at the end of the room.

Tekiō checked that the video-con unit was not switched on, nodding confirmation that it was not, to his boss, as he went into security mode continuing to scan the rest of the room. Tekiō's motto was 'be polite and friendly to all, if possible; but always have a plan as to how you would kill them, if required'.

He believed it to be a good motto, having served him well over the years.

Andō offered to them to pull across some chairs to the edge of the table and they all then sat around one end. 'Well, gentlemen, what is it that I can assist you with?' said Andō.

'My good friend Professor Yamaguchi-san says that you have a curious trinket that we may find interesting?' he said with a smirk.

Matachi returned him a knowing grin, realising the good professor had pre-empted their visit. He placed the small sample container he had been carrying (Tekiō now refusing to touch it all) on the table. He was about to unclasp the catches on either side when the Laboratory Supervisor held up his hand to stop him.

The man placed his metal lunchbox-sized container on the table, put on a pair of disposable gloves and a pair of safety glasses and then removed a Geiger counter from the box, very similar to the one the professor had used back at the university. Matachi could see Tekiō blanch at this, pushing himself back slightly from the table. At least this time he did not leg it.

He glanced in his direction and received one of his friend's 'I fucking told you so!' expressions in response.

The supervisor turned on the unit and ran it over the outside of the box. The machine made barely a click as he did so.

'Please do not be concerned,' said Murakami, looking worryingly at the openly agitated Tekiō. 'We have received a full report from the professor on the banality of the item, this is just a prudent precaution. An occupational – hazard – if I may use the term, of the necessarily assiduousness inherent within our industry.'

Tekiō, now received a 'this no time to be fucking around' look from Matachi in return.

'Of course, gentlemen, we understand completely, please carry on,' said Matachi.

The technician opened the lid on their receptacle to reveal the USB stick inside. He repeated the scan over its contents. It produced a slightly higher series of frequency clicks as he did so. He switched off the instrument and looking towards his boss said, 'No problem, very low-level indications.'

'Do you recognise it as one of yours?' questioned Matachi. Andō looked at his more junior colleague and nodded.

'Yes, it is a shielded data stick, generally only used beyond the confines of the operational support areas of the reactors or within the restricted radiological laboratories complex. The units are regarded as "captured", that means in normal operations, they would never leave the confines of their contiolled zones.'

'How do you think this one got out then?'

Again, the man glanced at his superior before answering. This was starting to get annoying, thought Matachi.

Once more the man only answered after receiving an approving nod from Andō. 'I really don't have any idea, all objects that are used within these areas are regarded as controlled waste. Despite being in a very low contamination usage and as such would be removed using a very rigidly defined process, its logging and movement out of the area for disposal would still be controlled. Depending on what it is and its size, it would be tagged and/or bagged, then placed in a container with a number of other such objects no longer required in the zone. This container would then be moved to what we call a 'pass through lock', situated on, indeed actually within the boundaries of, the restricted area. This chamber segregates the two areas, one regarded as clean, the other as dirty. From this point it is transported to collection areas designated for the level of contamination attributed to it before removal to regulated disposal.'

'Is there any other way it could have got out?'

The supervisor once again looked to his superior, remaining silent as no immediate response came from the man. There was an uncomfortable lull, as Andō kept his head downwards looking at the table.

Okay, thought Matachi, that's enough of this shit.

'Andō-san, I think I need to inform you that we are investigating a case of the very highest degree of criminality, in fact a murder case of the most heinous nature, any attempt to withhold information from us will be regarded as obstructing a police officer in the course of his duty, which is, I can assure you, a very serious offence.'

The man nodded his understanding and Matachi thought he had got the message. He could see the supervisor was now getting very agitated by the testing position he found himself in. 'Detective Matachi,' said Andō, breaking the silence, 'I realise that you have a job to do, however, please understand the extremely delicate and potentially dangerous work we do here. I am sure you will understand our need to be very careful in the context of any information we give out on this site. Perhaps if you would give us the data stick for a day or two, we could find out exactly where it has come from and what is on it and give you a full report.'

Fuck it, thought Matachi, he had heard enough bullshit from this management goon. He looked directly at Tekiō and jerked his head sideways. The big man got up and walked over to the door.

'That is a very kind offer, Andō-san, thank you, but unfortunately this is now a vital piece of evidence in a murder inquiry, so I cannot allow it to leave our custody. We only have a limited time we can spend here today (he emphasised the word *today* so that the man was sure they would be back), so in the interest of expediency, if you would be so kind as to accompany Detective Tekiō-san to another room, he will ask you some questions directly, while I finish off the discussion with your esteemed colleague here.'

Tekiō opened the door, and Matachi gave the man an encouraging smile to get him to stand up and leave them.

The man did not move at first, so Tekiō came over and stood beside him. Andō realised he was leaving the room one way or another, the other being dragged out by the hulking monster that towered above him. He quickly got to his feet and walked past Tekiō towards the door. Tekiō followed him closing the door behind them both as they left.

Once outside the manager ignored Tekiō's presence and took out his phone and started to make a call. He suddenly felt a vice like grip around the hand holding the phone.

'No calls,' said Tekiō, taking the cell out of the man's hand.

Andō was fairly sure that his rights had just been violated, but said nothing, as the uncomfortable essence of the intimidating gaze of the two-metre-tall detective glared down upon him.

'Oki doki,' said Matachi, cheerfully, trying to lighten the atmosphere, which had become decidedly uncomfortable, for the supervisor at least. 'Let's get down to business.'

'Who was murdered?' worryingly asked the supervisor.

'You don't need to concern yourself about that, I'm sure it is no one that you would know. Now where were we? Ah yes, you were about to tell me how the USB stick got out of a controlled area.'

The supervisor did not seem to be encouraged by this declaration about not being concerned with whom had been murdered, but regardless, he started to answer Matachi's question.

'All workers, without exception, must shower out of the controlled areas and take nothing with them. Though there are no cameras in the showers, there is extensive CCTV at every conceivable location on the site to ensure that this takes place. So being too large an object to swallow, I would say there would be only one way this could have conceivably been secreted out.'

'Boosted?' said Matachi

'Sorry?'

'Concealed inside the body, swallowed or inserted somewhere internally.'

'It's possible, of course, but why would someone want to?'

'Information can be a type of currency in my experience,' replied Matachi. 'I have no doubt that you have here quite a bit of intellectual property that would be valuable to the right group of people. Tell me, would there be any traceable designation for these devices?'

183

'Not as such, as you would have noticed there is no serial number on these units, and they are seen as free issue articles, treated as consumable stationery items, held in stock within the restricted areas.'

'I see, that is a pity.'

'There is one thing that may help somewhat though, if you try to locate a window of opportunity when it could have been removed.'

'Really,' said Matachi, he was definitely starting to like the guy now. 'What would that be, Murakami-san?'

'That type of data stick was only introduced in the last few months.'

'How can you tell?'

'The underlying colour, beneath the sticker that someone has placed on it, it's black. The same model as before, in size, shape and capacity all being identical, but the manufacturer for some reason, changed the colour from blue to black.'

'Ah, thank you, sir. That's useful information. How do I find out exactly when this new batch was issued?'

'I am sure Andō-san would be able to find that out for you, detective.'

'Yes, I'm sure he would as well. Thank you again, Murakami-san, that will be all for the time being. You have been extremely helpful.'

Matachi left the man in the room and went in search of his partner and the disgruntled HR manager. He found them in a deathly silent, small office adjacent to the conference room.

As he walked in Tekiō, who was standing by the door, handed him the man's phone.

'Ah, you have been getting to know each other, I see?' said Matachi.'

Andō glowered at him but said nothing.

'I must say it has been a very informative chat that we've had today. If you would be so kind as to assist us in our enquiries with just a few more elements, we will leave you to get on with your undoubtedly busy work that you do here.'

'That would indeed be wonderful, Detective Matachi. What is it that I can further help you with?' he replied sarcastically.

'Firstly, we are going to require the date when the black coloured batch of data sticks were first allocated into the restricted areas, which areas these were and a full list of all personnel who were working or visiting, however briefly, in those areas, from the time of the allocation up to the thirteenth of May.'

'That's a lot of information, Detective, it will take us some time to collate.'

Matachi could see the guy was stalling for some reason. He pulled his own cell phone from inside his jacket. 'I have been assured by' – he looked briefly at his phone, quickly scrolling through it – 'a Nishimura-sama, whom I believe is our government's Minster for Energy, that you will put all and any resources at our disposal and assist fully with our inquiries and any requests we may have.'

Andō looked shocked and confused by what Matachi had just said. How he wondered did a lowly detective have access to such a high-ranking government official?

Recovering himself he said, 'Really, what exactly does a murder inquiry have to do with the Minister for Energy?'

'I'm afraid I am not at liberty to divulge that information, other than to say this is a very high-profile case and we have been given access to some very senior support to aid our enquiries.' Andō was about to respond when the man's phone rang in Matachi's other hand. Matachi looked at the name on the screen. Handing the phone over he said, 'I believe that this is your boss…'

He snatched the device out of Matachi's hand and answered the call. The detective sneered at him.

'Yes,' he said into the phone. 'Yes, yes, sir… yes, yes, sir, right, straight away sir… exactly as you say, sir.' The phone went dead, and he looked at Matachi, now understanding why the man had regarded him with such open contempt and impertinence from almost the beginning of their meeting.

Matachi, it had transpired, held a powerful hand that he had hidden well until he needed to use it. First waiting until he had drawn them out, seeing what their initial reaction to his questions would be, then acting secure in the knowledge that at least for the moment he held all the cards. Andō could not help but admire the man's strategy and direct tactics when required. 'All you have asked will be done,' he said to the detectives after the call ended.

'Ah, thank you, Andō-san, I am most appreciative of your cooperation.'

They stood and bowed to each other and then the two detectives returned to their car.

'You could have told me you had already gone over their heads, you sneaky little shit, the way you were talking to them I thought you were going to drop us right in the boiling Shabu-Shabu pot for a moment back there,' said Tekiō as they walked back to the car park.

'Correct. However, if you had not been busying yourself, sulking and snoring all the way here, I would have discussed it with you. If you want to be in on the act, you must come to rehearsals, so let that be a lesson to you, dear boy.'

'I'll give you a fucking lesson in a minute – in how to remove one's elbow from inside of one's mouth – you arrogant arsehole. Spill it, how come the heavy artillery is lining up behind us?'

'Very soon after I started to report to Commander Ōno that a variety of our leads were directing us to the nuclear power station, he informed me that we would be supported by the very highest levels of government. On the way here I received another call from him – after I made apologies for your loud and disruptively unsavoury snoring, He said that he and his boss, and indeed also his bosses' boss, had been summoned to a meeting at Government House. He told me that he was not at liberty to say who else was at the meeting, however, the Minister for Energy would be contacting the General Manager of the Fukushima plant. And we would be assured of complete cooperation in all our inquiries concerning the plant.'

'Sounds like some gilded cages have been severely rattled there!'

'They would've been more than just rattled for us to be allocated this level of clout. There is a scandal looming here, this job is starting to emanate a particular kind of stink.'

'I fucking knew something was not right when we were given the job. Missing persons is well below our pay grade, even if she was a fucking governor. You knew it too, didn't you?'

'Of course, why do you think I accepted the job in the first place? Just so you could go paddling at the seaside?'

Tekiō gave one of his multipurpose grunts in response then said, 'We are now working a corruption case in addition to a murder, not to mention an AWOL governor and a few other suspicious deaths and disappearances.'

'You are correct, my friend, but just remember what I told you once about corruption in Japan.'

'You mean your theory that every senior politician, high-level businessman, government infrastructure and many major corporations, operate around levels of corruption as a function of its actualisation?'

'Correct, precisely that, nice to see that you do actually listen to what I have to say sometimes. Perversely a degree of corruption is now fundamental to the successful performance of all of them. To put it in perspective, of course, it is self-evident that all countries operate in and around a certain degree of corruption. There is a theory that states that, without a certain level of corruption embedded in any organisation, it will always ultimately fail. It's like cholesterol in your body, you can get good cholesterol and bad cholesterol, the one keeps the other in check. If you were to push them out of equilibrium or let them travel from their optimum band of benefit, the body withers.'

'Are you calling me, polyunsaturated?'

'My dear boy, please do take a look in the mirror at some point, no one would ever call you that.'

'Cheeky, scrawny, little shit,' retorted Tekiō indignantly.

Matachi ignored the insult. 'What I am outlining is that if the political grandees in the Japanese cabinet are now involving themselves directly in this, then those individuals, who are without question continuing to merrily draw on the threads of their own personal webs of corruption, could make the situation alarmingly unpredictable.

'The government has caught a whiff of the foul smell of a scandal, and we have been thrown in to shovel it up before someone important steps in it.'

'Well, let's make sure we don't get any of it stuck to our shoes shall we?' said Tekiō, pointedly staring at his feet.

'We have dealt with worse, brother, that's why they picked us for this case. Let's get back to base, the de-encryption program should've broken into those files we copied by now. I have a feeling that we are going to find some very interesting evidence within those documents.'

They handed in their security passes to the gatehouse guard and drove under the rising red and white patterned barriers, on to the solitary straight highway that connected this side of the plant to the rest of Fukushima Prefecture. It was ten minutes past two in the afternoon when Matachi steadily accelerated the Toyota up to the 60 km/h speed limit.

They had travelled approximately twenty kilometres from the plant and were climbing into the surrounding hills, when their vehicle began to slew from side to side.

'For fuck's sake what are you doing!' shouted a startled Tekiō, grabbing onto his door handle with the one hand, the dashboard with the other.

'It's not me,' shouted back an equally alarmed Matachi, as he swung the steering wheel frantically from side to side, trying to compensate for the wild oscillations the vehicle was being subjected to. 'It's the fucking road!'

CHAPTER TWENTY-TWO

11 March 2011 14.02

Takada watched the five men stroll into the hotel's restaurant, now converted back from the morning breakfast area. They were already arriving later than the two o'clock time they had given the maître d' earlier. To him they seemed to walk with the annoying nonchalance that was born of arrogant foreigners who just did not understand about the customs and traditions of his beloved Japan.

They were greeted nervously by Maeda and then seated by herself with the assistance of the other waitresses, though no one said anything about them being so late. Earlier there had been one hell of a row in the kitchen between the chef and the floor manager, after they were all told that they were required to work on past their normal finishing time of two-thirty. Although it was only the chef who had actually challenged the 'request,' they were all in silent agreement of everything he said to the manager – but probably not stretching to what he did.

It had started with the manager stating that because of their poor service of customers this morning, it was now imperative that they repair the reputation of the hotel by working the extra hours required to put the matter right.

Takada had responded that the floor manager was a gutless

dog, who could not even spell reputation let alone understand what it meant. He was a worm who would lay down whatever dignity he had within him to prostitute himself to the whims of scum.

The manager had then threatened to fire the chef on the spot. It was then that things started to get out of hand. Takada picked up a cleaver from the counter and walked over to the manager, his face a mask of repugnant loathing.

Maeda thought she was about to witness a murder in the kitchen, when the chef said, in a voice that held far more composure than the look on his face, 'Are you what the manhood of Japan has become?' And then with a blur of movement, he drove the cleaver into a wooden cutting block next to the manager so hard that it took two of the sous chefs to pull it out afterwards. The chef then said no more, returning to his duties. The manager scurried off to change his pants and everyone carried on with their work as if nothing had happened; other than to all agree it was the best bit of entertainment they had witnessed in their entire careers.

With the party seated, it was all going reasonably well with the guests all studying the menus, when one requested the Wagyu Beef Steak. It being one of the most expensive meals on the menu, and this being a complimentary lunch, Maeda said she would ask if there was any available.

She returned to the kitchen signalling to the manager to follow her.

'What is the problem now?' he asked.

'One of them has requested the Wagyu Beef,' she said. Before the man could answer, the chef piled in.

'Told you, they are nothing more than vulgar ungrateful Gaijin, the lowest of the low. Well, if you think I'm cooking Wagyu for that bunch of arrogant patronising pricks, who hold no respect of Japanese hospitality, you're going to be mightily disappointed.'

The manager did not disagree with his chef. The beef was very expensive, and it was not customary to take advantage of a situation in such a way. Also, his superiors may not be so supportive of his discretion on the free lunch if it ran to thousands of Yen. His contemplations on what to do next were swayed by the chef retrieving his cleaver, then announcing loud enough for the sentiment of his voice, if not the words, to be heard by the diners.

'The beef is "off", go and tell them – now!'

The man scurried away to tell the diners the unfortunate news on the Wagyu, while the chef took up a position in the kitchen doorway, with his arms folded around the cleaver.

'Shit,' said Maeda. 'It will all kick off now, I'm off to the bathroom for a while,' she said to one of her fellow waitresses. She began to walk away from her colleague towards the staff area at the rear of the kitchen. As she reached the door, she and the doorway suddenly moved to her left, then violently back the other way. Behind her people started screaming and shouting in panic. She fell to her knees as the building continued to shake powerfully from side to side. She tried to get back to her feet, but the movement of the floor beneath her was too strong. As she supported herself on her hands and knees, she heard the floor manager shouting, 'It's an earthquake.' No shit, she thought, his panic confirming her thoughts about him: 'Dippy idiot' she said under her breath.

Being Japanese, this was not her first experience of a quake; on the other occasions she had been outside, not in a building that had transformed itself into a bouncy castle. The hotel had now been shaking for nearly a minute, which, when one is experiencing an earthquake, seems like an eternity. The suspended ceiling now began to disintegrate, dropping styrene tiles and bits of steel framework down onto everyone. Customers and staff alike were crying out in fear.

She knew she had to get out, as did just about everyone else in the dining room, except for the foreigners. They stayed seated, desperately gripping onto their table for support, while everyone else crawled across the floor to the stairway exit.

As she reached the relative safety of the stairs, she looked back to see the manager was still shouting bullshit about what was happening. She felt someone should punch him in the face to shut the idiot up.

The man now turned his rantings towards the five foreigners, who did not understand a word he was saying as in his panic he was screaming in Japanese. Although from his extravagantly terrified facial expressions he would have done a Kabuki actor proud in portraying that there was something very wrong.

They were still not getting the message that they needed to get outside, when the chef arrived behind the manager. He grabbed him between the legs from behind with one hand and by the scruff of his neck with the other. He lifted him off the floor and threw him towards the exit.

She had not noticed before how muscular the chef's build was; his sturdy legs seemed able to keep him stable and mobile as he made his away across the room. She continued trying to make her way to the stairs, leaving the five bemused customers seated where they were.

The building was still swaying crazily from side to side as the chef now half ran and half stumbled past the manager who was now on his hands and knees. He grabbed him by the hair and dragged him along until he reached Maeda by the exit.

'Down the stairs! Move!' he commanded. Maeda looked back at the five men still sitting at the table. The chef seemed to read her thoughts.

'Fuck them, go – now!' he shouted, chucking the manager down towards the stairs by his hair, to join the flow of the rest of the staff who were already making their way to safety.

'Yeah, fuck them,' she said under her breath and followed the others down to the emergency exit.

At the bottom of the stairs, they joined a small group of employees cowering in the door well. Most Japanese understood where the main strength of a building was concentrated, it was taught to them from kindergarten upwards. Unfortunately, what they could not teach them, was how to remain calm under these deadly situations. They felt the shocks becoming less and several of her colleagues got up and started to make a run for it, attempting to escape for the relative safety of the street. She got up to do the same but the chef held her back. The first few made it to the centre of the wide boulevard outside the hotel, the next few were not so lucky. A large section of fascia that had come away from the side of the building high above crashed down onto them. They did not even get a chance to scream as the volume of masonry smashed them into the ground and piled up over their crumpled bodies, as if a dumper truck had unloaded its contents onto them.

Behind her she heard someone say in English, 'Oh, Christ almighty!' The five foreigners had finally got the message it seemed and had followed them out. She didn't turn around to look at them, instead kept her focus on the chef, who had now gone quite a way up in her estimation.

He now edged his head out and quickly glanced up above the building sides. Ducking back in he grabbed her by an arm. 'Move!' he shouted, at the same time dragging her with him.

They bolted out into the road. The chef took the most direct route to the middle lane, over the top of the fallen masonry interspersed with the crushed bodies of people who had just been killed or who were too badly injured to help themselves.

Maeda was given no time to think about it as she was forcefully dragged along by his ridiculously strong grip on her upper arm.

The remaining staff and guests who had been cowering there along with them had followed directly in their wake also crossing the field of carnage. There were many cries of anguish, along with horrified curses in Japanese and English, as they realised too late, what and who were in their path, but nobody stopped until they reached the safety of the roadway.

Chapter Twenty-Three

11 March 2011 14.46

Matachi, finally losing patience as he wrestled with the snaking asphalt, bared down onto the brake pedal as hard as he could. The Toyota slid sideways, coming to a screeching halt.

They both remained seated in the car as it continued to shake from side to side.

'Earthquake,' shouted Matachi.

'No shit, and this is a big bastard,' exclaimed Tekiō, both now realising what was happening to them.

Just to emphasise his point, the road started splitting itself in two, tearing along a jagged crack that suddenly appeared, running at an angle across the complete width of the road.

Both men exited the vehicle as the series of shocks dropped in intensity and eventually stopped. They approached the torn section of the tarmac in front of them. It was at least forty centimetres higher than the section they had stopped on.

'Do you think we can drive up over that?' asked Matachi. Tekiō inspected the now raised cross section of road.

'It looks too high, could bottom us out if we try it. I think we are going to need a log or some stones to make a bit of a ramp.' The two men began fanning out on the upward slope of the small hill they had come to a stop on, searching for anything they could use to bridge the gap. As they continued to search, other cars started appearing from both directions. The vehicles behind them coming to a stop behind their Toyota, which they had halted just before the fracture in the tarmac. On the opposite side of the road the first car had braked very close to the edge of the fissure.

The two detectives paid no attention to the rapidly evolving traffic, as they continued to scavenge for anything they could use to make a ramp. Tekiō made a cradle with his arms and Matachi loaded him up with various sized rocks and bits of wood.

After about ten minutes they had accumulated a sizeable amount in Tekiō's arms. As they began to walk back, the car on the other side of the highway began to edge forwards. They shouted at the driver to stop, but before they could prevent it, the driver inched the vehicle over the drop across the fractured road. The two of them looked on in astonishment, as first one wheel then the other rolled over the crevice, the vehicle, having no real momentum, instantly grounded itself along its chassis, pivoting at an angle before coming to rest with its left side turned towards the ground.

'What a fucking shit dribbler,' bellowed Tekiō, dropping his collection of rubble onto the road.

The back of the car was now sticking up into the air, one of its rear wheels spinning freely. The right-hand side of the car was leaning over at an angle. The driver's side door started to open, its weight now aided by gravity, flinging it wide and hard against its hinges. The impetus of the swinging door ejected a very frail looking old lady directly onto her face as she tried to exit the vehicle.

They both ran over to assist her, as she pushed herself up onto her knees. She looked furious. Looking directly at Tekiō she said, as he bent down to help her to her feet, 'Young man, I may be old, but I am not at all deaf!'

Matachi lent in close to Tekiō's to whisper, 'Sorry, Tekiō, but you're on your fucking own with this one, old boy.' He walked around them both to inspect how severely hung up the car was on the fissure.

From the security of the other side of the vehicle Matachi watched them. With the old lady now on her feet, she had bunched all her fingers together into the shape of a beak and was forcibly pecking Tekiō in the lower part of his chest, that being as high as she could reach, with all her strength. She laid into him about how he should be ashamed of himself using that sort of language, and even more so in front of an elderly lady.

Matachi was hoping that he would really screw himself up by telling the old lady he was a police officer, but, much to his disappointment, he just hung his head like a giant schoolboy and took the hammering. His only response a continuous litany of grovelling apologies.

Traffic was now snaking back on either side of the obstruction caused by the cracked highway and the stranded car. A small crowd of people had gathered together on the side of the road that overlooked the town. It consisted of a number of drivers and passengers from the mounting tailback of vehicles who had come forward to see why they were being held up.

Matachi then heard a collective groan emanate from the crowd, interspersed with sporadic shouts and cries. He went over to the group to see what was causing the commotion. They were all looking down the hill towards the coastline. A wail of warning sirens then began to resonate from the valley up towards them. He followed their gaze into the valley so he could see what had caught their attention.

Out of the haze on the misty horizon the sea had risen into an enormous wave that was rapidly moving landward. It was difficult to say how tall the wave was from their vantage point overlooking the bay, but Matachi estimated it to be at least twenty metres, probably more. It was not just the height of the wave, or the fact that the watery abomination should not have been there in the first place, it was the incredible size of the volume of water behind it that bothered him. It rose like an immense, aquatic cliff across the inlet. This formidable water wall loomed ominously, threatening to engulf the landscape and everyone within it with its relentless, surging power.

Helpless and horrified, the shocked gathering looked on as spectators, perched high in their giant natural amphitheatre, watched as the water relentlessly propelled itself inland.

Tekiō had joined him, also drawn by the commotion, accompanied by the old lady. Tekiō placed his right arm gently across her shoulders, as they too bore witness to the unfolding disaster. The elderly lady reached up with both her hands, laying them over Tekiō's hand. From the expression on Tekiō's face, Matachi was not sure who was comforting who.

'I'm going to call it in,' said Matachi, walking back to their car to use the police radio handset.

The water, relentless in its pursuit, surged into the town with an unstoppable force. Where the sea defences stood tall, the tsunami's immense pressure redirected its flow towards the estuary. This formidable onslaught reversed the course of the river, which had flowed steadfastly to the sea for millennia. Now, the swollen waters breached the riverbanks, spilling into the town with a voracious appetite, transforming streets into rivers and reclaiming the land for the sea.

As Matachi talked to the emergency operators, he was still locked into the morbid fascination of what was unfolding below them. He realised that the slowly seeping flow that began to creep through the streets, between the houses, would at first appear nothing more than some localised flooding.

Although individual people were a strain to make out at this distance, he could easily see cars and other vehicles, their occupants oblivious to the gathering danger, still driving around on the streets, innocently going about their daily business. Unaware that just in front of them were the first tentacles of the muddy waters wending their way between the buildings. It became macabrely apparent that the fate of those people was being sealed by their ignorance of the calamitous situation that was literally about to engulf them.

Tensions rose amongst the gathering of accidental voyeurs now lining the roadside, as they were forced to witness the emerging catastrophe. A panorama of individual tragedies now unfolded as the inward surging sea caught up with them.

A collective moan of despair echoed along the roadside as spectators witnessed the tragic plight of the town's inhabitants, helplessly caught in the maw of the disaster. Amidst the chaos, a perplexing reaction emerged from some bystanders – a nervous chuckle, seemingly out of place amidst such catastrophe. Matachi couldn't discern if this was borne out of sheer anxiety or a lack of empathy, as these onlookers appeared to mock the dire struggles unfolding below. Desperate citizens frantically manoeuvred their vehicles in a race against the rapidly ascending deluge. A few, by sheer luck or timely judgement, managed to escape, with mere moments to spare. Yet, as the water surged through the side streets, it created a merciless pattern – briefly allowing passage for some, only to ruthlessly cut off and ensnare the vehicles behind, before ultimately sweeping them away in its unyielding, roiling torrents.

The full brunt of the tsunami now began to take hold of the surrounding areas. With the sea defences totally breached, any lightweight wooden houses in its path were crumpled to matchwood, or lifted up from their foundations, to be floated away, almost intact, along with the many vehicles and small boats that had been dredged up into the abhorrent flotilla.

The extent of the annihilation that was unfolding before them tore at their very senses with an unyielding horror. There seemed to be no end to the destructive progress of the massive wave as it continued to make its way further and further inland.

Tekiō started to point out towards the southern side of the coastline; Matachi reluctantly took his gaze away from the evolving disaster to the direction that Tekiō was indicating. There in the distance, hugging the coast, was the shadowy outline of the

Fukushima plant, pinpricks of twinkling lights cascaded down its length, glinting through the gloom of the cloudy afternoon.

'Look,' he said, 'it has been swamped; the waters have passed well beyond its boundaries.'

Matachi viewed the spectacle in astonishment, he was sure he could see plumes of smoke or possibly steam rising above the buildings at intervals along the site.

'That's fucked it,' he said, turning towards Matachi. The old lady who admonished him earlier for swearing, nodded her head in solemn agreement.

The lights along the plant suddenly flickered, then all of them went out.

'That does not look great,' said Tekiō. 'How can a power station lose power?'

'It's a good point, old chap,' answered Matachi, 'but I don't think that's how these systems work. Though I would be surprised if they didn't have some very substantial power failure back up. It is a nuclear plant after all.'

'Yeah, you're right, I can just make out some of the lights coming back on now,' said Tekiō.

In the thickening gloom, they could barely discern the dimming lights of the plant's exterior, noticing that only about half of them remained illuminated compared to just a few moments earlier.

The wave now began to lose its impetus, turning the area in front of them into a huge lake of floating vehicles and houses, some of which were now burning fiercely as they came to rest with the zenith of the water's flow.

It became evident that the buildings constructed of concrete and steel had managed to weather this particularly barbaric storm, seemingly intact, from what could be seen above the water level. Matachi hoped that many of the population had managed to find some sanctuary within them.

The approaching drone of sirens from emergency response vehicles now drew everyone's attention temporarily away from the terrible scene. Down the hill towards them, travelling on the wrong side of the road to bypass the considerable traffic jam that had formed, came a small convoy of ambulances, fire trucks and police cars.

Matachi and Tekiō disengaged themselves from the crowd and strode over to meet them, pulling out their police IDs from their jackets.

The procession came to a standstill at the roadblock caused by the old lady's stranded car, as some of the police officers and firemen got out to inspect the reason for their immobilisation.

'It's fucking carnage down there,' Tekiō said to them.

'No fucking kidding, chum,' replied one of the firemen.

Matachi could see that the men looked quite shocked by what they had already witnessed and felt apprehensive about what they were about to encounter once they had made their way down.

The fire crews quickly assessed the cause of the hold-up and a group of them were already starting to physically manhandle the old lady's car out of the way. With a loud screech of metal on stone, they quickly pushed it off and wheeled it around between a gap behind the detectives' Toyota.

Another team of firefighters had begun to scoop earth from the roadside into sandbags. Once filled, these bags were swiftly passed to another group of firefighters. Working with precision and speed, they meticulously constructed a ramp, leading downwards from the elevated section of the road.

'Anything we can do to help?' asked Matachi.

'Thanks for the offer, but don't think this is really your bag, is it?' responded one of the uniformed police officers.

'Sure?' said Tekiō, butting into the conversation.

'Yes, I'm sure,' replied the policeman, 'but it was good of you to offer.'

They both bowed to the man. The officer bowed back, then said with a smile, 'Nonetheless, I would not have been happy to have been held responsible for you getting your suits dirty.'

200

Matachi and Tekiō wryly smiled back at the man. They returned to their car and waited for the convoy to move over the ramp to whatever tragedies awaited them in the hell being created below.

Part Two

Interlude

An earthquake is caused when one tectonic plate is driven under another, the forces involved are almost beyond comprehension, dwarfing anything humans have achieved or ever will. As this event takes place there comes a point when the force equalises, bringing the plates to a halt, where neither is really making any progress, while the billions of tonnes of mass behind each plate continue to push against each other. This enormous compression creates a pent-up marshalling of kinetic energy, the equivalent to the combined power of thousands of hydrogen bombs. Once this force is released, one of the massive plates jolts upwards. When this event happens inland the ground cracks and moves, mountains crumble and cities are toppled.

At sea it transfers its energy to the waters above it. If this materialises in the deep ocean it can accelerate the water into a shockwave, creating a wall of water that can radiate outwards in all directions, capable of reaching speeds of around 800 kilometres per hour. In the deep ocean, this dynamism is barely perceptible at the surface, it being dissipated into the vastness of the waters around it. Any sea-going vessel running in calm conditions within the vicinity of the seabed's disturbance would only notice an unremarkable swell. If they were operating in rougher conditions, they may not notice anything at all. But when the shockwave makes landfall the local conditions of the coastal areas will depict its next evolution, a tsunami.

Most shorelines have a gradual shallowing as they make landfall. This gradient reduces the speed of the tsunami, but in doing so raises its height, as the enormous pressure created by the speeding volume of water is pushed upwards when it meets the natural wedge of the shallows.

Depending on the local formation of the shoreline, combined with how forceful the earthquake was, the height of a tsunami can reach as high as thirty metres. However, even a relatively low wave can still demonstrate enormous potency from the continuous feed of kinetic energy that powers it.

The Pacific Ocean is the vast expanses of Suijin, the God of water. Like all his oceans it has three masters that rule its dynamism – Tsukiyomi the Moon, Raijin the Weather and Kenrō-Ji-Jin the Earth itself – with each power able to utilise the water's inherent malleability.

For the Moon and the Weather gods are without doubt powerful forces, dragging and pushing the waters of all the great oceans across the globe from continent to continent to batter coastlines wherever it comes ashore.

However, it is the World itself that decides where those oceans lay. It is by its own spin that the waters are played on the pull of the static one-faced Moon. It is the tectonic movement of its crust that brings design, to shape the giant basins that hold the water within, and it resolves the boundaries of the sea's land.

The compliant nature of the waters allows the Moon and Weather gods to constantly manipulate its movement, lapping Suijin's domain submissively around the globe at their command; driving the tides across the edges of Kenrō-Ji-Jin's realm. Allowing them to bring to all both storm and calm as they please.

This is because Suijin is easily led and enacts with Tsukiyomi and Raijin in carefree abundance. Their memory is as short as their time is immediate, so it is with easy nonchalance that they ignore their status in the Earth's continuous, imperceptible transformation, and forget their place in the order of things.

It is then that the Great Kenrō-Ji-Jin of the Earth will break its glacial inscrutability. And it is a wrathful lesson he gives, releasing once subjugated demons in its wake.

The Ogress Adachigahara

CHAPTER TWENTY-FOUR

11 March 2011 15.15

The becalmed fishing boat wallowed there, deep in the dip between the two huge waves, dangerously poised within a moment of suspended time. Her skipper frantically tried to bring the vessel about, flinging the throttle lever fully forward, attempting to bring the engine back to life, simultaneously spinning the ship's wheel. A final effort to gain enough control to face the next surging onslaught.

In his panic he had overcompensated the handling of the rudder, pushing the vessel around to starboard, exposing its portside towards the oncoming wave. The captain desperately tried to correct his mistake, but it was too late to take any meaningful action, as a great wall of water bore into the boat's side. The men below decks gave a collective terrifying scream as the vessel rolled over, piling everyone against the boat's right-hand bulkheads.

The force of the massive volume of water pinned the small boat on its side. The sheer power of this part of the great Pacific Ocean was being concentrated along the craft's length, overcoming the natural inclination of the ship to right itself.

Kurosawa now fully understood their terrifying predicament; he knew that when hard men come to scream in terror like young girls, death was near. Now captured by the sea and surrounded by the deafening storm of noise being generated by the tsunami, they were held there fast, for what seemed an eternity. Kurosawa, along with the petrified souls around him, were forced against the side of the boat's wheelhouse. Everyone, along with everything that was not secured down, thrashed around in a jumbled melee. Trapped within the confines of the overpowering pressure of water being generated by the tsunami, they were transported inland, riding the illegitimate tide that had been abhorrently born of the sea that day.

The colossal pressure bearing down on the *Michi Maru's* portside now began to gradually invert her, its power slowly turning the craft's sleek hull to face the sky. The men in the bridge began to slide onto what had been the ceiling of the small cabin, as the windows were smashed inwards, and the vessel turned fully upside down. Equal measures of torrents of water and frenzied madness now poured in around them, swirling them in a whirlpool of panic and desperation.

Kurosawa took a breath and attempted to brace himself, making an attempt to stay within the protective confines of the wheelhouse. The buoyancy of his lifejacket pushed him upwards against the deck, which was now above him. He found himself being helplessly induced to float upwards, pressed against the ceiling within an airless vortex that had formed in the wheelhouse. The force of the water now began swirling him around. He was trapped in a chaotic creation of thrashing water mixed with a foul soup made up of the now churning paraphernalia of the compartment. He looked around the confines of the wheelhouse for the others, however, he could see no sign of any of the crew, including the captain, in the surrounding murk.

He had now already been under water for nearly thirty seconds, but he felt no panic, he had been taught by someone very dear to him how to hold his breath underwater; a new skill that he had quite recently mastered and one he was now very grateful for. The craft seemed to be sitting with its hull above the water line and the decision to empty its holds of fish, now seemed without doubt the right one. He elected to stay within the protection of the bridge as long as he could, not knowing what carnage may now be occurring above.

He began to feel that the boat was losing momentum and appeared to be settling into its inverted state. He had now been holding his breath for over a minute, he could probably last a short longer, but felt that this lull would be an opportune time to get out. He prepared himself to make his exit out of the smashed doorway, but as he readied himself to launch his body through the exit, the vessel took a huge impact on its stern, the force of the hit pivoting the boat around, and as it did so, twisting the hull back into its upright position. He was thrown violently against the far wall, his life-vest keeping him afloat with the level of water as it drained away, allowing him to breathe air once again.

Kurosawa sat down heavily on the floor, as the remaining waters quickly drained out of the boat. He sat drenched and dishevelled on the deck and began to take stock of himself, checking if he had any injuries. Finding nothing seriously wrong, just some cuts and abrasions, he pulled himself to his feet.

The vessel was travelling in a forward direction, continuing to be pushed inland by the swell of the tsunami. He looked over the bow and saw he had joined a pathetic flotilla of broken ships of varying sizes, many of which had been smashed to matchwood. Looking back over the stern he saw a huge fish-processing ship coming alongside.

It must have been that what they had hit caused the ship to right itself. He could see no sign of anyone on the ships around him and there seemed to be not a soul left on the *Michi Maru*. Taking stock of his situation he saw that the hatches to the lower deck areas had been flung open. He scrambled over to them and shouted down inside to each compartment in turn but received no answer and saw no sign of any crew member in the water-filled hold.

He was alone and at the mercy of where this hellish ride

would now take him. As the *Michi Maru* was driven into the estuary, they were joined by a great mass of debris, flushing back down from the streets of the town, or rather where that part of the town had once been before it had been ravaged by the destructive power of the first wave.

The boat slewed uncertainly as it was driven into the narrowing estuary. It had taken on a great deal of water and now wallowed close to the level of the false tide, which was running dangerously close to swamping the deck.

He looked for an opportunity to disembark to a place of relative safety but saw nothing that could improve his current condition. It was then that he saw a flash of bright orange about twenty metres in front of the boat… it looked like a lifejacket.

He clambered over to the bow but lost sight of the vest as he did so. He scanned the swirling assemblage of broken human endeavours in front of him, desperately trying to catch another glimpse of it in the churning filth.

In the centre of the mass was a cream-coloured bus, floating like an iceberg, the rear third of its body jutting up at an angle out the water. The front of the vehicle, weighed down by its engine, had caught on some debris beneath the surface, holding it in place, allowing an entangled morass of smashed and mangled flotsam to swirl around it, creating a small floating island.

As the circling body of wreckage came around again – he saw him – it was the Nameless Captain!

He seemed to be in a bad condition, barely conscious, but still alive. He lay at the edge of the raft of jetsam, being buffeted by pieces of the jagged mass as it continued to snag bits of wreckage onto its edges.

Kurosawa believed the boat would run close to him, but not near enough to allow him to grab hold of the man. He searched the deck, trying to find something that the captain could grasp hold of.

He remembered seeing one of the thick-shafted fishing poles floating in the entrance to the hatchway to the hold at the centre of the boat. He quickly retreated to the flooded bulkhead and retrieved it.

He ran to the stern shouting. 'SKIPPER... SKIPPER... OVER HERE... grab hold of this.'

He pushed the rod into the water in front of him but got no response. He reached out again and prodded him with it, but all this managed to do was to push the captain further away.

Along with the continuous stream of human residue, the almost lifeless man now began to slowly float past the portside of the vessel, as the *Michi Maru* was driven inland by the powerful, steady swell of the water. Kurosawa continued to call to him, but he remained unresponsive. He inspected the fishing pole, particularly its high tensile steel hook which took up nearly half of the fifteen centimetres of the total length of the feathery lure.

He placed a foot on the pole, pinning it to the deck whilst wrapping the heavy gauge line around his hand. He tested to see if it was still firmly fixed to the pole's tip by pulling on it against the line's securing bond, where it was attached to the tip. Finding the binding still firm, he grasped the rubber hand grip on the casting end of the rod and whipped the line towards the floating fisherman. His cast landed a short distance beyond the man and he firmly drew the line back, trying to snag his clothing with the hook. The line and hook slid unimpeded over his lifejacket and Kurosawa drew it back to try again.

His first, second and third attempts also failed, but he continued to cast out towards the captain as he walked slowly to the stern of the vessel. He began to move steadily up the side of the boat, realising he was running out of time to land this particular 'human' catch. He tried a few more casts, this time putting more energy into the pole and ripping it back more aggressively as if striking at a fish.

Suddenly the pole bowed almost double as he felt a great resistance on the line, and the captain gave a slight lurch towards him. He pulled even harder, causing the man to gain momentum through the water towards the boat.

There was suddenly a great scream from the captain and he began to thrash around in the water, only becoming silent when his face was dragged momentarily over and into the filthy morass that surrounded him. He pulled his head free, coughing up the disgusting brew. Kurosawa paid no mind to the man's distress as he worked his hands along the pole until he reached the tip where the line was attached. Then, wrapping the filament around the side of a mooring cleat on the deck, he began to steadily haul the shrieking man alongside. He reached down and, grabbing his lifejacket with both hands, gave a powerful heave, dragging him up onto the decking.

Blood flowed freely mixing with seawater as it seeped out from beneath the captain's lifejacket. The hook had embedded itself on his right side, hooking into the edge of his armpit and upper chest.

The captain lay on the deck exhausted and semi-conscious. He looked in shocked unease at the lure's shank sticking out of his body, its feathers red with his blood, rising and falling with the man's exhausted breathing. His body bore witness to being sorely battered by his time in the sea amongst the floating debris. His face was scratched and bruised, with one leg of his trousers torn away revealing a line of lacerations along his outer thigh. He suddenly gave a pitiful high-pitched cry and started pushing his feet against the deck, seemingly trying to move himself away from the source of his torment. Kurosawa realised that man's general anguish was turning to panic at the perturbing sight of a steel hook sticking out of his body.

Without asking for permission to do so, he leaned over in front of the man's head to obscure his vision and removed the hook, sliding it down and out in one swift curved movement. Fortunately for the skipper, the hook was barbless, a requirement of the type of fishing they engaged in, to allow the tuna to be flicked off the hooks once they struck the deck. Because of this it came away effortlessly, true to its design.

He turned his attention to the man's injuries. Having nothing available to stem the flow of blood from the nasty gash under his armpit, Kurosawa grabbed the man's right hand and pressed it against the jagged wound.

'Here, keep the pressure on this,' he instructed the captain. 'You need to press the edges together, it's not as bad as you think,' he added half-heartedly, consoling not being one of Kurosawa's strong points. 'The bleeding will ease if you can keep holding it together.'

The captain was exhausted and bewildered but did as he was instructed. And then through his delirium he said, 'You gaffed me like a fish my boy! Reeled me in as if I was some wasted old marlin.'

Kurosawa did not respond, he calmly surveyed the man, and saw that the wound was not life-threatening. Though undoubtedly painful, as the hook had torn into the flesh and lodged under his pectoral muscle.

The captain followed his gaze to his wound and then looked back and gave him a faint grin, it was all the gratitude he had the strength to show.

Kurosawa nodded blankly back at him. He had seen far worse, he would live – that is if they could get themselves off this damned bucket, he thought.

CHAPTER TWENTY-FIVE

11 March 2011 07.15

It was a cloudy, overcast morning when Fujiwara Tadashi entered Reactor Four's high security level-controlled area. He and his team of eight personnel were experts in the handling of the nuclear fuel rods and their internal transportation within the plant and onto the site's internal port where the loading and unloading of the fissile material took place.

Today's procedure was the final part of this 'fuel rod shuffle' operation on Reactor Four. There was a defined programme which was run for each of the six reactors at the Fukushima Plant, specifically defining when fuel rods would be removed and/or replaced. This operation was normally undertaken every two years on each unit and with six units at the site, this meant that a replacement operation was carried out on an average cycle of four months. Each time this took place the process was supported by a small army of people, consisting of contractors and company personnel and would take approximately four weeks to complete.

This particular replacement was an unscheduled event, prompted by an issue with the plant's cooling system. It was determined that there was a fifteen per cent chance this part of the cooling system would fail to maintain the necessary cooling levels for the fuel rods it regulated over their expected lifespan. In the risk-adverse area of nuclear energy, this relatively insignificant system failure prediction was enough of an issue to move the risk category to the status of 'Very High', demanding an appropriate response. Consequently, it had been decided to shorten the operational life span of the uranium 235 rods, by removing them as soon as possible.

To enable the safe shutdown of the reactor, it had required a reduced and intensified reactor period around the use of the fuel rods. This amplified interaction would create an extra dimension to the already complex logistical situation.

The intensity of the process would reduce the source neutrons available for uptake by the uranium 235 rods, allowing them to produce an enhanced type of plutonium within its atomic structure. One with less of the more volatile PU-240 element, which does not readily present itself to weapons manufacture due to its high neutron emittance. This makes handling more complicated, and in addition causes it to be unsuitable for use in a nuclear weapon. The molecular deviation having a tendency to create a 'Fizzle' in a hydrogen bomb, the equivalent of a 'Damp Squib' in the nuclear weapons world.

This meant that the uranium they would be removing would have less than seven per cent of the contaminating PU-240, holding a greater amount of the more desirable plutonium type PU-239. This was classed as weapons-grade material, which would be required to be eventually added to the twenty–plus tons of weapons-grade plutonium Japan had stockpiled since the inception of its nuclear energy programme, at secret locations across the country, thus giving it the potential to create many hundreds of nuclear weapons if it ever felt the need to do so. The capability regarded by the Japanese government as a tacit nuclear deterrent held as a latent threat. As one politician put it, *'a turn of a screwdriver from possessing viable nuclear weapons...'*

Although now designated as weapons-grade material, it would not be handled any differently by Fujiwara's team to the methods they employed to handle the standard uranium rods. They already operated at the far extremes of safety that the protocols and guidelines of the nuclear industry demanded, and they were experts in this vocation.

The team were now in the 'final gowning room' having already removed their civilian clothes and all items of jewellery, in addition to any cosmetics. The group then donned disposable non-shedding underlayers and the captive shoes held on the 'clean' side of the low demarcation 'step-over' wall as they all crossed into the operational zones, making their way through airlocks to the first layer of controlled-atmosphere clean rooms. The team carried only their personal dosimeters, devices that measured individual radiation exposure. Those who needed prescription spectacles had an extra pair, along with their safety shoes, stored securely in the inner area. As they moved through the facility, they were enveloped in fully enclosed areas with controlled heating, ventilation and air conditioning (HVAC). This advanced HVAC system was designed to cycle the air volume hundreds of times per hour, purifying it by eliminating dust particles through its High-Efficiency Particulate Air (HEPA) filtration system, which captured 99.9 per cent of particles.

En route to the Reactor Room, the crew traversed through zones of cascading negative air pressures. Each zone had an air pressure 15 Pascals lower than the previous one, a strategic design to ensure the dust particles, potential carriers of contamination, were drawn into the building rather than expelled. This meticulous air pressure management was crucial for maintaining a contamination-free environment.

In the final gowning room, they assisted each other to put on their personal protective equipment (PPE) that they would wear during the operation. This consisted of chemically resistant one-piece hooded suits, gloves, steel toe-capped boots and respirators. Fujiwara and two others would also have radios to communicate with the Operations Centre.

The main part of the task involved removing the spent or

215

defective rods and relocating them to the holding tank, where they were kept inert by the controlled liquid environment they rested in. The next section of rods was then extracted and shuffled around into the now vacated silos. The last waltz of this atomic merry-go-round would be the replacement units which had already been placed in the reserve rod-holding tank, which would then be transported by the giant overhead crane into the final vacant tubes.

The crane was equipped with a lifting capacity of 200 metric tonnes, significantly exceeding its maximum anticipated load in the facility by more than double. This was in keeping with the engineering ethos, that every system had redundancy, back-up and over design, principles which were key to maintaining safety at the plant. It was widely believed that this philosophy was true throughout the site. However, unfortunately, that viewpoint, along with several other widely perceived beliefs, would turn out to be tragically flawed.

Today would be the final phase of the change out. All twenty-five of the units would be removed from their holding tank and inserted into a 'B class containment & transportation flask'. This unit would then be taken, suspended from the crane to the rear of the structure, rolling along on its massive dual rails that ran the full length on each side of the building. After moving beyond the location of two large isolation doors, the unit would be halted, pausing as the large structures were slid into place and locked into position behind the unit, sealing the reactor area off. The HVAC system would then rebalance itself to maintain the required atmospheric conditions in the now reduced space within the reactor area. Around the suspended cask the area was brought to the ambient pressure of the sea-level conditions outside, and only once this recompression was achieved would the hatch door be opened through the floor. It was big enough to accommodate the lowering of the five-metre flask through its orifice onto a specialised transport vehicle parked beneath. Once safely secured, from there it would be transported to the dockside for shipment. Fujiwara was thankful that the final stage of the operation had gone well for him and his highly skilled team. The site manager had already congratulated him on 'yet another immaculate undertaking'.

The time was now 14.30, they had done well to complete the task so quickly. With the containment flask firmly positioned on the transport vehicle, they drew upwards the giant suspended hook holding the bespoke jig that had been located on the flask, to allow the unit to be orientated from the vertical to the horizontal plain. The mammoth crane was now stored aside and the great trap door in the floor of the building closed on the now mobile flask of fuel rods below.

With a final personal check that everything had been left correctly, Fujiwara accompanied his team back through the defined decontamination route, shedding layers of protection as they went. There were no females in his group, so all the men then entered the male side of the final changing rooms and began to strip off their disposable undergarments before taking a shower. Each shower cubicle only released its outer door to the 'uncontrolled areas' after a minimum of ten minutes of showering had been completed under the high-volume water heads.

Fujiwara was halfway through his de-con shower cycle when the first alarms started to sound. At first, he did not recognise the tone of the siren, it took him a few minutes to realise it was the seismic monitoring system that had been activated. A sudden violent shaking of the shower cubicle he was trapped in, confirmed that they were indeed experiencing an earthquake. He hit the emergency release button on the inside of the shower cubicle, undergoing a proper decontamination had now become the least of his worries. He burst out of the shower door at the same time as three of his colleagues who threw themselves out of their own cubicles.

All four were covered from head to foot in a soapy lather and two of them collided together and hit the floor in a slippery naked entanglement. The two fallen men helped each other to their feet, any embarrassment that would have normally been felt at the incident overridden by their growing fear and anxiety.

Everyone had now grabbed a towel and began to furiously rub the detergent from their eyes and faces. The shockwave was still shaking the building as they threw on their workwear. Partially dressed, some without shoes, they ran out into the corridor beyond.

The shaking began to significantly reduce within the few minutes it took them to leave the area. Out in the hallway people were running in all directions, many in a state of panic. A voice over the PA system was telling people to adhere to their emergency exercise status. Everyone had been trained to follow a pre-prescribed drill in the event of an emergency. For most, it was to simply evacuate to their designated congregation area. For others, depending on their skills, roles and responsibilities, it could be more involved. For Fujiwara it was the latter. He gathered the remnants of his team to one side, now augmented by two additional members who joined them after completing their decontamination process alongside the first group that had already showered and cleaned themselves.

Their new responsibility was clear to him. The flask containing twenty-five significantly enriched uranium fuel rods was now outside the safety of the highly reinforced structures they normally resided within. Although he fully appreciated the incredible robustness of the design and construction of the flask, there was a risk that exposing it to the potentially extreme conditions generated by an earthquake may uncover unforeseen vulnerabilities.

He gave his orders. 'We need to get to the flask, check on its condition and assist in its safe transportation to a reinforced bay within the fuel rod recovery area.'

That particular building was set aside from the reactors, nestled between the two reactor blocks. Reactors One and Two and Three and Four were housed on one side of the site, the third block housing reactors Five and Six on the other side.

'We cannot leave the unit exposed,' he said, looking around the small group. 'It is our duty to protect it, come what may…'

The men in the team began to realise that they were about to embark on a challenging and potentially dangerous task. Though some of its members were clearly extremely frightened, they said nothing, a few then gave a couple of short bows of agreement before following Fujiwara down to the loading bay. This was where they had last seen the flask mounted on top of the transportation vehicle. It took over ten minutes to get themselves through the streams of people, either exiting the building or moving to their standby positions. One of the team members crashed through the emergency fire escape door that led to the outside. They all piled out of the door behind him into the courtyard beyond. The flask cradled on the vehicle was still parked at the back of the courtyard, below the enormous trap door it had been loaded through earlier.

As they began to run towards it another siren began to sound. There was no confusion over what this alarm meant; it sent a sudden jolt of foreboding through all of them – it was the tsunami warning alert!

On reaching the truck Fujiwara discovered that two of his team had disappointingly disappeared. He pulled open the driver's side door to find the driver still inside the cab. He had both hands firmly clenched around the steering wheel, his knuckles white, shaking quietly in an inanimate state of terror.

'Where are the rest of your team?' Fujiwara shouted at the man.

The man turned to him, relief evident on his face at the arrival of a senior member of staff. He undid the chinstrap of his safety helmet, and said, 'They have all fucked off… the bastards. As soon as the tsunami alert sounded, the whole lot of them did a disappearing act, including the supervisor.'

'Can't concern ourselves with that now, we need to drive these rods to the recovery bay, yes?'

He looked at Fujiwara finding comfort in the familiarity of being given a clear order from a senior.

219

'Yes, sir,' he responded. 'Good man. Now do that chin strap up, you may have use for that hat in a minute.' He grinned at the driver, who gave him a nervous, sickly smile in return, but did as he was told.

The cab of the vehicle was large with a row of back and front seats, enough for six people in total, the remainder of his team all jumped into the rear.

'Let's go!' he shouted above the wailing sirens, as he got in the front next to the driver. The man started the engine and the powerful diesel motor roared into life; two black plumes exhausted skyward either side of the cab as the heavy truck lurched into motion.

The combined weight of the truck and the flask filled with fuel rods was over forty tonnes. The transporter was not built for speed, it had six axles and twenty-four wheels, with the restricted speed of 20 km/h. It ground its way around Reactor Four, slowly trundling towards units Three, Two and One, through a landscape increasingly devoid of people, most realising the folly of congregating in groups at sea level during a tsunami alert.

Some had tried to find refuge higher up in the buildings, others had gone to the car park and collected their vehicles and were now trying to escape the complex in their cars, others were still on foot, running out of the site as quickly as they could.

It took them almost fifteen minutes to reach the fuel rod bay, only to find its massive steel doors shut fast. The transporter came to stop in front of the doors. Fujiwara leapt from the cab and ran to the control room entrance. The doors were closed and peering through the windows he could see there was no one inside. Access to the building was controlled by a keyed-in code in conjunction with an electronically programmed smart card.

Forty minutes had now passed since they first heard the tsunami warning alarms. He realised that time was running out for them. He heard someone shouting from above. He looked across to reactor building One, to find a group of people that had made their way onto the roof space calling and gesturing towards them. He could not understand what they were saying but from the excitable gesturing and pointing seawards, he had a terrifying understanding of what they were desperately trying to convey to the men on the ground.

He jumped back into the cab. 'We need to get the fuck out of here right now. Back this bastard up and get us to the main exit,' he yelled at the now petrified driver.

The driver did as he was told and they were soon moving down the access road towards the main gate.

'Won't this heap of shit go any faster?' called one of his team from the rear of the cab.

'Restricted,' called back the driver over his shoulder in response. It took them nearly ten minutes to reach the gate. Fortunately, the robust security gate remained open, positioned adjacent to one side of the main fence. Of the two rising barriers which covered both sides of the road, one had been smashed open and the other was fully raised. Numerous cars lay abandoned around the covered gatehouse security inspection area. As the truck drove through they could see at least one of the guards lying unconscious on the floor. It looked like he had been beaten up by a group of panicking employees trying to escape the facility when he had refused to open the gates.

One of the team wanted to stop and pick him up, but Fujiwara told the driver to keep going. The man was about to challenge this order, when the sudden appearance of water lapping past on either side of them abruptly halted any further discussion on the matter.

There was now a possibility that the truck and its precious cargo could be swept away by the incoming waters. The group's only chance of saving it, and hopefully themselves, was to drive inland and hopefully outrun the incoming tsunami.

CHAPTER TWENTY-SIX

11 March 2011 16.05

The final demise of the *Michi Maru* was almost serene in comparison to the dramatic events of the last few hours. The hull was now almost totally flooded, the mass of water drawing down the upper deck of the craft to mere centimetres of the level of the swirling tide around them, the boat's buoyancy almost totally degraded. Kurosawa looked down at the Nameless Captain where he lay against the front of the wheelhouse, gradually trying to recover from his ordeal.

He was a tough man, a veteran of the sea and the trials it could force a human being to endure. Kurosawa could see hints of the robust character of the resilient old mariner returning.

'You had better prepare yourself, captain,' he said. 'I think this ship is about to go down.'

'Poxy landlubbers, you're all the fucking same,' he replied. 'Ride out one pathetic wave and you think you are Christopher Columbus.' He forcefully spat out some blood and phlegm onto the deck, wiped his hand across his mouth and gave Kurosawa a wry grin.

'I see you are feeling better, captain,' said Kurosawa, heartened by the man's returning sarcasm.

'You had better do up that jacket, boy, if you are going to

survive in these waters, you're going to need all the help you can get,' responded the captain.

He did as the man said, as a small wave now began to gently ripple across the deck and the vessel ceased to float above the filthy tide. The boat's displacement, all but exhausted by the volume of water filling her holds, began to slowly submerge beneath the surface.

Kurosawa helped the captain to his feet and they made their way to the stern of the boat. The deck fell away from their feet leaving them floating free before they had reached fully aft. The shadow of the *Michi Maru* was still visible below them as it continued to make its ghostly journey inland, now beneath the water.

The two men tried to stay together as they were swirled along by the powerful eddies and unexpected currents, as all manner of items were carried along with them. The material familiar in its forms, yet alien in its presence, as they bobbed up and down in the great soupy waste.

As they struggled to push off or veer themselves away from the larger items that continually buffeted them, it became increasingly strenuous to hold onto each other. So, when the shattered end of a large uprooted tree struck them from behind, the shock of the impact pushed them apart either side of its broad trunk.

Kurosawa managed to grab hold of its rough bark and frantically heaved himself over the tree trunk in an attempt to grab hold of the captain. But it was to no avail, the captain drifted away from him as the tree was gripped by another fluctuation of the waters, floating him onto a different course.

'Remember, boy, the sea does not take prisoners, only souls,' the captain called to him as he disappeared from Kurosawa's view.

He realised there was nothing he could do for the captain now, so he began to think about how he could help himself. The tree had a large mass of bare branches at the far end and, recognising some semblance of safety there, he made his way along the trunk towards them. Grabbing hold of one of the sturdier branches, he managed to drag himself to the top.

The sizeable spread of the branches gave some stability to the floating tree, so he pulled himself further into the embrace of the nest of branches, leaving him clear of the water.

Perched precariously in his new sanctuary, he was also afforded some protection from being struck by the continuing floating barrage that swept around him, as the protective cradle now encountered a group of floating vans. Their orange colouration and descriptive nomenclature indicating that the vehicles all seemed to be from the same company, probably all having been washed away from their company car park at the same time.

As he stared at the alien sight, their greater collective mass began to push him to one side of the valley. It was shallower here, allowing the submerged section of the branches to entangle themselves within the ragged mess that had sunk below earlier. The trunk of his impromptu life-raft now began to swing about as the force of the tide waned, and it began to ebb back out to sea. The water as it departed now began to accelerate, and he quickly found himself high and dry on a small crest of crumbled and smashed deposits, not a hundred metres from the newly created shoreline over a kilometre inland.

Clambering from his perch, he began to carefully pick his way the short distance across a shoreline that had been transformed into some hideous refuge tip. It took him quite a while to make it across the tangled mess, but eventually he reached the safety of higher ground. As the tide of detritus gave way to civilised normality, he found the beginning of a small axis road, as its unaffected section emerged from the destruction behind him. He followed the road up into the hillside, a short walk taking him into what was left of the town. People here were now extracting themselves from vantage points, from where they had watched the disaster in relative safety, to come and give what help they could to their fellow inhabitants.

He approached a small group and respectfully asked them if he could use one of their cell phones. Several people considerately offered, also asking if they could be of any other assistance on seeing his bedraggled condition. He thanked them for their kindness, explaining to them that he was fine and that he just needed to call his mother to tell her that he was alright. He accepted one of the phones being offered from a still visibly shocked woman. Thanking her he walked a short distance from the group as he started to dial.

His call was quickly picked up, but he listened to only silence as he received no greeting from the other end.

'Where the fuck have you been?' came the sharp reply of a female voice.

'Yes, I've been worried about you too, sis,' he said. 'Can you come and pick me up?'

'Yes, but it may take a while to get to you. Do you need directions?'

'No, I have already triangulated your signal.'

'Okay, I'll stay here. I will have to hand this phone back, so do not follow that signal any more, stick to the position you already have, I will stay in that location until you arrive.'

The line went dead, and he tried to call Ikuko, but it went straight to voicemail. He hung up without leaving a message. Then thinking over his situation, the earthquake, his fortunate escape, and the fact he would be working with Azumi now for several days, he realised he needed to create a measure of distance from her for a short while. The borrowed phone indicated it was almost out of charge and he did not wish to use it all, that would be unforgivably discourteous to the lady who had loaned it to him. He redialled Ikuko's number and left a short message, it was a little direct and to the point, but it showed that he was safe, and felt sure she would understand why he needed some time to himself. Kurosawa returned the phone to its owner, thanking her profusely.

Someone wrapped a blanket around him and pressed a cup of

warm green tea in his hand. Two people then gently took hold of his arms and he allowed himself to be guided to a small tea house where a number of other survivors had also been taken.

He sat at a table at the back of the room, with the blanket pulled around him and cupping his hot drink in his hands. He began to process the events of the last few hours; it seemed he could not even get to enjoy his day off anymore!

He contemplated the tsunami, but his thoughts were not tethered to the havoc it wrought or the narrow escape he had from its deadly embrace. To him, it was a manifestation of nature's raw power or, perhaps, an act of divine will – perspectives shaped by personal beliefs. His own close encounters and life's journey had long ago crystallised his views on such phenomena, erasing any shades of doubt.

He was thinking more about how it would affect their operation. He was sure it would add complications to it somewhere. He was confident they would be more than capable to accommodate any issues that may arise. Sipping a little of his tea he immediately felt the warming benefits of the bitter brew as he surveyed the vista of destruction across the bay in front him. He hoped that his fellow survivor was also somewhere safe, he smiled to himself, comforted by the thought that it would take a lot to put that old sea dog down.

CHAPTER TWENTY-SEVEN

11 March 2011 16.05

Fujiwara and his crew had gambled their lives in trying to remove the fuel rods from the insidious grasp of the tsunami. The transporter, with its colossal weight of forty tonnes, remained steadfastly anchored to the road, impervious to the water's attempts to dislodge its enormous mass. The machine had been built to withstand almost any adversity, its giant 46-litre Komatsu diesel engine had managed to keep going even when fully submerged due to the electronic protection rating for its electrical systems and the snorkel configurations of the exhaust and air intake for its super chargers.

Fujiwara and the rest of the crew were sitting on the roof of the cabin, only the driver bravely remaining inside to keep the vehicle running. He now had just his head above the water. The driver was standing, holding his foot on the throttle to keep it pressed to the floor, his head half out of the open window. Almost immediately, the road vanished from their view, obscured by the sea's relentless surge that inundated the countryside ahead. In response, the driver relied on the lampposts, like beacons in the deluge, to trace the road's hidden path. Guided by these intermittent lights, he steered the transporter, navigating on a line-of-sight basis through the engulfing waters. However, once the line of lampposts ended, the road took on a series of bends and navigation became pure guesswork, soon leaving the security of the firm tarmac and rolling onto the fields.

Each of the vehicle's six axles powered the twenty-two wheels beneath, providing relentless propulsion even under such extreme conditions. However, in an abrupt twist, the front of the transporter plunged downwards, submerging the cabin in a watery grasp. Faced with no other option, the driver eased off the throttle. This loss of momentum, coupled with diminishing traction, led to the wheels embedding themselves in the mud. In mere moments, what was once a relentless advance turned into a helpless standstill, as the wheels became irrevocably stuck fast in the sodden earth.

Fujiwara helped the driver out of the cab through the open window. As the front of the truck was now submerged, they crawled up onto the cylinder containing the rods that was now sticking up at an angle out of the rising waters.

The six of them congregated at the ends of the cylinder, like sailors grasping onto the bow of a sinking ship. They were a sorry sight, all soaked to the skin and filthy from head to toe from the state of the water they had driven through. They fastened themselves as best they could to this last vestige of pitiful sanctuary and looked back at the Plant. Torrents of water deluged through the gaps in the massive structures of the reactor buildings, all manner of materials flowing with it on the surface. Worryingly, no lights could be seen shining from anywhere on the site, all power now lost, and he realised the back-up generators situated below ground, had without a doubt been overwhelmed by the relentless flow of the incoming sea.

His courageous group had achieved as much as anyone could have in the face of such adversity. Fujiwara believed that at least the flask had been moved far enough inland that its mass should hold it there and not take it out to sea when the tides finally began to ebb. Now huddled together they watched as the swirling torrent rushed towards them as its flow was redirected by the immovable contours of the rising hills. It brought with it a concoction of garbage, people's belongings, the remains of the rendered land and its human occupants. A matted and tangled wall of this waste was now steadily driven towards their forlorn metal island. With scant time to spare, saying nothing, each stood and jumped onto the semi-solid wave as best he could, desperately grasping at any debris that could give them some buoyancy. They were quickly carried away, scattered in different directions, individually fighting his own battle to keep afloat and not be crushed by the grinding jaws carnage around them. Fujiwara remained ignorant of the events that he had inadvertently now put in motion.

★ ★ ★

Within a small cottage situated on a vantage point overlooking the immediate facility, a man looked through the eyeglass of a high-powered telescope, the kind typically favoured by amateur astronomers. He watched the site as he did every day, noting mundane coming and goings, logging the movements of personnel, taking photographs using the telescope's capability to mount a camera. The telescope, perched on a vibration-dampened tripod firmly anchored to the ground, was a marvel of engineering. Originally designed to capture pristine images of stars millions of miles away, it effortlessly snapped crystal-clear pictures of vehicle registration plates from as far as thirty miles away.

For Kim Jin-sung today had proved to be a very unusual day, diverging totally from his daily mundane routine of spying on the Plant. He witnessed the major catastrophe unfolding before his eyes and had begun to set up the telescope to record the possible destruction of the facility, when the erratic movement of the large truck had attracted his attention.

It followed a path out of the main gate and along the access road to the countryside beyond, dogged all the way by the ever-increasing tide of water that had slowly begun to rise on each side of the vehicle as it made its excruciatingly slow escape. The machine finally surrendering to the inevitable as the waters rose around it and flooded into the vehicle's cab. He watched as some of its occupants had climbed onto the roof, partly to escape the rising waters within but also to give directions from a higher vantage point on where to steer the lumbering monolith. The road beneath them had by now been swamped by the incoming water and its tide of detritus, making it impossible for the vehicle to stay within the sanctuary of its tarmac surface. The large transporter kicked and bucked from side to side as its wheels responded to the uneven ground once it left the stable surface of the road. They continued to move forward, desperately attempting to outrun the tsunami, managing to make it over a kilometre inland before the vehicle became totally swamped by the rising inland tide.

He watched fascinated, as the driver was dragged out of the window up onto the roof, where the men desperately tried to cling to the vehicle. A combination of the fast-flowing waters and the churning wreckage that flowed with it, snatched each man in turn from its structure, swirling them into the vast currents rushing inland.

The vehicle and its exceptional cylindrical cargo began to disappear beneath the rising waters. The spy zeroed in on the position using the telescope's viewer and then locked it onto the location of the vehicle. He noted down all the readings on the digital controller and marked the settings of its tripod and laser range finder. He checked the DSLR camera fitted to the telescope which had been videoing the unfolding disaster. He switched it to stills and began to take a series of photographs of the area where the unit had come to rest.

If the cargo on board the vehicle was what he believed it to be, then it had been the most profitable and fortuitous day of his long and illustrious career. He went online and placed for sale an old Olympus Trip camera, with a note saying: 'No longer functioning may be good for parts, open to offers.' Within five minutes his computer pinged him an alert; there were two offers for his camera, one from collectormart.com and the other Bricabrac88. He accepted the offer from Bricabrac88 and settled down to await the visit from his handler.

CHAPTER TWENTY-EIGHT

11 March 2011 17.30

It was not possible for him to believe what he was seeing, how could he. If someone else related to him what he was witnessing now, he would have called them a fool or mad, or at the very least a liar. But as the Nameless Captain clung to the steel fire escape ladder attached to the sturdy reinforced concrete structure of the town's tsunami warning tower, he witnessed below him a swirling torrent of detritus crashing past on each side of the building. Stranded there with his legs and arms wrapped around the metal rungs of the ladder, he saw a manifestation that frightened him far more than the awful disaster unfolding around him. For on the nearby bank, emerging from the filthy waters came an entity of such abhorrence as to terrify him to his very core. For what he was seeing was not of this earthly realm.

It had happened very quickly, the outlandish creature emerging from the swirling waters. It moved with speed and efficiency, using a silky motion with smooth, fluent movements, like a droplet of free-flowing mercury finding its way down an uneven surface, only this entity was very peculiarly, seemingly flowing upwards against gravity.

It was a large beast, almost three metres in height and around a metre wide at the middle. It was covered in a long coat of silky fur, milky white to greyish black in colour. Almost oval in shape, hands and feet pushing at the four corners of its pelt-covered outline, similar to the structure of a flying squirrel. Only of course this was much larger. There was a slight doming around the region of its neck, which must have been caused by its head, as it morphed within its muscular upper frame.

It launched itself out of the water, using its hands and feet to quickly propel itself onto the bank, making its way towards a row of apartments. Then with one fluid motion blending into the next, it speedily ascended the side of the building with a powerful dexterity.

Its silky pelt seemed to shimmer with a pale creaminess that blended to a murky black, in a perplexing monochrome efflorescence. It disappeared from view for a moment as it effortlessly flowed over a wall onto a balcony on the third floor, then reappeared almost immediately. Moving along the front of the building using the doorways and window frames as anchor points, and with a series of coordinated efficient movements, it ascended to the top floor of the block.

It was then, unbelievably for the captain, that even after all the horrors he had experienced that day, he would still come to regard this moment to be the most terrifying event of his life.

The creature had seemed frantic as it moved up the building, frightened even, as anything would be, trying to escape the millions upon millions of tons of water and debris crashing around it. It too had been seemingly caught unawares by the epic disaster unfolding around them.

But now as it stood on the top floor of the five-storey building, pushing itself close to a small utility outbuilding sat on the roof, it spread its body across one of the walls and took a moment, seemingly to gather whatever faculties it possessed.

It was then, as the creature regained its composure, it perceived that it was being observed. It slowly turned its upper body towards the direction of the captain. Having scrambled to similar heights in their desperate bid for safety, they were both now situated at roughly the same level, though separated by a raging torrent of unforgiving destruction. They were at least fifty metres apart, but across that respectable distance the creature had still managed to sense his presence.

It stared at the captain with its large, almond eyes angled outwards into the dome of its head, they were large and dark with no white at all. It seemed to have a wide nose that spread in a shallow triangle beneath its eyes, all covered with streamers of gossamer fur, that flowed and fluttered as if each strand of hair had a will of its own, as its face seemed to ebb and flow in and out of focus.

And then as it held the captain's attention within its captivating gaze, an enormous mouth appeared as a cavity of bloody pink, exposing a top row of jagged scimitar-shaped teeth curving high under its nose, with the lower jaw sinking almost into the centre of the creature's abdomen. Its jawline was easily large enough to consume a fully grown person.

It seemed to be roaring at him, and although the captain heard no sound, he felt the terror of its emphasis. He was shamefully thankful for the presence of the horrifying estuary of destruction which raged between them, that was undeniably his only protection. The creature closed its jaws and continued to stare at him. It seemed to be contemplating what to do about its human detector.

It suddenly moved very quickly, climbing to the top of the small shed, seemingly to get a better view of a possible route to get to him. As it reached its new perch, the doorway to the structure burst open and a distraught family of a mother with a babe in arms and a father holding the hand of a small child, stumbled out onto the rooftop, a small wiry haired, anxious looking dog trotting out behind them. Unmistakably seeking sanctuary from the horrors below them, they had climbed the service stairs to the building's roof.

He tried to wave at them, shouted with a hoarse voice trying to sound a warning of what was behind them. They saw him and shouted and waved back, in what they thought was mutual recognition of their plights and the relative safety they found themselves in. At that moment their pet dog and the child, who had been clutching onto one of his father's hands with both of his, looked back, each sensing the presence of the creature behind them simultaneously. The child shrieked and the dog started yelping and whining. The parents turned to see what it was that was causing this new angst. But by then it was too late, the creature flew at them with a merciless ferocity that the captain struggled to comprehend. It was like a grizzly bear had been merged with the power of a turbine.

In a blur of savagery, the creature's claws and teeth swirled in circles of ruthless evisceration. He witnessed both parents and the small child torn to pieces and spewed over the balcony in a torrent of dismembered body parts and trailing organs, as if they had been ejected from a high-powered mincing machine.

He glimpsed the form of the new-born child that had been in its mother's arms, carried along within the ejected stream of mutilation, seemingly untouched. The bloody mess, along with the baby, splashed into the torrent below, and was quickly accepted into the foul stream, disappearing into the quagmire to be washed inland.

He turned his awareness back to the creature. The small dog stood beside it shaking, giving it a cursory glance as the beast turned and once again stared intently at the captain. The dog took its opportunity and bolted for the doorway from where it had just emerged and disappeared out of sight.

For all the blood and gore the creature created in its ferocious attack, there was little of it that had soiled its fur. The few splashes of blood and pieces of flesh that he could see on the creature's coat just seemed to slide off, as if it were covered in Teflon, leaving no stain behind. It gave one last lingering look at the captain, that instilled such terror in him the like of which he had never felt before, then it turned, dropping to all fours, slithered to the rear balcony, seemed to flow over it and vanished into the coming dusk as though it had never existed.

The captain climbed to the top of the tower and stood on the grating next to the soundless warning speakers. He turned his gaze inland, the horizon of destruction spread before him across the bay. He held onto the safety rail and lowered himself into a sitting position, finally giving in to a combination of exhaustion and terror. Blood still flowed from the ragged gash where the fishing hook had caught him. He tried to squeeze the flesh together with his fingers to stem the flow of blood. He thought about the stranger who had saved him, he hoped he had survived, though he held but modest hopes for the fate of his crew.

Had he really seen what he had just witnessed, or was it a trick of the mind, brought on by the fatigue and terror of his experiences that day? Feeling spent by his ordeal, his body demanded he accept the relative safety of his perch above the waters and his resolve finally gave in. His hand fell away from the handrail, and he slumped forward into blissful unconsciousness.

Within the tree line on the mountainside the mysterious creature took a long assessing breath through its nostrils, checking for a particular scent of a human male, before expelling the breath with distaste. It gave one last look at the obliteration before it, then walked to the cliff face, slid its svelte body around a large boulder and disappeared.

CHAPTER TWENTY-NINE

11 March 2011 19.30

On their return to the police station, the two detectives found the building virtually empty as all the uniformed staff had been allocated to assist with the disaster. Many of the civilian staff had also left, some to assist the emergency services and several because they had been personally impacted by the disaster in some way.

The building itself had only suffered superficial damage to its internal fixtures and fittings from the quake. Due to its importance in the national civil defence system, it had been constructed to even higher specifications than the earthquake-proof design standards in place for the construction of buildings in general.

As Tekiō and Matachi made their way through the deserted offices, they stopped to pick up various items of stationery they found in their path lying on the floor, thoughtfully replacing them onto desks and filing cabinets.

'Do you think we should offer to help?' asked Tekiō, as he pushed a line of drawers back into position on someone's desk as he was passing.

'I know it feels like we should,' said Matachi, 'but I think we would only get in the way, it would be more beneficial in the long term if we were to solve this case for them. One thing is for sure, normal police work for these guys will be a very low priority for some time.' They reached their small room at the back of the building. Tekiō unlocked the door and let them both in. There was little disruption in their office, apart from two of the monitors that were lying face down on the desk.

'Could be worse,' he said, as he shut the door behind them.

Matachi righted the two fallen monitors. 'Pull the laptops out, let's check them over,' he said.

Tekiō unlocked the filing cabinet where they had stored the laptops before leaving the office earlier that day and pulled the three units out.

Matachi took possession of the one they had left running earlier, deciphering the documents taken from Matsumoto's memory stick.

'It is down to twenty per cent power,' he said after logging on to the device.

Tekiō handed him the end of a live power cable and joined him in front of the laptop.

'Thanks,' said Matachi, taking the cable and plugging it in. 'Let's see what we have got then.'

The Spaniard had done its work and Matachi was able to move freely around the file, opening any of the documents he found embedded there. He created a new document folder and named it the 'Matsumoto Files' then dragged all the documents into it.

'There seems to be a great deal of information here,' he said.

'Looks like a cache of emails, some financial accounting data, and what looks like a series of personnel reports with various information on a number of individuals. You start working your way through the emails and reports and I will have a look at the finance data.'

Tekiō brought over another laptop and connected them both together via a cable. He did this without being asked, after years of working with Matachi, conducting himself to operate in cyber space in a secure manner was second nature to him. After being partners for over ten years they had learned a great deal from one another; Tekiō had reached almost geek level in his understanding of information technologies. Matachi for his part, had learned how to defend himself and to kill without hesitation if the situation required it. Both men were equally pleased with the progress they had made in mastering their new skills.

They settled down to start scrutinising the information on the files. This type of detailed probing required a high degree of concentration, a distraction that both of them were glad to use to focus their minds away from the horrors that had unfolded around them earlier that day.

It was the early hours of the morning when the detectives finally completed their exploration of the documents.

Matachi looked across the desk at Tekiō, who was holding his laptop in his hands, turning it to one side then the other whilst twisting his head in the opposite direction.

'Everything okay, old chap?' enquired Matachi. 'Flexible, and that's a fact,' he muttered, without taking his eyes off the screen.

'I feel like I have just spent the evening crawling through a manure heap, these finances are so dirty,' said Matachi. 'What about you, old boy, find anything of interest?'

'Absolutely, I think I have found quite a bit of filth myself…' said Tekiō cryptically before continuing. 'Some of it makes no sense at the moment, but there is a great deal of incriminating evidence on the involvement of Iwasaki Shizuko, the missing governor. She has appeared in a number of unsavoury enterprises, all linked to the construction of the Fukushima Plant. I also have the names of an assortment of people that are well worth a visit, some sooner rather than later.'

'Would one of them be called Uchida Zenjirō, by any chance?'

'Yes, his name is mentioned a few times, as is a Korean called Kwak Kyung-bok and, most importantly by far, a young lady called Ikeda Fuyuko.'

'What's so special about her?'

'Porn star.'

'Begging your pardon, sergeant?'

'She is a porn star; of some renown I might add. I have just spent the last half hour researching her and I can tell you now, she is a class act. Her stage and screen name is Luluero. She is an only child of mixed race, raised as a Catholic, attending convent school until sixteen. Her parents ran a respectable restaurant for many years in Tokyo. The father was Japanese and her mother was Thai. Both are now dead – probably of shock...' said a grinning Tekiō.

'What is so special about her – other than her ability to perform sexual acrobatics that is?'

'She is named in connection with Kwak and Uchida in a number of these emails for a start. It also seems that she has been involved with several of the men, who we now feel met their deaths in an untimely manner. What about you? How cooked are the books?'

'Done to a turn and thoroughly basted dear boy. Like I always say, "follow the money". How one makes it and how one spends it never fails to lead you to everything you wish to know.

'Our man, Uchida, has been a very busy chap. I am only paddling in the shallows for now, however, the information from Matsumoto is high level stuff, budgets, accounts, spend profiles and the like, not incriminating in their own right, but placed in there for a reason, like directions pointing to something deeper. Uchida is not a fool, he knows how to keep things below the surface, though when I attempt a few deep dives of my own, I am certain I will discover a picture of more than questionable activity.'

'Sounds like our guy,' said Tekiō.

'Yes, he may be. It has been tough going though, the guy is so reclusive, he would make a Hikikomori sufferer look like Donald Trump,' stated Matachi, referring to the Japanese trait for individuals to become social recluses, particularly as they got older.

'Do you think we have found the "Mr Big" in all of this?'

'Possibly, he is without a doubt, a very powerful and influential individual, however, he may be a cover for more serious players. He certainly moves around prominent circles, in both government and business alike, not that there is a great deal of difference between the two in Japan.'

'Any further information on the hardy Professor Takeuchi?'

'Yes, I have a little more background on her, it turns out she is a bit of a game old girl. It confirms her story around the accident. I feel she is a good woman,' said Tekiō. 'When I apologised for the damaged pot, she told me not to worry about it and would not accept my offer to replace it.'

'I think she may just have been reflecting somewhat on her day, after all someone had just tried to cut her head off and then re-enacted the battle of "Sekigahara" in her backyard. That sort of shit can inflict upon you a very mellowing perspective. The impact of some overweight clumsy ex-wrestler smashing up her garden was a mere triviality by then.'

'Actually, I think she genuinely liked me, I can have that effect on people.'

'Take it from me, Tekiō, no one genuinely likes you, and I have seen first-hand the effect you can have on the people around you… and let me tell you, mostly, it's far from endearing.'

Tekiō was about to protest this ill-mannered affront to his obvious ingratiating appeal and winning charm, when Matachi ignored him, asking, 'What else have you discovered on her?'

'This next bit is very interesting, considering what happened today. It says that before the accident she had publicly criticised the design and operation of the Plant, specifically in its ability to withstand flooding, naming the executives she felt were responsible for signing off on what she felt were the final "flawed" design and construction plans. After the accident she subsequently resigned from the company and began suing them for personal damages, for the injuries she received.'

'Interesting,' said Matachi.

'Also,' went on Tekiō, 'once she left the company, she became very heavily involved with local residents' action groups, opposed to nuclear energy. It looks like her in-depth knowledge of how the site was designed, built, and operated, handed the locals a range of brickbats, who then set about merrily aiming them at company executives and politicians alike. Their safety concerns surrounding the use of nuclear power was further legitimised by the professor's damning statements. This woman has managed to upset an awful lot of powerful people for sure. However, to send someone to have her sliced and diced would seem rather extreme, don't you think, even for a politician. I have no doubt that most of them would love to see her disappear, but even if one of them was stupid enough to have her killed, they must have been a real traditionalist to send a man with a sword to do it.'

'Yes, I agree,' said Matachi, 'there are plenty of potential motives there, without a doubt. However, these people may be corrupt… well, undoubtedly corrupt, but they are not generally killers. If they had wanted to really shut her up, they would have surely bought her off. Even the principled Professor would have a price tag on her conscience somewhere along its moral line.'

'If not them, then who? I think you're missing something here, boss.'

'What do you mean me?' said Matachi. 'Do I now take it that you have reverted fully to just picking up the heavy lifting?'

'You're the super sleuth, I leave the cerebral stuff to you; but I will tell you this for fuck all. When two men with swords appear out of nowhere in a vegetable patch, at some sleepy rural village and fight it out over a crisped up old lady and then disappear again without a trace, well, you can take it from me, we are getting into some deep shit here and make no mistake, hello…'

Matachi gave his friend a knowing look, saying, 'I have uploaded all the variables I have found into the program, so let's see what it churns up.'

'You do realise its two-thirty in the morning! I think I have had enough for one night,' said Tekiō.

'Yeah, let's call time on this for today. What was the score on the hotel, are we still able to use it tonight?'

'They said they are staying open when I called them. Looks like they are trying to help out where they can, but not to expect normal service. Stoic of them to stay open considering some of the guests and staff were killed by a falling balustrade trying to escape the building during the quake.'

'Life goes on and we have to sleep somewhere, and there is no way I am sleeping here tonight,' said Matachi.

'Let's go then,' agreed Tekiō, adding, 'What's our plan for tomorrow?'

'I think a visit to your Starlet is in order. Mind you I have no doubt that you have a little more "research" to carry out on her before you go to sleep tonight.'

'What makes you say that?'

'You have your laptop under your arm, I told you I was observant!' said a grinning Matachi.

CHAPTER THIRTY

11 March 2011 20.00

No one had come to rescue of the Nameless Captain from his precarious perch atop the tsunami warning tower. He had now regained consciousness a couple of hours after his body had finally given in. He pulled himself up against the frame of the tower and saw that the waters had all but receded back to the sea, leaving behind a shattered desert of human misery.

All around him lay a wasteland of broken and twisted remnants of human occupation. Cars, trucks and boats were strewn around, all in varying degrees of destruction, mixed in with the destroyed homes, factories and warehouses. The contents that they had once held, now brutally flushed out, to be amalgamated into the all-encompassing landscape of jumbled chaos.

The captain had felt relatively secure in his tower, which was probably the only 'good' that its construction achieved for anyone during the encompassing disaster. It had certainly not helped within its original utility. The sirens had sounded too late, and many people had disregarded its warning blasts, foretelling the impending menace, until the danger had been confirmed by the sea flowing around their feet.

He realised that lingering was no longer an option. With a clear line of sight, he worked out the best place to go to find a new sanctuary. Laboriously, he hoisted himself over the railings, back onto the ladder. The descent was slow and fraught with pain, leading him down to the sprawling landscape of refuse below. The closest position that resembled any form of normality was some higher ground to his left where the small fishing town's buildings began to thin out as they climbed into the banks of the hillside. The high watermark of detritus stopped there, in a band of destruction cutting across the town.

Lowering himself down onto the roof of a large truck, which had come to settle against the tower, he took a final bearing and started his long scramble across the terrain of everyday objects now turned into a gruelling obstacle course.

His route took him past the building where he had seen the abominably horrifying creature, barely two hours before.

He looked at the top balcony, witnessing a red slick running down the wall onto a fabric window awning just below, confirming the realisation that he had not imagined what he witnessed earlier.

Almost exhausted and still bleeding, he started his tangled climb through the massed wreckage of other people's lives. He pulled out a length of scaffolding tube sticking out of a jumble of bricks and stones that looked like they were once part of a house. This movement caused his wound to reopen. To stem the bleeding, he tore off a piece of what was left of his shirt to use as a dressing. Assisted by gripping one end with his teeth, he tied it under and over his shoulder, to bind it as best he could. Grasping the tube again, he began clambering, with some difficulty, over the sea of refuse that had been once his hometown.

Fortunately, although his clothes were in virtual tatters from his ordeal, his robust working boots were still intact. They covered a portion of his lower shins in addition to protecting his feet. Working with the steel tube to probe underfoot for unstable points and as a crutch when he needed to cross uneven areas, he steadily made progress through the surreal landscape.

It took him many hours to cover the three kilometres, in the gradually failing light, to the high-water mark of the horrific tide. During his journey he bore witness to gruesome and sickening sights. Stumbling through the aftermath, he negotiated past numerous corpses and dismembered remains. Each one stood as a grim testament to the tsunami's ferocious power, which had mercilessly torn apart these unfortunate souls.

It was very apparent to him that it was a miracle he had survived at all. If it had not been for the efforts of the inexplicable day worker who had come on board that morning, he realised that he would not have survived even the first few minutes of the catastrophe.

He gave a silent prayer that the man had also managed to survive, yet realising that particular person would be difficult to kill.

As he approached the edge of the great ruinous mess now pressed against the hillside, he was spotted by several groups of people who had congregated in a number of small groups. A mixture of survivors and emergency service personnel, both sets of people still shocked from their experiences, all trying to establish what they should do next.

The nearest people to him picked him out with bright flashlights and started calling to him, guiding him to their position. The effect of making contact with civilisation again, caused the captain to collapse, having reached the limit of most human's normal endurance many hours ago.

He lay back on a bent and twisted aluminium road sign that was partially buried and laying at an angle against a wall of mud and timber, as six people made their way down to meet him. They arrived with a rescue stretcher and gently lifted him onto it. They asked him some cursory questions regarding his condition, which he struggled to answer through fatigue and the onset of shock. Discovering that he was bleeding quite badly from where the hook had torn into his flesh, they carried him away to a temporary treatment centre.

Once in the hands of the emergency medical team, the captain's wounds were treated and he was given some water and a small bowl of thin soup, which was all he could stomach. They began to stabilise him by hooking him up to an antibiotic and albumin intravenous drip, trying to make him as comfortable as possible, and allowing him to rest. The medic's assessment of his condition classified him as a low priority for evacuation to a hospital, compared to less fortunate casualties lying around him. He was safe now, that was all that mattered to him. His body gave out again and he fell into a deep sleep of peculiar dreams; of huge waves that transformed into devils and monsters, that hunted and bore down on him again and again.

He woke the next morning in a feverishly terrified state, to find a medic standing beside him asking for his details. He did not know why, but he gave them a false name and false occupation. He had a dreadful foreboding that he was being hunted down, even though he had survived the storm.

As he lay there contemplating what to do next, looking around the makeshift aid centre, he realised that he had become the focus of an old lady sitting on a camp bed on the far side of the tented enclosure. She looked frail and unsteady even sitting down, holding herself in position with her two hands grasping the head of a walking stick, its tip jabbed into the wooden floor in front of her. As he returned her stare she rose from the bed with some difficulty, using the stick to pull herself upright. She began to slowly shuffle her bent over body to his bedside. Her back was so curved that it kept her face in line with his as she tried to look forwards, the metal tip of her stick stabbing at the floor with each step she took towards him.

She halted beside him. He made no effort to rise in greeting, instead remaining supine, with the IV drip hanging from the cannula in his arm creating a barrier between them. For a few moments, they silently appraised each other's battered forms. Finally, breaking the silence, the woman spoke, 'You have seen it then – more importantly, it has seen you.'

Shocked by her comment, fear gripped his body. 'Go away, you mad bitch,' he hissed at her through swollen lips. 'I have nothing to say to you. Leave me in peace, can't you see I am not well?' He responded by turning his head away from her.

'What I can see is a man who has been touched by the presence of the *Atrocitor*. And if he has a mind to survive then he should take heed of what I have to say.'

'You know nothing about me, I have been through a great ordeal. I just need to recover my strength so I can leave this place. I require nothing other than to be left in peace from the ramblings of a senile old bat, that is all I am looking for,' he said, with his face still turned away from her.

'Ah, yes, you are the tainted one then. Who are you to be calling me an old bat? You pathetic stinking fisherman!'

At this insult, he felt stung, but not by the words, more by the voice that delivered it. It held a very different tone than the old woman's voice of a moment ago. He turned back to face her, but she had gone. Instead before him was a significantly more vital looking female, her stature erect, imposing, with long black hair and emerald green eyes, but the white of the right eye tainted, bright bloodshot red.

'Listen you well to me, captain, if you value your existence. I can help you, if not I will just as happily leave you to a terrible fate, that, have no doubts, fisherman, surely awaits you.'

As he looked at the woman, it was as if he could only focus on her alone, the rest of the room became an opaque shimmering of ethereal shadows. It was as if everyone else had become like ghosts floating around them.

'I am listening,' he replied with some difficulty, as he pulled himself to a sitting position on the bed. He struggled to grasp the unfolding events. His recent experiences had been so bewildering and nonsensical that comprehending them was beyond his reach.

'As I said before, the creature you encountered is called the *Atrocitor*. They have lived between our world and theirs for millennia. They find comfort in the solitude of exploration deep beneath the land, within the cracks and fissures that cross the ground beneath our feet. Its kind has been trapped on this island from the time when the Earth had its last great adaption and created the rift that isolated its homeland on this island. Their objective for thousands of years is for the species to continue until the planet's surface shifts once again. They wish to be free to roam the great expanse of the "Full Lands" once more. They do not kill unnecessarily, just to feed and to protect their anonymity. To survive it must remain elusive, hidden from humankind. When the earthquake started, the movement of the ground drew it out. They have a natural attraction to seismic events, for that is the only thing that can repatriate them. The tsunami must have caught them unawares, the unexpected rushing waters flushing them out. That would have been how you came to encounter one of them.'

He stared at her open mouthed, this cannot be happening to him, perhaps he had gone mad. After all he had been through quite an ordeal. Was this just his mind playing tricks on him?

She stared down at the terrified fisherman. 'If you wish to survive then you need to help me. I need to be within the vicinity of one of these creatures and you can assist me accomplish that. They will only come to the surface for very specific reasons, one of which is to track down those who have seen them. Most who have had such an encounter do not survive; fortunately for both of us you did.'

The captain regained his voice to tell her, 'I can tell you now, for a fact, that you really do not want to be anywhere near one of those things, and I am certain that I have no desire to be anywhere near one again. So, for sure, I am not going to help you.'

'If you don't aid me in this task, then one night very soon, you will die a sudden and brutal death,' she hissed at him. 'You have already witnessed what they are capable of haven't you?'

'Yes, I have seen and that is why I have no intention of ever being in the proximity of one again.'

'You need to get a grip of yourself and most of all you need to trust me. Your only chance of survival is to do as I say, it is that or certain death for you.'

He said nothing in response, a sinking feeling as he accepted his fate, staring directly into her laser-sharp, piercing green eyes. 'You must make your way back to the coast, as soon as you are able,' she continued. 'Do whatever you must to find your way and stay there. The creature will find you there eventually, it has your scent now and that smell to them is like a fingerprint. In the daytime you are relatively safe, they are naturally nocturnal creatures, shy of the sunlight.'

He suddenly remembered the fate of the young family. 'Shy is not a term I would use to describe them; I have seen what they are capable of!' he responded to her angrily.

'Precisely, so make sure you are close to the shore at night, the water will give you some protection. When it does appear, you have my word I will be there, I can assure you its attention will be drawn to me.'

'Great, and what happens to me after it kills you, because I can assure you it will?'

'It won't kill me,' she said with a conviction that unnerved him even more.

'I would not be so confident on that score,' he said unconvinced. 'What do you want from it?'

'I need to deliver a message to it. Once I have done so, it should leave you alone.'

'Should!'

'Very little is totally guaranteed in both our worlds, but I am reasonably confident that it will let you go after I have engaged with it. Believe me, fisherman, it is the best offer you will receive and one that could lengthen your pathetic life.'

The captain looked down at his feet and said, 'I will think about it, I have to...' His sentence was cut short by her interrupting him.

'Get to the port, captain, to the port. I will see you there when the time is right.'

250

He looked up to protest at the demand, but all he saw was the old lady scuttling away from him, her crooked gait making her sway from side to side, as she hurried past the rows of occupied cots, towards the exit, and then she was gone.

CHAPTER THIRTY-ONE

11 March 1967

Kurosawa senior awoke to find Ichirō kneeling by the side of his futon, leaning over him with a hand placed gently on his chest. He had been screaming in his sleep again, every night was a test of his spirit to find at least some rest through the dark hours.

'I am okay now, my son, I am sorry to wake you again.' He took hold of his son's hands and pulled himself upright, he felt the firm grip from his son as he helped him arise. He could just make out the silhouette of his broad outline in the partial twilight, not yet eighteen and already twice the size of his father. Years of training from the best masters he could afford had transformed the child into a formidable young man. In the next few days, the boy would leave for Tokyo to start a degree in engineering, Kurosawa having firmly steered him away from the sciences he had been so keen to study. Japan was becoming a manufacturing powerhouse and he felt his son would find great opportunity there in the future.

'Go back to your room now, Ichirō, I promise I will not wake you again tonight. After all someone with your looks needs his beauty sleep more than I do,' he added, gently chiding his handsome son.

Ichirō forced a smile back at him, barely concealing the deep concern he felt for his tormented father. The war had taken a great toll on him, and it was no secret between them that its horrors revisited him most nights. His father never discussed what he had experienced during the war and Ichirō never asked.

The aftermath of the terrible experiences was written into the faces of all the people of his father's generation who had survived the war. Every adult he knew had locked those memories away deep inside. No one openly talked about it; it was as if the war had never happened. The clock had been reset on Japan, as if the people had accepted their eviscerated state where everything was broken and damaged. Their cities, even the very land itself, contaminated beyond belief. Its culture and society fragmented and the population shattered in a thousand ways.

The greatest damage had been inflicted upon the people themselves. The nation had traversed the extreme bounds of fear, reaching a point where no new terror could surpass the horrors already endured. In response, the community embraced a form of collective amnesia. Together, they resolved to accept their fate and endure the unendurable. Facing the insurmountable, they committed to rebuilding what lay before them. By mutually agreeing to leave the past behind, they turned their gaze towards a brighter future – symbolised by the rising sun.

Ichirō was part of the powerful new world his country was creating. He could see that despite his father's nightly terrors and failing health, he was proud that his son was part of this new vanguard, the one which would rebuild Japan. So, the dutiful son he was, he would never question his father's silence on his activities during the war. It would be many years later that he would have reason to cast those duties aside and have a need to demand answers of his father… but by then it would be far too late, his father would be long dead. The legacy bequeathed to him presented a pressing family dilemma, one that needed resolution to avert potential tragedy. The fate and wellbeing of his children couldn't be left to chance. He was determined to find a way to guide them onto the right path. What shape that path would take to keep them safe, was now his responsibility to solve.

CHAPTER THIRTY-TWO

11 March 2011

Having never regarded himself as a pious man, Uchida gave minor concern regarding the existence of any religion. If there were such things as gods, then they had certainly turned against him recently. During his career he had sequestered many rewards as personal vindications of his success, both professionally and financially. He felt it was just remuneration for the lifetime of hard work he had selfishly given for the success of others. The only deity he paid homage to was his avarice for power. Being wealthy was just a means to an end for him. A lever he used to procure the essential collaboration of business partners and politicians alike, along with a lesser web of willing quislings.

All had benefited from his acquaintance, for he had been generous in his support, and it had taken little persuasion for most of them to join him. They had been willing participants, disposed to aid him by the lure of greed, it allowed their conscience to envision alternative proposals and narrower perspectives in support of his Machiavellian endeavours. Or that had been the case until a few of them began to disappear or wake up headless. That had caused a wave of scrupulous morality to wash over his benefactors. That had indeed caused him difficulties, particularly with his overlords.

He had woken that morning after a sleep of deep reflection on his plan to deal with those issues. However, the unfolding day had brought an abrupt end to those machinations. His problem that afternoon, was that a wave of a very real kind had washed away, literally and figuratively, everything he had built.

The massive tsunami that had struck Japan's coastline, along with its overtly physical destructive impact, also held the capacity to sweep away every structure of concealment he had painstakingly built around his fraudulent realm.

The rushing waters had exposed what to him now seemed so obvious. There was a debilitating level of 'exposure' he had unwittingly designed into his plans. He now desperately needed a fall-back strategy to deal with such an unexpected catastrophic scenario. With the probability of many critical disclosures imminent, a multitude of associates now began to point fingers in his direction. This point had been made very clearly to him by Kwak Kyung-bok, the Korean front man for the most unsavoury of his co-conspirators. The knives were well and truly out now, quite literally in some cases, he understood full well that his associates would bar no belligerence in their effort to protect themselves.

For what had once been easily concealed was currently being revealed by the roaring waters of the tsunami. The calls had started to come in as soon as the catastrophic news was broadcast. A hoard of antagonists had appeared on every horizon, each with a unique reason to denounce him. Exposure to this degree of accusation would be enough to devastate him in its own right, financial ruin and incarceration were more than a possibility, and now even sweet life itself was at risk.

Self-pity had always been one of his many weaknesses. It was the emotion that he usually fell back into at times of crisis. His desperation overwhelmed him, as he washed around in his own sea of despair, being rendered useless by its buffering, as his fellow countrymen had been by the great wave. He emotionally sank, mentally struggling with how he should respond to the dangerous unravelling of his criminally fraudulent schemes.

He was overwhelmed by it all. He started to drink heavily and was soon in a stupor of desolation, wallowing in absolute hopelessness. His mind had begun drifting with one disturbing thought, that the only way out was to go under… quite literally. Japan had had one of the highest suicide rates in the world and, for many, it was still seen as an honourable route for a person to embark on. It was on reaching this decision that his survival instincts kicked in. Uchida's understanding of 'honour' was ethereal at best. He may be old, he thought, but he was still far too young to die, and definitely not by his own hand.

This acceptance of his situation, that he had come to the point of ultimate deterioration, was an important one for Uchida. It was what traumatised people understood as the 'far side of fear' – an antithesis of a Zen-like state. It was a place where a person acknowledged the hopelessness of their situation, but had freed themselves from the shackles of terror and started to act rationally within an irrational environment. This being the true domain of any survivor.

With his thoughts gathered, he pulled on the inflation toggle of his 'life jacket of self-preservation' and shot back up to the surface of reality. The old Uchida was back. He realised that he desperately needed someone to pull into this mess with him, so he could use them as a stepping stone to allow him to climb out of his quagmire of despair.

The first thing he had to do was to eradicate his footprints from everywhere he had been, and his fingerprints from everything he had touched, mainly by fabricating and substituting them for those of others.

He was a firm believer that when 'life provides you with lemons, find someone weaker than yourself and squeeze their juice into their eyes' even if it didn't benefit your current situation. Their discomfort would at least be a distraction to his own problems for a while.

This inherent trait of fierce vindictiveness had consistently proven advantageous throughout his life, and he was confident it would prove beneficial once again in this situation. Blame needed to be shifted, but to whom? Distance had also been created between him and his powerful backers. A firm wedge of isolation needed to be quickly hammered into place between him and them. He had no doubts that very soon after the tragic events had begun to unfold, contingency plans of their own would be coming into robust effect.

With a discriminative eye for the vulnerable, he reviewed the branches of his extensive network. He then proceeded to give this tree of wide-reaching associations a vigorous shake – patsies and scapegoats fell from it like ripe apples in autumn. He selected a few juicy morsels from the medley of low hanging fruit but his problem was the orchard no longer belonged to him. He would need to enlist some extremely unsavoury assistance to reap from it if he were to save himself.

Chapter Thirty-three

12 March 2011

It was the early hours of the morning when the TVs in the villa burst into life of their own volition. A mechanical voice calmly announcing that no one should panic, but a North Korean missile was about to pass into Japan's air space directly above them, then advising that they should make their way to the nearest shelter or reinforced building.

Kurosawa stepped outside into the inner courtyard of the villa, his sister, Azumi, joined him there. In the distance behind them they could hear the sounds of air raid sirens, their doom-laden harmony wailing out of the towns around them.

'You have to be kidding me,' he exclaimed. 'Why by all the gods would they fire their pathetic missiles over us now? It makes no sense.'

'Who knows what goes on in their insular brains?' she answered.

'Besides, I would have thought you would be far too tired after your short swim to be woken by these idiots.'

'Ah, that is so sweet of you to think of me with such endearment, dear sister. But strangely enough it was not the possibility of a nuclear attack that woke me.'

'The wellbeing of my beloved elder brother is always close to my heart,' she said with a mischievous sneer. 'What else troubles the magnificent Kurosawa Hikaru, Liege Lord of the Kurosawa Clan, he who heads the great and powerful force of – two! Aah, could it possibly be love?'

'It's true there is just the two of us but let no one decry the strength of our spirit. And no, it is not love that disturbs me, I feel something is different since the quake. I had thought it was an effect of yesterday's adventures, but it is not that. There seems to be a fresh rawness to the world.'

'Yes, I wondered if you felt it too. There is a change, a shift in the patterns of life. A puzzling vibration, whose difference creates an odd sense of disconcertedness.'

There was a sharp buzz from Azumi's cell phone and she removed it from the pocket of her kimono. She had received an 'emergency text' reiterating the emergency advice to seek shelter from a possible nuclear attack immediately. 'Now that really is disconcerting,' she said sarcastically.

'I suppose it's a type of retribution,' said Kurosawa. 'What goes around comes around.'

'We have paid enough retribution to those dog munchers in the North and the South,' she said and then spat into the sand of the Zen garden.

'Really!' He gave her a disapproving look, for the spitting rather than for her racist political views.

'Sorry, they just make me so fucking angry. The ROK would be nothing if we had not been so driven by guilt that we shared our technology with them – nothing! It would have stayed a desolate war-torn shit hole. It would not have even have become a republic.'

He looked at his sister, realising he was going to now endure one of her political rants.

'And then those cock-sucking puppets in the North, writhing in envy at the economic jewel we had helped Seoul become compared to their Pyongyang pigsty, decide to begin throwing missiles at us not at their fucking cousins in the South. The ones who spend every day rubbing the North's poverty-stricken faces in their avarice materialism; all the while standing behind the Americans shouting, "Fuck you" over the 38th Parallel.'

'Not bitter at all then?' he said, chiding her.

'It's not bitterness, it is just that I do not feel the guilt that you do over our grandfather's deeds – or for that matter Japan's war in general.

'War is war, there are no half measures, you either win or you lose, victims and protagonists fall on all sides, including Korea. Those bastards were in deep and dirty before the war, during it and after it, with both camps as corrupt as each other. When they had finished slaughtering one another, they made a choice. The South picked Dollars and the North chose Dogma, their mentality is still the same. I will never trust either side and Japan should do the same.'

'But that is not the reason why the two of us fight is it, sister? It is just the game we have decided to play. Our destiny and our family's destiny, is a destination that cannot be changed, only the course we take to arrive there is in our control. Always remember the consequence of collective guilt is as dangerous for us as the personal kind. When our grandfather sealed our fate because of his, it became the family weakness, we must not let it consume us as well. If our line is to survive, we cannot be controlled by this great weight of remorse. Whatever we do now we accept it for what it is, our nature. The wolf delivers no atonement to the lamb.'

'So, our penance is to thrive on menace and suffering,' said Azumi matter-of-factly.

'Yes, that is our curse, but we have chosen not to fight it but to work within it. If we do not, then we will be devoured by the very nature of it.'

'It was never much of a choice...' she said.

Kurosawa put both his arms on her shoulders, and looked intensely into her eyes, 'No, but even if it is the only one, it is the right one. We are Japanese, our family's lineage falls back from the two of us into eternity. Mistakes have been made along its path by them and our country, and we must carry the burden our ancestors have laid upon us. We have no option other than to be what we are.'

'What is that – conscionable psychopaths?'

He withdrew his hands saying. 'If you need a label, then wear one, Azumi, I will not. I am what I am, I need no marker to explain – and neither do you. We had no choice other than to accept it. It is the fate we consented to as children.'

'A great deal of what we do could be considered as evil.'

He did not like it when Azumi allowed old resentments to surface.

'There is no such thing as evil, like there is no such thing as good, alone each is as destructive as the other. Only their mutual dilution can bring order.'

'And whose recipe are we following for their concentration, brother, answer me that? Is there so much goodness in our lives that the untold buckets of blood we have spilled into this mix have not swayed its balance somewhat.'

'The pact has kept us alive, and I know you also feel the contentment it brings us. Its steadiness is our indicator, pain for joy, good for bad, laughter for sadness, all in equal measure to the limits of our capacity.'

'Which seems to have no boundary…' she said looking at him sadly.

'A covenant that has kept us from self-destruction.'

'As we well understand, deals with devils never end well, dear brother.'

'I can never understand why you have to keep challenging our situation. Have you ever really thought who is the real devil in this deal?'

Azumi shook her head saying, 'We only have a covenant because their creation turned out to be more powerful than they expected and has now become a threat to them.'

'This way allows us an acceptable existence, not real happiness

I agree, but at least contentment achieved by purpose. We have given ourselves meaning, when the alternative is madness, suicide or execution, each bringing an end to the Kurosawa line. Should that be our legacy?'

Azumi said nothing, they had had this conversation often, they both used it to reset their baseline to accept the covenant they had made, each in their own way. The sirens suddenly ended, leaving a silence that was more intense than the noise that preceded it.

'Japan is vulnerable,' he said.

'Japan is a hiding tiger, concealed amongst the bulrushes, watching its protagonists bare their arses at the reed bed. She looks on them with dispassionate inscrutability, as every day, unseen and unknown, her power and strength increases. And we are committed to protect her from her enemies and herself.'

'While we are on the subject of enemies, what are our next steps?'

'Well, it seems that your fencing partner may have been having quite a busy day when you made his acquaintance. The demise of Matsumoto-san was unexpected. We did not think he knew of anything worth losing his head over. The police are totally involved now including our pet detectives, the ones who found the guy. Their line of enquiries obviously led them to feel there is some connection to the corruption theme they are following. They are playing things quite tight. I am failing to gain access to their reports, that fact itself is a concern for us, these two are more than just ordinary cops.

We will need to keep a close eye on them.'

Kurosawa nodded in agreement. 'Yes, we will,' he said. 'Also, the sending of killers to undertake ritual execution by decapitation sadly went out of vogue quite a while ago. The man I fought was no amateur and far too good to be a Yakuza stooge. He demonstrated skill with the sword that almost equalled my own. That sort of ability does not occur in a person overnight. He was traditionally trained at some point in his life for sure.'

'We've thoroughly checked our databases and found no match for the individual fitting your description. It appears we're at an impasse, unless our colleagues in the detective department can shed some light on this. There's a possibility he's associated with the Koreans, but their motives remain unclear, especially since the others who disappeared were of significant value to them. Without a discernible motive, we're left with more questions than answers.'

'Perhaps another player has entered the game, sister.'

'It is possible, but if he has, then he is not doing us any favours with his Ninja evangelism. If it is his doing, then he has only left us a few leads worth pursuing.

'Besides since the tsunami hit the facility, I suspect the Koreans may start winding down their operations. Not sure what intelligence could be gleaned that would be of any use to them now, if the site is no longer working.

'In the meantime, I have put a measure of extra squeeze on Uchida. With the added pressure of the disaster to deal with, he may make a mistake that could lead us to some new leads, but it is a long shot. I don't think we are going to see a lot of action for quite some time, not until the aftermath of this earthquake is under control, I'm sure. You should take some time off, your little outing to the seaside may have taken more out of you than you think, brother. Go see your mermaid, maybe? I am going to return to the Mill in the morning.'

'No, I have let Ikuko know I am tied up for a few days, so will stick around, I think. But stay vigilant, sister, the unease we feel is unusual, not a common emotion for us. No time to let our guard down.'

'You worry far too much, brother, our guard is never down. As always, we feed the beast.'

'And the beast feeds us,' he unconsciously responded.

CHAPTER THIRTY-FOUR

12 March 2011

The two men stood in the spy's cottage, looking out of the large window of its wooden conservatory, considering the scene of incredible destruction before them. One held a pair of binoculars, the other peered through a high-powered telescope. The great tsunami had now retreated back out to sea leaving in its ravaging wake a chaotic landscape of total obliteration for as far as they could see. 'Are you sure that is the exact location?' said the man looking into the telescope, not taking his eye from the lens.

'One hundred per cent,' replied Kim Jin-sung, the spy who conducted his operations from the cottage. Lowering the binoculars he said, 'I recorded the exact position of it by zooming the telescope in and locking it into position.'

'So, you are confident that it is under this huge mound of crap?' questioned the man behind the telescope. He continued to scrutinise the dome of twisted trees, crushed cars, and the smashed remains of people's homes, that looked no different to the hundreds of similar mounds within the panoramic vista of destruction that lay across the land below them.

'And you have noticed no one coming to inspect the area?'

The whole area before them was filled with what looked like the bulldozed ridges of a landfill waste dump, coupled with the menacing profile of the smoking nuclear plant beyond it, presenting a truly apocalyptic scene.

A large team of workers wearing high-visibility protective clothing, accompanied by an assembly of bulldozers, had already worked its way down the access road towards the nuclear site. Re-opening the road was seen as a top priority for the authorities and they had been working around the clock in their efforts to clear it.

'No one,' firmly answered Kim. The man standing beside him was his controller; Kim knew him as Kwak Kyung-bok. The fact he would not normally take the risk of visiting at home underscored the gravity of the situation. 'This lot started steadily working their way to the site almost immediately after the waters had receded. But they carried on past the spot where the vehicle is buried without stopping to investigate. I am certain that no one in authority knows it is there.'

The man stopped peering through the telescope and walked to the kitchen table. Scattered across it were some very good images of the transporter and its cargo as it moved out of the site. He was joined by his colleague, who picked up one of the images and nodded knowingly to the man. There was no doubt in their minds what this was. Informants within the facility had already told them of the intended removal of the enriched uranium. Normally this information would just be logged along with all the other data they gathered on the facility. Information used by their intelligence agencies to build a picture of how this particular reactor site functioned and operated was very valuable to their own country's atomic development. In addition to this they were tasked in finding out the scope of Japan's potential nuclear weapons capability.

North Korea was engaged in a complex strategic game against Japan, its historical adversary and conqueror. Despite Japan's present constitution advocating non-aggression, it possessed the latent capability to rapidly develop an array of effective nuclear weapons, outpacing anything North Korea could feasibly achieve.

He understood that despite his country's aggressive rhetoric, without access to substantial quantities of high-grade uranium necessary for hydrogen bomb production, they would never instil the level of fear in their age-old enemy that they desired.

Yet, who could have imagined stumbling upon an opportunity as extraordinary as the one presented before them? They would have to move fast and extremely carefully to extract the flask under the noses of those Japanese fools. The framework for the extraction plan was already underway. It was based around taking advantage of the confusion and disarray that had been wrought by the disaster across the prefecture. It had been his own idea to use the situation to mask their operation, and to his considerable pleasure, the principle of the operation had already been approved by his superiors.

As they moved into the planning stage, however, there were some very real complications that would need to be resolved if his idea was to work. Many of their informants were no longer able to re-enter the site, so up-to-date information had been sketchy since the accident. Reports from the few spies left within the Fukushima facility indicated that they were losing the battle to control three of the site's six reactors, numbers One, Two and Three. The general conjecture coming from the media supported the intelligence on the ground. There were rumours that the auxiliary cooling systems for all three were failing due to lack of power. They had already vented contaminated steam into the atmosphere numerous times, an attempt to release some of the pressure building up in the reactor's cores.

On the one hand he saw this as fortuitous, it would pile further pressure onto the authorities thereby keeping them occupied. However, if the plant went super critical, that could cause them some serious grief. This prospect of an even greater catastrophe was already causing some concern with the authorities, but due to the overwhelming problems of dealing with the general destruction from the tsunami, they had been slow to react to the issues of radioactive contamination. However, if the reactor went critical and exploded, then they would undoubtedly shut everything down and fully evacuate everyone from the surrounding area, including emergency personnel. If that happened, it would greatly affect the efficacy of their plan.

He put down the photograph and returned to the telescope once more, this time surveying the Fukushima Facility itself. Smoke and steam rose above and between its buildings and several helicopters hovered above it.

One extremely good piece of news emerging from the facility was, as far as anyone was aware, no one had raised the question of the whereabouts of the extracted fuel rods. They must be working under the assumption that the material had been removed to the fuel rod holding area. A cursory check of its inventory would verify the rods were not there. As no full-scale search of the area had yet taken place, the men assumed that due to the massive emergency of a potential nuclear meltdown of one or more of the cores, coupled with erratic communications with dispersed staff, they had so far not discovered the major deficit.

However, both men fully understood that 'assumption' was the unadulterated mother of all fuck-ups. That being said, there was no doubt that a genuine window of opportunity had presented itself. If they acted swiftly, they could feasibly secure a significant quantity of the plutonium-enriched uranium. Consequently, all available resources were being redirected under his command. Their nation's nuclear programme had been struggling, barely managing to produce minimal amounts of plutonium through its slow, inefficient uranium enrichment process using centrifuges, and from their few under-performing experimental reactors. Now, acquiring the elusive flask and bringing it into Korean possession had become the top priority for the Hermit Kingdom. He was aware that the Supreme Leader was closely watching their efforts, demanding hourly updates. Kwak was acutely conscious of the dire consequences awaiting them all if they failed in this high-stakes operation.

At that very moment units were mobilising across Japan to

come to their assistance. It would not be for lack of support that this venture would fail, in truth he was very optimistic of its success. On extremely short notice, they had envisioned a plan capable of delivering success. There was the inevitable trade off, caused by the immediate timescales they would be working to, meaning that sacrifices would have to be made to accomplish their ambitious goals. Their strategy hinged on decisively eliminating any hindrances that might jeopardise the mission's success, irrespective of the associated costs. He and his commanders concurred that they needed to abandon any facade of subtlety in their tactics. The primary goal was the acquisition of the enormous nuclear flask and securing it for Korea. To this end, they were prepared to make any sacrifice necessary to ensure the success of the operation.

Short term solutions to local issues were to be executed wherever it was deemed necessary to support the success of the assignment. The implications of such actions on their current initiatives on the Japanese mainland, were now regarded as irrelevant. Espionage programmes that had been running for years involving the 'big seven' – infiltration, surveillance, subversion, coercion, kidnap, assassination and sabotage – could be stripped of any resource on his authority alone if required.

Indeed, there were many loose ends that needed to be urgently cut away, regardless of any future repercussions. Uchida was now becoming an obvious and immediate liability. The man was engaged in frenetic activity in an attempt to save himself, but it would be to no avail. Matsumoto's disclosures had been the final element that had sealed his fate.

The partnership with Uchida had been immensely beneficial for both sides over the years. Uchida, a master of manipulation and deception, skilfully maintained a low profile while weaving his intricate network of corruption. His profound influence in political and business circles initially drew them to him, and a mutually advantageous relationship was established. Through their extensive interactions, he had become an invaluable asset within Japan's nuclear industry. However, this dynamic began to shift when the full extent of the information that Matsumoto had acquired came to light.

The situation revealed that Uchida had grown overly confident in his ability to control his surroundings. He had fallen victim to the hubris that often ensnares those in power, developing a disdainful attitude towards those he manipulated. While such carelessness was unacceptable in their eyes, his value might have compelled them to help him navigate through these complications. However, the unforeseen geological event, with the distraction it caused in his operations and the opening it presented to them, sealed Uchida's fate. There was no chance of redemption for him now. They had already sent one of their best operatives to eliminate him at the first viable opportunity. The greater priority now was the damning information that the now deceased Matsumoto had compiled. Any evidence of Korean collusion with Uchida had to be urgently found and destroyed. Execution squads had already been brought in to clean that particular mess up along with the removal of the snooping reporter, Kurosawa Azumi. Yet another of Uchida's failures, who seemed impotent in preventing the brazen journalist from asking far too many sensitive questions. Their standard orders in this type of operation were to keep any elimination as low key as possible. They had been given unprecedented autonomy to do whatever they considered appropriate in accomplishing their task. One of the teams had been working on infiltrating the reporter's home for some time and were well advanced in their preparations.

These were all distractions that had to be dealt with immediately, although not to the detriment of the 'Extract Team' they were now assembling. Removing these annoyances would give them the space they needed to operate in the short term and free up the greatly needed manpower.

The technical aspects of this elite unit had been expediently brought together to find and remove the flask. Every Korean agent on the Japanese mainland had now been reassigned to some aspect of this mission. All operatives were highly trained individuals, able to adapt quickly and effectively to new environments. He had scant doubt that before this episode was over, the task before them would test their capabilities beyond the limits foreseen by the motherland.

'When will the Extraction Team be ready to go in?' asked Kim, interrupting the man's thoughts.

'Some are already here, infiltrating the emergency response units. The main convoy arrives tonight. It left Tokyo this afternoon and you will be kept fully informed of any changes. You understand that your role as overseer to this mission is now vital. For the next few days, twenty-four-hour observation is your designated role. To assist you I have assigned some support who will be with you directly.'

'That would be most helpful, sir, thank you. How long do you think it will take to complete the mission?'

'The extraction of the flask must be completed by tomorrow evening. The final part of the plan will take considerably longer, at least a week. There is much work to be done after we secure the flask; it will also take time for the offshore assets to mobilise and come into position without causing any suspicion.'

'This will be a great achievement when we have accomplished it, probably the greatest in the history of our nation since we drove the Imperialist dogs out of the North.'

'Yes, it will be a great accomplishment, and have no concerns that your part in this venture will be recognised and rewarded.'
'Thank you, sir, but serving the Supreme Leader is reward enough,' said Kim, giving the correct response to his superior.
'Of course, that requires no confirmation, his eyes are always wide open,' said Kwak, his voice holding a note of trepidation. He knew too well what the consequences of failing the Dear Leader would be.

Kim gulped involuntarily, totally understanding the gravity of the situation and the terrible penalties that would follow failure.

Kwak saw the impact of his statement on the man and tempered it with a tight smile, saying, 'Good fortune, Kim, I will return in a few days' time. In the meantime, keep me fully appraised of developments through the normal channels.'

CHAPTER THIRTY-FIVE

13 March 2011

The detectives had traced Ikeda Fuyuko, aka Luluero, to the Motochi area, south of Fukushima City. It was getting dark when they arrived at the new residential block on the edge of town. They pulled up at the end of the block and walked back to the entrance. They looked along the list of residents on the intercom list, found the name there of Ikeda Fuyuko and pressed the buzzer alongside it. Both holding their badges up to the CCTV camera they pressed it a few more times, with still no response.

'Let's sit in the car, finish our noodles and wait a while,' said Matachi.

'I'm not that hungry,' lied Tekiō.

Matachi, shook his head at him dismissively, realising his partner was having one of his conflicting eating moments. 'Sure you're not,' he said. He headed back to the car. 'Let's not waste them though, I will finish yours off for you, how's that?' He never felt guilty about abusing Tekiō, especially around his eating disorder.

Tekiō said nothing just following behind Matachi, wondering how much pressure he would have to generate if he held his head between his hands to make his best friend's eyes pop out.

Half an hour later, just as Matachi was noisily finishing off

Tekiō's noodles, he saw in the rear view mirror a girl wearing a beige trench coat, open at the front, revealing a figure-hugging miniskirt and crop top. She had a swing bag under her arm and wore knee high boots with ridiculously high block heels and soles, making her seem far taller than she actually was.

Matachi slurped in the last of the noodles and dropped the disposable chopsticks into the cardboard noodle box, throwing it onto the dash.

'That's our girl,' he said.

Just as she approached her apartment block entrance, she stopped to take a phone out of her bag and answered a call. She said a few words, then returned the phone, and carried on walking past the apartment block, turning down a side street just in front of them.

'Strange...' said Matachi.

Getting out of the car Tekiō said, 'Bring the car around to pick us up, while I detain her.'

Tekiō fell in about twenty metres behind the woman and began walking swiftly after her. Matachi started the car up and began to turn it around, looking to pull into the street ahead of them so they could quickly get her into the car once Tekiō had detained her.

'Pardon me, miss,' said Tekiō, trotting up to within five metres of the girl. He got no response, instead she increased her pace slightly and seemed preoccupied with her handbag. He tried again to attract her attention. He was now steadily gaining on her, a couple more strides and he would be right behind her. Now within almost touching distance on her left side, he tried to hail her again.

'Miss, excuse me, miss, please don't be alarmed I am a police officer,' he called as he reached out to gently put a hand on her arm. Then the lights went out.

★ ★ ★

Later, in the local hospital's emergency centre, a doctor was having a detailed discussion with Tekiō, explaining the complex effects of a Taser hit on the human body. The doctor emphasised that an individual's physical bulk was just one of many factors influencing the Taser's impact. Using charts and models the doctor illustrated how the Taser's effect varied depending on a range of elements, highlighting the diversity in individual susceptibility regardless of size. The place was bustling with medical activity, but both the doctor and Tekiō were focused intently on their conversation.

The doctor pointed out that if you were to put the results of all the Tasering events in the world into a graph, you find at one end, maybe one or two per cent would be very susceptible, sustaining serious injuries and/or death, in the middle would be the vast majority who would just collapse, their nervous systems disrupted and overwhelmed by the fifty thousand volts passing through them and at the far end you would have those who it would have hardly any effect on. These were a type of human super insulators, walking Faraday cages in effect.

Luckily for Tekiō he was not sitting in the more susceptible end of the scale, had not died, but neither was he immune to such devices. He felt that his sheer size, not to mention his strong constitution, should have protected him. The only cages he knew of were the ones where you took an opponent on, and if he had met this 'Faraday' in one, he would have gone down hard and fast.

The doctor realised that his patient was not making a great deal of sense. He surmised that it was possible that the man was suffering from the after-effects of his incident, or it could be that he was just an idiot. The man was a police officer after all. He prudently kept these thoughts to himself, this one was distinctly a larger than normal specimen and clearly from even the brief conversation they had, he deduced that man had more than a strong predisposition towards violence. The doctor resumed the stitching up of Tekiō's forehead, as he continued to patiently explain to him, for the third time, that the fact that he had never once been knocked out in all of his Sumo career, having fought in hundreds of contests, was irrelevant. His nervous system was very average, the type that did not much like having billions of electrons fired into it for several seconds.

Tekiō lay on the bed and was about to slip another proviso into the doctor's thesis, when Matachi came through the treatment room door. He looked fresh and clean, flashing multi-coloured cufflinks at the ends of his crisp, white shirt sleeves, where the bright cuffs protruded beyond yet another tailored suit; this one with a silver sheen that changed shades as the harsh lights of the treatment bay played on its fabric.

'Ouch,' he said, coming to the bedside and holding one hand across his jacket so his bright red, pencil-thin tie didn't swing onto the bloodied dressings laid out on the paper shroud of the suture kit that was open across Tekiō's chest.

He inspected the row of stitches running down the right side of his forehead. 'Looks painful, is it?'

'What do you think?' said Tekiō trying not to move.

Matachi considered the doctor's handiwork, as the medic continued to methodically suture the wound. He confidently slid the curved needle through the two edges of flesh, finishing the procedure with a short flurry of coordinated finger movements to complete and precisely place the knot.

'Do you realise, Tekiō, you're the only guy I know who, by the action of smacking his head on the floor, could actually improve his looks,' said a grinning Matachi. 'I would say at the very least, the doc's fine work here has taken a few wrinkles out.'

'Should have seen the other guy,' countered Tekiō.

'Ah yes, the "itsy bitsy" slip of a girl you nearly killed.'

'People should not go around willy-nilly zapping policemen,' said a wincing Tekiō, as the final suture went in.

'You know for a moment there I thought she had got away. I looked up and down the street, thinking where the hell had she disappeared to, but all I could see was your groaning body slumped on the floor – but no sign of her! How peculiar I thought, there was no way she could run far in that outfit. A mini mystery right there on the sidewalk. Then the great detective that I am, by the power of positive deduction, realised what had happened to the poor girl… you'd eaten her!' exclaimed a laughing Matachi. 'I must admit, I felt really guilty then for having taken those noodles off you earlier. It troubled me that by withholding such sustenance from you, I had pushed you over the edge like that.' Matachi gave him another toothy grin.

'You really are a bit of an arse, aren't you, boss?' said Tekiō.

'Okay, but at first it really did look like you had devoured her. Your body showed a suspicious bulge as you lay there; I saw slightly more of a curve to your lower back than normal. Anyone else other than a great detective such as my good self would have missed that clue you know,' he said with a wry smirk.

'How is she?' asked Tekiō.

'She will be fine; she had managed to roll herself into the foetal position as you collapsed on top of her and your gut sort of absorbed the girl into it without crushing her too much. She was reasonably well asphyxiated though; your blubbery belly had made a pretty good airtight seal around her you see. Anyway, forget about your concerns for her, what about me? I'm telling you my back will never be the same again after levering you off her, you fat fucker!'

'Can't see how it is my fault that you are a spindly little weakling, I've seen more muscle on a Sakanaya's shop floor, and those bastards are tight, they waste nothing,' said Tekiō, feeling that he had to try and defend his size. 'You clearly couldn't have tried that hard – there is not a mark on your suit.'

'Give me a lever and I will move the world, Aristotle,' said Matachi.

'Harri who?' said a puzzled Tekiō. 'Why am I being continually quoted about people I know nothing about?'

'I pulled up one of your arms, locked it against the joints like you showed me with that Aikido stuff, pulled back against your shoulder and over you went and out she popped! It was beautiful, like a giant walrus giving birth.'

Tekiō called to the doctor, who had now completed his suturing and was tidying up the detritus from sewing his head back together. 'Hey Doc, don't go just yet, I may have another job for you.' He scowled at Matachi, the new vivid scar on his head giving an added touch of menace to his face. Matachi ignored the intimidation and carried on with his story.

'And that's not all, then I had to give her CPR to resuscitate her. She was well on her way to the land of her forefathers I'm telling you; as anybody would, having their head pressed into your groin for any length of time.'

'Boss, did you give the kiss of life? Mouth to mouth like?' said Tekiō with a sudden evil smirk on his face.

'Yes, why?'

'You do realise she is a porn star, don't you?'

'And?'

'Oh nothing, but do you really think your theory is right about the HIV thing? Stand by it, do you?'

'Just fuck off,' said Matachi, heading for the door. 'I'm going to have a word with the girl and try not to fall over again. You may look like a Weeble but you don't tend to roll back upright when they push you over!' he declared, as he stormed off down the corridor.

Tekiō lay back on his bed, alternately wincing and laughing, as the doctor shook his head at him.

CHAPTER THIRTY-SIX

13 March 2011

Uchida had masterfully woven through the ethereal framework that propelled his ascent to power. Emerging from a crippling depression, he immersed himself in a meticulous strategy to reclaim his influence. His shrewd manoeuvres had brought in key players to operate almost exclusively under his directives. Uchida skilfully negotiated with the bankers, buying time as he strategically liquidated assets from his offshore ventures. Although these actions would yield minimal profit, he accepted this as a necessary compromise. His priorities had undergone a radical shift; now, avoiding prison – or securing his very survival – outweighed any financial gains. This was a reality Uchida was prepared to embrace, as long as it kept him out of jail and alive.

In the days following the earthquake, more details of the damage caused by the series of giant waves that hit the two nuclear sites on the Fukushima coast became evident. Fukushima II had managed to safely shut down its four reactors and had not been seriously affected by the rising waters. However, the condition of the Fukushima I plant was far graver. Although it too had managed to shut down all of its six reactors, the units had been totally swamped by the waters that breached the sea barriers, again and again. He was not expecting the catastrophic news that followed this event. The reactors had started to go into meltdown, unquestionably a direct consequence of the flaws in the design which had allowed the critical areas to flood. The significant impact of losing auxiliary power, preventing the emergency system to operate, being one of the main issues.

Confronted with the inevitable fallout of these issues, he opted to defer their resolution to another day, prioritising more urgent matters related to his immediate well-being. Uchida had set in motion a series of strategies aimed at mitigating the current crisis, and it appeared that these manoeuvres were starting to bear fruit. Just as he was beginning to gain a semblance of confidence in his precarious situation, unforeseen developments started to emerge, adding new layers of complexity to his already challenging circumstances.

Followed by the sudden demise of Matsumoto – there was always someone who just could not keep their head in challenging situations, but Matsumoto had rather taken that adage to the extreme. The two clowns masquerading as detectives had almost wet themselves with excitement when they had discovered the hapless executive.

He had been told by his informants within the local police force, that in fact one of them had managed to slightly contaminate the crime scene with his clumsiness. He evidently had not been in possession of the single brain cell they shared between them; the more confusion they caused the better as far as he was concerned.

A larger issue had been that following his destruction of Matsumoto's political aspirations, the man had attempted to report the issue up the political chain. Unfortunately, the person he took his allegations to were on Uchida's pay role. The same individual had participated in creating a scenario that caused Matsumoto's downfall. After carefully listening to Matsumoto's tale, Uchida's lackey started personally berating him on what a fool he was in what he was trying to do.

Matsumoto had taken offence at that, which his associate

found amusing, and openly started laughing in Matsumoto's face. This had been far too much for Matsumoto to take, losing his temper completely, he had pulled out a data stick and waved it in front of his associate's face. He told him in no uncertain terms that he should savour this moment of hilarity, so he could remember it when he and the rest of his gang of swindling, corrupt swine were behind bars. Their treason would lose its amusement when it put them all in prison. He emphasised that he had enough information to stop them laughing for a very long time.

After his outburst, if Matsumoto had not turned up dead, it wouldn't have been long before he met his demise. That problem had been solved for him by somebody else, but the whereabouts of that memory stick was now paramount.

Having informed Kwak of the situation, Matsumoto's home had been thoroughly searched, not only by the police, but also by Kwak's men, but no trace could be found of the missing data stick. It was possible that it was in his office at the Municipal Civic Building, so a plan was being devised to search that as well. The fact that Matsumoto had made the accusation of treason indicated that he had at least an idea of what was going on. If the man knew of nothing else, that fact alone was extremely concerning. There was also the possibility that it had been removed from the crime scene by the assassin after he was murdered. From what Uchida could gather, it appeared to have been some sort of ritual execution of Matsumoto, though the apparent lack of any visible struggle was a perplexing prelude to such a violent killing. It led him to the conclusion that Matsumoto had accepted his fate. It was even possible that he may have knelt before his nemesis, willingly accepting his macabre lot. Then there had been the failed attempt to remove Professor Takeuchi's head. He had fleetingly entertained the thought of eliminating her himself. However, he had imagined a more subtle end than beheading, such as an overdose of her own medication perhaps or some sort of induced heart attack.

Well, that was out of the question now, with not one, but possibly two, psychopathic sword-wielding maniacs running feral across the prefecture!

Security surrounding the woman was stringent, demanding a degree of violence to reach her that, at present, didn't justify her elimination. Uchida, aware of this delicate balance, sought to meticulously orchestrate every facet of the situation, including the body count. He understood that there existed a threshold for unremarkable accidents and mysterious deaths before they aroused undue suspicion – a limit he anticipated needing in full to tie up his own unresolved issues.

He was certain that these assaults would not be mistaken for accidents. Millennia had passed since sword-based violence was considered acceptable behaviour. Yet, it was with a mix of disbelief and contempt that he realised these violent acts were the least of his worries. Disturbingly, it had come to light that some of Plant I's uranium was either missing or, at the very least, untraceable in their records.

There was of course an in-depth investigation being carried out, where all employees had been questioned and asked to give statements concerning their understanding of events on that day. Details of the damage caused by the series of giant waves that hit the two sites were still rather vague, but it transpired that a fuel cell exchange was in process when the wave hit. Some of the surviving members of a fuel cell recovery unit explained for safety reasons they had placed the uranium rods inside a protective flask and loaded it onto a transporter vehicle. The whereabouts of this vehicle was still as yet unknown. Any CCTV data recorded around the majority of the site had been destroyed. Robotically controlled machinery was just starting to be used in and around the epicentre of the exploding reactor, and it was just possible that the transporter and its precious cargo had somehow been driven into this area and that traces of it could possibly be discovered there.

There was also a possibility that it had been washed into

the waters beyond the dock area. This was being checked via the use of submersible robotic vehicles, though it was deemed unlikely that even the power of the tsunami could have taken such a heavy vehicle back towards the Pacific.

The situation was already shocking, but it took a graver turn when it was revealed that this was no ordinary uranium; it was enriched with weapons-grade plutonium. This distressing reality sharpened the focus of many, especially considering his connections with known felons. Uchida had successfully convinced the concerned parties to keep the details under wraps until a comprehensive grasp of the situation was achieved. Having secured control over the dissemination of this critical information, it was now imperative for them to maintain their grip on it. Controlling the narrative surrounding these calamitous events was essential for steering towards any favourable outcome.

CHAPTER THIRTY-SEVEN

13 March 2011

'Ikeda-san, how are you now? You are looking greatly improved on your earlier condition,' Matachi enquired of the porn star, who had earlier been crushed by Tekiō. She was being treated in another cubicle, a few rooms down from where his partner was being attended to.

She gave no response to his question, not even seeming to acknowledge his presence. He changed tack to something less sympathetic.

'You do realise that assaulting a police officer is a serious offence?' he said, his tone slightly harsher, with just a subtle hint of menace.

This seemed to at least get his presence acknowledged. She now looked at him from the corner of her eyes only, her head remaining resting on a stack of pillows as she lay back on the bed. She had an IV hooked up to her right arm and a pulse monitor on her left index finger. Her makeup had been removed from her face which made her appear very plain. Incredible what a dash of war paint can do for someone, Matachi thought. He would not have given her a second glance on the street. She now looked nothing like the pictures Tekiō and he had seen online, but then he imagined everyone looks different without a dick in their mouth.

This distasteful vision began to make hin[...]
as he recalled what Tekiō had happily reminded [...]
moments ago. He was not so much worried about catch[...]
disease from resuscitating her, it was more the thought tha[...]
knew where her mouth had been… He tried to suppress the
memories of the pornographic images he had witnessed and
got back to trying to get her to talk.

'Particularly as you tasered him. The possession of which is
also a criminal act.'

'It's not illegal to own one, you fuck-witted plod, just to use
it. And if your friend Jabber, had not chased me down the street
and assaulted me, I would not have had to zap him, would I?'
She spat the words at him with real venom, like someone who
was used to dealing with difficult situations.

He realised that his intimidation tactics were not going so
well; it was time to change his approach, he thought. He opened
the cover of his tablet and pulled up her file which he had
downloaded from the police criminal data base. The picture of
her there was one of the few they had found that did not include
any form of genitalia in the shot – she must have been on her
day off when they took it, he thought.

'We could still charge you,' he said, 'assault with a deadly
weapon. I see from your file that you have a couple of convictions
for drugs and prostitution offences.'

'Girl's gotta make a living,' she responded contemptuously.

'It would not look good for you,' he continued, 'if a charge of
GBH against a police officer in the legal course of his duty was
added to your rap sheet.'

'If you were going to book me you would have done it by
now, so save the warmup act for the cretins you shake down
on the street. Your human blimp back there nearly killed me, so
my counter claim for police brutality would tie you two fuckers
up in litigation until the hairs on your balls turned grey. Look
you, I get to deal with a lot of arseholes in my business, so I
know one when I smell one. Though you impress me as more of

arsehole. So, what the fuck do you want from
‥‥y?'

‥‥tachi closed the cover on the tablet. 'We are looking for some information on a Korean called Kwak Kyung-bok. We have sightings of you meeting him at a number of areas around Fukushima City.'

She was about to respond with some other witty profanity but checked herself. There, for the briefest of moments, he thought he saw some emotion other than anger ripple across her face. 'I know a few Koreans but none with that name,' she finally replied.

Matachi reopened his tablet and flicked his fingers across it. 'Here,' he said, 'do you recognise this man?' holding the tablet for her to look at. He knew she had no choice other than to say yes, he had lied about the sightings with Kwak , but she didn't know that.

'Yeah, I know him, we had a few dates together, nothing steady, you know just some laughs.'

'You mean he was a client of yours?' declared Matachi.

'Like I said, a girl has gotta make a living, it's a tough out there. Not many favours found in my life, nothing is for free, even love,' she replied defensively.

'Not really what one would call love is it, more like services provided…'

'What the fuck would you know about it, "Hikikomori Boy", you've spent far too long sitting in front of that TV firing off your "wrist rocket". I can tell by your skin; it's got that grey tinge that comes off the flare of one of those oversized high-definition screens. You don't get out a great deal, do you? I would guess that the closest you got to love was a virtual relationship with some distorted "Manga Bitch" with a wasp-shaped arse, a waist narrower than your granny's mind and tits up to her chin,' she almost shrieked at him.

'I think you are mistaking me for a member of your admiring fan club,' Matachi retorted.

To give her credit she had hit the mark somewhat, but there

had been scant time for Manga stories when you are writing a PhD, though he had, and still did, spend a great deal of time in front of a computer screen.

'Enough about me, your boyfriend, tell me his name?' Again, a slight hesitation before answering, 'Okay, it's him, Kwak , Kwak Kyung-bok, that's what he told me anyway. He did not strike me as any sort of criminal, he was just after some companionship, shits and giggles, you know, and a fuck now and again. Why, what's he done?'

'Nothing illegal as far as we know, we just need to find him so we can ask him some questions. Merely clearing up some loose ends, you know how it is with cops, we like things neat and tidy. Where can we find him?'

'Blind Stag,' she said.

'Where's that?' asked Matachi, making a note on his tablet with its stylus.

'*No eyed deer*, dummy. Are you sure you're a cop, because you're thicker than a Gurkha's foreskin, you know that!' She started laughing at her jokes.

Matachi was not amused. He turned his stylus over and ran the electronic eraser over what he had written on the tablet. 'You're so funny, you really should be on TV. Oh, I forgot, you are, and you are actually fucking hysterical. My favourite scene is the one where you are co-starred with that greased-up pig by the way.'

She stopped laughing and changed her tone. 'I don't know where he is, he has not contacted me for a few weeks, and we only meet up at hotels that he chooses. It's a shame he's not been around though, he's a good customer.'

'Ah, that special love that never fades,' he responded, now looking down at her from alongside her bed. 'What does he do for a living? His occupation?'

She picked at the sticky tape around the cannula needle in her arm, not looking at him she said, 'He told me he works freelance for telecoms companies, travelling around a lot, selling data packages, he tried to explain it, but it all sounded like nonsense to me.'

'Which companies did he work for?'

'He did not say, and I did not ask, who cares about that boring shit. I'm not interested where they make their money only that they have it, and the more of it they have the better I like it, okay. Hey, that's some nice threads you have on there. Armani? Looks like my Korean friend is not the only one to have a bit of coin, right? Maybe you would like to party later? After all I was not really that conscious the last time you made some advances on me.'

Matachi made a distasteful face, remembering what Tekiō had said earlier, he made a mental note to really 'thank him' later for it.

'It is tailored Dior, and thanks but no thanks. I am going to need a complete list from you of all the places that you met Kwak-san, including dates, times and how long you spent in each other's company.'

'What's wrong, detective? Go on, give building that robot in your bedroom a break for one night. Hey, get a whiff of this.' She lifted the thin blanket to her chin and wafted it up and down. 'It's called gi...rrrr...lll,' she drawled as she raised the blanket to just below her eyes and tried to look at him with a provocative innocence.

He locked onto her gaze as she failed to pull off the pretence, unable to mask the unsavouriness of her character from shining through her attempted façade. Matachi looked at her red-rimmed eyes void of makeup, noticing a hint of jaundice around the whites. She looked more Hammer Horror than Betty Boop, he thought. Patently not one for the live performances then, the close-ups he had seen of her face in her explicit videos had captured her looking a lot younger, the magic of television he supposed.

'The sooner we get started the quicker you can go, unless you would rather do this at a police station?'

'I thought you said to me that you knew where we had been meeting?' she challenged.

'Let's see if your list matches mine, shall we, if nothing else, I'm always up for a bit of cross referencing,' he said with a slight smirk on his lips.

She gave a disgruntled snort and then began answering his questions.

CHAPTER THIRTY-EIGHT

11 March 1988

It was late in the evening at the end of a warm summer's day and Kurosawa Ichirō was trying to help his wife and daughter clear away the pots and dishes from their supper. The meal had been the usual nightly affair, when their happy little family group came together to discuss the gossips of their day. That was except for Hikaru, who now seemed to become more and more withdrawn. As he had matured into a young man, he had without a doubt developed a distinct melancholy, conduct his father advised his wife was just some typical teenager behaviour. His weak attempt to deny to her and moreover himself the deeper concerns he held for his son.

Never having a great deal to say at dinner times, his demeanour was one of a sulky, introvert individual who had not really altered greatly from when he was a child. However, he seemed content in his own world, and as long as he remained polite and courteous, he was left to be himself. Tonight, he was different somehow, consuming his meal mechanically in almost total silence. Far more withdrawn than normal. Later, when the meal was finished, he quickly excused himself to his room, leaving the clearing up to the rest of the family.

At a knowing glance from his wife, Ichirō said nothing in chastisement at this rudeness, instead changed the mood by deliberately getting in the way of the two women clearing up. He was soon being chided by his wife and daughter for his interference in their practised, efficient routines of cleaning and tidying everything away. He continued to tease them on purpose, banging the pots together and accidentally dropping bits of food onto the floor, making light of it all as he did so, laughing and pulling buffoon faces behind his wife's back, making his daughter Azumi giggle. His wife looked at him as he acted the clumsy oaf, bumping into his daughter next to the sink, both of them now sniggering together.

He was no clumsy oaf, that was for sure, but he was the sweetest loving human she had ever known. He was the lightning rod of happiness that held the family together. Finally, she lost her patience and sent him to collect more logs for the wood burning stove. The night was getting chilly, and they loved to sit around the fire after supper before retiring to bed. Ichirō went out to where a neat, long row of firewood was stacked against the side of the house near the kitchen, a mosaic artwork of taupe timber ends, each one precisely cut to the same length. He was starting to fill the small basket when he heard a slight sound coming from the other side of the Zen garden. Out of the gloom near the far wall, he saw three figures approaching the house, all of them coming to a halt at the edge of the sunken garden. Each man was dressed in a smart suit with a colourful necktie secured with a ridiculously large knot. He faced them saying nothing. He could hear his wife and daughter still loudly chatting in the kitchen. He did not know the reason for their presence, and he did not care. Three men had come uninvited, climbed over his wall, trespassing onto his property. Though he had no idea what they wanted, he knew exactly what they were about to get. He shifted slightly to face them, still holding the small basket of logs in his left hand.

'Don't do anything you might not live to regret, old man,' warned the man directly opposite him, his face wearing a leering lopsided grin.

The smiling man dropped down into the Zen garden, while his two accomplices walked along the enclosure towards the other side of the house, both lightly skipping down the steps that led onto the wooden training area. He then began to walk through the freshly raked sand that Ichirō had meticulously created earlier that evening, uncaringly kicking through the elegant waves. He stopped suddenly with a cry, as a seasoned lump of oak log hit him squarely in the face. He fell to his knees and spat out what was left of his grin into the sand from the force of the blow. He looked at the blood-splattered sand in disbelief, before him lay the ivory shards of several of his front teeth. He forcefully expelled the remaining blood-stained fragments from his mouth. Simultaneously, his right hand swiftly moved beneath his jacket, deftly drawing a concealed short sword from its hiding place. The two other men swore loudly and, turning towards Ichirō, also produced short swords of their own. Ichirō started to move to meet them head on, holding a log in each hand. A moment before he was about to step down onto the training ground, he heard Hikaru call out.

'Father, here!'

He glanced over to see his son sprinting across the opposite side of the training area. His son's figure was distinguished by the large Katana tucked securely into his belt, and another held firmly by its scabbard in both hands. In a fluid motion, Hikaru gracefully dropped to his left knee, his right leg poised forward. He then raised the sword, still in its scabbard, high above his head. With a deft flick of his right thumb, he unlocked the blade and swung it forward with controlled force. Gripping the scabbard tightly at the peak of the sword's trajectory, he propelled the blade out, sending it soaring like a shining arrow, hilt first. Ichirō , almost caught off guard, quickly released the logs he was carrying and smoothly caught the sword by its hilt, skilfully using the momentum to swing it in a wide, sweeping circle. He then positioned the blade vertically in front of his face, offering his son a westernised fencing salute – a mark of respect for an exceptionally executed move.

He dropped into the sand, where the toothless man was half stumbling towards him. Enraged at his injury, anger now blinded him to the fact that his assailant was no longer holding a piece of wood in his right hand, but a metre of razor-sharp steel. Ichirō flicked the blade out to his right, then slashed it downwards, cutting through the man's sword hand. The man gave an ear-piercing scream as his thumb and all the fingers on his right hand now joined the remnants of his teeth in the sand. The man cried out in anguish as he fell to his knees trying to stem the flow of blood from the stumps of where his fingers once were. Ichirō turned his attention to the two remaining intruders who were now closing in on him. The sound of another Katana being drawn behind them altered their progress.

The two men reflected on the size of their smaller blades against the deadly Katana, being held unwaveringly point first towards them. They knew from first-hand experience they were no match to the boy's skill alone, and if it was the father who had trained him, well… quite simply they were fucked.

Trying to ignore the screams of their comrade now clutching his hand, they exchanged worrying glances with each other. They had begun to lower their weapons, when some muffled cries from the direction of the house drew everyone's attention. Two more men were dragging Ichirō's wife and daughter out onto the decking, their hands were covering their mouths and they held blades to their throats. Ichirō and Hikaru leapt back onto the raised dais, both thinking through the best way to protect their family. The sound of someone forcibly expelling cigarette smoke came from within their kitchen, and an unarmed man holding a cigarette appeared from behind one of the sliding doors.

'Good evening citizens,' greeted the man. He was dressed in similar fashion to the others, but he held no weapon that could be seen, and his demeanour was open and inappropriately congenial. 'I sincerely apologise for the intrusion on your supper,' he said with a slight bow. 'If you would return to us what is rightfully ours, we will disturb you no more this evening, pick up our lost digits, collect our broken teeth, along with my men's shattered honour and leave.'

'Nothing here belongs to you,' responded Ichirō, barely containing his fear and anger.

'I'm afraid that is where you're very much mistaken Kurosawa-san, is that not the case, Hikaru?'

Everyone turned their attention towards Hikaru.

'What have you done, Hikaru?' half choked, half cried Ichirō at his son.

Hikaru lowered his gaze to the floor along with his sword, unable to meet his father's glare.

'Let them go and I will come with you,' he said without looking at anyone directly.

Nobody moved, the blades remained held against the women's throats.

'Now, I said! Or I swear no one will recognise what remains of you when I have finished.'

The mobster flicked his cigarette into the Zen garden and pulled a pistol from the back of his waistband. He shook the weapon in the direction of the restrained females.

'Release them,' he commanded his henchmen.

The two men let them go. They ran to Ichirō's side, his wife openly weeping in shock, confused and frightened by the events unfolding around them. Azumi calmly stood slightly to the side of her father, her arms folded, with her right hand inside her sleeve.

Ichirō began to realise what his son had done.

'Why, Son?' he pleaded. 'Why would you do this to us? Have we not cared and nurtured you, giving you as much love as any family could possibly give their child? This is how you repay us for cherishing you so, by becoming a gangster?'

Hikaru sheathed his sword and without glancing at his family strode quickly into the kitchen.

'This is not the life for you, my son, not the path the gods have chosen for you. Please believe me, you'll regret this moment for the rest of your life if you leave us.'

'I am sorry, Father, even though I know what you say is true, please believe me when I tell you that that there is no choice for me other than this.' The voice that replied from inside the gloomy house did not sound like the young Hikaru they loved, but of a man resigned to a terrible fate.

After Hikaru had left with the gangsters, Ichirō did a sweep of the house to check if anyone was still inside. In Hikaru's room he picked up his son's short sword. He had left almost everything behind, only taking the long sword and the clothes that he had been wearing.

What was his son thinking of getting himself mixed up with the worst of Japanese society? After the war, not everyone had been willing to embrace the prospect of building a new prosperity for Japan. There were many who had been so brutalised by what they had done and what they had been experienced, they fell beyond all redemption; the evil that had been innately within their nature, given full reign by their exposure to the brutality of unadulterated war. These few individuals found themselves at hostilities end, unable to wind back into the source of original humanity they once held dear. That is why he had worked so hard to focus his son away from these fates.

He carefully lifted the sword and partially unsheathed the blade. Beneath the pristine shine of the steel lay the intricate detail of countless microscopic folds, a testament to the *Kawagane* – the hardened outer layer. These patterns were a silent witness to the myriad times the metal had been meticulously folded and hammered out in the rigorous forging process, embodying both the art and the science that had gone into its creation. A similar process he had subtly attempted in nurturing and developing his son.

Unfortunately, that process to guide him, to keep him true and faithful to a better path, had clearly failed. There was no escaping what was happening to his son now, Ichirō knew the bitter truth. Hikaru seemed inevitably ensnared in the self-fulfilling prophecy that his grandfather had set in motion. He became more than a mere participant in this destiny; he embraced it, compelled by the solemn promise he had made to the old man on his deathbed.

He had only told his son that his grandfather had wanted him to learn the old ways of the Samurai and to wield an exceptional sword he had made for him; the parting gift for the grandson he would never know. He never mentioned the darker aspects of what his father had told him of the burden that would pass to his generation, this was something he would leave for later.

To own such a weapon required a certain responsibility, for owning it was one thing, being worthy of such a weapon was quite another. Ichirō wanted to ensure that his son earned that merit, and that would be gained by the diligent application of the arduous and meticulous training required to effectively wield such a weapon – using body, mind, and spirit.

Ichirō wished he had been able to treat him in the same kind ways in which he had raised his daughter. Perhaps that was what drove him to seek a life outside society with the Yakuza. Was it the rigid training and preparation he had imposed on him that had driven him away? The fact that he had meticulously trained him to become an exceptionally skilled swordsman undoubtedly played a significant role, making his son a highly desirable candidate for recruitment into their ranks.

He also felt regret for Azumi, the girl was nothing but sweetness and light to all. She projected joy to those around her, in equal measure, in the same way the boy had walked in an ambiance of perpetual intemperateness. Surprisingly they never argued with one another, each accepting the demeanour of the other without question. There was undoubtedly a strong bond between them. Much to his annoyance he would frequently find Hikaru instructing his sister in the martial ways he had acquired, worrying she would get injured. He never put a stop to it as it seemed to bring satisfaction to both of them. He would often find them talking together on their own, although it always seemed to be Azumi doing the talking and Hikaru listening very intently. He found their conversations were benign to say the least, for whenever he came into earshot of their discussion, they appeared to be concerned with topics such as food, making friends or Manga comics. It concerned him that they may both be lost in the isolation of their naivety, not comprehending the real world that awaited them beyond. He feared for them both constantly, and now he had failed his son, he only had Azumi left. He vowed to protect his innocent daughter, no matter what, her genteel vulnerability was all he and his wife had left.

Chapter Thirty-nine

13 March 2011

Matachi left the porn star and returned to see how Tekiō was doing. He met him coming the other way down the hallway. 'I need a drink,' he said.

'Hey, let me tell you, old chap, you had it easy, getting tasered was fuck all compared to interviewing that bitch.'

'You don't look too bad to me,' growled Tekiō sarcastically, as he lightly touched the dressing over his right eye.

'Looks can be deceiving, I have been thoroughly beaten up, believe me. You can't see the wounds they are on the inside, but I have been emotionally scarred by my charming heart-to-heart with the adorable Ikeda-san. They say that beauty is only skin deep, but ugliness cuts to the bone and I can confirm that she is one piece of bitter and twisted arse.'

'All the same, it's a nice-looking arse though. Before she zapped me, I was locked on to it as I followed her down the street.'

'Well, that's two "Pigs" who liked it then, she should start a piggy fan club. Hey, you could be her piggy mascot, like Tripitaka's Pigsy, I can see it now, a modern-day twist on a Buddhist journey to enlightenment.'

'Screw you,' said Tekiō, 'and you would make a better

"Monkey" than I would a "Pigsy" that's for sure! So did she actually disclose anything of interest to the case?'

'Correct! She told me everything by telling me nothing.'

'Don't start with that pseudo-Sherlock shit. My head feels like it's been hit by a paving slab… and, oh bless my soul, that's because it has been hit by one! In addition, it's late and it's been a very long fucking day… and as I said, I need a drink. So, if you could give being sleuth of the fucking century a miss for a while, and just tell me what you fucking well know… please, boss.'

'You know, Tekiō, for a Japanese, you really do lack the natural projection of those ethnic functional qualities, of politeness, formality and reverence for one's superior, that one would normally expect from a subordinate,' responded Matachi, managing to look down his nose whilst looking up into the face of his giant partner, showing his best arrogant police superior officer face.

'I'm fucking warning you now,' said Tekiō in a raised tone, who, in his growing vocal frustration, also inadvertently fired a splutter of spittle between the gap in his front two teeth, the majority of which, at least, went over Matachi's head. It had indeed been a long day, what with his earlier tasering and the following consequences of bouncing onto the flagstones, had left Tekiō more than a little tetchy.

He felt that the day's events had excessively stretched his normally easy-going demeanour. After all it was not generally representative of his typical working day to: drop a severed head, get contaminated by radioactive material, absorb 50,000 volts and split your eyebrow wide open all in one shift! Now Matachi's pitiless teasing was rubbing his customarily tranquil soul right up the wrong way. So, it was with widened eyes and clenched fists that he stood around in front of Matachi and said, 'Give me one more piece of shit and I will pull the cheeks of your arse right up over your ears. I fucking guarantee it, boss!'

Matachi pulled his neatly folded handkerchief from inside his pocket and mopped off the few spots of spittle that had failed in their trajectory over his head. 'You really should seek some professional advice on that temper of yours, old chum,' said Matachi. 'As I was saying before I was so rudely menaced,' he quickly carried on to his next sentence before Tekiō could react to his latest barb, 'the girl's full of shit. She is calculatingly evasive and deceitful and gave out scarcely more than we already know about our Korean friend. Without a doubt she is very protective of him, which then would beg the question why she would care for one of many clients in her side-line of prostitution? What distresses her so, that she would go to such lengths to protect him? Could he mean more to her than just another trick?'

'You have more questions than answers, it sounds like.'

'I have a few leads for us to look into, but she hasn't disclosed a great deal that we didn't already know. We need to run his name through some telecom companies, but it's probably an alias. We also need to get a tail on her asap.'

'Did you mention Uchida's name to her?'

'No, thought it best not to. If he is as important as we think he is, then any mention of a connection to them or to us would get back to him fast. I believe it would be better if he isn't pre-warned that he is a suspect.' Matachi placed a hand onto his friend's upper arm. 'Let's go back to the hotel, I think we both could do with calling it a day and, by the state of your face, particularly you.'

★ ★ ★

Ikeda did not leave the Hospital Emergency Department until after midnight. The Korean intelligence officer watched her pull the collar of her coat up around her neck as she waved at a taxi stationed at the front of vehicles waiting at the taxi rank. Its light went out as it moved forward to pick up his next ride. Before the taxi had completely stopped beside her, Ikeda had already pulled open the door, not giving the driver time to open it for her, much to the man's annoyance, and jumped into the back seat. The Korean saw her lean forward towards the now agitated driver to give her address. As she sat back, the car quickly pulled out of the hospital grounds to join the spartan late evening traffic.

'Target acquired. Over,' he said into his throat mike beneath his full-face motorcycle helmet.

'Roger that. Over,' came the reply into his earpiece.

He flicked his thumb at the starter button on his motorcycle; the powerful engine instantly responded with a deep initial roar, before settling down into a latent powerful throb. Kicking it into gear with only a slight twist of his wrist, the machine powered after the taxi, its acceleration leaving his right leg trailing as the machine leapt into motion.

He pulled in behind the taxi a few cars behind. He had no need to get too close. He was riding a Yamaha R1 sports bike, its 1,000cc engine could deliver 190 brake horsepower and was capable of reaching in excess 100 kilometres per hour in under three seconds. With a top speed of 300 kilometres per hour, it was the ideal tool to follow another vehicle as long as it did not go 'off road'; in Fukushima City this was unlikely.

He waited for the vehicle to pull off the highway at the junction for the district of Motochi where Ikeda lived. When it did so, he accelerated past the trailing cars with ease, to overtake the taxi on the exit ramp. Now that he had confirmation that she was heading for her apartment, he used the speed and manoeuvrability of the bike to race to her home before she arrived.

He updated the rest of the team – 'Target is heading for apartment. Over.'

He too had some questions for Fuyuko and they would be considerably more demanding in nature and application than those of the police. The order had come down that nothing would be allowed to interfere with the operation that was now entering into a critical stage. The woman had become a liability now that she had drawn the attention of the law. This was no time to allow such liabilities to go unchecked. The order had been given that the time had come to dispose of her, in addition any usefulness she had once held for them had been superseded by recent events. Unfortunately for her the game had changed, the stakes were greater now. This was no longer a simple spying operation, the goal being to glean information and manipulate players. A significant operation of enormous magnitude was evolving. They were totally committed to its success and all available resources were being directed at achieving that objective. The order had been issued to mitigate any potential risks, and, if that required sacrificing certain assets, then it was deemed necessary. Time was an immediate enemy, forcing them to play the short game, to the detriment, if necessary, of any other ongoing assignment. He had been given new orders, with no ambiguity on the directive, or the consequences of failing to follow them.

He cut the ignition on the motorcycle, gliding almost silently to come to a standstill at the sidewalk, as he watched the taxi pull up directly outside her building's lobby.

'We have her in sight. Over,' informed the voice in his ear. 'Remember the taser. Over.'

'Roger that. Over and out.' The voice went dead in his ear as he watched two men appear on either side of the apartment building as their target walked quickly to the doorway. She seemed to be struggling to find her keys in her bag, when the men closed in on her. She suddenly spun around, stabbing outwards with her taser. One of the men deflected her arm away and grabbed hold of it firmly, as the second man hit her squarely under the chin with the palm of his hand, knocking her out cold instantly. Her legs began to buckle as the men moved in close to her, taking hold of her arms and hooking their own under her armpits. They lifted the slightly built woman so her feet were off the floor, moving her with ease to the side door of the Toyota Hi-Ace van which was conveniently parked outside her building. Within seconds they were inside, the door closing as they pulled way into the night.

The motorcyclist waited for a few more moments, surveying the scene for any witnesses, before he too sped away in the wake of the van.

Chapter Forty

14 March 2011

Truth, it is said, is the first casualty of war, and Uchida was managing to get a firm footing on its blathering throat. He had finally begun to control the narrative, managing to use his influence with the media outlets. He needed to shift their attention from the technical details of the disaster to the human stories, which were abundant in such a catastrophe. Of course, he couldn't control all media, especially the independent foreign press. Their staunch support for free speech made them particularly resistant to influence.

Nevertheless, he had a significant advantage: many major shareholders of the primary Japanese media outlets were under his influence, allowing him to sway their reporting and narratives. This control proved vital, especially in the following weeks when the reactor explosions became a global spectacle. The subsequent chemical explosion, which produced a mushroom cloud-like formation, seemed almost like a personal challenge to him!

Despite this, it turned out to be not that difficult to keep control of at least the local media. After all, only a few people had been actually killed as a direct result of the explosion at the plant. Some of the employees, not all, had done what they had been paid to do – their jobs. Those who had died or were injured while doing their duties, presented him with another opportunity to spin the story away from himself. He had managed to turn their 'heroics' into deflecting accounts of 'daring do', all helping to focus attention away from the main issues.

There were just a few small problems that, for some reason, persistently niggled at his self-assurance. The company could not yet confirm the whereabouts of a batch of spent uranium rods that had been replaced on the day of the tsunami. Considering the devastation wrought upon the facility, this was understandable. He was sure it was just the overzealous nature of the organisation in action. He was confident that absolute verification of their location would be confirmed shortly. In addition, there was also the issue of some of the still missing personnel who had been working in the reactor areas. There were some that had still not yet been accounted for. Everyone else was either alive, some it was true to say barely, or confirmed dead. The bodies of all the other workers had been eventually recovered, some in somewhat unusual places, several of them a few kilometres inland from the plant. These were some of the cowardly people who had left their posts and driven for the high ground but failed to make it. Most had got there quite quickly, having driven at breakneck speeds, not stopping for hell or the reality of the high waters chasing them. These employees were all now accounted for. They had also been warned not to tell of their escape for the sake of exposing their own cowardly embarrassment as well as the company's tenuous position following the disaster. As for the general population in the vicinity of the plant, many had died from being caught by the pace of the rising waters, but none attributed to the explosion at the plant… well not yet anyway.

A significantly larger issue was dealing with the public outcry that followed the forced evacuation from the ever-expanding exclusion zone, which had turned into a far more serious problem to deal with. Gone were the days when the common folk put up and shut up. Now, not only did they have the audacity to openly criticise the company and its actions, but also began to organise themselves into focus groups, directly lobbying politicians to take action. They discernibly saw an opportunity to make money for themselves, to supplement the meagre handouts that the government offered to individuals to build their shattered lives following the actual tsunami.

The antinuclear factions had jumped upon it, of course, and politicians, seeing the full force of the now weighty pendulum of public opinion bearing down on them, began to fear for their pathetic careers and had listened to the ignorant masses. There was no doubt that the pressure would force the nuclear energy companies to a near total national shutdown.

He saw that all of this would require managing, the growing fury would need to be deflected away from where the real blame was genuinely attributed. The raft of culpabilities steered onto rocks of derision and disparagement, macerating any truth, by diluting it with falsehoods and fake news. It would not be easy, but he was beginning to build a strategy to which may just actually work.

His Korean partners had made clear their uneasiness, but they now seemed to be placated after his discussion with Kwak. Indications from them now were that they felt content in his strategy for containing the situation and he began to feel a growing confidence as his plans fell into place.

His train of thought was abruptly derailed as he gazed into the face of a casually dressed man who had seemingly appeared out of nowhere, like a phantom materialising in the living room of his apartment.

Without any warning, a solid steel dart flew out and jabbed him in the left eye, returning equally as fast via its elastic tether and instantaneously sprung back out, hitting him a second time in his right eye. The range between them was less than a metre, and to the victim the double strike felt like a single blow, it was delivered so quickly. The pain was excruciating, far worse than anything he had endured before. It felt like someone had stuck a pitchfork in his face. It had happened without warning and far quicker than he could react to prevent it. He reacted now though, by bringing both his hands up to eyes as he reeled backwards. He rubbed his hands into his eyes, trying to physically push the horrific pain away and was sickened to feel the glutinous wetness of his ruptured eyeballs on his cheeks. Both hands now holding the front of his face, he threw back his head releasing a blood-curdling scream, just as his assailant knew he would.

With his head momentarily lifted in response to the pain, he formed a triangular frame with his raised forearms and the horizontal line of his collar bone, exposing his throat at the centre, creating the assailant's second target, just as he had intended.

His attacker allowed the deadly steel weight attached to the end of the rope dart to again recoil to its full length behind him. The range had increased to nearly two metres now, as the terrified man staggered backwards. He fed a few more centimetres of the cord attached to the steel dart and flicked it out again, hitting the man just below his Adam's apple, instantly crushing his throat.

Uchida's terrified screams were halted by the sudden inability to pass any breath over his vocal cords or draw a final breath into his chest. The pain inflicted by the rupturing of his eyes, that had been so foremost in his consciousness, now became less all-consuming as the sudden need to breathe became his priority. He fell to his knees as he started to lose consciousness, slowly sitting back on his ankles as his strength began to drain from his body. His folded legs were spread wide in front of him, the strain he would have normally felt in his thigh muscles now deemed irrelevant as his life force passed from him. He tipped slowly backwards, coming to rest with his head not quite touching the floor.

The assassin watched him die. It was part of his craft to understand all human endeavours. Although death was just death in the end. He should know, he had seen a great deal of it in his career, but still never failed to be surprised at the uniqueness of the final moments of a person's expiration.

He looked at the steel dart he had caught in his hand after the final strike. It was pendant-like in shape, similar to a large fishing weight, buffed to a dull hue. The hammer end was domed, designed to act like a cosh, not to penetrate flesh. This component of the weapon, the dart itself, was probably over a hundred years old, part of a set he had drawn from the quartermaster.

The rope dart was an ancient weapon, used by many countries around Asia in various forms over the millennia. Though deadly in trained hands, it was a speciality weapon with limited effectiveness and had not been a real favourite in his professional circles. The benefits to him were that it could be easily concealed within the minimum of clothing and its obscure design removed it from suspicion as a tool of death if discovered.

However, what was now attached to the end of the dart, had given it a bit of a renaissance. Instead of the original length of hemp rope traditionally used, modern technology had added an extra piece of utility that had transformed its capabilities – in the right hands of course. The enhancement was accomplished by attaching a high-performance elasticated cable constructed in a composite of dense natural rubber, combined with a dual helical binding of nylon threads, finished off with a covering of a black silicon coating, transforming the rope dart into something far more versatile.

The size of the elastic cord could be varied, this one was 15 millimetres in diameter and 3 metres in length, stretching to 5 metres when fully extended. With a little innovation and a few modifications of his own, he had made the weapon a deadly tool in his adept hands; a master in its use.

The assassin took a sterile wipe out of a packet he held in an inside pocket of his coat and started to clean the weapon down. A strong smell of ninety per cent rubbing alcohol rose into Min Hyun-woo's face as he pulled the lanyard through the sterile wipe. Min was a diligent man; he knew this to be a fact as he was at least forty years old and still alive. He had no idea exactly how old he was, for he was taken from a North Korean hard labour camp at a very young age, possibly around five years old. It was hard to say, he had scant concept of 'age' at that time and his memories from then were fragmented, though rather vivid. The permanent state of terror that his parents seemed to be in being one of his strongest memories. A fact reinforced thirteen years later when he had been required to murder them for committing crimes against the state.

They had not been the first humans he had murdered, of course, the camps were full of 'enemies of the State' and he had already lost count of the number he had dispatched during his training. The only part of this process he remembered were the different techniques and weapons he practised with. After all that was the most important part.

They had transgressed against the Supreme Leader, and it was only fair that their transgressions be rectified through a significant sacrifice to the state. By becoming subjects for extermination, they contributed to the vital process of forging model Korean citizens, exemplars like himself.

He was officially a member of the National Academy of Collective Farming. A front for the training of some of the most effective spies and assassins that had ever existed. The dead man in front of him now a testament to the rigorous standards he had been instructed in.

He looked at his watch, it had taken him all of fifteen minutes to access the building, using the copied access cards and keys they had created back when Uchida had first become an asset to them. A standard prudent approach in dealing with associates, part of a range of interventions put in place for the soul purpose of dealing with a situation such as this arising.

What could not be regarded as standard was the blatant manner in which he had been ordered to undertake the assassination. He abandoned all pretence of stealth in favour of speed. It was inevitable that the authorities would soon notice his presence in the building, and, with that, the revelation of his identity was only a matter of time. A substantial operation must be underway for his superiors to act in such an unprofessional manner. Dropping the weapon down one arm of his long-sleeved shirt, he began to make his way back to the street where his colleagues would be anxiously awaiting his return.

CHAPTER FORTY-ONE

14 March 2011

He had always envisaged his meeting with Uchida as the final act of his latest enterprise. A moment he had originally planned as the final deathly step, once Takada had systematically removed all the other players in the web of corruption the man had assembled around him. It was to have been an accumulation of violent actions, a process that would have eventually brought him a delectable moment he had intended to savour. That plan had evaporated quickly once he fully understood Uchida's implication in a far more heinous crime. An evolving development that had made him the starting point of a new venture. In Takada's doctrine of honour, treason was the most abhorrent of crimes. While it was true that any violation of the code incurred the most severe penalty, the key distinction for him lay in how he responded to each specific offence. He drew power from his actions, each violent act bestowed on him a degree of energising vitality, with the measure of that force increasing in direct proportion to the transgression he punished. The offence of treason was near the pinnacle of that reward system and offered him the chance of a far greater emotional recompense than mere white-collar crime, however insidious it had been.

He would leave the corruption and sleaze to the detectives

to unravel, if nothing else they should be able to use the information on the data stick to assist them – if they had managed to decipher it of course. He would follow the trail of treason, gaining substance from eliminating as many of the Japanese and foreign players as he could before the authorities became fully engaged. But this time he would work downwards from the top. He glanced at the short sword as it lay in the footwell of his noodle van on the passenger side and envisaged it cutting down through Uchida's sternum.

He was about to exit his diminutive vehicle, when something about an individual on the opposite side of the street triggered his tripwire of cautious vigilance. He quietly re-closed the door and began observing the man more intently. He was parked in the business sector in downtown Fukushima. It was midday and busy, the reason why he had planned this time to take down his prey. The man caught his attention, despite the fact he was moving in the sea of people walking to and fro on the sidewalk; he strolled with the practised ability of one trained to merge into any urban environment. To most people, he would have been just another worker taking a lunch break or returning to work in the busy business sector and its numerous cafés and restaurants. An innocuous nobody, floating past in the concealing waters that were the crowds. Mimicking the speed and gait of those around him, ghosting in and around the multitudes as gaps in the throng opened up, moving with just enough urgency to allow him a modest increase in speed without drawing attention to himself.

Now that his quarry had moved far enough away from him, he got out of his own vehicle and began to follow, using similar techniques to move through the crowd. He kept a respectful distance, continuing his observations as he did so. To a master of the human condition, like Takada, not only was it obvious that the man was in a hurry, but also that he was extracting himself from a serious incident. Takada's senses told him that the man had killed and had done so very recently. To him he may well have been carrying his victim across his shoulders, as he moved out onto the edge of the payment, coming alongside a dark blue Toyota Hi-Ace van. He moved as quickly as he could to the far side of the street, to get a side on view. The name 'Fukuo Maritime Engineering' was painted on the side of the vehicle, with a telephone number for inquiries below the company's name.

The two men in the front of the van now drew his attention. They were mere amateurs in relation to the individual he was watching now. He should have picked them up on his first sweep of the area in his noodle van. He had spotted the van earlier, but the men must have been hiding inside. The passenger looked back as he operated the automatic side door from the cabin. The door smoothly slid open and the man neatly hopped in, the door closing behind him as the engine started. He had to move quickly, the traffic was busy, so it gave him a few precious moments to move across behind the van before it managed to pull out. He quickly targeted a lady who would arrive at the rear of the Toyota at the same time as him, purposely bumping into her, causing her to drop her bag. As he and the woman began to outdo each other in profuse apologies, he stooped to pick up her bag, at the same time placing a magnetic tracker under the rear of the van.

He finally managed to disengage himself from the woman. As the van slowly pulled itself out into the flow of traffic, Takada activated the tracker software on the responder now in his hand. He was rewarded with a flashing red dot highlighted on a road map of their current location as the van drove out of view.

His original plan to apprehend Uchida in his home, from what he had seen he now deduced, was no longer a viable option. Best to check he thought, so he made his way to a payphone booth and placed an anonymous call to the emergency services. He told them he was a resident in the building and had heard screaming coming from Uchida's apartment and that he could now smell smoke in the area. They asked him for his details, but he said he did not want any trouble he was just a concerned citizen doing his duty and then hung up and returned to his noodle van.

Within ten minutes a police car and then a fire engine drove past him towards Uchida's apartment block with sirens blaring.

He turned on the emergency radio scanner he had brought with him, onto the local police radio band. He heard them request for the caretaker to come up to the apartment and let them in, seemingly not having any success in gaining entry themselves. The coms went quiet for a while, and then he heard a more frantic call for an ambulance to attend. This was quickly followed by a request to escalate the area to a serious crime scene.

It was obvious that someone had beaten him to Uchida. The fact that they had killed him was unexpected, surely, he was more valuable alive than dead. The man had not been in the building long enough to achieve any meaningful interrogation. He thought they may just have wished to retrieve something physical from the apartment, kill him, and leave.

Feeling terribly cheated by not getting to Uchida sooner, Takada quietly fumed in anger at his loss. Not only had he failed to kill the man, with Uchida now literally a dead end, he had nothing tangible to support the conjecture and supposition on his other leads. Some time spent with a living Uchida had been critical to the next phase of his plan. He took some deep breaths and calmed his mind. Someone was going to compensate him for that loss, that was a given. There were at least three 'someones' he needed a word with immediately. He fired up the noodle van and started to pick up the route of the Toyota from his transponder.

PART THREE

Interlude

Japan had been forced to accept a humiliating unconditional surrender in September 1945. Since then, its people have dedicated themselves to the colossal task of rebuilding the country. In doing so, they have not only created an economic powerhouse but also accomplished this feat in a remarkably short period of time. Along the way Japan's corporate executives in just about every sector of business, along with the political grandees of the more powerful governing bodies, had become the Shoguns of their time. They thrived under a system that granted them such impunity, reminiscent of an era dominated by warlords and ancient clans. This power significantly propelled the country's progress. However, it came with societal costs, challenging many fundamental aspects of Japan's deeply conservative culture.

Numerous members of Japan's business and political elite had formed a clique steeped in self-perpetuating decadence. They proliferated their excesses without fear of reprisal, manipulating the media and exploiting the deeply ingrained cultural aversion to causing direct embarrassment or loss of face. For many the pendulum had swung too far; it is said that for every action in nature there is an equal and opposite reaction. This is a logical response, one that is always eventually delivered by society, through the instinctive manifestation of the human condition to reset from within.

Unfortunately, the rise of democratic liberalism in Japan would never be strong enough to fully counter these historically ingrained dynamics – that would take the unleashing of deeply felt evangelical irreverence, a force that corruption naturally draws to itself.

.

The oceans provide sustenance to the land, but only the fool would think of it as a gift. Water gives and water reclaims.

Only the gods ever knew when is the time to watch the sea and when is the time to sail it. For choice and change are the eternal coinage of eternity, but look and beware, the denizen deep is scattered with tactless fools of calamitous fortune. When spent, some stare in bewilderment, others to the gloom of perpetuity.

It is so that one must be tactful in what one wishes for, and yet not so careful as to lack the courage to wish at all.

Feint heart will flounder as fortitude excels, rewarding those brave enough to make attempt; to write on their part of the universe in its own script. They and they alone will be told if they have written well – or not.

Then when all is said and all done, after the reckoning and disturbance, obligatory; a period of rebalancing must return the order of all things.

The Ogress Adachigahara

CHAPTER FORTY-TWO

15 March 2011

The large semitrailer slowly ground to a stop. The huge vehicle creaked and groaned, with a jerky hissing of pneumatic brakes as it halted. The Volvo tractor at the front, coming to rest alongside the two policemen who had waved it down.

Attached to the tractor unit was a low loader trailer, upon which were secured a JCB digger/bucket combo and a small crane. All the vehicles looked like they had seen better days, with their weathered and flaking paint, cracked windows and other numerous dents and scrapes along their exteriors.

One of the policemen grabbed hold of the mirror bar on the truck's cab and hauled himself up onto the footplate looking into the driver's side window. Inside, along with the vehicle's driver, were two passengers.

'Where are you going with this lot then?' he asked the driver. 'Good day, officer, my name is Katsuji,' answered the driver. 'My good self along with my brothers run a small building company near Tokyo,' he said, gesturing to the two other men in the cab. 'We are volunteers, going to the disaster zone to assist in any way we can.'

The policeman gave a noncommittal grunt in reply to their answer.

'You see, officer, a member of our family, my mother's brother, lives in Naraha and we have not heard from him since the disaster.'

'I see,' said the policeman. 'And you think you're going to find him with that?' He gestured to the equipment on the back of the trailer.

'Ah... oh... no sir, we do not think we would be able to find him directly, though we feel that any assistance we can give generally may help in some way. The more people searching, the more chance there is of discovering what happened to him. And if we find any other poor souls along the way, then all the better for everyone. We heard there is a lack of machinery and skilled workers, and we bring both,' the driver said, gesturing to the equipment on the back of the truck and to his co-workers in the cab with him.

The policeman seemed genuinely touched by the sincerity of the man. He had witnessed first-hand the devastation caused by the tsunami and he knew there were many people in need of help, but he still had his duty to perform. 'Ah, yes, very good Katsuji-san,' he said with a short series of bows, 'but I will still need you to show me your licence and registration documents for all vehicles, including the two on the back, if they are yours, and I want to see everyone's ID cards please.'

The men began to frantically dig into their pockets and start searching through the glove compartment of the truck. One of the men pulled out a rucksack from behind the seats and began looking through it. The policeman waited patiently until they had put together a small pile of documents for him to inspect.

The policeman took the small stack of worn and dog-eared papers to his colleague by the police car, spreading them out on the bonnet as they both thoroughly examined them.

They then walked around the trailer checking all the vehicles' registration plates matched their paperwork, carrying out a cursory inspection of the rig to ensure it was in a roadworthy condition. After satisfying themselves that everything was in

319

order, the officer who had stopped them neatly re-folded the documents along their worn seams and climbed back onto the foot plate, handing them back to the driver.

'Okay guys, you can proceed,' he said, then found he was unable to stop himself adding, 'It may be worth considering it's time to apply for a renewal on some of those documents, they are barely legible now.'

The driver gave a resigned bow of acceptance of the rebuke, responding simply, 'Ah, yes, yes, we will Officer-san, as soon as we are finished assisting.'

The policeman now felt embarrassed by the triviality of his comment, having been made to consider the relative circumstances. He bowed again to the driver. 'On your way then,' he said as he jumped down to the road.

'Oh, and guys… good luck!'

He waved the truck and trailer on with a sombre look.

All the men inside bowed and smiled in gratitude at being allowed to continue as they drove past.

'Stupid cunt,' said one of the passengers after they moved well beyond the police roadblock. Katsuji sniggered. 'Traffic policemen, wherever you go, anywhere in this country, they're all as dumb as fuck,' he added. Katsuji's real name was Nam Chui-min and he worked as a senior officer for the North Korean Intelligence station in Tokyo. He, like the others accompanying him, was one of many such operatives now hurriedly reassigned to this mission. As they rolled on into Fukushima Prefecture, the men carefully replaced the documents back where they had recovered them from. Some of them were real, but there were also a number of very good forgeries. Their seemingly haphazard placement was part of the charade of their cover as working-class men just trying to do their bit for their beleaguered fellow citizens.

They were making good time and, if they were not stopped again, would make the first rendezvous point with the rest of the team as planned.

CHAPTER FORTY-THREE

15 March 2011

The Municipal Civic Building that housed the Local Department for Energy, was located on the fourth floor of Fukushima City Hall. It had a very basic level of security, which was standard for low-level local government buildings. There was no intruder alert system and limited CCTV positioned at the front of the site or within the reception area.

However, for the intruders this was a covert operation, they had to infiltrate the building without leaving any trace of entry whatsoever – at least until the first phase of the operation was complete. They were part of a six-man team, three of them were to gain entry to the building and carry out the search, of the remaining three, two were to provide over-watch, the remaining member being the driver for the insertion and extraction phases. The building had been previously reconnoitred by the group, both on the ground and by studying original blueprints of the building.

Then they had been given two options for the end phase of the mission, dependent upon what they discovered during the covert search. The first option was to leave as clandestinely as they entered, erasing all evidence of their movements as they did so. The second option was rather more pyrotechnical, but also had to be carried out covertly.

The three men now converged through the darkness, to a poorly lit access door situated in a rear utility area. The deadlock on the louvred door was quickly and skilfully picked by the access team, aided by the fact they already knew its make and design. The building's rudimentary security system had already been remotely overridden and was under the control of the over-watch section.

The engineering room they now entered held the two large gas-fired boilers that provided all the heating for the eight-storey municipal building, one of which made a loud roaring sound as it fired up, its gas burner clearly showing a stabbing flame through the inspection glass as it responded to the hot water thermostat calling for more heat to be fed into the system.

They each pulled a set of night vision goggles from their modestly sized tactical rucksacks, donning the headsets over the plain darkly coloured hoodies each wore. They switched the goggles on, being careful not to glance at the fiery brightness emanating from the small sight glass of the working boiler.

From this point they quickly accessed the maintenance corridors beyond, which led back into the main building, where one of the internal fire escape staircases was situated. Knowing that the building was completely empty of any personnel, the three quickly jogged up the stairway to the fifth floor. Entering the office area, they moved efficiently through a series of corridors and open plan areas until they arrived at Matsumoto's corner office.

The lock to this was also quickly and efficiently picked, allowing the three men to enter the room and search it with ease. Everything that was opened or moved, was replaced in exactly the same position as they found it; they were only looking for one item. One of them removed a small metal cash box from the bottom of a filing cabinet.

The box was locked, but again this proved no obstacle. Inside there was some petty cash, a worn notebook and what they had been searching for, a single data stick, dark in colour and slightly larger than normal. One of the men secured the stick in a pocket of his rucksack, another removed an identical memory stick from one of his pockets and placed it in the tin. The third member of the group photographed every page of the notebook, then replaced this back into the box returning it to the filing cabinet in exactly the same position as before, leaving no trace of their activities.

One of the men activated his throat mike. 'Option two,' he whispered, 'I repeat option two, over.' The other two men nodded their understanding.

'Confirm – option two. Over and out,' came the curt response in the man's ear. The trio quickly retraced their steps back down to the basement floor utility area and located the archive storage area.

It was a large room with row upon row of ceiling high racking, containing essential hard copies of archived documentation the municipal administration was required to keep stored for at least twenty years. The intruders rolled a wheeled access ladder down one of the aisles of tinder dry paper to the far wall.

One of the men mounted the ladder and pushed up against the lightweight false ceiling tiles; a single tile lifted from its frame, giving access to the void beyond. He deftly moved his body up the ladder into the upper space. He now faced a metal box that ran the full length of the building wall, disappearing at both ends into other rooms beyond. This was the building 'busbar' electrical distribution system, which ran power around the building to all its areas. He then used a screwdriver to loosen the screws on some of the busbar's protective panels, loosening them but leaving them in place. The team knew that the busbar provided high voltage power to all the building's utilities. Within this network each of its three copper strips provided 200 volts of power, available to be tapped off at intervals wherever required to provide power for the electrical requirements in every room. They repeated this action at intervals several times along the length of the busbar system. Each time a section was exposed, the ceiling tiles were replaced very carefully within the grid.

Once this task had been completed, they quickly returned to the boiler-house, where one man climbed on top of the active units. Once there he removed a small wooden wedge from his rucksack and forced it under the override lever of the main pressure relief valve. The unit had a small design fault, an error they had noticed during their extensive reconnoitre. The steel pipe leading off from the safety valve, that would exhaust any pressurised steam away from the boiler, had not been plumbed into the atmosphere but to a small drain in the corner of the plant room floor. For normal operation this would not have been an issue, but the wooden wedge now caused the valve to continually relieve, pushing over 5 BAR of saturated steam into the room.

Using a pair of steps and ladders left by the maintenance crew, the other two men worked as a team to loosen the screws on the length of connecting busbar that ran through the boiler house. This cover was completely removed, exposing the three strips of electricity conducting copper within.

Steam now began to fill the room from the ceiling downwards. As the moist vapour began to permeate the busbar system, it began to arc and splutter as it made contact with the live wires. The three men squatted low beside the exit, removed their goggles, and waited until the moist atmosphere caused the steam to be drawn into the rest of the busbar system, causing the reaction to take place along its entire length. The thin metal covering around the busbar in the boiler house began to melt and drip molten steel onto the floor below. Within the archive store the same process had also begun at various points along its length, the loosened covers allowing oxygen-rich air to enter the cavity and feed the electrical fire within. As the temperature rose to over a thousand degrees centigrade, it drew in ever greater amounts of oxygen and globs of white-hot molten metal were soon dropping down, burning through the light fibre tiles to set fire to stacks of paperwork stored on the shelves below.

As acrid smoke began to build up, along with the steam inside the boiler room, the men let themselves out, locking the door behind them. The group made its way onto the access road where their Toyota Hi-Ace van was waiting for them. One of them pulled open the side door and slid it fully back on its rack and they all jumped in.

Peering out the of the van's doorway, the group could see flickers of flame spring up through the windows of the archive store, as their handiwork enabled the fire to take hold. The building was fitted with a sprinkler system, but the 'PLC controller', that in turn ran the water pumps for the sprinkler system, had also been disabled remotely. No siren sounded, and no sprinkler burst into life, within ten minutes the building was irretrievably ablaze.

The men closed the door on the van and unhurriedly headed off to their rendezvous point with the over-watch team in the firm belief that another successful mission had been accomplished. However, there were a few more operations that needed tackling before their work would be done.

Parked at the central level of the municipal building's multi-storey carpark was a small noodle delivery van, it sat out of view, towards the middle line of car parking spaces. In the front of the vehicle, Takada watched the intruder team drive away through a pair of old, but still very serviceable, war-time reconnaissance binoculars. He held them to his eyes with his right hand until the Toyota was out of sight. These guys are really getting busy he thought, as he watched the flames start to consume the building. He realised they were on a mission to mop up anything that could connect them to Uchida, but that was of no real interest to him. He would need to keep following them until they led him to something more noteworthy than petty arson.

Utilising the tracker, he had installed earlier that day, he had been following the van continuously as it dropped off its original occupants at several locations and was now being used by this new crew. As it began yet another journey, he pulled out of the car park and again began tracking it.

The van had been heading out towards the outskirts of the

prefecture for an hour or so, obviously heading back to where he had followed them earlier that day. He kept well out of sight allowing the tracker to do the work for him. He glanced at his watch; it was just after midnight; he knew only too well that darkness was always the best camouflage for such operations. He continued to maintain his distance, at least a kilometre behind the van, when suddenly out of the gloom he saw the Toyota heading directly towards him on the other side of the road. Takada readied himself for a confrontation as the van quickly approached, but it passed him by, travelling in the direction he had just come from.

He checked the tracker signal on his tablet resting on the central console. It showed no change at all, it was steadily continuing on its way as before. The van was identical to the one he had been following, its company name recognisably displayed on its side. The vehicle had not hailed its brother as they had approached one another, as one would have expected if they were part of the same company. This said to him that both occupants knew each other but did not wish to draw attention to themselves. He made a snap decision, halting his own van and spinning it around to follow the other vehicle. The night was young and still full of secrets, he hoped.

CHAPTER FORTY-FOUR

15 March 2011

On the fourth full day after the accident at the Atomic Energy Facility, the access road 252 from Shimonogami town to the Daiichi facility had been re-opened. The Korean spies' eighteen-wheeler had dropped off the JCB digger and small crane beside a thin clearing on the side of the motorway, almost adjacent to the junction with the 252, close to a pile of wreckage that had once been the Ōno train station.

It was approaching dusk as they finally got the two vehicles driven off a set of ramps they had fitted onto the rear of the trailer. Once the heavy plant was firmly on the roadside, the three men assisted each other to restore the ramps back onto the trailer.

Katsuji and one of the team would now proceed to drive the digger and crane down the 252, while the third member took the Semi to a pre-scouted location three kilometres away, where there was enough room to turn the unit around and park it up in readiness to be called back for the pickup.

The front bucket section of the JCB was filled with high strain strops and chains, a small diesel generator, spare cans of fuel and some demountable lights, along with a selection of light tools placed on top of them. Tied onto the back of the crane was a small set of oxyacetylene cutting equipment and in the space within the cab were stored two petrol-powered thirty-centimetre diamond disc cutters, plus a twenty-litre jerrycan of spare fuel. Inside the cabins the men had stored their personal equipment and enough supplies to last a few days.

They steadily trundled down the road, the powerful lights on their vehicles highlighting a ghostly wasteland of devastation to either side, creating flickering sharp shadows that contrasted starkly with the dark, straight, clean lines of the asphalt road before them. They carried on for about three kilometres until they reached a group of five men in high visibility jackets, standing on the side of the highway. They were staring at a small mound of wreckage, almost discernible from the surrounding sea of devastation.

The two men brought their vehicles to a halt and then jumped out of their cabs, swiftly walking to the side of one of the men wearing high viz. The man held a relatively unsophisticated GPS unit in his hand which he was studying intently. Without even looking at the two men who had joined him he said, 'That's it, that mound of crap two hundred metres in front of us.'

'Are you sure?' responded Katsuji.

'If they are certain of the coordinates I was supplied, then I am sure we are where they say we should be.'

'Fair enough,' responded Katsuji. 'Let's get a wiggle on then, this is no place to be fucking around at this time of night.'

The men got to work, one of them taking the point position at the front of the group, holding a Geiger counter. He picked his way with some difficulty through the carnage, as the others assisted him in creating a path through the debris until they reached the mound. The unit crackled as it indicated the presence of the background radiation now present in the atmosphere caused by the release of radioactive contamination from the now openly decaying reactors on the coastline. He adjusted the unit to fade out this relatively low level of contamination. They were under no illusions that, if the flask had been damaged, they would be receiving a much stronger response. He gave the signal that it was safe to proceed, at least for the time being.

They now needed to steadily, but carefully, work their way into the area they were targeting and as the going got tougher, they called in the heavy machinery to assist them, beginning to remove piece by piece an array of smashed buildings, crushed vehicles, destroyed furniture and kitchen appliances, all mixed in with a morass of rendered vegetation and stinking mud. They made good progress and in less than an hour they had discovered the rear of the nuclear containment flask.

The leader of the group pulled out his cell phone, quickly thumbed a short text and sent it. It read, 'Father your prayers have been heard.' This was picked up by the spy on the hill who had been keeping watch for them. He got a jolt of excitement at the news, then quickly relayed it onto the rest of the team, which included the driver of the Semi, putting him on 'standby' to move immediately when they required extracting.

They had intentionally started their work late in the afternoon so it would be dark by the time they reached the critical phase of their work. Their main concern were the numerous helicopters that had started to come into play around the crippled plant. If spotted by them or any other observers, hopefully the group looked like a small team searching for survivors, one of many in the area undertaking similar work. So, they gambled that they would not attract attention to themselves if they were spotted just digging around.

This was an acceptable risk for the daylight element of the plan, but the cover of night would be needed once the flask had been located; keeping on schedule was an absolute requirement if they were to hit the critical timing markers set within their plan. Fortunately, for the moment, helicopters were not required, or were deemed too risky for nocturnal operations by the authorities and they retreated with the coming of dusk. The removal of the prying eyes in the sky above with the cloaking comfort of darkness to shroud the task of retrieving the flask would be key to the success of their mission.

A cell phone delivered a strong vibration to the leader's right hand, it was the coms he had been waiting for from the spy on the hill. On witnessing the departure of the final helicopter from the area, he had sent a text saying, 'His mother was looking greatly improved now.' This was a signal that the skies were now clear and there were no other obvious interlopers in the vicinity.

The man with the handheld Geiger counter approached the rear of the flask. It was a very sophisticated device, as well as being a gamma radiation spectrometer, it had the capability to detect Alpha and Beta emittance. He scanned the area, listening through a headset connected to the device and monitoring the multiple screens on its face. He re-tuned the receiver to cover the full range of any possible contamination and, finding no signal that the flask had been breached at this point, he clambered up onto the pile of debris that covered the tractor unit, walking along its length as he repeated the scanning operation.

'Nothing,' he said, after the few minutes that it took him to walk the length of the raised area. Then he added, 'Well, nothing to be concerned about anyway, just some background stuff coming out of that place.' He waved the wand of his detector towards the outline of the smoking nuclear power station in the distance.

'Right,' said Katsuji, 'let's get this fucker out.'

The fading twilight gave away to an eerie darkness, as they quickly and efficiently worked to uncover the complete flask. Their personal head torches added even more silhouettes, shapes and shadows, from a deranged kaleidoscope of a shredded field of once human existence, as they quickly and efficiently worked to uncover the complete flask. The transporter itself, except for the rear of the vehicle, was left buried, exposed only to the level of the retaining mechanism holding the flask in place on the vehicle's mountings.

During their excavations to reach and uncover their prize,

any smaller pieces of rubble and flattened material, was recycled by the crew to line a narrow path, creating a pontoon to the roadside. The crane now began to tee itself up in readiness to move forward when called for, whilst a pair of spotlights were run out to the flask, their cables running alongside the improvised track. The generator was hand-cranked into life, with a few quick pulls of its rope lanyard, causing the spotlights to first flicker and then erupt into a powerful cascade of luminescence around their trophy.

The team began to attach strops and chains to the conveniently positioned steel lifting eyes located on each corner of the unit. One man stood at the centre of the flask, holding in both hands a large steel ring where the converging cables were now held in place. The crane switched on its headlights and rolled forward onto the makeshift road, its four large wheels making it rock from side to side as its weight was displaced by the uneven surface. On reaching the rear of the flask, it extended its lifting boom, a hydraulically powered ram driving forward a solid square of telescopic steel, until the large hook, situated at its end, could be coupled with the retaining ring. The crane driver guided it into position and the man holding the retaining ring slipped it over the hook. The driver was now directed to lift the boom until it just bit at the tensioned weight beneath it.

Members of the team positioned themselves around the flask with their cutting gear, and in a shower of sparks the rear retaining bolts were first sliced away. Observing no apparent untoward movement of the flask, the retaining coupling at the front of the unit was also carefully removed in the same manner. The crane driver was ordered to gently take the strain by lifting its powerful arm. The flask gave a slight jolt as it was released from its retaining cradle. Guide ropes that had been fitted to each end of the flask, were now kept taut by the men holding them, controlling the swing around from its central hanging pivot point. The crane driver steadily brought the load closer to him to gain a more secure centre of balance, then, slowly reversed the vehicle and its dangerously precious cargo back towards the road.

As the remainder of the team used the JCB to bulldoze piles of debris back over the transporter and then the makeshift road they had constructed, the crane began to trundle the two kilometres back to the junction where it joined the main road.

The Semi-trailer driver nervously waited on the main highway for the slow progress of his next load to arrive. There would have been no room to turn his rig around if he had driven to the extraction site directly and it would have been impractical to have attempted to reverse the unit back onto the main road. It would have taken just as long, with the added risk of a jack-knife of both truck and trailer. If that had occurred it would have likely had catastrophic consequences for the whole mission.

He could just see the crane approaching the intersection now, its dimmed headlights silhouetting the large cylinder in front of it and its accompanying sentinels on foot guiding it, holding firm lanyards trailing off either side, preventing the steel monolith from sluing from side to side.

He fired up the truck's powerful diesel engine, making his approach to place the vehicle's trailer directly across the junction. The large machine came to a halt astride the road with a series of jerks as its powerful brakes snatched at the unladen trailer. A final roaring hiss of expelled air informed the awaiting crew that the unit had come to a final stop. The team quickly manoeuvred the crane into position and began placing the uranium-filled flask on top of the flatbed. Using a selection of large wooden blocks and wedges, plus the strops and chains they had brought with them for the purpose, they chocked and secured the flask firmly into place.

Finally, they drew over it, a single tarpaulin, large enough to cover the load entirely. Once this was fastened in place, Katsuji, along with his other original companion, climbed into the passenger side of the cab, re-joining their colleague. The driver selected one of the lower gears, of the twenty-two that the gearbox held, and the diesel engine gave a powerful rattle as he applied the throttle with his foot. The rig gave a series of small shudders as they began to slowly pull away.

The greatest theft of a physical atomic entity in the history of nuclear energy was underway... and going to plan.

CHAPTER FORTY-FIVE

15 March 2011

The owner of the boat had been very pleased with the deal he had secured for his beached and marooned vessel. Although damage to his boat had been light, the expense of recovering it and then relaunching it back out to sea had outweighed the overall salvage cost for the vessel.

He watched, as his boat, the *Shiroboshi Maru*, now firmly anchored onto the very large low-loader trailer, began to drive away through his now destroyed village of Futaba. He had been astonished when he had been made an offer for the vessel, it had exceeded anything he could have got from the insurance claim. Recently the authorities had informed him that it was his responsibility to remove the boat from the centre of town, where it had eventually beached itself from the receding waters. Failure to remove it would result in a prosecution he was told by the authorities. At the time he had laughed in their faces when notified of this. Did they not realise he was already ruined, along with everyone else in the village for that matter? Bloodsucking bureaucrats, he had told them, declaring with biting scorn that even his own excrement held more worth and integrity than they did as humans. He had shrugged and walked away telling them to do their worst. Whatever they did was of little consequence. You cannot fell the same tree twice he had shouted at them.

But despite his brazen affront to the authorities, the fate of the boat did worry him. The vessel had come to rest at the intersection to the only bridge into the village. It would have to be moved to allow reconstruction of the village to take place. The fact that everyone in Futaba knew, in reality through his bluster, this truth dragged heavily upon his conscience. It was his duty to his community to deal with the issue. So, when the group of men had made such a generous offer, and in addition would take responsibility for its imminent removal, he had almost bitten their hands off.

The very next day, a team of men with a crane had arrived to recover the *Shiroboshi Maru*. Fortunately, after his craft had been swept inland by the wave, its keel had become stuck on the rubble of a collapsed building. As the waters receded, it had amazingly come to rest almost upright and virtually intact. This presentation greatly assisted in the retrieval of the boat. The team the buyer had brought with him had worked quickly and efficiently. Within a few hours the vessel had been lifted off the junction and placed onto the trailer ready for transportation.

He had been amazed at how efficiently the team had worked at the task. He was thoroughly impressed by their skill and efficiency, which led him to approach the supervisor, seeking his business card. Eager to commend their work, he mentioned to the supervisor that such talent would undoubtedly be valuable in other projects. The supervisor, embodying the humble grace characteristic of Japanese culture, responded with a smile and a modest bow, typically offered in gratitude for praise. Regrettably, amid the busy activities of securing the craft to the low-loader, the supervisor and his team departed, inadvertently leaving without providing their contact details.

This had seemed odd at the time, but the man put it down to them being extremely busy. Their loss, he thought, as he walked back through his devastated village, in wonder at how one's fortune can change so quickly. The vagaries of the gods were beyond his understanding, he thought, as he calculated the size of the deposit needed for his new fishing vessel. Nam and his team had hired an abandoned industrial site within a large commercial yard, that held a spacious workshop at its centre. The company that had previously owned it had been hit quite hard by the tsunami, with most of its mobile ship repair vehicles washed out to sea. The sign above the office entrance said 'Fukuo Maritime Engineering'. Their business had been used to maintain the hundreds of fishing vessels that had worked out of the local harbours, most of which had now been largely washed out to sea. It was remote and deserted, ideal for the project they now had to undertake.

Two hours after retrieving the beached craft, they drove their very useful and versatile eighteen-wheeler Semi into the yard. On opening the large roller shutter doors to the main maintenance bay, they carefully reversed their latest acquisition deep inside.

The team immediately set to work. Beginning with the first task of removing most of the top deck of the vessel, but in addition maintaining its condition, so that it could eventually be refitted. This was not going to be an easy project, but they had selected the most suitable craft available. Admittedly they did have an extensive range to choose from. The shores of Fukushima prefecture were littered with now high and dry hulks of almost every description. However, they had a list of very defined criteria for selecting the correct vessel. That specification needed to be met, to enable any chance of success for their plan. The boat they had eventually chosen was as close a match as they could have wished for. It was now up to them to achieve success in this next crucial step.

The original team they used to extract the flask were versatile, willing operators, but they lacked the required skills for the task ahead of them now. They had been required to urgently supplement the crew with professional maritime engineers. It had not been easy to bring these specialists into the country without raising any suspicion from the authorities, particularly at such short notice, but their expertise would be invaluable.

The group set about hollowing out the inside of the vessel, removing everything below the upper deck, with the critical exceptions of essential elements required to power and control the ship left in situ. Once that was complete, the internal structure would be strengthened with steel bracing until they had created a reinforced compartment deep within the craft.

It had taken them nearly two days of working in shifts, continually working diligently and effectively twenty-four hours day, before they had finally managed to insert the nuclear flask into the bowels of the ship and rebuild the superstructure around it. Returning the vessel, to what they hopefully believed, would be a sea-going fishing boat once again.

The next step would be the final crucial phase, and he had requested even greater support to accomplish it. Speed of execution was critical to their plan, he understood time was a thief whose appetite could never be slated. To add to his woes, additional complications were emerging like worms in old bean curd. There was now a high-level list of actions that required urgent attention. He would now require all the resources his country could provide if he were to help achieve his nation's ultimate goal.

CHAPTER FORTY-SIX

17 March 2011

The two detectives had been informed by one of the hotel's managers that it was with the deepest of apologies that they would unfortunately be extending the reduced service at breakfast for at least a few more days. The man had been extremely sorry for any inconvenience caused. However, due to a lack of staff caused by the tragic incident at the hotel and the wider impact of the earthquake, they would be running a condensed mealtime provision for at least a week, limited to beverages, fruit and pastries for the time being. Matachi and Tekiō placated the man's embarrassment with the customary empathetic sympathising and consolation, telling him it was perfectly understandable under the circumstances, and they had not been inconvenienced at all. This came as quite some relief to the manager as he stared at the large, freshly stitched gash over Tekiō's forehead. A sight which had not exactly made him any more socially appealing. Fixing his smile and giving a few more low bows he retreated backwards into the restaurant. 'That's breakfast screwed then,' said Tekiō, once out of earshot of the manager. 'I am fucking starving; I could eat an elephant and chase the Mahout.'

'Do you ever stop thinking about your stomach? At least not eating here keeps you away from the disgusting Nattō you so love to pour down your throat.'

'We will have to make a pitstop on the way. You don't like me so much when I'm hungry.'

Matachi, was about to inform Tekiō that he was not that enthusiastic about him under most circumstances, when his cell phone started ringing. 'Hello, Detective Matachi speaking,' he answered.

He listened intently to the speaker on the other end of the line, saying little other than 'Yes' at intervals until he finally thanked the caller and hung up.

'We're not going to get any breakfast, are we?' said Tekiō, understanding from his boss's demeanour the gravity of the call.

'Correct! I'm afraid not old boy. It looks like we will be meeting Uchida this morning, instead of later on today.

'Dead?'

'Oh yes, deader than the style your tailer uses.'

'I don't have a tailor.'

'That dear boy comes as no real surprise,' said Matachi, looking at his friend's baggy unkempt suit.

'Has this one kept his head?' asked Tekiō, ignoring the dig at his dress sense.

'Err – pretty much – ish. The forensic chaps have the report for us.'

'That was quick!'

'Not really, he died four days ago and we're only being told now! I got the impression from the call that they only enlightened us because they had been forced to.'

'Thought you were looking slightly aggravated on the phone.'

'I can assure you, not as "aggravated" as commander Fukumoto-buchō will be shortly, when he has his pants pulled down by his superiors.'

Later that day the two men were sat at a picnic table, having stopped at a lay-by. They were on their way back from Uchida's apartment and had stopped at Tekiō's insistence at the roadside takeaway. They began to consume the assortment of snacks and beverages they had picked up from the 'Yatai' snack shack situated at the end of the bay. Except for the old couple running the shack, the place was deserted, and they had chosen the furthest table away from the van. It was testament to the men's constitution that, despite what they had just witnessed at the local morgue, they had not lost their appetites.

'You have to admit that was quite novel,' said Tekiō, stuffing his third Okonomiyaki savoury pancake into his mouth and talking around it. 'Never seen injuries on a stiff like that before. Three hits precisely inflicted with devastating consequences.'

'Any idea on the weapon used?' questioned Matachi, ensuring he was out of splatter range of the voraciously chomping Tekiō. Violence and gore always seemed to have the reverse effect on his appetite, he really did have quite the neurotic eating disorder.

'My first thoughts were a low-calibre weapon, just powerful enough to make a penetrating entry without causing an exit wound. But the strikes to the eyes were non-lethal, not strong enough to damage the brain, almost superficial... though he probably didn't think so at the time. It was the hit to the throat which killed him. Everything vital to life is on the surface in that area. The larynx had been heavily struck, crushing the thyroid cartilage, instantly cutting off all air from entering the windpipe. He would have become unconscious in under a minute, dying very soon after.'

'If not a gun, what then?'

'Best guess, is a blunt spear.'

Matachi stopped mid-bite into his Yakitori kebab. 'So, you are the weapons and tactics expert here and your best guess on the murder weapon is a blunted spear?'

'A weapon that was narrow at its end, fairly blunt and solid, delivering blows with considerable force, caused those injuries. The precise nature and the power that had to be used, indicates that they occurred in quick succession. Jab... jab... jab...' said Tekiō, demonstrating the strikes, by taking his chopsticks out of

340

his Ramen noodles and poking them in the direction of Matachi three times.

'Well, dear boy, there were no reports of anyone entering the vicinity of the building, running around with a fucking spear in their hands, blunt or otherwise.'

'As I keep pointing out, weird shit follows us around.'

'Undoubtedly correct, however, if we keep losing suspects at the rate we currently are, then this case will very soon close itself by default, with all the main suspects now dead.'

'Good,' said Tekiō, slurping in a mouthful of noodles. 'No leads left to follow. Case closed and we can go home before we become irradiated. Have you seen the pictures of that Plant? Its spewing god knows what into the atmosphere around here.'

'Yes, I think you are accurate there, dear boy. I believe the case we have been sent to decipher is finished, because it is about to solve itself!'

'I think the radiation has affected your brain, boss. What the fuck do you mean solved itself? We have got at least three dead – the governor who has almost definitely been killed, we are just missing her body; one attempted murder and several additional missing persons, unaccounted for – with not a clue to who has done any of it. Please explain to me how this case is solved?'

'Finding murderers was not our prime mission, they were just leads, means to an end, Tekiō. We were sent here to bring down bigger game than two a Yen assassins. The trigger men are unimportant.'

'I like taking down killers, it's my favourite part of the job,' said Tekiō waving his chopsticks in the air.

'That's as maybe, but we are not here to indulge in pet activities; well not unless they just happen to present themselves in the prosecution of our legal duties. Look we have already established that the power plant was central to what was going on here. All our leads directed us to the facility or came from it. The USB stick holds details of years of evidence, everything from financial mismanagement to extreme corruption, with Uchida's stench smeared all over it. Building a case against him was key to unravelling this, to getting close to the high-level government corruption involved here. We have no one implicated of more importance than him and now he is dead. That tells us something important.'

'I'm not sure where you're going with this, you're just stating the obvious,' replied Tekiō.

Matachi continued with his theory. 'A man like that, one with his scheming abilities, was a player, someone who knew how to protect himself and those around him would have been very aware of that. The tsunami changed everything for them, yes, all their unscrupulous behaviour has been laid bare. But they would still not be able to move against him for fear of what would be revealed subsequently if they did. That would have brought the whole stinking web of corruption down on all their heads.'

'Then why did they have him murdered, if it seals their fate as well as his?'

'Exactly my point, old chap,' went on Matachi. 'They didn't have him killed. But regardless they will now suffer the consequences of whatever mechanism Uchida put in place to protect himself. It is just a matter of time before they are exposed and the whole decrepit structure comes down on those who built it.'

Tekiō chased the last of his noodles around the bowl and flicked them into his mouth. 'If his associates did not do it, who did then?' he mumbled.

'Whoever it was does not care about the aftermath that will inevitably follow. Either it was done to draw attention to the crimes being committed, which is what I now believe was the motive driving the deaths and disappearances prior to Uchida's, or I feel the game has changed. It is more likely that he had knowledge of information that was so important, it was enough to have him silenced, and to hell with the consequences that would eventually follow his death. That would mean that there is an element at play here that we have missed, but is of such importance that no sacrifice is too great to protect it. That does mean that there are two separate scenarios emerging here. Possibly overlapping in places, but ultimately independent of each other in their goals.'

'Regardless,' Tekiō half belched, 'if it is, case completed, then are we not starting to engage in some "mission creep" here? Should we not make our report, pack up and go home?'

'I thought you liked to mix it with the bad guys?' said Matachi, not waiting for a reply before saying, 'If I'm correct in what I think is unfolding, then we may have a serious issue with our Korean cousins. We need to find Kwak, and quickly. Our best hope of that is through this Luluero woman. We are now reliant on the surveillance I requested on her, to guide us to him. Your new girlfriend is more important than I first realised. Her and the trowel are the only leads we have at the moment. Let's see if forensics have sent us anything.'

Tekiō gave him a snort of derision at the comment and began eating his last rice cake, as Matachi activated his tablet. He was greeted by an alerting 'ping' sound coming from the machine. He opened an attachment on an incoming email.

'Looks like we've got a trace on the blood from the trowel,' he said.

'Great, who is this hero who likes to get his jollies by chopping up old ladies?'

'His name is – what! Redacted; age redacted; occupation redacted; address redacted – what the fuck is this, it's just scanned pages of blanked out lines!'

'Let me see,' said Tekiō, putting down his noodles and taking the tablet from Matachi. He swiped his sausage-like fingers across the screen flicking the scanned sheets back and forth.

'There is nothing in it, it's just bullshit. The guy undeniably exists in our database somewhere, but someone has been over all the files at some point with a black marker,' said Matachi.

Tekiō continued to study the scanned pages of blanked-out detail, then said, 'What about this bit here, they have not fully covered this bit up, in the family background section.'

'Give it to me,' said Matachi, taking the device back. He stared at the spot that Tekiō pointed out, the black ink was slightly faded at this spot over some printed words. He zoomed in on the screen and by widening the spot between his two fingers explained, 'I can just make out the word "Yuzen". What does that mean?'

'Let's look it up,' said Tekiō, 'put the word into a search engine.'

'It's the name of a specialised fabric dyeing process. Let's see how specialised.' He expanded his search for manufacturers of the dyeing technique. 'It says there are only four manufacturers in all of Japan who use this technique, none locally, seems it was too specialised and expensive causing many companies to have closed down.'

'Try searching for the ones that have gone out of business,' suggested Tekiō brightly.

'Obviously!' retorted , looking at his friend condescendingly over the raised tablet. 'Bingo, there was a site in the Kenmochiyama area not thirty miles from here, closed down ten years ago, some sort of pollution spill killed it off! It may be a long shot, but we have nothing else to go on now, so let's go and check it out.'

'Fall down seven times, stand up eight,' said Tekiō. 'Don't start with the fucking proverbs – please!'

CHAPTER FORTY-SEVEN

16 March 2011

The squad's new mission was not an overly complicated one, infiltrate the complex, locate the woman, and then kill her as neatly as possible, preferably with one of their trademark-orchestrated 'accidents', or their equally popular method of a plausible murder scenario. They had set about staking out the abandoned textile mill with a covert surveillance plan that covered all areas of the complex.

The six men had viewed her movements from every angle for three days, with four of the men, in two-man teams, always on station directly observing through military grade optics. The nearest of them no closer than half a kilometre. They also had one man acting as 'Tactical Controller' situated in their Toyota Hi-Ace van, parked two kilometres away on a remote side road. He watched remotely via a live streaming from the camouflaged battery-operated surveillance cameras that had been planted around the site. These had been systemically installed as her movements and location had offered opportunity to do so. The TacCon also ran the coordination of the group using their integrated radio system. The final member of the team was classed as the 'Floater', or spare man. He rotated with the covert observation members if required, though generally, once in position the men were trained to stay in the same location for days. The Floater also provided any resupply support as required, reverting to a reserve asset to cover any unforeseen events that might occur.

The best scenario seemed to be to contrive a simple drowning accident next to the river. The main problem with this option would be first restraining and then transporting her to the river without causing any damage to her body, that would not be in harmony with a trip or a fall into the water. Even something as mundane as a bruise in an inappropriate place, could be spotted during the autopsy that would inevitably follow the discovery of a dead body. This in turn potentially led to questions that may detract from their illicit fabrication of an authentic accident.

The basic method for this type of contrived accident was to be able to deliver a single blow to the head, hard enough to render someone unconscious, but not hard enough to kill or break the skin to allow a bleed to occur. Then carefully transport the comatose individual to a pre-chosen location of the 'accident' and hold their head under the water until they drowned.

This method they saw as the most favourable scenario, however, as usual to meet the high level of professionalism their craft demanded, a unique attention to detail would be essential to achieve the required unequivocal standard of deception.

Two options were proposed for the take-down. One was to strike in the daytime, as she went about her now well studied routines. The benefits of this option were that she would be fully clothed, so her transportation to the river would be undertaken very quickly with a minimum of fuss. The downside was that their approach to come within striking distance would carry a reasonable risk of them being seen before they got close enough to bludgeon her. They were all trained to approach with stealth, but any grappling or manhandling of her that took place would curtail use of the accidental drowning scenario.

The other option was to make their approach when she was asleep, then once they had rendered her unconscious, change her clothes to daywear and transport her to the river. The upside of this was that they had hidden a camera in her room so could tell when she was asleep, then use the remote surveillance and integrated coms to guide them in, right up to her bedside. The weaknesses of this option were less problematic, they would just have to undress and redress her, put the night wear away and remake the bed, leaving the room to appear that it had not been slept in. There was the matter of it being dark, but night vision goggles would be worn to negate this.

To leave a DNA trail, in both cases the wounded area of her head would need to be scraped against the alleged point of contact of her demise, in this case the side of a waterwheel, before she entered into the river.

Their back-up plan would be to initiate a classic predatory assault leading to a murder and robbery MO. They would knock her senseless, sexually assault her and then strangle her to death, being careful to leave no trace of any of their DNA on the body. Finally, the house would be ransacked of any valuables. Not as neat as the accident method, but as long as no clues were left as to their involvement, extremely workable.

After a short debate, the consensus was that the night action was the least risky. There was no point in waiting through the fourth day to carry out the attack, as nothing more would be gained from further observation. The team were confident they knew her every habit and routine. So, it was agreed unanimously that the operation would be carried out that night.

In the centre of the complex a two-storey office administration building had been converted into living quarters. Downstairs there was a kitchen/diner and lounge area and on the first-floor theatre were the bedrooms and bathroom.

The stairway to the bedrooms was made of stone and made no sound under the soft-soled shoes that covered the feet of the two men stealthily making their way to the top of the steps. The CCTV controller was still feeding them real time telemetry on the status of the girl.

'She is still out for the count, fast asleep, laying on her front,' he informed them through their earpieces. 'Standby.'

The woman had not moved in the last half an hour, since the team had started to move in from their start points, almost two hours ago.

The Tac Con had been in constant communication with them from the beginning of the operation, ensuring that they were fully up to date on her exact movements, since she got herself ready for bed.

No real variation in her routine was noticed from the previous days, apart from one small incident, where, after knocking over a small cup of tea onto her pillow, she had changed some of her bedding before she had turned in for the evening. The futon and quilt were not stained by the tea and so she had just gone to the linen cupboard and taken out another pillow to replace the wet and blemished one. It escaped their attention that the pillow had already been stored with a pillowcase over it. Neither did they think it was relevant that the pillow was blue while the rest of her bedding was white. After that incident she continued with her normal routine of opening the bedroom window before retiring. The team patiently waited for four hours, observing her through the night vision capacity of the hidden camera. The Tac Con was trained in recognising sleep patterns. It understood the sequence of different behaviours that individuals demonstrated as they moved through the layered gateways to come to the slow wave sleep cycle, a 'non rapid eye movement' phase of sleep, when the mind has dropped into its deepest level. The human brain starts to generate ever-increasing amounts of delta waves, relaxing the body to a groggy, debilitating state; the point when we are most vulnerable and slow to react if woken suddenly.

They observed her lying face down with her head resting on its right side, sandwiching the pillow between her two arms, which were folded across each other, under the pillow above her shoulders.

'She is ready, stand by, stand by – go, go, go,' signalled the Tac Con quietly.

The lead man on the two-man group acknowledged the order to proceed with a single click of his transmitter button at his throat. Receiving the order to proceed directly into his brain via the bone-conducting receivers held against both sides of his upper jaw. The device allowed his ears to be free from obstruction, removing the impedance that a standard headset, in or around his ears, would limit his ability to pick up important ambient sounds.

The two men were completely dressed in black from head to toe, with just a band of darkened skin, dulled by light-absorbing shades of camouflage cosmetics, showing through the eye slits in their balaclavas. They were suitably armed with a single side, doubled-edged knife, one also carrying a leather-covered cosh filled with half a kilo of lead shot. They had kept it light for speed and deftness, leaving the heavy artillery with the back-up team. Their breathing disciplined and measured, a control they had defined over years of training, they silently opened the door and entered the woman's bedroom. Each moved to either side of her bed. The man on the left teed up his cosh by raising it about his head, cocked to deliver the single blow required for their plan.

The second assailant readied himself with hands free, to seize her if she moved... then she moved.

The Tac Con suddenly found himself blind, deaf, and dumb, all the screens on the laptops before him had turned to a fuzzy haze, he called via the net, 'Abort, abort, we are compromised. I repeat abort.'

But he got no response from any of the other five members of the team. He quickly exited the van, picking up his Chinese variant AK 47 assault rifle as he did so and started to jog towards the complex.

The man on the right-hand side of the bed was already dead, so he could not remember the woman rising up backwards from the bed onto her knees. She had risen so fast it was as if she had

349

been released from a catapult. Her two arms unfolding from around her pillow, she struck with the speed of a praying mantis. Two thin slivers of hardened steel, sharp as razors on both edges had flown from her hands. The man on the right had taken the narrow blade in his left eye, the twenty-five centimetres of steel firmly embedded up to the hilt into his brain.

The second man on the left, was not quite dead yet, the blade had been deflected slightly by his throat mike. It had entered his neck but missed his spinal cord. He now looked in disbelief at the slight female before him dressed in pink Pokémon pyjamas, resting on her knees with both her arms outstretched level with her shoulders. He had dropped the cosh, and with both his hands now clutching at the handle of the knife sticking out of his neck, he watched her suddenly spin around, pivoting on her left knee, her right-hand whipping outwards. She struck his hands where they held onto the blade protruding from his throat, causing the blade to slice through his vertebrae. The angle of the strike delivered a blow that almost decapitated him, but for the remains of his muscles on the left-hand side of his neck.

She rolled off the bottom of the bed, avoiding the two expanding pools of blood on either side, to reopen the linen cupboard. Reaching to the rear of the cupboard she pulled out a SIG Sauer P227 and a Wakizashi sword, the smaller brother of the Katana.

The second team remained in position outside of the dwelling, awaiting the order to enter the building and initiate the next phase of the operation, maintaining radio silence as per the plan. They had no idea they had been compromised – that was until the lead member's head exploded right in front of his partner. He looked upwards to the source of the gunfire, neatly presenting his forehead as a second target for the next hollow point tipped round from the woman leaning out of the window, brandishing the SIG in her right hand. She stroked the trigger, watching dispassionately as his head also disintegrated in a shower of bone and brain.

On hearing gunfire, the fifth member of the team now realised things were not going exactly as planned. He tried to hail his comrades over the net; but received just worrying static in response. He drew and checked his side arm, a Glock 26, putting a 9 x 19 Parrbellum round in the chamber and re-holstered it. Picking up his AK 47, he did the same for that, loading one of the thirty 7.62 rounds held in the magazine and started to move towards the building.

The Toyota HiAce van drove into the car park at the front of the complex. As it rounded the stone-walled approach road, its headlights picked out a small woman with a large gun held across her chest, a pistol hanging from one hand, with a short sword pushed through the waistband of her pyjamas. Behind her lay a torso lacking most of its head, bleeding profusely across the tarmac.

The vehicle pulled up in front of her. Its lights extinguished along with the noise of the engine, as she walked towards the side door of the van. The driver got out and came around to stand beside her.

'Trouble at mill?' said Kurosawa Hikaru, sliding back the door of the van, to reveal a lifeless, bound, and gagged man dressed in dark clothing.

'Bring him in,' she said. 'But before we ask him some questions, I will need to clean the place up a little. Will you help?'

'You always did give me the shit jobs around here, sister,' he said, shaking his head from side to side, making his long fringe float across his angular face, as if the mop of black hair had a life of its own.

'It was all you were ever good for, brother! Now put him in the dye room. There are many questions that require answers, hopefully he can provide some of them. If they are targeting us directly, then we have a major problem unfolding here. Something important must be in progress.'

'Well, whatever it is, we are going to be well armed to face it, and no mistake. These guys meant business.'

351

He handed her a second AK that matched the gun she was holding and reached in to grab their prisoner.

'A resupply is always welcome,' she said as she shouldered the weapon by its sling. 'Though we must thank our friends for their technological investments that watch over us.'

'Always nice to get a heads up when unwanted visitors come to call, sister.'

'Yes, but it is always the mess they make afterwards that is most annoying,' she said as she walked away to start clearing up the bodies. 'Oh, and brother, don't forget to turn that jammer off, I'm told it is powerful enough to intercept every radio signal within a twenty-mile radius. We don't want to draw any more unwanted attention, do we?'

'I will, sister,' he called back to her. He looked down at their captive. 'And you are about to have the worst and last day of your life, friend,' he said to the now semiconscious man. He noticed that the dull hue of the man's aura flickered slightly, as his subconscious registered danger at the comment. He caught hold of the man's collar and dragged him away to their makeshift interrogation room.

CHAPTER FORTY-EIGHT

17 March 2011

They drove out to the old cotton dyeing factory, having found the address easily online, also discovering the reason why the mill had been shut down. It was set in a quiet rural area, several miles from the nearest town. The reason for its location had been its good source of fresh, clean water for the dyeing process, though this reason had also been part of its downfall. For that 'fresh clean water' was similarly important for the villages and hamlets it meandered through on its way to join up with the other tributaries making their way to the sea on Fukushima's coastline.

Their inhabitants had been complaining for many years about the 'brackish taste' their once beautiful fresh water now had, but no evidence could be found of any contamination, a change in the water's 'taste' being a very subjective element to prove. Then one day an accident at the plant had caused a solution of almost pure dye to leach into the river. The dye was instantly caught by the clear waters, which instantaneously turned a vivid green colour. The tainted wave sped down the valley by the river's natural flow, staining everything it came into contact with.

The incident had occurred late at night. When the locals, preparing for their morning routines, had fetched water from a nearby stream to make breakfast and brew tea. Unknown to them, the water was contaminated with a dye. This dye, although harmless, had a remarkably strong pigment. It was typically used by sewage engineers to identify leaks in waste pipes due to its vivid colouration and ability to starkly discolour other substances. The following morning, a number of residents experienced a startling revelation. After consuming the water, they observed their urine had turned a luminous green. This unusual phenomenon caused widespread panic, leading many people to seek hasty medical attention, fearing a severe problem with their health. It was only discovered later the true cause of their concerns; the water from the stream infected by the dye spillage.

The disaster had caused a huge local scandal, even though no one had been seriously hurt – though a good many of the locals said that the discovery of expelling a stream of translucent green had caused more than a little psychological damage – the plant was quickly shut down by the authorities, never to be reopened. The owner had objected, stating that the leak had been caused deliberately, accusing the locals of purposely sabotaging the plant to get it closed down. But she could not prove anything, and it remained closed. Following this, claims and counter-claims had been going through the courts for years, but still nothing had been settled. The owner's name, he noticed, was one Kurosawa Azumi, the daughter of Kurosawa Ichirō, who had run the business successfully for many years before he handed it over to her in his will after his death. She had kept it operating quite successfully for several years until the time of the accident. As the detectives approached the site, they could see that it was a labyrinth of greying timber buildings, a water wheel stood unmoving, adjacent to near the bank of the river. They drove along the side of a traditional stone wall that led along the fields adjacent to the site and into the car park. Pulling the car to a halt across two spaces, they surveyed the frontage of the main building with a collection of smaller ones scattered around it. They were all constructed using traditional techniques working with nature's most abundant raw materials: wood, stone ,and iron.

They surveyed the area from the car in silence. The place reminded Matachi of a reconstruction of a feudal Japanese village, that modern-day Shokunin would have used their inherited skills to build. The place held an air of foreboding about it, that made him uneasy. There seemed to be no sign of occupation, but he felt they were being watched by the very buildings themselves.

'This place gives me the shits,' blurted out Tekiō, breaking the eerie silence and making Matachi start. 'Wouldn't want to spend any time here after dark that's for sure.'

'Then it's a good job we arrived here fairly early, isn't it?' said Matachi trying to be bullish to hide his unease. They both opened their car doors and got out at the same time.

'Let's have a look down past the water wheel, and Tekiō, I have an uncomfortable feeling about this place, so make sure you bring "Herman" with you.'

'You know I never leave home without him, boss.' Matachi nodded, saying, 'Check, check.'

'Check, check,' responded Tekiō, patting the left breast pocket of his jacket.

They headed towards the water wheel and down past weather-beaten, but still serviceable, buildings intersected by low stone walls, that ran at angles from the buildings. Peering in through the windows they witnessed various bits of manufacturing paraphernalia and machinery, each item appeared to be clean and serviceable.

'It's like a fucking museum around here, just look at this stuff,' said Tekiō pushing his face against another window to view the odd treasures within. He took his phone out and started taking pictures of the rooms' contents.

At the water wheel Matachi stopped and looked down into the dry weir, with its entry and exit locks firmly closed against the deep water on the other side. Tekiō carried on down the alley of the stone buildings swanning from window to window, still taking pictures as he did so. He had got about thirty metres ahead of him when Matachi heard Tekiō cry out… 'Girl!' He started to run back towards Matachi, who stared bewilderingly at the sprinting fat man. It was then he realised that if Tekiō was running from something, then it was something worth running from. Matachi was about to turn around to also put a bit of serious distance between him and whatever his partner was sprinting from, when, as Tekiō passed by him, the man reached out with one of his enormous arms, scooping him up off the floor. He tucked Matachi under his right side, carrying him along in the direction of their parked car. Matachi appreciated the sentiment, but being crushed under one of Tekiō's armpits like a folded newspaper was starting to lose its appeal, on account that his lungs were no longer able to take in any air. He thought he was about to pass out when he was dropped unceremoniously onto the ground near the side of the car.

'What the fuck is it?' he managed to gasp.

Tekiō was peering over the roof of the car, hands fumbling for his personal weapon.

'Get on the blower right now and tell control there's a woman running around with a fucking rocket launcher down here,' he shouted at Matachi.

'You screamed "Girl" you fat idiot, if someone has a rocket launcher, I believe the gender designation is by default, irrelevant and the correct nomenclature I believe is R.P. … fucking G!'

'RPG!!' yelled Tekiō, as a small girl with a big rocket launcher over her shoulder, came around the side of the building they had just sprinted past and took a very deliberate aim at their car.

'Fuck me,' cried Matachi getting up and starting to run for one of the low, ornate stone walls lined the side of the track behind them. He had almost reached it when he was overtaken once more by Tekiō. There was no denying the bastard was fast over short distances, as he witnessed his friend clearing the wall a millisecond before the blast from a huge explosion carried him over it as well.

Matachi lay on his back on the other side of their impromptu ballistic barrier, as bits of their Toyota rained down on them, trailing fire and smoke as they did so. He scrambled back to the comparative safety of the wall, next to Tekiō. The man had curled himself up into a foetal position, face down into the dirt, pressed up against the substantial stonework, looking for all the world like a large hibernating bear. Matachi now drew his sidearm and started shooting in the direction of where he had last seen the girl.

'What the fuck are you doing, you're going to draw her attention to us for fuck's sake, you dumb runt!' said Tekiō's muffled voice. 'It may have escaped your attention, but we are somewhat outgunned here!'

'No, I think not. What has escaped your attention, you chicken-livered oversized cretin, is the fact she only had the one missile.' Tekiō raised one of his massive, slab-like arms, revealing his face as he leaned forward to gaze at Matachi. His head tilted at an almost upside-down angle, a tense, wide tight grin stretched across his face, pulling his lips back over jaws that were clenched tightly together.

Matachi glanced down at him briefly, a bullet cracked through the air, passing frighteningly close to his head. He shouted at Tekiō, 'Hey "Pennywise" get that fucking cannon of yours into action.'

Tekiō had not had the time to draw the service pistol holstered under his right arm during their sprint for safety, he now ignored it, instead moving his hand deep under his left armpit he pulled out 'Herman' a Pfeifer-Zeliska .600 Nitro Express pistol. It was a revolver that was at the extreme end of handgun design, engineered to be able to fire hunting rounds, ordinance normally used for killing big game.

The reason for having 'Herman' at all, was because of an incident early in their relationship, involving a disappointing shootout with some heavily body-armoured individuals. After landing several hits on the Kevlar-clad criminals without any noticeable results, the limitation of their service pistols was blatantly obvious. Later, after the men had disappointedly got away, Matachi had suggested that perhaps they should look at acquiring an 'upgrade'.

After some extensive testing of a number of potential weapons, covertly brought onto a police range, the Austrian weapon was chosen. The effect of being hit by a .600 Nitro Express bullet would be devastating on anyone, even someone wearing body armour and that was exactly the effect they were looking for.

The weapon was far from being a standard police armament and not an insignificant purchase at 4,000,000 Yen, with even its shells retailing at an eye-watering 6000 Yen a round. An official purchase of such a weapon was highly irregular, but then everything about their unique set-up was. It was agreed that sometimes the ends must justify the means, and the protection of their ability to safely operate and continue to have such amazing results must be protected, so the weapon had been approved.

After their poor performance in their last gunfight, an incident that could have easily gotten them killed, Matachi saw the weapon as a solid investment. The fact that, as a revolver it retained its cartridge casings, was also very appealing, particularly when one was using not exactly a strictly legal weapon.

It weighed around five kilos and was fifty-five centimetres in length, being essentially a collector's piece for firing on a range. It was not a weapon that could be handled effectively or safely in a tactical environment by a normal sized person. However, it was not a normal sized person who now held it, arms outstretched on the wall, both hands supporting the weapon. The gun looked impressive even with most of its outline lost in Tekiō's huge hands. With large booms, the gun started to put 58-gram slugs down range at 2,139.7 km/h. The blockwork wall behind the girl began to shatter under the impact, as the huge bullets smacked into it showering her with bits of rubble. Matachi could see that the smoke from the burning Toyota was obscuring Tekiō's usually excellent aim.

'Cover me,' he shouted as he moved behind Tekiō, trying to outflank the girl on the right-hand side. Adding as he did so, 'And watch what you're doing with that fucking cannon, your aim is shit today.'

The girl slipped back into a doorway and disappeared as he made his move to the right.

'You just have to hope she does not have a re-load for that fucking stove pipe,' barked Tekiō after him. 'Because if she does, you are on your fucking own.'

Matachi zigzagged for the cover of the first building that ran adjacent to their protective barrier in front of them and began firing with his pistol at the doorway. Tekiō had now used up the five rounds the weapon held and was reloading. Because of their weight and bulk, Tekiō only carried ten more bullets, Matachi held another five of the cigar-sized rounds in a small leather pouch attached to the back of his belt.

'Move!' he shouted across at Tekiō, putting a few rounds from his 9-mm into the doorway.

Tekiō landed with a thump against the building wall by his side. Panting hard he said, 'We need to get some back-up, PDQ, boss.' 'That will be quite difficult without a radio, they were all in the car. You had better make a "One Ten" call on your phone.'

Tekiō nodded in the direction of the water wheel. 'I dropped mine when I grabbed you.'

'Shit!' responded Matachi.

'It was you or the cell phone, what would you have preferred?' said Tekiō testily. 'I have reloaded, let me cover while you call on yours.'

The two men switched places and Matachi holstered his pistol and searched for his phone. Not finding it in his inside jacket pocket he started to search himself more frantically, patting all his pockets in turn with both hands.

Tekiō glanced at him.

'What's with the "fisherman's fag dance"?' he said. 'Don't tell me you have fucking dropped yours as well?'

'Fuck knows where it is, could be anywhere after the acrobatics I have just performed.'

'Without back up, we are seriously in the shit, it must be between the wall and the car somewhere, nip back and have a look.'

Tekiō was right, there was no doubt they needed help, and fast, he readied himself to dash back.

'Okay, cover me, on three: one… two… three!'

Matachi started running back the way he had come. At the same time Tekiō started firing around the corner with his standard issue pistol. Matachi made about five metres, when a burst of automatic gunfire tore up the ground in front of him. He halted his run and got back to the safety of the building, achieving the return journey a great deal faster than he had headed out. 'Fuck that,' he said breathlessly on his return.

Tekiō looked worryingly at his boss. 'Sounds like an AK,' he said and took a quick glance around the corner. 'She is down by the wheel, tucked up in that fucking weir.'

Another salvo of bullets stitched up the side of the building where Tekiō had just put his head. The steel jacketed 7.62 rounds splintering off the corners of the stonework.

'It's definitely an AK and this girl is not fucking about. What's the plan?'

'The girl is no lady that's for sure,' said Matachi as he cupped his hands up to his face and shouted. 'POLICE, LAY DOWN YOUR WEAPONS AND COME OUT WITH YOUR HANDS UP, YOU ARE UNDER ARREST.'

Tekiō, looked at Matachi in disbelief and covered his head with one arm to protect himself from the splinters that he was certain were about to be blasted off the stone corner of the building again, a strong feeling telling him that was going to be the main response to his boss's stupid demands of the girl.

'Is that the best you can come up with, and you say you're the brains of this outfit… you fucking tube!'

They lay there, pressed up against the stone, tense, and

cringing, awaiting another burst of automatic fire. But nothing happened. Matachi gave an encouraging nod to Tekiō indicating he should take another look around the side of the building. Tekiō did not exactly feel emboldened by the gesture, demonstrating the fact, by moving his fist vigorously up and down at the wrist, to Matachi's face. However, with a discerning scowl towards his boss, he did as he was asked.

Drawing the other pistol, he gave a darting glance around the stonework, then held his head out a millisecond longer, pointing both weapons in line with the movement of his head, scanning the area as best he could. He turned back to Matachi saying, 'I think she has fucked off, can't see any sign of the bitch. Go, get the phone now!'

Matachi made his pistol safe and secured the weapon into its holster, then was up and sprinting back towards the metre-high wall, quicker than dysentery with daps on. On reaching it, he performed a graceful swan dive, clearing the wall's top with ease. From the proceeding crunch, loud winded grunt and cacophony of foul language that followed the clearance, Tekiō assumed that the landing had lacked a little of the same grace as the dive. He could not see what was happening beyond the wall, but after a few seconds he was relieved to hear Matachi shout, 'Got it, calling it in now.'

'I would not do that if I was the person on the other side of this,' said a voice quietly, but firmly behind him.

Matachi felt the deathly cold touch of steel at the side of his neck. He slowly moved his head to look down the length of a long sword, at the end of which was a man with his left knee to the ground, pointing the blade at arm's length, parallel with the thigh of his outstretched right leg. The stance was reminiscent of a European-style fencer. But this was no dandy's rapier in his hand, it was a Japanese Katana, arguably one of the finest and deadliest swords ever created.

With uncomfortable effort he brought his gaze up to the man's face. From what he could see, from under the dark tendrils of black hair that dropped across his captor's features, was the angular appearance of a handsome fiend. Unexpectedly sharp teeth slowly formed a dangerous smile on the man's face; a sneer that Matachi found more threatening than the sword against his throat.

'Place your weapon on the ground and then call to your fat friend with his super-sized cannon to do the same,' the swordsman said.

'Kurosawa-san, I presume?' said Matachi.

★ ★ ★

The little rocket girl took back her cell phone from him. He had just spoken to the director of intelligence at the Cabinet Intelligence and Research Office. He thought there was something odd about these two and now he had been informed that they were operatives of CIRO, Japan's spying organisation. He thanked her with a polite bow, she glared at him in response. Matachi had thought the brother was scary, but his sister was in a different league. Curiously he could see that Tekiō was smitten, the lecherous idiot had all but dropped a wing for her. Having beauty and the beast rolled into one must be his type. He started to fantasise on what that courtship would look like, and the unlimited potential for ridicule he could force his friend to endure, when her cell rang again. Without a word, she again handed him the phone.

'Hello,' he vacantly said, as the voice of his boss, Commander Ōno, came into his ear, which brought him back to immediate concerns.

'Is that you, Matachi?'

'Yes sir. It is my good self, sir.'

'What on earth is going on down there? Since your deployment the whole bloody prefecture has imploded around you!'

'With all due respect, sir, I don't think we can be held responsible for the tsunami.'

'I was not talking about the tsunami; I was referring to the political shit storm that is erupting back in Tokyo. You have managed to put your foot into a wasp's nest it seems. It looks like Commander Nomura has been running a sideline in espionage, trading secrets with the Koreans. The civil elements may have led us to this, but they are now irrelevant. You are to hand over all information to the Kurosawas and give them any assistance they require. It looks like there is a spy network that is desperately trying to extract itself and they are quite content to burn every bridge in an effort to do so. You may not have heard, but the Municipal Government Building went up in flames last night. We need to find out what the hell is going on down there. The Koreans are up to something, and it has to mean a lot to them if they are acting so blatantly.'

'I think the information we are deciphering from Matsumoto's USB stick will hold some weight to that hypothesis, sir.'

'It is no hypothesis, Matachi, you understandably have not been introduced to the six dead Koreans the Kurosawa twins have stashed in the Mill.'

'No, I have not, sir. Regrettably our introduction was a rather fraught affair. We have had little time for any cultural exchanges to take place – as of yet, and I did not know they are actually twins, sir.'

'Believe me, Inspector, when I tell you they are of one mind.

It would be prudent for you to keep relationships cordial, so to speak. And as they have informed you, they work for CIRO, so share with them totally and openly any information you have on this case, is that understood?'

'Yes, sir, absolutely, sir.'

'Good. One other thing, you were also correct about Nomura, leaking information to Uchida. Unfortunately, before we got to him, he had withdrawn your surveillance on Ikeda Fuyuko, he has also passed on the information you requested from forensics on Kurosawa. You had better inform them of that, because that may be how the Koreans tracked them down to the Mill. It is possible that they have gleaned more intelligence on them both from Nomura's actions of which they were not fully aware.'

Matachi looked at the two strange siblings who now stood talking to Tekiō. Perhaps, he thought, he might need to delegate the passing on of news that he may have possibly dropped the two psychos in the shit.

'Yes, sir, I will inform them immediately.'

'Very good, Inspector. Oh, and Matachi.'

'Yes, sir?'

'Good luck.'

'Thank you, sir.'

He handed the cell phone back over to the bat shit crazy sister. Both siblings stared at him without any expression on their faces at all. There was definitely something not right about these two, he thought.

'Thank you,' he said. 'I just need to have a quick word with my sergeant here, he can complete his update for you and then it seems we are all yours.'

CHAPTER FORTY-NINE

18 March 2011

The villa was in total darkness when Ikuko pulled her car up outside the front entrance. Once she had stopped, she looked in the rear-view mirror and firmly stated out loud that she was not a jealous woman. A point she had continually reiterated to herself as she journeyed through the late evening into the early hours of the morning, all the way from Shima to Kurosawa's home.

This was not jealousy, she had tried to convince herself, during those long hours travelling the hundreds of kilometres, this was a point of honour. She was not someone to be taken lightly. She did not give love freely, but when she did, she did so with an intense passion. A fervour that demanded through its powerful sincerity, appropriative reciprocation.

It was not merely that she was under no illusion that she had been treated poorly, …and on listening to his message over and over, she now had scant doubt, she had been. It was also the sentiment of it. He had sounded so dispassionate, soulless, and preoccupied, as if she had been listening to a completely different man. Not the one she knew and loved so dearly. That message on the day of the disaster and been his only attempt to contact her. For a full week now since that day she had not heard from him. She had tried to call him several times but could not even leave a message, his phone seemed to be permanently switched off. It was infuriating.

The continuous brooding was making her feel consumed with resentment. There was no doubt in her mind that she was totally justified in seeking some answers to his behaviour. Unless she was a complete fool, she believed he cared for her, and she had responded to that affection. She was not the needy type, but to be totally ghosted since they last spoke was not good enough, not for her that was for sure. She felt herself starting to cry, tears forming in her eyes. This was not her, she never cried, not even when her parents had died. Enough of this nonsense, she thought, stop feeling sorry for yourself and act. That was when she had decided to take matters into her own hands and got straight into her car and headed for Fukushima to confront him.

Five long hours of furious driving later, she had found herself in a state of enraged indignation, banging fruitlessly on his front door. The place seemed very well lit inside and around its perimeter, but there was absolutely no sign of occupation. Where the hell was he? He surely could not have gone far. Where the hell was there to go around here anyway since the disaster had created such havoc in the area? To hell with it, she had come this far and was not going to be swayed by a minor issue like the bastard not being home. She decided to try and call him again.

She pulled out her cell phone and dialled his number. She was desperately trying to work out what to say to him if he answered, when she heard a sound behind her. Believing it was Kurosawa she turned to face him, only to be confronted by two men wearing black balaclavas. Before her mind could engage with what was happening and turn it into some physical reaction, they had a hold of her, gripping her wrists tightly. Then, grabbing her by the hair, one of them kicked the back of her knee joints, forcing her onto the ground. Her body finally started to struggle, using the blast of adrenalin her primeval response to danger had automatically produced – flee or fight. But it was no use, both options were no longer viable as they pinned her to the ground and handcuffed her hands behind her.

★ ★ ★

Takada had been observing the two men for some time. It had been quite an amateurish stakeout of the villa in his opinion, it had been far too easy for him to get into position to monitor them and the house without raising any suspicion from the pair. They were patient, he would give them that, making just one sweep around the premises to confirm that it was not occupied. They continued to lay in wait, hoping to catch its inhabitants once they returned. Whilst they were making their recce, he had taken the opportunity to fit another of his trackers to their van as well. He had then retired to his position in the wooded area opposite to see what would develop, knowing his own perseverance would eventually bear fruit.

Just before dawn he was justly rewarded for his diligence. The woman who arrived at the villa looked to be in some distress, as she banged loudly on the door. He watched dispassionately as the two men broke cover and apprehended the female, quickly and efficiently restraining her. After a short exchange between them they dragged the frightened and struggling victim to their van and threw her into the back. One of them jumped in with her, the other climbing into the driver's seat and starting the engine. It was going to be a long night, he thought, as he checked his transponder. A green and red light blinked back at him. The green one remained stationary, he zoomed in on the screen and saw the red one begin to move away from him.

CHAPTER FIFTY

18 March 2011

The Koreans had not been gentle with Fuyuko during her interrogation with Kwak . She had answered every question in absolute detail, from the moment of her detention by the police, to the time of her release. She had given him a full description of the two detectives who had come for her and her analysis of what sort of individuals the two men were. She had held nothing back from Kwak, responding as if her life depended on it, which she fully understood it did.

When he had finished questioning her, Kwak seemed satisfied with everything she had said. But she knew it would not be enough to save her, the cold way he had thanked her and then said goodbye, left her in no doubt that they intended to kill her.

She had given it her best shot, taking every opportunity to focus her answers to Kwak directly, desperately trying to make him understand that she was still of value to them. Had she not worked on some of their most prestigious 'honey trap' operations, her particular expertise put to use in extorting invaluable information from many businessmen and politicians, even a few females had been taken in by her? But she could sense the situation had changed, she did not know what it was, but it was enough for her to be seen as a liability.

In some respects, it was an odd relief, the realisation that she had done as much as she could to save herself and stay within the organisation. At least she now knew where she stood, out in the cold and alone. It was not the first time she had found herself so. The choice made for her; she now began working on her own rescue plan before it was too late.

★ ★ ★

Bound, gagged, and blindfolded, Ikuko had been transported face down in the rear of the van, with a man's foot resting on her upper back. Every time she made any sort of move to help with the discomfort of laying prostrate across the floor, it was met with an even greater pressure on her ribcage, accompanied by a coarse command to 'keep still'. It felt like they had been travelling for over an hour before they finally came to a stop, by which time she had lost all feeling in her upper back and arms. Her mind struggled to comprehend what was happening. Why had the men taken her, more importantly where were they taking her and to what end? It must be something to do with Hikaru. He was mixed up in god knows what, that was for sure. The presence of the men outside his house, more than likely the reason for his manner with her earlier. If he was in trouble, why had he not told her? It was always the bloody quiet ones that were real trouble, she thought.

She felt the breeze when the van's doors were opened, it brought with it the unmistakable scent of the sea. The two men roughly dragged her out of the car onto her feet. She stood, her body swaying slightly, as a wave of pins and needles swept across her upper body. This uncomfortable, yet oddly relieving feeling, marked the return of her circulation after the sudden release of pressure.

The two men took hold of an arm each and half walked, half dragged her across a short piece of what felt like some concrete and then what sounded like the hollow echo of a wooden walkway, until finally the unmistakable feeling of moving across an aluminium gangplank. She was in no doubt that she was now on board a boat of some description.

She felt the sudden pressure of a hand on her head, as it was forced forward and down as she was taken below deck. Her nostrils began to pick up the sweaty, rancid odours of unwashed bodies and the unmistakable scent of sex hung in the air around her. She sensed the presence of several other people in the confines of the cabin. It had been extremely difficult to breathe with the wad of cloth in her mouth, and now it had drawn up all her saliva, her tongue and inner cheeks were stuck to it making her want to gag.

She was pushed onto a thinly cushioned seat, the abruptness of the move causing her to sit against her bound hands. She heard someone say, 'At last, some fresh meat.' Then another voice saying, 'Let's have a look at her then.' Someone undid her blindfold, and the gag was roughly removed. She swallowed hard attempting to relieve the dryness in her throat and desperately tried to focus her eyes to the gloomy interior.

There was a bed at the far end of the room with a naked, motionless female lying on it, her legs spread wide apart. Her face was bloody and beaten and she seemed to have no part of her body that was not covered in scratches or the discolouration of bruised flesh.

'This one is not to be touched,' said a voice behind her. 'She is for the programme. Understand?'

She looked around and saw two men standing there, they must have been the ones that had kidnapped her, she thought. A small chorus of begrudging murmurs went around the cabin from the three other men present.

'Keep your attentions on the whore,' he said, pointing at the bound woman on the bed. 'She is to become fish food soon, so do what you like with her. But I better not find a mark on this one or there will be trouble.'

'Are we still leaving in the morning?' asked one of what seemed to be the boat's crew.

'Yes,' he said, then with a disdainful glare at the others he stopped speaking in Japanese. Though Ikuko no longer understood what was being said she realised the men were talking in Korean. 'All is still as planned. Get ready to cast off as soon as we return,' he continued in Korean.

Ikuko was now extremely distraught and tried to speak, wanting to ask what the hell was going on. However, her tongue was far too swollen and strained to make any sound at all, other than a croaking guttural groan from deep within her dehydrated throat.

The man glanced at her, now unmasked, his face appeared hard and uncompromising.

'Make sure she is adequately cared for; it's going to be a long trip,' he said, as he left the cabin, his partner accompanying him out.

She felt the eyes of the other three men fall on her. She lowered her head, not wanting to catch their eye and invite an interaction from them. What was she to do now? Ikuko had no idea where she was, and she was in no position to free herself. What had she gotten herself involved in? For the first time in her life, she felt all was lost.

★ ★ ★

Fuyuko lay there, feigning unconsciousness; the men had enjoyed treating her badly over the last few days. Gaining their pleasure from inflicting their sadistic sexual machinations on her. She did not think they realised she was a professional porn star and had been a sex worker of one sort or another since she was an adolescent. These men did not know what rough sex was. They were fucking amateurs compared to her as they would soon find out. She had played along with their pathetic attempts to cause her pain and suffering, feeding their pitiful desires, with crying and screaming at all the appropriate places. One of her better performances she had thought. Yes, they had hurt her, caused her pain without a doubt, gang rape had its own depraved tempo. But now she had them exactly where she wanted them. The fools had stopped checking her bonds as she feigned a weakened state of vulnerability, luring them into a false sense of security over her. They now saw her as just a plaything, of no danger to them at all. She had been waiting for just the right moment to spring her trap, when the unknown girl with the blue hair and the unusually broad shoulders, had been dumped amongst them.

She had listened intently to what was being said from her position of seemingly being in a state of oblivion, crumpled on the bed. She had no idea what was going on now, but palpably, the normal pattern of operations she had been involved with was over. A sudden and dramatic change occurred, the reason for it was beyond her comprehension. It was the deadly consequences of it that concerned her now.

The girl appeared to be regarded as some sort of bonus to their plan. She knew the Koreans had been running a programme which involved the kidnapping of Japanese citizens and transporting them to the North for some time. Perhaps they were sweetening whatever the fucking deal they were operating now, with her.

She looked terrified, but considering the situation, she maintained more control over herself than one would have expected. Cheer up, sweetheart, this may turn out to be not such a bad day for you after all, she thought, as she waited for the kidnap team to leave. She had not met any of the men now in the cabin with them before. Up to this point, her sole contact had been Kwak, who served as the intermediary connecting her with the businessmen and politicians. These individuals would be coerced through blackmail into working for Uchida, a scheme she was now a part of.

None of the men were concerned with concealing their identity, which would have been concerning if she had not already known what her fate was to be. Though conversation could not be said to be her jailer's main interest in her, they did tend to use Japanese when speaking to her. She was sure they knew she could understand Korean but maintained a charade of ignorance by not responding to anything said in Korean. Two of the men, Ko Ha-kyun and Du Jea-min, now remained below with them, as the Korean they called Jin Wook, whom she understood to be the leader of the merry trio, accompanied the second group back onto the main deck. One of the men from the kidnap group began to ask questions about the state of the vessel. She could not hear everything, but it seemed the craft was going out to sea as soon as possible, ready to come to the assistance of another vessel if and when required. The men's voices faded, something about a request to inspect the towing lines, then she could make out nothing more.

If she was going to escape these idiots, then it had to be before they cast off. Once at sea she would have no chance, they were already tiring of her, and they may just kill her and throw her overboard once they were a safe distance offshore. She had been working at loosening the rope on her right hand whenever she had been left alone. Her captors' first mistake was to have not tied the bond tight enough, the second was not checking to see if it was secure when she pretended to be unconscious. It was not much of an edge on her situation, but she had no choice other than to make the most of it.

The sound of footfalls on the upper deck and the boat starting to sway indicated that the men had made their way back ashore. The appearance of Jin in the hatchway, calling for one of them to come up and assist him, confirmed it.

The two men had a brief conversation about who should have the 'final run at her' and with a smirk, Ko said Du was welcome to her and made his way topside.

The door to the cabin opened and Ikuko looked up to see Du standing there. He gave her a leer glance and replaced the gag and then started to grope her breasts. For a moment Fuyuko thought he was going to disobey his orders and turn his attention to this new girl. She gave a fragile moan and rolled onto her back with her legs falling open in an enticing manner. It was enough of a lure to draw Du to her, to Ikuko's relief. Moving across the cabin, he undid his belt holding his trousers, which also held a nasty looking knife and began to climb onto the bed, she could see he was fully aroused, but Fuyuko's focus was on the knife.

It had been many years before, back in the clubs and brothels of Bangkok, that Fuyuko had first entered the sex trade. She had always been a wilful child and a great disappointment to her hard-working parents. She had not cared about what they thought, then or now. She took to the sphere of vice with a will, working in the 'ping pong' bars around the many seedy districts of the city. She soon understood there was a craft to her chosen vocation, and she became studious in acquiring its knowledge. Within a year she had become a star attraction at Bangkok's 'Long Shot Bar', an establishment with a reputation for a particular form of entertainment. Unfortunately for Du, she had become a master at performing this particular skill.

Spitting on his hand, Du climbed onto her. You are going to need a lot more lube than that, you cockroach scuttling cunt, she thought. Opening herself wide so that he could fully fit inside her, she secured his searching lips on her own. Suddenly releasing half a breath, she sucked his tongue into her mouth. Du immediately became aware something was not right and started to withdraw from her when he felt a vice-like grip on his penis. The woman then proceeded to bite down hard onto his tongue. He started to panic, the sudden pain from both areas was excruciating and he began to flail around hitting out at her. He desperately needed to get her to release him, but she was like a fucking limpet.

During her time at Madame Clow's, Fuyuko's act became the club's best attraction. She could fire ping pong balls as fast as her assistant could load them into her. The balls flew in every direction around the bar. You could always tell the regular customers, as they were the ones with beer mats prudently placed over their drinks. That was the first part of her act; the second was when a bottle of beer was handed around the audience and punters were invited to remove the steel cap with their bare hands. The unopened bottle was then placed onto the floor of the stage. She would then slowly squat over it, drawing the bottle deep inside her. She would then rise majestically from around the bottle, as beer frothed from its now opened top, to a great crescendo of applause and cheers from her admiring fans. Then to their great delight, she would reach her fingers inside and remove the steel cap, flicking it with a thumb, directly into the audience. There was no doubt as Du was finding out, the woman had specific talents.

Du had somewhat lost his ardour as he thrashed around trying to get away from the creature that had locked onto him. Unfortunately for him, if he had managed to keep his tongue in his head, he would have been able to scream. He eventually managed to push himself up onto one arm while he held the other one up to his profusely bleeding mouth. He was so preoccupied with the pain he failed to notice that Fuyuko had freed her right arm and was now working his knife from its sheath. With a deft slicing action, she ran the blade down between them, his attempt to pull away giving Fuyuko all the target she required. There was a gagged scream and Du flew backwards onto the floor as she cut the tether between them. Fuyuko quickly used the blade on the rest of her bonds.

An already traumatised Ikuko looked on in horror as the battered woman sat upright. Reaching inside a cheek, she removed a lump of flesh that had been most of Du's tongue. She threw it mockingly at her assailant on the floor, now writhing in agony, clutching at what remained of his groin and gagging on the blood from his torn-out tongue. The knife, now in Fuyuko's hands, suddenly caught his attention and, realising what was about to happen next, Du desperately tried to crawl away. He felt a foot on his chest, and he looked up to see Ikuko looking pitilessly down on him.

'Way to go, girl!' said Fuyuko, as she quickly crossed to the hapless man and straddled his back. Pulling the man's head

375

back by the hair, she leaned in close to the side of his head and whispered in a hoarse, evil voice, 'I never give freebies, fucker, you'll have to pay the full price,' as she pushed the blade slowly into the side of his neck and with a quick sawing action out through his throat.

Blood flowed around Ikuko's feet as the man quickly bled out. She looked up to find Fuyuko in a wide-legged stance, arms stretched outwards at her side, the blade held tightly in one fist. She was soaked in blood from her hair down to her toes. It was a terrifying sight to behold and to Ikuko she looked like a type of primeval gladiator, victoriously gloating over her kill. Despite her shock at what had just happened and the scene of carnage before her, Ikuko could not help but feel an overwhelming sense of admiration for this woman.

Before she could say anything, Fuyuko acted quickly, straightening Du's pants and searching for the keys to Ikuko's cuffs. Finding them she quickly released her. Pulling her gag down, she held a finger to her lips and beckoned for her to follow. Ikuko nodded in understanding. Silently Ikuko pointed to a set of car keys in a pool of blood on the floor. Poking her head furtively above the hatchway to the cabin, Fuyuko could see one of the men at the bow of the craft, of the other there was no sign. She could see a Toyota van parked on the quayside. She glanced back down at Ikuko now holding a set of car keys in front of her. Ikuko stared back at the almost naked, blood-drenched creature before her. She looked possessed, like a painting she had once seen of Izanami, the god of death. She was utterly terrified and unsure of what she had got herself mixed up in. She locked eyes with Fuyuko, receiving a horrifying grin in return, as she beckoned to her to follow her up onto the deck of the boat.

Creeping slowly and staying low, they worked their way along the side of the boat towards the gangplank and the van parked alongside. They had just reached the narrow platform, when a cry of alarm went up behind them.

'Run!' shouted Fuyuko, turning to face the direction of the shout.

Ikuko burst into life, scrambling down the metal gantry without looking behind her. Once on the quayside she risked a glance only to see Fuyuko bent backwards onto her hands like a crab, her torso thrust upwards and towards the man advancing on her.

Back in the day, the grand finale of Fuyuko's nightly performance, was to lay back onto the table and insert a banana into her vagina. Accompanied by a beaming grin and a drum roll, the fruit would become a yellow missile, which she would fire across a Mexican wave of hurriedly lowered heads, to explode with a resounding splat on impact with the far wall of the bar. There would be no rapturous applause to accompany this act, but it was by far her best performance to date. Jin did not have time to duck Du's shredded penis hitting him full in the face with such force that he flew backwards in horror, retching and screaming on discovering what had struck him and then stuck to his face.

Exit stage left, thought Fuyuko, as she regained her feet and went after Ikuko, only to find her struggling with Ko. The man had her in a bear hug, lifting her off the ground.

'I've got this!' Ikuko shouted at her. 'Go. Get the van started.' Fuyuko waved for an instant, knife in hand, looking to slash the man without hurting Ikuko. Suddenly Ikuko lifted both her feet off the floor and pushed off the side of the handrail, driving herself and Ko over the quay into the dark waters below.

Silly girl, thought Fuyuko, as she moved down the gangplank. She had almost made it to the bottom when she was violently pulled back by a strong grip on her arm. She was about to turn on her assailant when she was suddenly released and sent flying onto the concrete of the quay. Puzzlingly she still felt the presence of the man's grip on her arm, then she saw the reason why, his arm was still holding onto her.

A high-pitched scream of terror drew her bemused attention

to the gangplank. In front of her a stocky man with a long sword was methodically dissecting Jin one joint at a time. Bits of him flew into the air around him like a chainsaw going through a trifle, until only his torso remained intact.

What was left of Jin begged for mercy. Takada answered by spitting in his face and pushing what was left of him over the side into the water.

'Bravo! Bravo!'

Takada turned to see a partially naked woman sitting on the quay, cloaked in blood, and waving a severed arm at him as if it was a trophy. 'The last act should always be the best,' she said to him.

He drew his sword outwards, flicking the blood off it with a sharp strike of his left hand, drawing it across the top of his scabbard with the precision of the master swordsman he was. He sheathed the sword and brought himself fully upright, returning the lady's salute with a deep bow.

'I wonder if you could be of similar assistance to my new friend down there?' she said pointing into the oily waters of the dock. Takada moved to the edge, but all he could see were a few bubbles coming up to the surface.

'I'm sorry,' he said, 'I think they have been down there too long; your friend is gone.'

Fuyuko, came alongside him and said, 'Pity, I was just starting to like her.'

Ikuko and Ko had tumbled into the water between the ship and the quay, their momentum pushing them out into the harbour. Ko fought to get back to the surface, dragging himself from her embrace. As he frantically struck out for the surface, Ikuko reached up and, with a grip that was powerful enough to rip a crustacean from its rocky lair, grabbed hold of his testicles. The searing agony jolted Ko, urging him to gasp for breath and unleash the scream that his body ached to release. Yet, as he desperately tried to inhale, no air filled his lungs. Instead, the briny waters of the Pacific flooded in, stifling his cry and amplifying his torment. As the lack of oxygen sapped his strength, Ikuko pulled him back down to her eye level, as she calmly floated in the water. Cocking her head slightly to one side as their eyes locked, she watched him helplessly drown in front her. She gave him another twenty seconds just to make sure, before she released him to sink below her. He fell away, slowly sinking into the gloom, as she then drifted gently to the surface. She emerged to find a shocked, thickset man and an amazed Fuyuko, now with a short coat around her shoulders that hardly protected her modesty, staring in astonishment down at her.

'What the hell have you been doing in there, you silly cow!' shouted down Fuyuko. 'Come out at once, before you catch your death!'

CHAPTER FIFTY-ONE

18 March 2011

For over a week the Nameless Captain had languished in self-contained solitude, hiding out in a temporary refuge for the now many homeless, that had been set up in the town's community centre. It was one of a number of such places that had sprung up following the disaster, in an attempt to give comfort and support to some of the beleaguered surviving inhabitants of the battered prefecture.

The centre had quickly filled up with displaced and dispossessed residents, each person a distraught receptacle possessing a tale of individual tragedy. He had shared in their trauma over the last few days, asleep or awake, each seemed resigned to constantly reliving the horrors that had befallen them and their loved ones. The captain had watched as the days had passed and its occupants moved from a state of debilitating shock, which had stupefied them from comatose dormancy, to one of grim wretchedness. A condition of misery that he now knew only too well.

It was then, through the fog of desolation that had settled amongst them, that the voices of the dead could be heard. Each night several of the catastrophe's victims were visited by the lost. Their ethereal infection, becoming renewed anguish for the others, as each relayed tales of hearing loved ones call to them across the sea, the forlorn sound of the pitiful crying of babies, or for some, a collective wail of despair, a siren of the lamented, sounding across the land, that caught in their souls. He had stayed there helping where he could, by just listening to these forlorn people, not questioning the tales shared with him. This new terror became too painful for many, though gave outlandish solace to some. For the captain it confirmed what he already understood he must do. The land had been cracked open, its raw rift releasing entities from the vale of spirits to that of man. For some reason unfathomable to him, he had been chosen for a task. The epiphany of his fate was clear to him, that he had been made a part of the balm required for the land's healing. This understanding renewed some of his lost vigour. He was hardly refreshed but had been filled with new purpose. He could not explain why, but the time had come to leave his bereft companions and start to make his way to the sea once again.

It was late in the evening when he arrived at Higashimachi. He had spent all that day hitching rides when he could, resorting to walking when the traffic on the roads around the prefecture became sparse. But finally, his haphazard journey to the coast was complete. He had been vague about any specific destination to those who had been kind enough to pick him up, telling them he was looking for lost relatives who had lived along the coast.

He now found himself in one of the few coastal towns that had been relatively untouched by the disaster. Making his way to the quayside, he took a seat on one of the free steel mooring bollards that lined its harbour walls. He saw the sad predicament of many berths that were empty of cables, with only a few scattered vessels moored along the harbour's length.

Weary, hungry and thirsty, he wondered what he was to do now. This was the place he was sure it had drawn him to, as sure as the Moon pulls at the tides. Resigning himself to wait patiently, he allowed the minutes to yield into hours. A gloomy dusk had started to foreshadow the oncoming evening when he began to hear a commotion further down the harbour. It was too gloomy to see exactly what was going on, most of the lights were off, still suffering from the lack of power to the area, but there was no mistaking the screams and cries of terrified people. Without questioning why, he rose and began to jog towards the commotion. It was clear from the potency of the sounds of human anguish, that someone was in considerable distress. As he got nearer, he began to make out figures in the gloom, they were kneeling over the quayside pulling a girl out of the water next to a fishing boat, not unlike his *Michi Maru*.

He was about to ask if they needed any assistance, when he found himself looking down the wrong end of a sharp-looking sword. He skidded to a halt, with the blade almost touching his throat. He held his hands up either side of his shoulders and said, 'Peace brother. I have no quarrel here. I heard the screaming and have just come to help.'

The short, burly man with the sword moved himself away from the two women, saying nothing as he pivoted the point of the sword, so it was now in the captain's face. It was then he noticed that both girls were drenched; one with water, the other in blood and everyone was looking at him suspiciously. 'I can see this is none of my business,' said the captain, 'and I have trouble enough of my own to deal with, friends, I can assure you. Just let me be; to mind my own concerns and I will be on my way.'

'He is not Korean, but he may be one of them,' said Fuyuko The captain looked at the woman who had spoken. 'I am not one of anybody. I'm just another trade-less fisherman,' he said, with an air of righteous indignation.

'Maybe. Regardless, you are coming with us,' said Takada.

Before the captain could answer, Ikeda said, 'And where exactly are we going?'

'To ask questions, receive answers and deal out retribution.' The two women looked deep into each other's eyes; both saw the fanning flames of anger wrought by a woman scorned. 'Just give us a moment to get cleaned up and we will be right with you,' said Fuyuko.

They both walked back along the quay and re-entered the boat together.

'Don't be long,' he called after them.'

He had not thought earlier when he had begun to follow the van, that he would be spending time that evening waiting for females to make themselves presentable. He returned his attention to his new captive. The man had seemed to him to be the stoic type, but now his face was whiter than mare's milk.

'If you are innocent, I promise on my honour all will be well for you, fisherman.'

'I don't think so,' said the captain, staring beyond Takada to the line of wooden storage buildings along the quayside. He started to back away from the sword that had not left his face since he had arrived.

'I would not do that, pilgrim,' said Takada, watching as a look of terror seeped into the man's features.

'And I would not do that,' said the captain continuing to back away.

'Do what?'

'Have my back turned to one of those!' said the captain pointing over Takada's head, with a visibly trembling hand. An unexpected rustling sound came from behind him, pulling Takada's attention away from the captain. On the apex of a wooden roof was a creature of such abnormal proportions and structure, the like of which his senses failed to comprehend. It started to flow down the side of the building, like a giant bear that could move with the dexterity of an ape. It landed on the ground accompanied by a rustling sound. It seemed to be ignoring Takada, looking beyond him, to the man now beside him. It's alien, almond-shaped eyes seemed to recognise the captain. An inshore breeze swept past them, carrying the men's scent straight to the creature's nostrils, which twitched in acknowledgement. Takada turned to fully face it, his back to the quay's edge, his stance changing to accept the challenge of imminent deadly combat. His mind did not try and analyse what was before him, triggered automatically by the mortal threat, his awareness took him to the deep Zen state where life and death became one and the true warrior embraces all fates. He lifted his sword to the full guard position and gave a blood-curdling Samurai war cry, as he readied himself for battle. Nothing now existed for him, other than the power of this moment.

Then, as the creature readied itself to pounce, they heard a female voice behind them, its tone strong and compellingly gripping them all. 'You have done well, captain, even after all your doubts. I congratulate you on being an exceptional tethered goat,' she said, her words now mocking, but still potently beguiling.

'Where the fuck did she spring from?' said a now extremely alarmed Takada, as he made to circle away from the small gathering. He was sure the woman was glowing.

The witch ignored him and continued to walk towards the creature, gliding in front of Takada. Once directly in front of the creature she addressed it directly. 'I have been sent to return you, Atrocitor, for this is not the time for a creature of eternity to roam freely in this realm. Now is not your time. You must restore yourself to the realm of shadows, the surface is not ready for you yet. A mistake was made and I bear the regret of the gods for the disturbance caused. They ask for your forgiveness for their clumsy error, but you must return now. There will be a time to present yourself here once again, when the humans have done their worst and lifted their wretched vale. I bring apologies from those who cast you out, a mistake they are sincerely sorry for. Miscalculations can occur, even for them and I have been dispatched to guide you back.'

If the woman wanted an answer, she did not wait for one as she continued to walk towards the creature as she spoke. Takada was thinking this would be a good time to make a run for it but was transfixed by what he was witnessing.

Stopping just before reaching the creature, she was seemingly uncaring of any threat it might pose, and turning to the two men said, 'Fisherman, your part is played, go now and never look back. Samurai, I will have need of your services before this day is over.'

Without waiting for an answer to her request, she carried on into an alleyway between the buildings. The creature, with a final glance, blinked its eyes at the captain and then duly followed her. Both disappeared into the gloom.

'What's going on?' said a voice from the boat as Ikuko and Fuyuko re-joined them on the quay. They had cleaned and dressed themselves as best they could. They would readily admit that they would not win any fashion show, however the two men did not appear to acknowledge their return at all. They just stood gawking at an alleyway.

'Everything okay? Did we miss anything?' asked Fuyuko to Takada who seemed to be frozen to the spot. 'I brought these for the fisherman, just in case.'

She held up a set of handcuffs. Takada came out of his stupor and took them from her, throwing them into the water.

'We are not taking him with us any fucking where, and we need to get away from here as fast as we can right now.'

'What happened?' asked Ikeda.

'I will tell you about it on the way, but I can assure you, there is no way you will believe me,' he said briskly striding to where he had left his noodle van.

CHAPTER FIFTY-TWO

18 March 2011

Firmly clasping a Katana securely between her knees, Ikuko sat alongside Takada in the front of the noodle van. Fuyuko was in the back sitting on the floor, lodged between the stainless-steel cupboards and a serving hatch. She held the tracking device and was giving a running commentary as to where the other bugged Toyota was now. As Takada drove them way up into the highlands of Fukushima, the target vehicle had not moved since they had started out and they were now close to where it was Kenrō-Ji-Jin.

Takada was still not sure why he had made the decision to follow the van carrying Ikuko in the first place, but it had turned out to be a very fruitful one. It had started off fairly normally for this type of operation by first getting himself into a good position to observe what was going on around the boat. He had witnessed the blue-haired girl being taken on board; the men returning very shortly afterwards without her. They had wasted no time in driving off, and he had decided to stick with the boat. The reason for the girl being held intrigued him. He had decided to get a closer look and was making a stealthy approach towards the vessel, when all hell broke loose. The women had come onto the deck and almost immediately found themselves in a desperate fight with the Koreans. By the time the blue-haired one had pushed herself and her attacker into the water, he was already sprinting across the quay with his Katana drawn, ready to join the altercation. He was still trying to process what he had seen after that. The delight he felt from chopping the Korean into bits had been short lived, along with the enjoyable feeling of gratitude from the two girls he rescued. Since then, the information Fuyuko had freely provided, had filled in a lot of gaps on the termination of Uchida. The blue-haired one was also connected somehow, but even she did not know how. It was very apparent that the Koreans were up to something big – but what?

He was still trying to process the encounter with the creature, not mentioning to them what had happened when he had been left with the fisherman. He was still not sure it really happened, perhaps he was suffering from some sort of stress disorder, no doubt brought on by being far too pleasant to people as of late. He put the event to one side, he needed to concentrate on the task in hand. It was difficult to comprehend, but he was feeling an overwhelming sense of destiny approaching and he was determined not to be found wanting.

They soon found themselves driving through a light industrial business area, with each unit's courtyard widely spaced from the next.

'It's in there,' said Fuyuko peering out of the side hatch window as they passed a padlocked, large, double steel gate barring access to the unit. Takada did not slow down as he drove by. He continued on until he found a courtyard that he felt was far enough away to conceal them and pulled in, parking his van between two buildings, out of sight.

'Stay here,' he said, getting out of the van. He retrieved his sword from Ikuko and leaned in through the door, saying, 'Won't be more than ten minutes.' He closed the door quietly and disappeared into the darkness.

He made his way through the adjoining perimeters of the surrounding business units until he was next to the one that held the Toyota van. The buildings backed onto each other obscuring any view into the unit. Leaving his sword tucked in behind a drainpipe, he scaled the side of the closest building, clambering up one of the vertical steel girders on its external cladding. Dextrously moving hand over hand, at the same time jamming each foot into the gap between the steel and the block work wall, he gained access to the building's roof within seconds.

Laying on his front, he gently pulled himself along its surface until he could look directly into the yard below. From his vantage point he could see a fishing boat had been loaded onto a large trailer, with a powerful looking truck attached to it. There were several identically marked HiAce vans parked around the unit. It was impossible to distinguish which one was the van he had attached the tracker to and he counted at least ten individuals engaged in different activities around the truck and trailer. All of the men moved with a strong sense of urgency as they went about their tasks; it looked like they were readying themselves to move off in a convoy.

Four more men then came out of one of the buildings, each one holding the unmistakable silhouette of an AK-47. They got into one of the Toyotas and, as one side of the gate was opened for them, they drove off heading towards the coast.

Scouts, he thought, off to set up pickets for the convoy no doubt. He quickly made his way back down to the ground. Retrieving his sword, he jogged back to his own van. Opening the door, he handed his sheathed sword back to Ikuko. 'Did you see the van come out?' he asked.

'Yes, looks like it's going back the way we came. To the coast,' said Fuyuko. 'Are we going to follow it?'

'Yes, I am. I really need to drop you off, but for the moment, I'm afraid you will have to come with me.'

'I thought we were going to get some pay back,' said Fuyuko. 'Oh, have no fear, fierce one, you will, and this is how I am now going to get it for you.'

He started up his noodle van and drove back the way they had just come.

The trio had been following the Toyota as it made its way down towards the coast. Being the only vehicles on the road at that time, travelling with their lights switched off, it had not been difficult to stay out of sight. They watched as it came to a stop about a kilometre in front of them, pulling into the side of the road.

Takada stopped the noodle van and looked across at the two girls.

'I think it is time that you got out and left this to me,' he said. 'Whatever it is that they did to you back on the boat, there are now bigger concerns in play. Concerns that I must put a halt to.'

'Do you think the men back there and the ones in that car are part of the same group that held us?' asked Ikuko.

'Yes,' answered Takada.

'Is it your intention to kill them?'

'Yes.'

'In that case you will not be fucking doing it without us; we want to see those bastards dead,' said Fuyuko. 'We can help you.'

'We are tougher than we look,' added Ikuko.

He stared at the women. They were both quite dishevelled and still stained with blood; they looked as wild as a couple of Yonaki babās. 'I would find that really concerning,' he said.

He felt the determined stares from them intensely focusing on him. 'Okay,' he said, jumping back in the noodle van and starting the engine, 'there is something you could help me with, I'm sure.'

As Takada made his final approach to the side of the Korean's vehicle on foot, he could hear the high revving sound of his Suzuki coming in fast. The women had timed their run to perfection. They shot past driving flat out, drawing the attention of the men in the van long enough for him to pull back the side door and jump in.

'Surprise!' he shouted as he kicked the man in front of him into the other; both fell to the floor. The two men in the front had been looking out the windshield, distracted by the noodle van flying past at high speed. With a single sweep of his blade, he beheaded both driver and front passenger before they had even thought to turn around. Following the arch of his sword around, he used its momentum to change his grip on the hilt, with his right hand holding it like a long dagger and his left braced with the palm against its end. He then drove the blade down and through the heart of the man he had kicked to the ground. The man beneath him was fumbling for his weapon and desperately trying to get up. But it was too late, pulling the blade out of the first man's ribs, he swept around, neatly parting his head from his shoulders, to add to the other two.

After he had finished loading the two bodies from the front, he pulled the driver out of his seat onto the ground. He let the last of his blood flow out his severed neck and then picked him up and threw him into the back with the others, followed by the two heads. Jumping into the vacant seat he wiped their blood off the steering wheel with a balaclava that was on the dash and started the van up and went after his able accomplices.

CHAPTER FIFTY-THREE

18 March 2011

The three men sat around Kim Jin-sung's small dining table, in his quaint hillside cottage, each held a lit cigarette and a glass of sake. In front of them was an ashtray fashioned from a wide, flat seashell set into a wooden base and a half-empty sake bottle. It was early evening and, beyond their vantage point in the building's conservatory, a long line of industrial artificial brightness could be seen through its windows, the piecing arc lights bearing witness to the presence of the crippled nuclear plant on the coast.

One of the men, Min Hyun-woo, a man regarded by them as a most accomplished assassin, stubbed his half-smoked cigarette out in the ash tray, disturbing the ashen layers of its many predecessors.

'It's too late for them now, their response has been too slow,' said, Kwak. 'The fools have not even discovered the whereabouts of the displaced rods. In fact, they are still not entirely sure that the rods have gone missing in the first place.' He held out a packet of cigarettes to his co-conspirator.

'They are looking for the transporter. When they find it, they will see that we cut the flask free with a blowtorch, that will be the proof they need that the uranium fuel has been taken. Only then will they stop acting like idiots, pathetically willing the fuel rods to turn up in the wreckage of their plant or at the bottom of the sea. Then they will have no choice other than to admit the loss of a considerable amount of weapons-grade plutonium. Until then we have time enough to finish our operation.'

Min took a cigarette and lit it. 'Yes,' he said, 'I agree the spineless chimps will not escalate their failings to the Japanese authorities, let alone Washington, until they are totally sure it is missing. The kind of search and investigation required for this would take days for them to organise, even without already having to deal with two national catastrophes.' He blew a plume of smoke into the smoggy air above them.

Kim, nodded in agreement saying, 'He is correct, Japan is reeling from this double disaster, punch drunk and on the ropes. The country's capabilities and resources are near collapse, they will never intercept the flask now. They will not know where to start. They will eventually have no choice but to admit the rods are missing at some point, but not for at least a few more days and by then it will be far too late. We are covering our tracks ruthlessly, leaving nothing that could alert them to our plans.'

Kwak took a sip of his sake, adding, 'The clean-up teams are working overtime now, eliminating anyone we suspect of having knowledge of our operations. Most of them have completed their tasks and have been reassigned to protect the cargo and secure its passage to Higashimachi. I have talked to the whore, and she has not told the two detectives anything. Soon she will take her final curtain call. I have sent word to Nam to eliminate the girl we found outside the Kurosawa family villa. It would have been nice to send a little icing on the cake back to our homeland, but we have orders to take no chances on anything that could remotely interfere with the mission. They will dump them both once the *Daimyo Maru* has taken up its position at sea. After this briefing, Min and I will make our way to Higashimachi to oversee the launch. After tonight, destroy all evidence of our operation and disperse to your extraction routes. I am sure we will all meet again in the presence of the Supreme Leader to be honoured.'

Kim rose from the table and addressed the two seated men. 'Regardless of the efficiency of the clean-up teams, I still say a rising body count will attract attention from police and security forces alike, as sure as shit attracts flies, I am…'

The sudden appearance of a lone female approaching from the darkened interior of the cottage's living room skewered the remainder of his sentence in the back of Kim's throat.

'I'm afraid that is not all it attracts,' said the attractive young woman, pointing two, not so pretty pistols directly at them.

She focused her handguns, each on Min and Kwak and held them firmly there. Not being covered by either of the weapons, Kim saw his chance and broke for the conservatory door, ripping it open and throwing himself through it. Azumi stood resolute and unwavering, her intense gaze fixed on the two men before her. She stared at them with a terrifyingly calm expression, which did not alter even as, within a few seconds, Kim returned by flying through one of the windows, smashing him into a heavy telescope. The man lay under the optic, bleeding profusely from multiple wounds on his head and face, the consequence of being beaten, cut by glass from the broken window and his impact with a metal tube firmly bolted to the floor.

'Welcome back,' she said, in a not very welcoming manner. 'I was disappointed that you felt you had to leave us so soon.' The man struggled to regain his feet, grabbing onto one of the legs of the tripod for support, still reeling from the recent open palm strike to the back of his skull, the task was quite a challenge for him as his senses were swirling like a well shaken snow-globe.

'Ah, such a gentleman,' she said to the struggling man. 'But please don't get up on my account.'

The man continued his struggle to rise, until the sensation of a cold hard tap underneath his jaw, rendered him still. Rolling his eyes downwards, he saw the blade of a very long Katana resting flatly underneath his chin, with its edge laying inwards, not quite touching his throat. The reason for his sudden ricochet back into the cottage now standing beside him.

'Look at me,' said the swordsman, with an encouraging light flick from the point of his sword.

Kim turned to face him. The look on the man's face was as identically void of emotion as the mask worn by the girl.

'I believe this is Kim Jin-sung, the owner of this quaint charming cottage,' said Hikaru.

'That means that you,' said Azumi, as she gestured with the pistol pointing to the man on the right, 'must be Min Hyun-woo, which then makes you Kwak Kyung-bok,' she said looking down the sight of the other weapon. 'The man with the plan and friend of the stars... well a few porn stars at least.'

'We need to wrap this up, I need to make a call,' said Kurosawa to his sister, his voice urgent.

Azumi picked up on the disconcerted tone from her brother. It was unlike him to sound so agitated, particularly on a job.

Kwak looked into the barrel of the pistol held in her right hand, pointing straight at his face, it was a Glock. In her left hand was a smaller, but no less deadly .38, both of which she held close to her body. The girl made jokes lightly, but clearly was not looking for laughs. His mind, recovering from its initial shock, was now looking for an opening. He knew that at least two of his associates were well armed with an array of weapons, which were concealed about them. He decided if he saw just the smallest of openings, he would attack the girl, relying on the other two to take down the guy with the sword.

The fact that they were still alive gave him some hope, they obviously wanted them that way and the more time went on the greater their chances of survival.

Azumi realised they needed to get on with it. 'Okay, in that case, we need to simplify things,' she said, not taking her eyes off the two men in front of her.

There was a sudden movement that the two men at the table caught sight of from the corner of their eyes. It was instantly followed by the sound of a high-pitched, sharp whoosh in the air, followed by the sickening sound of flesh and bone being sliced by hard, sharp steel.

Kim was a thin, slight man, his body did not seem to trouble the blade with any resistance as it caught him through the left side of his neck, down through his trunk and exited out under his right armpit. The two halves of his body fell forward together, sliding off one another as they hit the floor by the side of Kwak. Blood now flowed freely from the dismembered torso, pooling under the table around both men's feet.

Min recalculated their chances of survival as Kurosawa moved behind him to go outside to use his cell phone.

'Two is company and three is after all a crowd,' she said, smiling and nodding her head in the direction of their dissected companion. Her smile morphed into a hideous sneer, her eyes never leaving the two men until Kurosawa returned from making his call. 'No answer,' he said simply on his return.

There would be only one person her brother would wish to call; she understood Ikuko must be in some sort of trouble. 'Then we need to move,' she said.

The Koreans heard small zipping sounds from the direction of the swordsman now standing behind them.

'It would be very unfortunate if you were to make any movement now… at all,' said Azumi to them both, as sets of plastic zip ties were lowered over Kwak 's head with the tip of Kurosawa's sword. Attached to it were two smaller zip tie loops. 'Put one around your own neck first and pull it tight,' she directed him.

He did as he was told.

'Now put your right hand in one of the others and pull that tight too. And now put the other hand in and pull it tight with your teeth.'

He again did as he was told.

'I said, tight!' she hissed at him, the first sign of any emotion from the girl. They fully understood the abilities of the men they were dealing with and were not taking any chances with them.

Kwak grabbed the end of the plastic again with his teeth and pulled it tighter.

'Now lean forward until your forehead is on the table.'

A second set of zip ties now appeared at the end of the sword above Min, and the larger loop also lowered over his head.

'And repeat,' she ordered, the sickly smile returning to her face.

Min now felt the wrong end of a gun barrel pressed firmly against his neck. Amateurs after all, he thought. They had got too close; this was not how you walk out a killer such as himself. Believing that the time had come for him to act, he readied himself.

Kurosawa pulled the trigger, firing the sedative into Min's bloodstream. The sophisticated compounds took effect immediately. He quickly did the same with Kwak .

As the men collapsed into unconsciousness Kurosawa started to make another call.

'Ikuko?' asked his sister simply.

'Yes, she must have driven to the villa after I hung up on her yesterday. Why would she do that?' he said, waiting for his call to be answered.

'Oh, I have no idea, brother,' said Azumi raising her eyebrows at him in incredulity at his lack of understanding.

'Retrieve the bug while I check in with Matachi and Co.' Azumi heard him give a description of Ikuko, as she picked up the slim microphone, she had slid under the door to enable them to listen to the spy ring's conversation before they gate-crashed the party.

Kurosawa handed her the phone. 'She may have been on the boat, but there is no one there now.'

'Take them to the van, I will organise a collection for these two for later. Our friends will be pleased to receive such high value assets. I will redirect the detectives to the industrial estate. Other assists are moving in, but it will take too long to get them into the action, the closest back-up is hours away, at best. Those two detectives are capable enough and are all we have for now. I will call it in on the way and send them the transcript. We are on our own for now. And if what we heard is correct – we are really in the shit.'

CHAPTER FIFTY-FOUR

18 March 2011

The small convoy of truck and trailer and the last of the useful Toyota vans from the fleet they had inherited at the site began to move out of the compound. Lead units had already left and were located at strategic points along their proposed route to Higashimachi. The giant engine of the Volvo truck powerfully growled in tune with the driver as he quickly worked his way up through the gears, picking up speed as the machine led off in the direction of their ultimate destination that night.

The crane had already been dispatched a few days earlier, using a legitimate haulier to transport the unit to the port side, where it had been unloaded and parked at a prearranged area away from general view. The unit was now making its way under its own power down to the dock side in readiness for its next vital role. Its task, to remove the boat and its precious cargo and place it into the waters of the port.

Nam had been concerned about the disappearance of the covert team sent to the Mill, but nothing would be allowed to interfere with the mission. The order from control was to proceed with the plan as previously arranged. This meant that no changes were deemed necessary to timelines or any of the many specific elements needed to complete this final phase.

The only change was Control's insistence that security would be increased. Additional covert personnel would be put in place along the route to add further layers of protection for them and their uniquely valuable asset.

The mission's general security was now fully under his command, but he readily agreed with their suggestion and the extra teams were already moving into place. Despite the concerns, his confidence had been buoyed by how well the plan had worked so far. He was sure that within the next few hours they would have successfully launched their precious ward. However, that held conviction started to be challenged when they had travelled half the distance to their objective. As they followed a long bend in the highway, they were confronted by a neat row of decapitated heads laid out across the road in front of them. It was a gruesome sight; some of the men still wearing dark woolly hats with balaclavas beneath and one still had his headset clamped to his ears.

On being confronted by this human speed bump, the driver began to change down through the gearbox, slowing the vehicle and its precious cargo down, accompanied by a crescendo from the revving diesel engine and sharp blasts from the air brakes being applied.

Nam screamed at him to speed back up immediately. The driver duly complied. Putting his foot down on the accelerator he rolled the truck over the heads with a series of sickening crunching splats. He then started to hit a pile of decapitated bodies, that had been left in a heap.

As they watched in horror, the front of the truck hit them with a sickening meaty smack. They were so engrossed in the ghastly spectacle before them, neither of them noticed in the rear view mirror a squat man with a large sword tucked into his belt, narrowly missing to gain a foothold on the rear of the trailer.

Takada swore loudly as the truck disappeared around the bend without him. A complete lower jawbone that belonged to one of the heads, had come to rest with its chin on the floor and a perfect set of white teeth pointed upwards. It seemed to be taunting him with its half grin.

'Your yanking my chain, you little fucker,' he said, launching it skywards with a kick.

He jogged back to where he had hidden his noodle van as the trailing HiAce went by in the Semi's wake, followed by the screeching of tyres as it too tried to manoeuvre around the now compressed bodies of their comrades.

'How many of those fucking vans are there!' Takada exclaimed as he wedged his sword down the side of the passenger seat. Firing up the compact three-cylinder engine, he sped out onto the road, the miniature van slewing from side to side as it accelerated in pursuit. The large transporter maybe restricted to the wide main highways, but he was not in his considerably more compact vehicle. He pulled off the highway onto the network of narrow lanes used by local farmers to service their fields. If he could remember all the routes, he may just beat them to the port.

As he watched the large unit followed by the HiAce scream across the junction in front of him, Takada realised that his recollection of the farm lanes had not been as reliable as he had hoped. He pulled back in behind them, the fishing boat towering over the surrounding buildings as it sped through the streets of Higashimachi.

He now had no choice but to let the convoy run its course to its destination, then come up with a new plan from there. However, with all elements of surprise now lost it was going to be a challenge to work out how he could stop the launch on his own.

He pulled back out of sight and let the convoy roll on. There was no danger that he was going to lose it now.

CHAPTER FIFTY-FIVE

18 March 2011

There was a continuous sound of bumps and slaps, as the two unconscious bound men were thrown around the rear space of the Toyota. Kurosawa was driving the vehicle as fast as it would go, crunching through the column-drive gear selector, as he squeezed everything he could out of the van's transmission along the windy back roads until they connected with the main highway to Higashimachi.

After a few kilometres they came across an identical vehicle to their own parked in a lay-by, with two men standing behind it. Kurosawa pulled in behind the vehicle about ten metres back and turned off the engine.

'Ikuko may be in there, I need to get close,' he said as he jumped out.

Azumi held her pistols on her lap and watched as he approached the two men.

'Annyeong,' said Kurosawa, greeting the men in Korean.

Dreadful accent, thought Azumi. Suddenly a third man appeared from beneath the chassis of the truck behind the first man, rolling sideways into the road, coming to rest lying face down. He quickly raised a pistol at Kurosawa and started to shoot. Kurosawa spun away from the attack, but suddenly collapsed onto the road.

Rounds from the prone attacker began to impact through the windshield of their HiAce. Azumi threw herself from the vehicle onto the verge, as bullets from a second shooter entered the vehicle exactly where she had just been sitting.

She rolled into a kneeling position and began to return fire with both pistols at the same time.

The first man out of the truck, who had seemed unarmed at first, now held an automatic pistol in his hands and was firing furiously at her. The cracking noise of the bullets as they passed over her head were drowned out by the almost simultaneous discharge blasts, of what were now several weapons all firing at once. Bullets cracked into the van behind her as she sprinted for the cover of the verge-side.

The first man did not get a second chance to correct his poor aim, as a tight group of explosive-tipped rounds erupted in his chest and face. Before his shredded body had hit the road, Azumi rolled into a small depression in the grassy verge and began engaging the third shooter, who had gone into hiding behind the vegetation on the opposite side of the road. She continued to pour fire towards his location, highlighted by the muzzle flashes. Her .38 now empty, she discarded it, carrying on returning fire with the automatic until the gunfire abruptly stopped.

She quickly took the opportunity to change magazines on the Glock, when the man who had been lying in the road, unable to get a good aim at her, jumped to his feet, vaulted the stricken Kurosawa and ran towards her firing his weapon.

She realised that she would not be able to reload her weapon in time to meet her attacker, so she flicked the weapon towards his face and launched herself towards the man, hoping for the slim chance of getting close enough to kill him with her hands. The man easily avoided the flying pistol and, with a sickly grin forming on his face, he drew down his weapon taking aim to fire. Azumi realised she was not going to get close enough to him to make her attack count, when the lights abruptly went out in the man's face, his body lost all control and he fell forwards into the lay-by. There appeared to be a length of dark string coming out of the back of the man's head. Her eyes followed the line back towards where her brother was lying – conceding that there may be some benefits to the traditional approach sometimes.

She retrieved her weapon and quickly reloaded it with a fresh magazine. The firing from the other side of the road had now ceased. Still covering the area, she cautiously approached her brother.

'Where are you hit?' she asked. 'I'm good,' he replied.

She glanced down at him, and saw the right-hand side of his head was covered in blood.

'I can assure you that you have looked much better. Where did you get that from?' she asked pointing at the lump of metal sticking out of the back of the Korean's head.

'I took it off one of the spies,' he said, weakly pulling on the line attached to it. The cord expanded, but the mace did not move, just jerked the man's head gruesomely backwards.

'Leave it, brother, I will get you another one, darling,' she said as she helped him to his feet and started examining his wound. 'Let me take a look. I think it is a ricochet that hit you; they didn't seem to be terribly good shots. Keep some pressure on it while I check on our cargo.'

Azumi opened the side door of the van, to find both men unhurt, but still out cold. 'Yep, I was right, terrible shots,' she shouted back to her brother.

'Come on, jump in we need to get going,' called Kurosawa. 'Coming,' she said, with a shake of her head before she slammed the door shut.

CHAPTER FIFTY-SIX

18 March 2011

What a heap of shit!' said a disgruntled Tekiō from the passenger side of the Subaru Impreza. 'There is no fucking room in here at all. Why couldn't we have taken the van? At least then I could have got in the back, plenty of room in there.'

'Look,' said Matachi, 'they told me they needed it and I don't think we were in a position to really put up an argument. Though at the time, I did not hear you say anything at all about it, other than, it was very kind of her to offer us the car. Of course, the fact that they fucking blew ours up did not seem to cross your mind, did it?'

Tekiō did not answer. Even with the seat fully back he was bent double, supporting his forward weight by holding his hands on the dash of the car.

'Look on the bright side, it is very fast, and it seems we are now off to rescue your other girlfriend!' said Matachi.

'That is if their intel is correct,' said Tekiō. 'How the hell do they know that she is there?'

Matachi drove the car out onto the highway. 'I did ask them, but they seemed rather cagey on that front. Probably want to protect their source no doubt. Always best to not take risks with informants, they can come to harm so easily if they fall into the wrong hands. They were confident, though, we would find three Korean men and the girl on a fishing vessel called the *Daimyo Maru*, moored at the quayside at Higashimachi. She also told me it would be helpful to get another prisoner, but to take no chances, just the one would do. Definitely a woman after your own heart there, Tekiō, old boy. Though I didn't realise they already had anyone in custody? I do rather get the feeling that they are not being entirely straight with us.'

Tekiō did not respond to the jibe, saying, 'That's Spooks for you, it goes with the territory.'

Matachi nodded in agreement. 'I must say it was nice of them to confirm that it was the brother at the professor's place, that means we still have one less unaccounted crazy running around with a sword.'

'And a blunt spear,' added Tekiō.

'Correct, sergeant, we mustn't forget that. It is possible that the remaining crazies are all working for the Koreans perhaps. Maybe they are off to see them now. Did they possibly mention where they were going to you?'

Tekiō shook his head with some difficulty. 'No, I know as much as you. There is something big going down, that's for sure. However, nobody has the fucking foggiest idea what it is. But whatever it is, it is going down tonight – they were totally sure about that for some reason. They must have persuaded one of their assailants to talk, that is what I would have done. How long before we arrive at Higashimachi?'

Matachi thought that was possible, they had not seen all of the bodies, just told by Azumi that there were six dead. 'It is going to be another hour or so I'm afraid, old boy.'

★ ★ ★

It was fully into the evening by the time they had reached the port. 'This looks like the one,' said Matachi. 'Yes, the *Daimyo Maru*, this is it.' He stopped the Impreza opposite the boat and he, together

405

with a greatly relieved Tekiō, got out, although Tekiō found he had to roll out of the car onto his hands and knees to do so.

Matachi came around to Tekiō's side of the car, watching his friend in amusement. 'Dignified,' he said, looking over to the craft before them. 'Shall we?'

He started walking towards the gangplank; Tekiō grunted to his feet and followed him. They both urgently drew their side arms on seeing the blood pooled around it on the ground. Nodding to each other, they quickly climbed onto the craft moving along each side of the cabin area, covering each other as they did so.

'POLICE!' shouted Matachi. 'If there is anyone onboard or below show yourselves now!'

Matachi took a few more steps forward, then felt an unsettling squelching feeling under his right foot. Apprehensively he looked down at his Armani boots. 'I don't think there is anyone here,' he said. 'And I think they left in a hurry.'

'What makes you say that?' asked Tekiō.

'Well, for a start, one of them was in such a rush to leave, he has left his dick behind. Let's check the cabin,' said Matachi. Tekiō came over and covered the entrance to the cabin as Matachi went below. 'Yuk,' he said looking down to where Matachi had been standing.

'It's carnage down here,' he shouted up. 'There is a guy with his throat cut and... oh he's also missing a penis,' he said re-emerging.

'Another mystery solved,' said Tekiō.

Matachi came back up on deck, re-holstering his weapon so he could use both hands to steady himself on the guard rail. He started to clean the sole of his boot on a cleat, when his cell phone rang. He looked at the caller ID, it read 'Hansel & Gretel'. 'It's the Gruesome Two-some,' he responded.

'Detective Matachi,' he announced, followed by a moment's silence while he listened intently. 'Yes, one dead male here. Possibly Korean, but no porn stars, and no, afraid not, definitely no girl with blue hair. All I can give you is that there has been one hell of a fight here. There are no other bodies as such, but far too much blood around for just one death, not sure yet where the other bodies are.' Matachi paused to listen again. 'Very well, I understand, we are on our way.'

'What's up?' said Tekiō.

'Well, the chuckle brother has lost his air of inscrutability that's for sure. We have a new mission it seems. One which is likely to get us killed.'

'Really! I like it already,' said Tekiō. 'Who's the girl with the blue hair?'

'Not sure, but looks like she is someone important to the brother, he sounded rather tense I must say. Your new girlfriend took the phone at the end of that intriguing conversation, and she told me that we are to proceed to a location she is texting through now. There, apparently, we will find a boat on the back of a truck. We are to stop it from moving at all costs. She emphasised the "at all costs" aspect quite a bit. Think she may be going off you.' Tekiō looked very concerned at the news.

'Cheer up, old chap, I am sure you can patch it up, it will be fine. True love never runs smooth,' said a smiling Matachi.

'It is not that, of course I will be fine,' said Tekiō, unholstering Herman, removing the magazine and checking it before replacing it and chambering a round. 'And so will we,' he said looking intently down the long barrel. 'It is the fact I have to get back into that fucking post-box on wheels that pisses me off.'

The Subaru was making good progress up into the hillside, eating up the distance, its powerful turbo-charged engine thrusting it onwards along the twisting roads that led into the hills.

'We are not far,' said Matachi, as they pulled off the side road onto the main highway. 'How are you holding up there, old boy? Looks damned uncomfortable if you ask me.'

'Guts!' said Tekiō.

'What, no wait, hold it in, let me pull over first,' said a panicking Matachi.

'No, guts! Guts in the road,' said Tekiō gesturing through the windshield at a long length of intestines lying in the road.

'Bloody hell, do you think it is human?'

'Yes, I'm pretty certain,' said Tekiō.

'How can you tell?'

'Arm.'

'What?'

'Arm. Back there, at the junction we just passed, there was also an arm lying in the road,' said Tekiō, thrusting his thumb in a backwards direction.

Matachi did an expert handbrake U-turn, spinning the car around. With his foot to the floor, all four wheels bit into the tarmac as he sent them back down the road, trailing a cloud of smoke.

'Enjoying the Impreza then,' said Tekiō, as he was pushed uncomfortably into the car's door by the manoeuvre.

'Sorry, change of plan I think, old boy. I feel we need to follow the trail of meaty breadcrumbs, if you spot any more do let me know.'

'Can't see any more bits of people, but there is a girl with blue hair and a porn star hiding behind those bushes – right there,' said Tekiō, pointing to the road on Matachi's side as they shot past.

Matachi brought the car to a tyre-screeching halt, then quickly threw it into reverse gear, burning rubber as he shot the car down the road.

'Missed the acting class on how to be a bush then, Luluero!' shouted Matachi from the window.

'Fuck you, fat pig,' hissed Fuyuko, as she dragged a reluctant Ikuko by the hand to their car.

'Really great to see you too, luv,' said Matachi, as he got out and pulled his seat forwards so they could get in the rear of the car.

'Not a lot of room in here,' she said, ducking inside.

'Fucking tell me about it,' said Tekiō, again squeezing his frame back into the front seat.

'I think it is better than the noodle van,' said Ikuko.

'And a lot less bloody than the Toyota,' added Fuyuko.

A difficult move for Tekiō, but both men were now looking at the two dishevelled females sat in the rear of their car. 'What the hell are you doing here, Fuyuko?' asked Matachi incredulously.

'And who exactly are you, miss?' added Tekiō.

Ikuko was about to explain, when Fuyuko silenced her by placing a hand on her knee. 'Later, Ikuko, we don't have time for *War and Peace* now.' She turned to address the two detectives, 'We need to get to the port, right now.'

'Why?' asked Matachi. 'We have just come from there. It is all very quiet, well at the moment anyway. By the way, we seem to be finding bits of people just lying around on the road we just drove up and on a boat in the harbour. I'm no expert, but I would say they were fairly important to those individuals they once belonged to. Parts you would miss, if you see what I mean. Would you know anything about that?'

Ikuko found something interesting to stare at on her lap, as Fuyuko answered, 'Look, a lot of shit has gone down tonight and a great deal more is about to. I can fully answer all of your questions, but for now we need to get to the coast and help him.'

'Help whom exactly?' enquired Matachi.

'The swordsman, the guy who saved our arses back on the boat. He is chasing those fucking, shit-munching Korean bitches, taking that boat to the port.'

'I see,' said a perplexed Matachi, as he unpicked the litany of profanities from her statement, getting to its principal significance. He looked at Tekiō. 'We need to turn around. Tekiō, call your girlfriend. Ladies please do fill us in with all the details,' he said, firing the car back into life.

★ ★ ★

'Where is my fucking crane!?' screamed Nam into the receiver.

'It's on its way to you, sir, you arrived sooner than we expected,' came the reply over the handset.

The trailer was positioned alongside the quay, leaving enough room for the crane to lift the boat off and into the water. His remaining men busied themselves releasing the clamping devices that held the boat securely to the trailer. Around them armed men took up position in a perimeter, creating a protective screen for the delicate operation.

Nam had now lost contact with several more of his teams, in addition to the remains of the recce team section he had ordered. The support boat section, based at the dock had disappeared completely. It was not looking good; he felt sure another attack of some sort was imminent. The fact that the place was not swarming with military and police already made him assume that he still had a chance to launch the craft, which was the main objective of the mission. He was willing to lay down the lives of his remaining men to achieve it. If he could just get the fucking hulk into the water, he would be in with a chance of success. He watched as the crane manoeuvred itself into a position where it could lift the craft off the flatbed trailer and drop it into the dock's basin. The process moved slower than molasses in winter. Every lost moment putting them closer to failure.

CHAPTER FIFTY-SEVEN

18 March 2011

The Subaru slowly rolled along the highway, passing next to a smoking, bullet riddled HiAce and a number of bodies lying at either side of the road. Both detectives looked out of their respectively rolled down car windows.

'I believe we are getting close,' said Tekiō staring at the dead bodies in the road.

'Any of them your pals?' asked Matachi.

'No, it's not them,' said Tekiō. 'And this van has a different registration.'

'Pity, that means we are going to get a rollocking for being late from your girlfriend.' Matachi closed his window as he sped the car onwards to Higashimachi. 'Your saviour is a busy boy,' he said to the two women in the back.

'I don't think they are his work,' said Fuyuko.

'How could you possibly tell?' enquired Matachi.

'They were in one piece, more or less. They seemed to have all been shot, I don't think he owns a gun, just a very long fucking sword.'

'How quaint,' retorted Matachi.

★ ★ ★

Takada watched the crane trundle down from its position in the maintenance section of the shipyard. It was not built for speed but was making steady progress towards the transporter rig. He realised it would be futile to storm the positions the Koreans had set around the craft, but he had managed to work his way in close. Maybe he could sabotage the crane he thought, that would undoubtedly curtail their plans to launch the fishing vessel.

He watched as a blue Subaru Impreza appeared about hundred metres behind it. Who the fuck are *they*, he thought?

'That looks interesting,' said Tekiō as they approached the rear of the crane. 'Do you think it is anything to do with what we are actually doing here?'

An incredibly loud WHOOSHING sound, accompanied by a trail of smoke, shot over their car, closely followed by a massive detonation as the crane erupted in a bright and powerful explosion.

'Not anymore,' said Matachi, as bullets began to ricochet off the bonnet of his car, causing both women and Tekiō to start screaming.

'I think the Kurosawas may be here,' said Matachi nonchalantly, as he pulled the car quickly into a side street.

'I told you she had a reload for that fucking stovepipe,' said an excited Tekiō.

'Did you say Kurosawa?' asked Ikuko. 'Yes, do you know them?'

'I fucking well know *him*!' she replied.

'Love is in the air,' said Tekiō.

'What did you say?' said the furious looking Ikuko.

'Perhaps this would be an opportune moment to let you girls out,' said Matachi, as he brought the now steaming and smoking vehicle to a juddering stop.

Takada flicked bits of burning crane off him. He was trying to figure out what the hell was happening when the assault started. AK-47s opened up on the Koreans from at least two directions

412

at once. He could not see exactly where it was coming from as the source of the fire kept moving, but they were professionals of that he was certain. Controlled bursts of fire were decimating the security force at the perimeter and they were dropping like wheat under a scythe. It was looking like his work was done, when he felt a presence behind him. He spun around, his sword coming into the guard position in front of him. 'Fuck,' he said under his breath.

'Peace to you, Samurai,' the Witch said to him. The Atrocitor loomed behind her, like some furry silhouette. Its large, almond eyes bore down on him from over her head, like twin cannons on the nose of a jetfighter. 'I have need of your services,' she said. 'A small task, that should be an easy chore for one such as your good self.'

'I have the feeling you are telling, rather than asking,' said Takada, forcing himself to a statue-like stillness.

'A simple task, I… or should I say we… just require a few souls, two should do it. Though they must be alive and possibly malevolently wicked at their core.' She waved in the direction of the battle evolving below. 'There will be some types that would fit the bill down there.'

'I will see what I can do,' he said lowering his sword.

★ ★ ★

Matachi watched as the two girls ran up the side street away from the gunfire.

'Come on, we are missing all the fun,' screamed a very excited Tekiō as he ran to the corner of the nearest building and started unloading Herman down range at the Koreans.

'Wait for me, you fat fucker,' shouted Matachi, coming up out of the trunk of the Subaru with an assault rifle of his own and some webbing full of magazines. 'The twins left us this just in case, wasn't that jolly decent of them?'

With half his force already dead or wounded and no crane to launch his ship, all seemed lost to Nam. They had almost done

413

it; the transport was in position and the restraints had all been removed in readiness for the lift. The timing had been perfect with the tide at its zenith, ideal conditions to put to sea.

Looking at the fishing boat all ready to launch, it was then that he knew what must be done. He grabbed hold of one of his team and started giving orders to start the truck. The man turned to do as he was ordered when his head simply exploded. What the hell are they firing at us, thought Nam, wiping blood and brain out his eyes?

He called to the ship's crew to get on board and start the engines, then he sprinted to the truck's cab, bullets landing all around him as he ran. He knew what the reward for failure would be for him, he accepted his fate and threw himself into the cab.

'I see your aim has returned, old boy,' said Matachi encouragingly as he saw Tekiō hit one of the Koreans in the head with dramatic effect. 'Now let's wrap this thing up.'

Takada had stayed under cover and in the shadows as the assault had unfolded. It looked like it was going to succeed, but then he realised what the Koreans were trying to do.

With a burst of black smoke from its massive diesel engine erupting from the machine's exhaust stacks, the truck started to move forwards. Slowly at first, but as it went up through the gear ratios it started to gain speed until it was hurtling along the quayside. The waste bins and rows of benches along the bank were smashed out of the way as it headed for the end of the quay, a hail of bullets lighting up its cab.

Without hesitation it flew off the stony rampart into the sea. Its momentum and weight sending it to land almost flat on the water with a huge splash. Once the spray had fallen away, it revealed the fishing boat alone and afloat, swaying from side to side, but underway heading for the Pacific. The truck had totally vanished into the bay.

Tekiō ran to the edge of the quay and took aim at the disappearing vessel.

'I would not do that if I was you,' said a female voice at his side. 'Not unless you want another nuclear disaster on your hands that is.'

The four of them walked back up the street to where the Kurosawas had left the remaining HiAce with their two dead Koreans. Behind them was an apocalyptic scene of destruction that none of them seemed to even notice.

'We have failed then,' said Tekiō.

'Failure is a matter of perspective, big man,' said Azumi, smiling at him.

Matachi glanced at the pair, I do believe they like each other, he thought.

They all turned as they heard a woman's voice call out, 'Hikaru! Hikaru!'

A breathless Ikuko, ran towards the group, with Fuyuko trailing behind her.

Lowering his rifle to the floor, Kurosawa faced her, allowing her to run into his arms. 'You're safe!' he stammered, so relieved to see her.

Ikuko reached up to the badly tied, bloodied bandage around his head. 'Are you okay?'

'Yes, it is nothing, really,' he said holding her wrists in his hands. 'I was worried about you. Why did you come to the house?'

She suddenly remembered why she had, but before Ikuko could answer, the others came to a stop at the van in front of them. It was shaking from side to side and peculiar slurping and rustling sounds came from within. Then, a shout of – 'Put away the bread knife' – an old Korean peasant greeting came from the back of the vehicle.

The four spread out, Kurosawa pushed Ikuko behind him and drew the sword he had strapped across his back. Takada stepped out from behind the van with a large grin spread across his face.

'Greetings, fellow Samurai,' said Takada to Kurosawa, drawing his own sword. 'I see you have tied up two more loose ends,' he said, pointing his sword at the van.

415

This was answered by an accompanying chorus of safety catches being released.

Ikuko slipped past Kurosawa and ran to Takada's side. 'You two have met!' she said in surprise.

'A meeting of sorts,' said Kurosawa. 'Move away from him!'

'I will not. He has saved my life many times today. You will let him pass.'

'What has he done with the prisoners?'

'I have done nothing with them. They were a necessary offering of appeasement to it. A modicum of sustenance to keep it fortified for its journey, I believe.'

'It – what on earth is *it*?' asked Kurosawa.

'You really don't want to know,' said Ikuko, walking forward, taking his arm, and guiding him away from the scene. She glanced at Takada who gave her a knowing nod. 'Now let's all get the fuck out of here, before *it* comes back.'

CHAPTER FIFTY-EIGHT

19 March 2011

The captain of the Korean submarine moulded his forehead and cheekbones into the rubber shroud on his periscope. His breath drew in the familiar comforting smell of fresh machine oil embedded in the soft latex, as he watched the fishing boat approach the significantly larger tanker. He had been tracking the boat since it left the coast of Japan yesterday. He had been well within Japanese territorial waters when he had made contact with it, but this was far from a unique event for him, the crew and this vessel in particular.

On board the tanker he observed a seaman topside starting to deploy a large crane, which had been specifically fitted to the ship. The vessel itself retained the appearance of one of the rusting Korean hulks that routinely made clandestine runs to rendezvous with Chinese vessels in international waters, where they took on mainly oil and other contraband commodities. Despite its deceptive appearance suggesting it would not survive another storm, the tanker was, in reality, an exceptionally seaworthy vessel. It had been greatly modified, with one of its holds being greatly shallower than it seemed, containing only half the oil of the others. This was because it encompassed a false compartment beneath it. The detachable bulkheads had already been removed to allow access to the hidden area deep within the bowels of the ship. Once replaced it would look like any other oil smuggler, even if boarded. As the grey dawn blended with the monochrome sea, the submarine captain watched the fishing vessel rise and fall in the light swell. The modified craft pushed its engines to the limit as it conveyed its oversized cargo towards the tanker. He was unaware of the specifics of the cargo being transferred, but knew his orders: to be in the area and, if necessary, to exhaust every effort to guarantee the transfer's success. This commitment extended to risking the destruction of his boat, the lives of his crew, and his own.

He continued to survey the progress of the struggling fishing boat, which was still about a kilometre away before coming alongside the tanker. He suddenly felt someone wrenching at his arm, he was about to pull away from the telescope to punch the insolent dog who would dare accost him in such an inappropriate manner, when the large tanker seemed to lift into the sky.

He watched in total disbelief as the ship disintegrated into a horizontal fireball of debris and bright yellow flames, the very surface of the sea itself was now alight. A fiery mattress of conflagration now rose and fell with the swelling ocean, as bits of the craft that had exploded into the sky above, now lost its momentum and returned seaward, creating a rain of fiery splashes as they hit the surface and then disappeared forever.

He was finally wrenched away from the scene by the insistent seaman, who had now managed to pull him aside. The man looked like he was in a state of panic as he shouted, 'Captain, sonar has three objects approaching fast!'

The captain barely managed to utter, 'How fast?' before his own vessel erupted into a colossal ball of explosive energy. The blast's colossal force created a towering dome of water, rising twenty metres high, which then collapsed into a churning maelstrom of oily, frothy, grey-brown water. This turbulent whirlpool was strewn with small, shattered and singed fragments of debris swirling in its midst.

On board the *Shiroboshi Maru* the crew of three had gone into shock on witnessing the sudden and violent Armageddon that had unfolded around them. They were further stunned, when a Virginia class Hunter Killer submarine leapt out from the surface of the sea alongside them, soaking the crew on deck with the spray of displaced water thrown into the air by the breaching submarine.

The crew stared in astonishment at the towering vessel that had appeared so violently on their port side. The smaller fishing boat began to wallow in the swell caused by the settling Leviathan, as it swept under their vessel's hull.

The 'emergency blow action' had not been carried out for entertainment value, the manoeuvre had been undertaken to distract the crew on the fishing vessel long enough for the Navy SEAL team on board the USS *Texas* to deploy. They had been waiting below decks for the precise moment that they could move up onto the conning tower and the main deck. A full platoon of Navy SEALs swiftly manoeuvred into strategic positions, dividing into two meticulously coordinated sections. The larger unit, with expert precision, readied an impressive arsenal of light arms, aiming them intently at the unsuspecting North Korean fishing boat. Meanwhile, the second unit, with equal efficiency and stealth, swiftly deployed a Zodiac inflatable boat from the concealed port side of the USS *Texas*, ready for a covert approach. As the six-man assault team secured their positions on board, they executed the drill with the practised efficiency born from countless hours of rigorous training. With every member in sync, the craft was primed for launch. The Coxswain ignited the engine, and the raiding vessel thundered to life, its nose rising sharply as it surged forwards along the submarine's sleek length. Skilfully, he manoeuvred the attacking inflatable so that it was parallel with the *Shiroboshi Maru*, seamlessly slipping under the protective cover of the formidable gun line now established along the submarine's starboard side.

The sudden high growl of an out-board motor and the

appearance of an assault group aggressively bearing down on them, seemed to bring the Koreans out of their stupor. One man unwittingly signed their collective death warrants by attempting to pick up his weapon.

Before he even had a chance to raise the assault rifle at the Americans, the SEAL Team opened up with a fusillade of small arms fire, engaging each member of the crew at once. A lethal combination of SR-25 Sniper Rifles, Mk-46 machine guns and CQBR Carbines sent a cascade of steel into each of the three men's bodies. The marksmanship of the specialist team was exceptional; each frogman careful not to hit any part of the fishing vessel below the waterline.

The moment was short and deadly and, as the firing ceased, the coxswain brought the assault team alongside the fishing boat. Instantly the boarding party sprung onto the vessel before their own craft had even stopped. The men spread out across the deck, one SEAL firing his weapon into the body of one of the prone Koreans. No chances were being taken as the team moved to clear the fishing boat. Three of them made their way below to complete their search.

The captain of the *Texas* had made his way out onto the conning tower of his boat, and was surveying the scene below through his binoculars. He waited patiently as the assault team completed their search. One of the men now re-emerged out of its hull and he heard the man's voice come over the net, via his earpiece saying, 'Payload secure, all Tango times three down. Over.'

'Roger that,' he heard the SEAL commander respond.

The captain gave the order to get a line on the fishing boat and secure it to the side of his submarine. They were to wait there for the arrival of the USS *Ponce,* an amphibious transport ship which had been launched as an emergency from Okinawa earlier that day. It was now making good headway, steaming hard towards the precise coordinates it had now been given. The ship's cavernous hull was more than able to take the vessel on board and then secure its precious and volatile cargo.

The USS *Texas*'s sister ship, the USS *Hawaii*, maintained a stealthy presence, remaining submerged and vigilantly patrolling the vicinity. Equipped with advanced photonics masts, the USS *Hawaii* conducted a thorough scan of the surrounding area, capturing details with far greater precision and clarity than any traditional periscope could ever achieve. This state-of-the-art technology provided it with a critical advantage, allowing for unparalleled surveillance and threat detection in the vast expanse of the ocean. It had already fired three MR48 torpedoes into the Korean sub. It was ready to fire again if required from its powerful armoury of torpedoes and cruise missiles, into any other vessel that identified as a threat or that ventured into their protective exclusion zone. But none would come, the captain of the second Korean Sub, held in support some twenty kilometres away, had heard enough and had already turned around. Now submerged a hundred metres below the surface, the vessel surged ahead at full speed, desperately fleeing from the imminent peril it had unexpectedly encountered. The captain, acutely aware of the formidable adversaries lurking in the depths, understood that the silent, relentless hunters of the deep – the American submarines patrolling the Pacific – were already poised to eliminate him permanently should he pose any threat. He navigated with a mix of fear and determination, knowing that these relentless guardians of the ocean's expanse were unmatched in their lethal efficiency.

Burdened with his new mission – the bearer of news of failure and the uncertain, potentially grave consequences that might ensue – the captain found scant solace. As he contemplated the daunting task ahead, he began to question whether retreat might offer a more favourable outcome. The weight of his decision loomed large, stirring a tumult of doubt and apprehension about the path that lay before him, and the repercussions it might bring...

EPILOGUE

21 March 2011

The four of them sat around a small meeting table in Azumi's office at her mill. They had reconvened there at her request a few days after what was now known as the – battle of Higashimachi.

Matachi was feeling very uneasy about being back there, the memories of his last visit still very vivid. He had said as much to Tekiō, who had informed him that he had a bad habit of harbouring resentments, and he should let bygones be bygones. Did he think he was that stupid, thought Matachi? He was onto Tekiō, the lecherous lump, it was all too clear why he was so amenable to returning to the place.

'Thank you for coming,' said Azumi, 'I'm sure you have been very busy debriefing your superiors on the situation.'

'Did we have a choice?' said Matachi, giving a small bow to Kurosawa. Remembering the last time, he met the man here, he had held a sword to his throat.

He would have gone on, but the painful pressure of a very large foot squashing down on his instep momentarily caused him to catch his breath.

'We are more than delighted to be of assistance,' Tekiō interjected, then easing off the pressure on his partner's foot just enough to allow him to take a breath again.

'Wonderful,' said Azumi with a tight-lipped smile. 'We felt it would be good to update you on a few developments since the other night.'

Matachi glanced at Tekiō broadly smiling back at her. He had never realised the guy had so many teeth in there. 'You mean our total failure to prevent an event that could have dire consequence for the rest of the planet,' he replied. He felt the pressure momentarily return to his foot.

'Yes, about that,' she said. 'You see, there are not going to be any consequences, well, not for us anyway.'

'Really, please, do tell, because by my recollection, the last time I saw our stolen plutonium, it was merrily chugging out into the Pacific?' said Matachi.

Azumi raised her eybrows at him, 'Operation Catcher Up,' she said.

'Pardon me?' said Matachi.

'No offence to anyone present,' said Azumi, focusing slightly longer on the two detectives than was comfortable. 'But we could not just rely on us to stop the Koreans. Hence, operation "Catcher Up".'

'I can assure you, Azumi-san, none taken,' responded Matachi curtly. 'But please do elaborate.'

'It took CIRO some time to piece all the information together, but, once we appreciated this was more than just a political corruption racket we were dealing with, that changed things. The speed of response required meant we were on the clock, and had to move quickly with what resources we had on hand.' She nodded at the two men.

'There was no time to bring in the military, and they already had their hands full dealing with the disaster,' said Matachi, 'so you used us.'

'I'm afraid so, however, I would put it as utilised. It was fortunate for us that you had already been assigned to the area, so able to assist us with the goal of trying to stop their operation on Japanese soil. That would have been the safest option, and politically the best outcome for the nation, partially in light of the major disaster we were already struggling with. It is self-evident that losing a batch of weapons-grade plutonium to the North Koreans would have been an even greater catastrophe, with consequences that would have ranged far beyond our shores.'

'But not your only option?' said Matachi.

'No, it could not be with what was at stake,' she replied.

'So, you called in our American cousins,' stated Matachi.

'Yes, once we shared with them the information on what we thought was going on, they started searching for suspicious North Korean merchant and naval activity. Several vessels of interest were found, and the United States Navy took it from there.'

'It's been recovered?' asked Matachi.

'Yes, it is safely in the possession of the Americans now.'

'I would wager that was a messy operation,' said Tekiō thoughtfully.

'There was some collateral damage in the process, we could not take any chance after all. The total complement of the Koreans who managed to escape with the pay load are dead, and furthermore there were some losses from their naval assets, that they sent to rendezvous with the fishing boat.'

'Yes, those Yanks don't waste time messing around,' said Tekiō. 'Maybe it should have been called operation "Batter Up"!' he proposed.

'Quite,' said Azumi. 'But the Koreans are flagging no indications about the loss of their vessels or any involvement in the attempted theft of the plutonium.'

'That would be them admitting to a huge loss of face,' said Matachi. 'From our perspective I can see how the naval incident can be concealed, but what about the enormous gun fight on the quay?'

'Let's not forget the scattering of body parts around half of Higashimachi,' added Tekiō.

'Officially it is being reported as a turf war between the Yakuza and a Korean organised crime gang who were trying to take advantage of the local chaos and move into the area,' explained Azumi.

'I see,' said Matachi. 'Very neatly done... And I take it the question of the missing plutonium will be quietly side-lined?'

'Administrative error made in the heat of the moment, by the highly stressed staff. Given the circumstances, readily understandable, and more importantly believable,' said Azumi. 'As for the initial reason for your involvement here, once the government investigation into the catastrophe at the nuclear facility concludes, they will establish the fact that inadequate design and build processes used in the construction of the reactor plant were the cause of its failure to perform to the standards required to meet such an emergency. That means that the organisational web of corruption and murder run by Uchida Zenjirō and his cronies will come out eventually as a huge national scandal.'

'That is all very well, but we have not established who exactly murdered whom!' said Matachi. 'All we have is a number of suspects, one of which was the mysterious man who rescued Ikuko and the delightful Ikeda Fuyuko,' said Matachi.

At the mention of Ikuko and the mystery samurai, Matachi saw Kurosawa stir slightly; the guy had let his sister do all the talking so far, but was about to say something when she cut him off.

She focussed very intently on Matachi and said, 'Unfortunately, you must end any inquiry into this individual immediately.'

'Don't tell me – he is an asset of yours!' said Matachi.

'All I can say, is that he once worked for a different department.'

'Really, well, all I can say is, he may have gone a little, "extracurricular" don't you think?' he replied.

'What with all those heads turning up minus their bodies,' thoughtfully added Tekiō, with a smile and nod.

Azumi did not return the smile, which Tekiō found hurtful. He was only trying to help after all.

'That is interesting, considering his interaction with your brother,' said Matachi. 'May I offer some feedback that you may wish to improve on your interdepartmental communication...'

The pressure momentarily returned to his foot, as Tekiō was trying his best to keep on the right side of Azumi.

With a wince, Matachi, changed the subject slightly. 'We would like to make a request to interview the two Korean spies you detained at the cottage. At least, give us that.'

Again, he saw Kurosawa become uncomfortable at his comment.

'That will not be possible, in fact it would be impossible,' said Azumi.

'Why, what have you done with them?' asked Matachi.

Kurosawa now spoke for the first time. 'We did nothing with them – but something did.'

'Something – what sort of "something" exactly?' inquired Matachi. 'The last we heard was that you were bringing them with you to the port?'

Azumi shared another glance with her brother before answering. 'It's classified.'

The siblings seemed unnerved, which was undeniably out of character for these two. A display that Matachi himself found unsettling, now knowing them as he did.

'Amazing, case closed, all neatly tidied up and sectioned off into a bento box of unattainable delights.'

'Matachi-san,' started Kurosawa, 'we are extremely grateful for you and Tekiō's assistance in supporting us in this operation. I would also like to thank you personally for the rescue of Ikuko,' he said with a small bow. 'This month of March has been nothing short of a catalogue of remarkably extreme events, cataclysmic in their nature. Unfortunately, despite your current knowledge and understanding of what has happened, there are still elements of this case we cannot share with you, at least not at this time.'

'I thank you, Kurosawa-san, we appreciate the sincerity of your words. However, I do not think we will be working together again, do you?'

Kurosawa looked back at him with an intense stare, saying, 'This operation may not have had the outcome you were looking for, however, understand I... we are indebted to you. If at any time you need anything from us, please do not hesitate to request it, Matachi-san.'

Before Matachi could respond, Azumi cut in, 'I think we have all made some useful connections,' she said, slightly smiling at Tekiō.

Tekiō began to go puce, which caused a blushing chain reaction with Azumi.

Matachi began to feel embarrassed for them both, and Kurosawa was experiencing an emotional overcharge from the excitable auras now on display.

'I think this meeting has concluded,' said Matachi.'

High above the mill, beneath a shaded, dark grey cliff, the Atrocitor drew in the faint breeze that swept across the four individuals below. His wide nostrils flared as it categorised each distinct scent. Large horizontal eyelids, flickered across the beast's deathly dark almond-shaped eyes, as it observed the four make their way to their vehicles and drive away.

He watched them depart and then slid effortlessly through a fissure in the rock face and disappeared.